SCORPIO

LARA GIESBERS

ISBN
978-1-958122-46-4 (Paperback)
978-1-958122-45-7 (eBook)

Dedicated to Lawrence William Brunette Jr.

The man who never gave up on reading

TABLE OF CONTENTS

Cast Of Characters 1

Book 2...7

1397 9

Chapter 1 13

Chapter 2 19

Chapter 3 27

Chapter 4 51

Chapter 5 61

Chapter 6 81

Chapter 7 99

Chapter 8 121

Chapter 9 151

Chapter 10..165

Chapter 11..175

Chapter 12..181

Chapter 13 205

Chapter 14..225

Chapter 15..265

Chapter 16..283

Chapter 17..289

Chapter 18..309

Chapter 19..321

Chapter 20 337

Chapter 21..347

Chapter 22 357

Chapter 23 365

Chapter 24 375

Chapter 25..383

Chapter 26 397

Acknowledgments... 409

CAST OF CHARACTERS

Jason Mauldon. Vineyard owner living in the village of Denholm Glen. Married to Thena Coe Mauldon and father of Philip, Michael, and Nafaria. One of the Craft, he has wisdom and tact in dealing with people above and below his station in life. He also had a special gift for premonition.

Thena Coe Mauldon. Jason's wife and mother of Philip, Michael and Nafaria. One of the Craft, she is a healer and well versed in herbs. Her family was murdered in a brutal massacre; she was raised by Lord and Lady Briton.

Philip Mauldon. Eldest son of Jason Mauldon. Philip's talents are hunting, fishing, and anything outdoors. He married Nadia Saintclaire, and became a horse trainer and tutor for his uncle, Count Lucerne.

Michael Mauldon. Second son of Jason Mauldon. Michael's abilities are intense study and discerning arcane knowledge.

Lillia Sallen Mauldon. Wife of Michael Mauldon, Daughter of Reinard Sallen.

Warrick Mauldon. Jason's father.

Donovan Mauldon. Jason's grandfather.

Marek Mauldon. Jason's great grandfather.

Reinard Sallen. Village elder of Denholm Glen. Father of Lillia Sallen, uncle of Colin Greene, and great uncle of Nina Westen Catalane.

Bennett Luxton. Village elder of Denholm Glen.

Bryant Saintclaire. Horse master of Illith, married to Cassandra and father of Nadia. One of the Craft and has an uncanny intuition which allows him to prepare for future events.

Cassandra Saintclaire. Wife of Bryant Saintclaire, mother of Nadia. Cassandra possesses knowledge of herbs and their properties, especially lavender.

Nadia Saintclaire Mauldon. Daughter of Bryant and Cassandra Saintclaire. Married to Philip Mauldon and a horse trainer and tutor for Count Lucerne in North Agea.

Samson. One of two of Bryant's most trusted hired men. Along with Ian Keller, he sent away Bryant's servants and burned the manor in an attempt to keep Count Vedan from claiming Bryant's land.

Ian Keller. The other most trusted of Bryant's hired men. He and his wife Julia aided Alana Deveraux in freeing Lillia Sallen before she was to be executed.

Julia Keller. Wife of Ian Keller, she was employed by Count Vedan.

Alana Deveraux. Daughter of Count Deveraux who defied her father and saved Lillia Sallen before she was executed.

Sebastian Cavanaugh. Laborer from Denholm Glen who aided Alana Deveraux in freeing Lillia Sallen before she was executed.

Rohn Catalane. King of Nereheim, he became acquainted with Jason when he moved to Wildemere.

Susanna Catalane. Queen of Nereheim, originally from North Agea.

Andrew Catalane. Prince of Nereheim, son of Rohn and Susanna.

Nina Westen Catalane. Great niece of Reinard Sallen and wife of Andrew Catalane.

Joel Blackstone. A young blacksmith apprentice who befriends Jason. He becomes his enemy when his wife dies while Thena tried to save her.

Leanna Blackstone: Joel's wife and friend to Thena.

Lord Robert Stowe. A noble in Wildemere who does not trust anyone of the Craft.

Lydia Stowe. Robert's wife and mother of Ephratha Stowe Saint Marc.

Elias Wheaton. One of the Craft and owner of the antiquarian library in Wildmere.

Colin Greene. Second under the captain of the royal guard of Nereheim.

Citizens of North Agea:

Lian Saint Marc. King of North Agea, married to Clara Saint Marc who is the younger sister of Susanna Catalane and father of Jared.

Clara Saint Marc. Queen of North Agea, younger sister of Susanna Catalane and mother of Jared.

Jared Saint Marc. Prince of North Agea. Married to Ephratha Stowe Saint Marc.

Ephratha Stowe Saint Marc. Daughter of Robert and Lydia Stowe. Married Jared Saint Marc and moved to North Agea.

Coleman Cade. Captain of the royal guard of North Agea and childhood friend of Jared Saint Marc.

Rowen Cade. Old friend of Lian Saint Marc, and father of Coleman Cade. He has a special interest and ability with plants and flowers of all kinds.

Count Lucerne. Husband of Contessa Mauldon Lucerne, not of the Craft. Contessa was sent to live with the Count's family and eventually married his son.

Contessa Mauldon Lucerne. Wife of Count Lucerne, aunt of Philip Mauldon. One of the Craft, her special ability lies in the study of alchemy and the very intricate details that make up the world.

Malcom Stone. An apothecary in Arioth, and brother-in-law of Rohn Catalane. One of the Craft who left Nereheim and moved to North Agea to avoid persecution.

Nathaniel Stone. Son of Malcom Stone married to Nafaria Mauldon Stone. One of the Craft, his special ability lies in herbs, and intricate study. He is driven by the desire to be powerful enough to protect and avenge those of the Craft who were persecuted in the past.

Nafaria Mauldon Stone. Wife of Nathaniel Stone, Daughter of Jason and the youngest child. Nafaria's abilities lie in cultivating herbs for use in healing.

Oberman. An old and powerful sorcerer who received his power directly from the god of blood.

BOOK 2

Wisdom's Nemesis

"There is a way that seems right to a man, but in the end it leads to death."

Proverbs 16:25

In the year of our Lord 1395, Jason Mauldon, of the Craft, was betrayed and murdered by a man he trusted implicitly. Joel Blackstone was grief stricken the night his wife died with a child that was to be their first. In his grief, he sought revenge on Jason and his household for letting what was precious to him waste away.

Jason's family was dispersed between North Agea and Nereheim. Philip, the eldest, was sent to North Agea, where he and his wife Nadia became horse masters and tutors for Count Lucerne. There he was united with an aunt he never knew.

Michael, the middle child, returned to Denholm Glen, to the family vineyard. He married Lillia Sallen, his longtime friend and only master of his heart. He focused his mind on alchemy and searched the darkest parts of the Craft for arcane pieces of knowledge—for he was convinced he would need to weather the darkness to find the light.

Nafaria, the youngest, was reunited with Nathaniel Stone and the two were married in the rose garden of the king at Arioth in North Agea. She pursued her love of herbs and drawing. With Nathaniel's help, she built a bountiful herb and flower garden. It was a reflection of Nafaria's beauty as well as her wisdom for practical healing; just as she was both wise in her craft and beautiful to behold.

Each child chose their path and walked with confidence. Meanwhile, a shadow settled over the sister kingdoms holding a greater evil than the treachery of Joel Blackstone. The day would come when both evils would meet face to face. The story continues...

Part 1

1397

Footsteps echoed through the castle hall, ending at the door of the throne room. A young man bowed his head to the guard standing squarely before it. "I am Michael Mauldon. I have been summoned by the king." The guard nodded in acknowledgment and opened the door. Michael walked into the presence of King Rohn Catalane and bowed his head.

The king watched him approach. "Michael Mauldon, thank you for coming so quickly."

"That is the nature of a summons, your majesty."

"That is an answer I would expect from your father."

Michael did not respond. The king went on. "I miss your father more each day. More than wise counsel, I miss his compassion. Among the nobles I see in society, it was he who made me feel as if we spoke man to man; not just master to servant."

"Father enjoyed your company as well, your majesty. He often said the goings on of royalty is not what you expect once inside the castle walls. He was especially fond of relating Queen Susanna's latest tale of mischief."

"The queen enjoyed your father's visits as much as I did."

After an awkward moment of silence, Michael asked, "Is there something you wish of me, your majesty?"

"There is. I remember when you came with your father after he inspected the Wheaton Estate. When he asked you to relate your discovery, I was impressed with your knowledge at such a young age. Your father related new things you learned over the years. You have grown in wisdom and carry yourself before men of stature with the same honor and respect your father did. These are qualities found in one worthy to be named Court Adviser."

"Your majesty, are you suggesting I become your next Court Adviser?"

Rohn nodded his head. "You are young, but you exhibit the qualities of a Court Adviser. Will you accept this position?"

"My king; you accord me with great honor. However, it is a position not to be taken lightly. I have questions I would like answers for."

"Ask your questions."

"I mean no disrespect. The last Court Adviser was your brother-in-law. Those who remember say he left after you disagreed over the use of power. What made Malcom Stone leave his family? He was like a father to me and Nathaniel was my best friend. What drove such a wedge between you?"

"You perceive much to ask this question. Malcom came to my court when he was young. His prudence and compassion were unmatched in all of Nereheim. I needed a prudent leader. My father helped me understand how to judge whether a man was trustworthy and honorable. He taught me to trust motive and belief just as much, if not more, than age and one's station in life. That advice helped me see Malcom's potential. We were close in age and related well together. Having a peer with such moral excellence at my disposal helped me grow as well." Rohn paused a moment before going on.

"When the plague broke out in Burnea, Malcom did everything he could for those people. He did not believe it would come as far as Wildemere. It claimed my sister a few weeks after she gave birth to Nathaniel. I was distraught. In my grief, I begged Malcom to use his power to bring Sasha back from the dead. I told him I knew there was power that could do such a thing. He called that power forbidden and said it would be a curse to the living as well as the one brought back. He would not usurp the decision of YAHWEH by going beyond natural law to bring back someone from death. Not even for Sasha, and he loved her so much. Our arguments became fights, and he saw this as an impasse. He could no longer serve one who was not willing to listen to YAHWEH's wisdom.

He took Nathaniel and left the day he came back from the Wheaton Estate and implored me to seal it. Malcom feared nothing—but his eyes held great fear when he returned from the estate. I followed his instruction without question. He settled in Denholm Glen, and lived a simple life as he helped those around him. I went on in my pride, never disturbing him. Over time, I came to see the folly in letting him stay away. I missed his company. From time to time, I would hear of young nobles of the Craft who held promise of diplomacy, but upon closer inspection, there was always a flaw. Perhaps the only flaw was I missed my brother-in-law, and always hoped he would return to court. In time, bitterness overtook me and I let Nereheim do what it pleased with the wise ones."

"Your disagreement was over the use of the power YAHWEH gives to those of the Craft?"

"Yes."

"Your majesty, do you still believe it is just to break natural law for the ones we love?"

"I do not know what I would do if I were placed in that position again." Rohn sighed. "Would I try to bring back one I loved? I know the more noble choice, but not if I could choose it."

"To choose what is right when it breaks your heart is a very hard calling. To seek justice for being robbed of a loved one is not wrong. To seek blood for that loved one is for YAHWEH alone. To go outside his natural order is not for us to choose. I would be of no use to you as Court Adviser. I would make the same decision as Malcom without question."

"I will weigh your words and think on them. I believe your way is the better calling, not whether I can accept it."

"I understand your majesty. It is not always for us to comprehend what YAHWEH's will is. His ways are higher than our ways[1]. This is why the ancients were commended for their faith—their confidence in things they did not understand[2]." Michael bowed once more, and left Rohn to ponder his words.

---

[1]   Isaiah 55:9

[2]   Hebrews 11:2

CHAPTER 1

The sky was black, revealing a dazzling display of stars. A cloak wrapped snugly around the frame of Lord Reinard Sallen kept the chill at bay as he finished his observation. He discovered long ago the many uses of his rooftop. He retired there when he needed fresh air to breathe and a clear head to think. Lillia preferred it when stargazing. Few chose to look for him there when they needed him; but he was never closer at hand. After all, how often were the careworn simply able to look up and find their quarry?

His special viewing glass magnified the night sky, making the stars easier to see. His brow creased as he concentrated. Lately, stars were coming together in singular fashion. Whispers came from traveling merchants of odd happenings in the villages along the Anenderes River. Were the two closely related? It was no secret the heavens worked its will on large bodies of water. Did they have a connection to the Anenderes itself? He decided to call on one of his peers to help solve this mystery.

Lord Bennett Luxton drank his tea as he sat in his great room lit by a candlestick on a table next to him. A quiet knock on his door interrupted his thoughts. His eyebrows raised in curiosity. Precious few knew he kept late hours. He walked to the door and opened it. Reinard stood in the doorway.

"Good evening, Lord Luxton. Please pardon the late intrusion," said Reinard.

"I should be glad for the visit. What is on your mind?" Bennett stood aside to let his guest through the door. They walked into the great room and sat down. Reinard handed him a rolled piece of paper.

"Queer sightings in towns near the Anenderes River have been reported lately. While stargazing on my roof, I noticed large stars are coming into alignment. I have charted some of them on that paper. Do you know what this phenomenon is?"

Bennett studied the paper. "It seems we are falling into another period of transcendence. The alignment of planets and stars holds sway on the Anenderes River. Its effect can be quite strong, depending on the season, and what is happening in Nereheim."

"What do you mean?"

"Your son in law will be of greater help than I. The Mauldon family annals are quite intricate and have helped me in the past. Michael's great grandfather, Donovan Mauldon, devoted his youth to the Anenderes River and studied the strange happenings before during many phases. He noted the transcendence. I remember something happened to Donovan that brought him home to the vineyard to live out the rest of his days. I am certain the secret to that decision is also written down. Go to Michael. Ask to see these annals. Perhaps the two of you can decipher the mystery together."

"Is this a dangerous time?" asked Reinard.

"It is an occasion when people will see and receive messages from the dead who went before them. It is said that if a spirit wishes, during transcendence, it can willingly appear to someone they wish to speak to and give messages of warning or comfort. To see the dead is never a good omen. Nereheim may be heading into a dark future."

━━━━ ✦✦✦ ━━━━

Samson sat in front of a little cabin he built in the mountains. The fire was warm, casting an orange glow in the darkness. He loved sitting outside most evenings. Now that summer was drawing to a close, he came to treasure these times. He spent the last ten years of his life in the quiet of the mountains. There was no intrigue to find him, and he was content to live by what he could catch with his hands. Still, by exiling himself from mankind, he found there was little purpose to his existence.

He thought of Ian Keller and his wife Julia. They found a new life in Denholm Glen, the scene of so much bitterness and hate for those of the Craft. In the village of Illith, Count Vedan's own lust not only brought about the end of his life, but the life of Lord and Lady Saintclaire. That loss would be felt in the next generation all over Nereheim. For no one could train horses the way Bryant Saintclaire could. Samson vowed the day he razed the manor to the ground, he would not walk among mankind again. He thought it best to take his chances with the coyotes and wolves. At least he knew their motive from the moment their eyes found his.

The moon was full—he almost had no need of firelight. The Kellers came to mind once again. They were not without their problems when they first came to Denholm Glen. Ian told Samson a fantastic tale of how he helped the Viscountess, Alana Deveraux, thwart her father's plan to execute a young girl he believed to be of the Craft. That young girl grew into a beautiful woman who became the wife of Michael Mauldon, the studious son of the vineyard owner. Samson stared into the fire, smiling. "I wonder if he ever learned to ride?"

What good would be accomplished by breaking his vow and returning to the human race? He did not relish the idea of quitting his solitude for a sniveling master who did nothing but count pennies while his workers toiled for him. He needed to work for someone he respected. He wanted to work for someone he could believe in. Perhaps he should go to Denholm Glen and offer to work for Michael Mauldon. Though Michael spent his time in study, he still respected each man's place in this world. It was one of many traits Jason Mauldon passed on to both his sons. This he knew from the things Ian told him about Michael's vineyard. He was not as hearty for the outdoors as Philip, but he diligently learned every task on his property. Though Samson doubted he could bake yeast rolls like Sylvia did.

"Samson." Samson started and looked around him. He clearly heard his departed master's voice.

"Yes, my lord?" he said aloud.

He looked across the fire and slowly rose. Bryant Saintclaire stood on the other side of the fire. "Is it really you, my lord Saintclaire?"

"Yes."

"How is this possible?"

"The sacred writings say all things are possible with YAHWEH[3]. You must not let the past stand in the way of the future that awaits you. Count Deveraux has diligently put things in order in his new district. He has righted many of the shrewd dealings Count Vedan left as his legacy. Deveraux has only one thing left to do. King Rohn charged him with the task of rebuilding my home for Nadia should she choose to come back to Nereheim. Because of his distrust of those of the Craft, he has purposely left this as his last task. He needs a foreman to begin the process. I ask you to leave your life in the mountains, and join your fellow man once again.

You lived on my land your entire life. You love it as much as I did. There is no one else more capable for this endeavor. Rebuild my home."

"What if the Count has already chosen someone for this project?"

"Attach yourself to the task any way you can. The time is coming when you will be needed in Illith once again."

A cloud passed over the sky in the path of the moon and Bryant Saintclaire disappeared. Samson rubbed his eyes once more. "My lord?" he called into the night.

"Rebuild my home."

"It will be done, my Lord Saintclaire." He put out the fire and went inside. Tomorrow he would start back to Illith.

---

[3]   Matthew 19:26

CHAPTER 2

It was early as Reinard rode out to the Mauldon vineyard. He did not wonder whether Michael was awake. Despite the early hour, master and servant alike were known to get an early start to their daily activities. Since Sylvia's death, Maia kept the manor running efficiently for Michael and Lillia. She turned out to be a very capable young woman who made the transition from one manager to the next seamless. For this, Reinard was truly grateful.

He rode up the cobblestone pathway to the vineyard and left his horse with the stable hands. He was greeted as he walked through the servant's entrance.

Maia smiled when she saw him. "Lord Sallen, I am not accustomed to seeing you so early. Is there something I can help you with?"

"I need to see my son in law."

"You will find him in the library."

"Thank you, Maia." Reinard paused a moment to grab a warm yeast roll on his way through. Her laugh followed him down the hallway.

Michael sat in a chair watching the fire, a very distant and pensive look on his face. Reinard took that moment to finish his yeast roll.

"You have the look of someone who has spent the last few hours pondering a great conundrum." Michael looked over at the door where Reinard stood.

"Father, I did not hear you come in."

"I realize my visit is early."

Michael smiled. "I did not think you rose out of bed until the cock crowed. What brings you here so early?"

Reinard pulled a folded paper from his shirt pocket. "For the past month, I have charted the stars. Travelers passing through Denholm Glen tell of being visited by people they knew as dead. This chart shows a curious alignment of stars and planets alike."

Michael looked at the figures on the paper. It was mostly a series of dots sectioned off into something like map coordinates. Four larger spots caught his attention. The way they were drawn was not in perfect alignment, but if this was a chart of what happened over time, they soon would be. His brow furrowed as he looked at the paper.

"Have you ever heard of transcendence?" asked Reinard.

"It is a period where the heavenly bodies come into perfect alignment," Michael replied.

"Lord Luxton suggested that I ask to look into your family annals for Donovan Mauldon's discoveries about transcendence."

"You think the incidents may be related?"

"Lord Luxton has a long memory to match his many years. He studied the stars when my father was still alive. If he believes the two are related, we should look into it. He also said something else."

"What was that?" Michael rose and walked over to one of the shelves in the room.

"To see the dead is never a good omen. Nereheim may be entering troublesome times. That is why I want to know what Donovan Mauldon knew."

Michael took a volume off one of the shelves and handed it to Reinard. "This volume contains Marek and Donovan's life. This is where you will find everything related to Donovan's early life and travels. What he recorded about the Anenderes River should be here. However, I will go to my study and retrieve his diary. Perhaps there is more information there. I ask that this book stays here. Do you mind?"

"Nothing would please me more than a few hours of uninterrupted perusal of a book sure to be fascinating," replied Reinard.

"I will be back after a while to see what you found." Michael left the room.

Reinard opened the great book. It began with Lord Marek's life. It recorded Marek's accomplishments from his youth—how he was able to tame and train even the most obnoxious beasts. As Marek grew older, there were many times he was called upon to calm wild animals that became a threat to his village. He made the most spirited animals bow before him. Reinard remembered Bryant Saintclaire. Did Marek possess the same intuition that allowed Bryant to become the most noted horse master in Nereheim?

As he read, Reinard discovered the Mauldon family did not always dwell in Denholm Glen. Marek, his wife, and their young son Donovan lived in a village residing along the Anenderes River near Wildemere. From a young age, Donovan sat along the river, mesmerized by it. He spent his time in careful study of the Craft and became an accomplished rider, but always made time for watching the river. He wrote in a special book as he did this.

When Donovan was sixteen years old, his mother died in a plague that spread to their village. Marek sold their home and moved west. Donovan was heartbroken to leave their home by the river.

Settling in Denholm Glen, Marek began a vineyard. He noted his son's melancholy, but Donovan set himself to the task. He worked for two years before finally telling his father he wished to travel. He was drawn to the river and wanted to continue to study it.

Marek wrote that Donovan set off on his eighteenth birthday seeking answers believed to be found only along the river.

During late summer a few months later, Donovan returned home. Marek was overjoyed, but asked why he returned.

"I witnessed a most singular experience, father. You would never believe me if I told you," replied Donovan.

He said no more, but was happy to settle back into the life of a vineyard owner next to his father. Marek never asked again, and Donovan never mentioned the mystery that brought him home. Their relationship became closer than ever, with Donovan learning everything about the vineyard.

As Reinard read on in the book, the script changed from tight to more free flowing. In one sentence he realized why. Two years after Donovan's return, Marek went to bed one night and never awoke. Donovan's script recorded his father's death and reason for returning.

It is amazing the turns our lives make. Each one mixes with another to become what we know as fate. We are bedrock sure of one thing until we chance to turn around and see something we know to be impossible.

I had such an occurrence on the fifth of September, two years ago. I was on a secluded road little more than a path among tall grass. It was said to lead to the ruined city of Herron. My horse, Drifter, was very unsteady. I barely kept him on the track. I finally dismounted and led him myself, such was his apprehension. After two hours, we came to a clearing and I saw the sparkling water of the Anenderes River. I stood, for a moment, spellbound by its vastness, the way I watched the waves as a child. After a few moments, a voice behind me gave me a chill, for I remembered it well. I slowly turned to see my mother who died two years ago.

"Hello, my son."

My eyes filled with tears as I whispered, "Mother, is it really you?"

"Yes. I came to tell you to return home to your father right away. He misses you greatly. Take care not to tarry along the river, or you may return home to ill news. I love you my son."

I blinked and she was gone. Her voice sounded as a whisper on the wind as it said, "GO."

I returned home to find my father well and the vineyard prosperous. I was relieved, but puzzled, about the incident. I know I saw my mother, but I could never tell father. He would believe me mad. I chose to write the account here, for my future kin. May the information it contains serve you well.

Reinard paused his reading and looked up. Michael entered the room with a small book in his hand.

"I think I may have found something of interest."

"I may have too."

"You first," replied Michael leaning against his desk.

"Donovan Mauldon recorded seeing his dead mother appear before him, and warned him to return to Denholm Glen. He dated the account on September fifth, as he traveled the road to the ruined village of Herron."

"The fifth of September."

"Yes. Does that mean anything?"

Michael turned the pages of the book in his hand. "This book reads like a journal. It is filled out by date, but it records patterns in the sky and describes strange stories, sightings and tendencies of the Anenderes River. There is something listed under the fifth of September the year 1305 that looks like a chart." He turned the book around to face Reinard. "Does this look familiar to you?" Michael held the piece of paper Reinard brought next to the book in his hand. They were identical.

"At the time he recorded this, Donovan may not have realized what transcendence was. However, it seems this event he records coincides with a time of transcendence for that year."

"What did his mother say?" asked Michael.

"To return home before his father was lost to him. Marek died in his sleep two years after Donovan's return."

Michael's gaze grew pensive as he spoke. "There is an epic poem told about the Anenderes River. One of the lines says, 'the spirits have been known to whisper, short messages to us creatures.' It seems Donovan was forewarned by his mother of his father's coming demise."

"Merchants have whispered about the dead being seen as though living. Lord Luxton was correct to believe this was somehow related."

Michael nodded. "I wonder just what this time of transcendence will bring to Nereheim."

CHAPTER 3

A small cottage sat amid wild fields—the very essence of solitude. A gentle breeze kept the sun's heat at bay as birds sang among the scattered bushes and trees.

Nafaria sat in the middle of her herb garden, inspecting the lavender plants. They were coming along nicely. Soon, she would have a hearty crop to experiment with.

She started her garden to use its herbs and flowers in various tisanes, elixirs, and remedies for her father-in-law to sell in his apothecary shop. Malcom Stone's name was powerful among the people of North Agea. His reputation for healing powders and elixirs was well known. People traveled great distances to see the apothecary who knew his medicines intimately.

Nafaria unwittingly became just as well-known. She helped people in nearby villages or anyone who passed by their cottage where she and Nathaniel lived. Many were drawn to her delightful smile and gentle nature. Those who could not afford to travel all the way to Arioth believed her to be nothing less than a gift from YAHWEH to help them.

She met Matthew and his father Silas this way. They were on their way to Arioth, but were forced to stop near the cottage and ask for aid. Silas had an infection in his leg so strong he could not go further unless it was treated. Nafaria invited them in, treated the infection and urged them to stay the night with her and Nathaniel. His leg was healed by the next morning. Silas was so grateful; he and Matthew offered to help Nathaniel in the fields. The arrangement worked well for everyone.

The gentle breeze brought another moment of refreshment. A horse galloping roused her from her thoughts. She saw a lone rider with long red hair. Jumping up, Nafaria quickly made her way out of the garden to the road.

The horse slowed and the visitor let herself down with grace and ease. She threw her arms around Nafaria. "Hello little one!" she exclaimed.

"Nadia, what are you doing here?" asked Nafaria.

"Your aunt Contessa sent me to Arioth for an elixir that will help Sela sleep through the night. She has been restless lately. Since you are on the way, I wanted to give you something."

Nadia turned to her horse and opened a pack that fastened to its side, and pulled out a thick book. She looked at it reverently then put it in Nafaria's hands.

Nafaria looked down and saw the stem of lavender embossed on the leather cover. "Is this Lady Cassandra's diary?"

"Yes."

"Nadia, this is your mother's book— her wisdom. I could not possibly take it."

"I thought about this greatly and talked it over with Philip. We are both horse trainers and we are out in the wild with living animals day after day. Father's wisdom helps us every day, but mother's sits on a shelf and we hardly seek it. You will put it to good use, I am confident of that. This way, her knowledge stays in the family and will not be lost among a collection of books never to be opened. Philip agreed with me. We both feel you will derive far more use from it. Philip has knowledge of the woods and all the plants found in the wild. We will pass that knowledge on to Roland and Rowena. If I ever need this book for anything, I know where to locate it. You are gaining a strong reputation for yourself as a healer like your mother and Malcom. You can use this wisdom to benefit all," said Nadia.

"Thank you for this book. I am so interested to learn your mother's secrets," said Nafaria.

"Mother used lavender for everything. The smell of that flower reminds me of home. She mixed a special calming elixir for father to calm the horses when they were restless. Perhaps we can make it for Sela."

"If I have all the ingredients, we can make it here and save you a trip to Arioth."

Nadia smiled. "It will be time well spent with my little sister." They went into the cottage.

Nafaria put the book on a large table in the kitchen. She went to a cupboard in the corner of the room and took out a bowl and other tools. Nadia opened the book and turned it toward Nafaria.

"This is the elixir."

Nafaria looked at the ingredient list and directions. Then she pointed to the opposite page. "What is this?"

"A powder mother derived for father to use when the horses could not be calmed any other way. It is very powerful; strong enough to quiet a mad boar. Father had to use it on one that ran wild through Illith once. He had to get close enough to it to throw it in the animal's face, but it worked excellently."

"It sounds like a very powerful sedative." Nafaria scanned the list of ingredients. "I have the ingredients for this as well. Would you mind if I make some for you? I think Nathaniel and Malcom would find this very interesting."

"It would be a useful gift to carry back to Philip. Lately the villagers around us have asked him to quiet restless animals."

Nafaria began the elixir. She quietly combined the ingredients, looking at the book every now and then. Nadia leaned back against the wall by the sink.

"How do you like being here?"

"It is very much like home. People are curious about who I am and what I do. Because I help Malcom, I often get visitors. I thought of spending some time in Arioth to work in his shop and learn from him. That would give me the opportunity to see Ephratha more."

"Lady Contessa speaks highly of her. She seems like a very modest and delightful girl."

"Ephratha knows exactly where she stands in life. She is not always confident in herself, but has great respect for things she does not understand. Her mother taught her the practicality of respect. She knows it is earned, not given. Therefore Ephratha forms opinions based on a person's actions, not on their appearance. This is wise, but sometimes even actions can be misjudged and a person with false motives can catch her off guard by quickly winning her approval. It is not the worst character flaw a person can have, but it can be a dangerous one at court." Nafaria took the pot and walked over to the corner, positioning it over the fire. The low flame was perfect for heating. Soon, the cottage smelled of lavender.

"That smells so good," said Nadia.

Nafaria stirred the liquid as it cooked. When it was ready, she grabbed a thick towel and brought the pot back to the table, adding a small amount of wild honey to it.

"It must cool before putting it into jars. I will give Malcom some for his shop."

Nafaria cleaned the bowl and tools and dried them. Then she studied the recipe for the powder once again. "This recipe looks like the elixir, only in powder form. The quantities of herbs are much higher, making a more powerful sedative. It could be used as a sleeping powder, but you must use a very small amount." She measured herbs into the bowl she just cleaned, then picked up a pestle and ground the ingredients until it was a fine powder. She found three small jars with cork stoppers and measured the powder into them.

"Mother always had this powder on hand. My father came for it often," said Nadia.

"Now you have some for Philip as well. Do you need this recipe?"

Nadia shook her head. "I have this copied into my own diary as well as the elixir."

Nafaria walked over to the pot and stirred the elixir. She ladled it into jars on the table. She then lined a sack with a cotton towel. Carefully, she put the jars in the sack and handed it to Nadia.

"You may still want to go to Arioth and speak with Malcom about what may help Sela."

"I will take my chances with what you made."

Nafaria hugged Nadia. "I am glad we had this time together. Send my brother greetings for me. I miss you both."

"Come visit us when you have the chance. Count Lucerne's land is quite spectacular."

"We shall see," replied Nafaria.

Sunset painted the sky in rich reds, oranges and purples. Old Oberman took in the spectacle from his favorite cliff at the edge of the woods. His weathered skin saw far too many winters for mere mortal comprehension. He accomplished much with his long life, amassing greater knowledge and wisdom than he ever dreamed. With it, he bore his share of sorrow. Such was the way of the wise and powerful. They often left the souls of the naïve scattered in their wake as discarded refuse. He did amazing things in his life: he built kingdoms— shattered nations. He stole sacred things believed unattainable by human hands. His great master showed him terrible truths. Oberman dared to seek out the darkness and reaped his reward: power. YAHWEH was great, but his master revealed secrets denied him by his creator. For those left who knew what dangers lay in the whisper of his name, Oberman was more than mere myth or legend.

In the days of his youth, his ambition was to rival the wise King Solomon. He wanted to be the wisest, most powerful being to walk the earth. His ambition led him to Herron, that legendary city of the sacred bell. Oberman wished to sit at the feet of the first of the Craft to come to Nereheim, who discovered the bell and built Herron as a monument to its creator. For all his desire, he was mocked and cast aside, deemed unworthy for the deepest secrets Herron guarded from the world. Shunned by the old men who counted him unfit for their wisdom, he swore they would pay for their oversight in blood.

Visited by a hooded man with eyes of red fire, he was challenged to make his own wisdom and be the greatest sorcerer in the sister kingdoms. "Your name will be whispered among the mountains in the West, to the Anenderes in the East. Let it be terrible indeed."

"What must I do?"

"Steal the sacred bell, and wield its power against Herron. Too long have fools revered this great discovery. It is a tool to be used, not a relic to be worshipped. Take the bell, call forth the spirits, and destroy the city."

The thought of the bell in his grasp provided the nerve Oberman needed for such an audacious act. He walked boldly to the edge of the quay and stood before the bell. He reached out his hand and after a moment, plucked it from the pedestal and took the hammer from its place. After striking the bell, a great cloud of unnatural host gathered before him, each one lusting for destruction.

Loose them on the city. Oberman heard the whisper and obeyed, giving the command for them to go forth and destroy.

"Not one stone shall be left upon another!" he screamed into the swirling maelstrom that left in a flash to make the city of the learned and wise a haunted ruin—a blight in the hearts of men.

Now, two hundred years of his life stretched his skin over his bones like a worn leather hide. He learned so much and was ready to go to dust. The

Grimoire Macabre, the symbol of all the dark secrets and wisdom of the master of this world, would go to another. Many came in search of great power, but his master examines the hearts of his successors and chooses or rejects without mercy. All were rejected. What would his successor be like? Would he be focused? Would he be driven? How much intelligence would he possess?

Oberman remembered a studious, wealthy, young man from his past. He possessed great skill and was tactful with everyone he met. He sought deeper truths in a way Oberman related to. Joseph Wheaton proved an apt pupil with every test he was given. He drove himself to the edge of madness for the power to save; such was his single mindedness. Oberman was convinced his successor was found.

As his final test, Oberman asked Joseph for the reason he should grant his wish and reveal his secrets. Joseph shared an incantation he wrote in the oldest runic language known to the world of alchemy. It was reminiscent of the greatness of Herron's past. It gave the wielder the power to see into another's mind and manipulate that consciousness. Oberman taught Joseph the ritual to summon his master. He was unaware another was chosen, even more focused and driven. Oberman asked no questions. He bowed to his master, and waited these last years for his successor to seek him. He smiled as he believed the time was at hand.

———————— ·+++++· ————————

The full moon through the window cast a glow revealing the outline of Nafaria's body as Nathaniel watched her sleep. He reached out his hand and gently stroked her cheek. Her skin was soft and warm. He moved closer and kissed her forehead.

He watched her often while she slept—a slight smile on her lips. As if all the tragedy in her past were a distant memory pulled from her mind and discarded like so much refuse.

Tears formed and rolled down his cheeks. He wanted to protect her from the rest of the world. His precious jewel was finally in his grasp, and no one would hurt her again.

As he pulled her closer, he felt the heat and softness of her body. Tears continued as he kissed her neck and face, gently, so as not to wake her.

Laying in the dark, with her in his arms, his thoughts drifted to the man who would be his father-in-law, if he were still alive. Jason chose to live in anonymity in Nereheim, always hoping to serve his country. Trust in the wrong person cost him his life and Thena's as well. He chose to love and hope, but those traits failed him in the end. His country did not respect his life, nor would it protect the wise ones living in exile within its borders.

Those of the Craft were given supernatural power by YAHWEH to protect mortal man from themselves. They were to be respected, not mocked or despised. Too long had his kind buried this power and only tapped the surface to help comfort those with minor ailments from time to time. Or to seek higher wisdom to teach their mortal neighbors how to get along with one another. He must unleash his real potential, if only to protect the ones he loved.

"I will protect you from them. You will not die by hanging or burning," he whispered. He drifted off to sleep, breathing her airy scent.

He awoke later, but Nafaria still slept. He saw clouds and light rain through the window. Fog hid the trees around the cottage.

Nathaniel loved a rainy day. The overhead sky, a nondescript gray that one spent hours gazing at not realizing time passed. He crept out of bed, dressed quickly and left the room, grabbing his black cloak from a chair near the door.

Nathaniel pulled his hood over his head as he walked through the woods behind their home. It was a peaceful place, but one day he and Nafaria would be in a position to afford greater.

He walked along, his mind on the future. He felt himself standing at a crossroads. What should be his next pursuit? He knew he needed to protect Nafaria, but what power and wisdom would be great enough to do so?

He became aware he was not alone. Another traveler in a long black cloak with a walking stick moved out of the mist into view. He saw nothing of the stranger but his hands.

"Greetings sir, you pick a strange day to be traveling," said Nathaniel.

"It would seem you have done the same," replied the traveler. His voice was rich and soothing.

"I enjoy walking in the rain," replied Nathaniel.

"As do I." The stranger moved closer. "I have sought you, Nathaniel Stone, for I know what is on your mind. You are within reach of the power you seek. Find the old hermit named Oberman. He will show you his secrets. His house is a day's ride beyond the hills to the West. Do not delay; lest you be too late to receive his wisdom." The stranger walked on as if he needed not linger.

"Wait sir, what on earth are you talking about?" asked Nathaniel.

The stranger laughed as he turned and faced Nathaniel with blood red eyes. "Find Oberman, he will know."

Nathaniel sat up in bed gasping for air, his body covered in sweat. He became aware he was in his bedroom, with Nafaria at his side. Outside, a steady gentle rain fell. He gulped air and finally lay back down.

Nafaria opened her eyes and smiled at him. "It sounds like rain." Her brow creased when she looked at him. "Is something wrong?"

"It was only a bad dream. Help me make it go away." Nathaniel clutched her closely and kissed her neck gently, his fingers caressing her long hair.

"You are so wonderful," she sighed.

He smiled and laid his head on her chest, feeling the steady beat of her heart. He stroked her hair and whispered, "Tell me a secret."

"A secret?"

"Something no one else knows about you. A little detail I can guard with my life."

There was only one thing Nafaria knew was her greatest secret. Her mother warned her never to tell anyone of her elderberry aversion. Surely that did not include her husband? Nathaniel was chosen for her the way she knew she was chosen for him. Though she had her parents' blessing, she knew YAHWEH himself chose Nathaniel for her. How could they have found each other after so long if not for his design? She had nothing to fear with Nathaniel. He was her perfect love.

"There is one thing about me no one else knows." Nathaniel looked at her as she continued.

"Do you remember the day you gave me this ring?" She pointed to her right hand.

"Sylvia said you were sick and thought you would not be able to play."

"I was very sick the night before. My heart raced and I was covered in sweat. I tried to go to my mother, but I stumbled in the hallway near my parents' bedroom. I tried calling her but was too weak. Then I vomited so much I coughed up blood."

"What made you so sick?"

"Sylvia was making elderberry jam that day. I never had it before, and she offered me some before dinner. My parents were convinced that was it. Mother told me I almost died that night. If I would have had as much jam as I wanted, I very likely would have."

"That is so strange. Cooked elderberry is supposed to be very good for health."

"My parents were perplexed about that also. That is why they told me never to reveal my secret to anyone." Nathaniel put his head down next to hers and looked into her eyes. "I searched for you a long time and now I have you. Being married to you is like a breath of fresh air. Do you think I would poison you?"

"No, but my parents did insist."

"Thank you for entrusting me with your secret," he whispered.

⸻ ⊹⊹⊹⊹⊹ ⸻

The sky turned lighter as it rained into the afternoon. Nafaria looked out the kitchen window and sighed. They lived less than a day's ride from Arioth, but she felt even further away.

Nafaria wondered what Ephratha was doing. Did she enjoy her new life as princess? Was Jared busy with the affairs of the kingdom? Did she feel Jared's weight of responsibility also?

Warm hands and strong arms wrapped around her body. Nathaniel's breath was warm on her neck.

"Is something wrong?" he asked.

"No. I just miss Ephratha. I have not seen her since we moved here."

"Would you like to spend a few days with her?"

"I would love that, but do you not wish to come?"

"I have struggled this week with a question in my head. There is something I need to do, and I must go alone. While I am away, you can visit Ephratha and Jared."

"Silas and Matthew can mind the garden and field for us. How long will you be gone?"

"I think a week will suffice."

"I can part with you that long, but it will feel like an eternity."

"I shall be back soon," whispered Nathaniel in her ear. She smiled as he kissed her neck and the rain continued outside.

<hr>

The next morning Nafaria packed clothes in a velvet bag given her as a wedding present. She took the bag to the stable where their horses were. Nathaniel and Silas were there, going through last minute details. Both smiled as she approached.

"Nathaniel told us you both intend to be gone for a while. Will you be alright to ride to Arioth alone?" asked Silas.

"I will be fine. One single rider is going to attract trouble whether they be man or woman," she said.

"Matthew could go with you," said Silas. His voice held concern.

"That is not necessary."

Silas looked at Nathaniel who shrugged his shoulders. "If she says no, I will respect that. However, I do expect you to be careful and not invite trouble." He looked at Nafaria carefully.

She moved toward him and playfully kissed his nose. "I promise to be careful. It will be fun to catch Ephratha by surprise."

Nathaniel pulled her close to him and hugged her. He kissed her forehead and whispered, "I will never forgive myself or the man who harms you."

"I love you very much. I do hope this time apart will be a rare occurrence."

"It will. Now go and have fun with your friend."

"Let me fasten your sack for you." Silas pointed to the sack in her hand as he took it and fastened it to the saddle while she climbed on the horse.

"Be safe," said Nafaria.

"I will be here when you return," said Nathaniel.

She smiled again, coaxing the horse into a smooth trot, heading toward Arioth. Nathaniel watched her go. He needed answers, but he would miss her. The last thing he saw was her hair in the breeze while her horse increased its speed.

⸻ ⬥⬥⬥ ⸻

The late afternoon sun was bright. Coleman stood next to the sentry on the castle wall. From this height, he saw a vast distance. Arioth was not on a hill, but the open fields made it easy to see every direction, making the castle more defensible.

"The day has been uneventful, Captain."

"So it appears." Coleman continued his watch of the fields through his glass.

"Do you expect trouble?"

"My duty to the king demands my vigilance even when there seems no need of it. Continue to keep watch."

"Yes Captain."

The blue sky was beautiful and without a hint of storm on the horizon. Still, Coleman was restless, making him wary. Something sinister threatened the peace of North Agea. His thoughts were interrupted by the sentry.

"Captain, a lone rider approaches."

Coleman took out his glass and looked in the direction the sentry indicated. A smile crossed his face.

"Who is it?"

"Someone the princess will be very happy to see when she returns." He descended the stairwell on the wall and went to the gate.

<hr>

The smile on Nafaria's face grew wide as the castle came closer. Warm wind threw her hair behind her as the sun kissed her cheeks. She was excited to see her friend and find out if there was anything new. Good tidings make time pass quickly.

Nafaria saw Coleman at the castle gate. She slowed her horse and stopped next to him. "Coleman, it is nice of you to meet me." She hopped down off her horse.

"The pleasure is mine, my lady. Are you here alone? Where is Nathaniel on this fine day?"

"He is in need of answers he seeks on his own, so we agreed to time apart. I came to visit Ephratha. Is she here?"

"The family is in Nereheim for Prince Andrew's wedding. We expect their return tomorrow. The king and queen insisted Jared and Ephratha join them for the wedding. Neither was happy about the trip."

"I suppose not. Jared and Andrew do not fare well together."

"I will do my best to entertain you in their absence. However, I have the watch after dinner."

"All I need is a room to sleep in, and direction to the royal library. Perhaps I will learn more about the healing plants and herbs here."

"From what I hear, your expertise as a healer and herb cultivator is quite impressive already."

"One can always learn more."

"Nathaniel is very lucky to have a wife who contents herself so easily."

After leaving Nafaria's horse in the stable, Coleman brought her to the guest room nearest Jared and Ephratha's room. "Dinner is in an hour. Afterward, the library awaits you."

"Thank you, Coleman. That sounds lovely."

⸻ ⊹⊹⊹⊹⊹ ⸻

After dinner, Nafaria sat in the library before a candlestick reading a volume of herbs. The details of the book were intricate, reminding her of something one might read from one of the Craft. She marveled that such a book was in the king's library.

She paused as she heard a faint whisper. After a moment, she returned to her reading. The sound grew louder, threatening her concentration. She walked to the doorway and peered down each direction of the great hall, but it was empty. She sighed and sat back down.

Nafaria looked at the book. A draft of cold air came along with a definite whisper, *"Nafaria!"* The voice sounded like her mother. She closed her eyes and sighed. The whisper brought back sweet but painful recollection.

"Mother?" she whispered as she looked around the room. In that moment, she longed to hear her voice again.

"Beware the dark Master. He seeks your child. Beware lest you fall victim to him."

How was it possible she heard her mother's voice? Both her parents perished before she escaped to North Agea. Yet, she also knew with

YAHWEH, all things were possible.[4] Nafaria smelled a hint of apple blossom.

She closed the book and returned it to the shelf. She wrote the words—beware the dark master, on a piece of paper sitting on the table and left the room.

⋅⊹⊹⊹⋅

The airy scent of wild lilac greeted Nafaria as she opened the door to the apothecary shop. Malcom smiled when he saw her.

"Nafaria, this is a surprise!" He swallowed her in a hug. "Where is Nathaniel?"

"We agreed on time apart so he could be alone to sort through something on his mind. He suggested I visit Ephratha and Jared."

"Are you just arriving?"

"I came yesterday afternoon. Coleman entertained me. They are with the king and queen in Nereheim."

"Yes, to celebrate Prince Andrew's wedding. Ephratha was looking for a gift for the bride before they left."

"What did she settle on?"

"A perfume made of lilac. Apparently, the bride is very fond of them."

"That is just like Ephratha to give something to put one at their ease."

"Did you stay the night in the castle?"

"Coleman would have it no other way. He wanted to make sure I was taken care of."

---

[4]   Mark 10:27

Nafaria became silent. After a moment she said, "Something happened last night. I was reading in the castle library after dinner when I heard mother's whisper. I know it is impossible, but I could not mistake her voice for wind in the hallway. Also, I smelled apple blossom in the air."

"Your mother was hanged and burned in an apple grove in Wildemere. Nathaniel and I first encountered Lydia Stowe there. She told us what happened to her."

"I remember that place was such a comfort for me. It was peaceful amid the bustle of the market."

"If it happens again, you should write to Michael and ask his advice on the matter. Talk among the gypsies traveling between Nereheim and North Agea grows of the wise one from Denholm Glen who is a vineyard owner and busy schooling himself in arcane knowledge. He even studies their ways."

"With Lillia finally at his side, Michael has nothing else to content himself with. I know something of that myself." She pulled two glass vials from her pocket. One contained a liquid, the other a powder.

"What is this?"

"Nadia came to see me with a valuable gift—Lady Cassandra's diary. She was coming to see you for something to help Sela sleep, but we made an elixir from one of Lady Cassandra's potions."

Malcom picked up the vial containing the liquid. "This is the elixir?"

"Yes. I thought you might want it on hand for your shop. If you like, I can make more for you."

Malcom held up the other vial. "Is this Lady Cassandra's relaxing powder?"

"Yes."

"This has been said to stop a wild boar. Thank you, Nafaria. I am sure I can find use for these. Continue to make them for me."

"I will. I must go now. I want to be at the castle when Jared and Ephratha return."

Malcom gave Nafaria another hug. "Come see me before you leave for home again."

She smiled at Malcom as she left the shop.

⸻ ·⊹⊹⊹⊹⊹· ⸻

Coleman came to Nafaria as she climbed the stone steps to the catwalk along the castle wall. "Good morning, Nafaria. You are up earlier than I expected."

"I have been up earlier than you imagine. I came outside for a stroll." She looked at the fields surrounding the castle. "What a lovely view. I understand why you choose sentry duty on a day like today."

"During times of peace, the sentry has much time to think. During times of conflict, he is the first alert of enemy approach and must able respond quickly."

"Has there ever been a time of conflict?"

"Not in my career. We are most fortunate that Rohn and Lian will not war against each other."

"Have they always been close?"

"They have never been close; but each one respects the other, even when they disagree. It is never tense when both kings are together. Each one loves his wife deeply, so they work at their friendship."

"We are lucky to be living in such a time."

"Indeed. Such times give way to darker ones."

The sound of horses caught Coleman's attention. He looked through his glass and spied a carriage with the king's crest on the side. "The royal family returns."

They hurried down the stairs as the carriage drove through the gate, stopping in front of them. The door opened and Jared stepped out. He smiled when he saw Nafaria standing next to Coleman.

"Ephratha, it seems we have a guest!" he exclaimed. Ephratha took Jared's hand and stepped down. She straightened after both feet were firmly on the ground. Nafaria saw her belly was a small round shape.

"Nafaria, this is a lovely surprise! When did you get here?" asked Ephratha as she wrapped her arms around her friend.

"I arrived yesterday to find you gone. How was the wedding?" asked Nafaria.

"Nina looked enchanting, and was so wonderful to be around."

"What about Andrew?"

A sour look crossed Ephratha's face. "He was tolerable when Nina was around. She seems to bring out whatever good qualities he has."

"Nafaria, it is good to see you, unexpected as it may be," said King Lian as he emerged from of the carriage.

"Thank you, your majesty," replied Nafaria with a slight bow. She turned back to Ephratha. "You look so well! I can hardly believe you will be a mother soon."

"I can hardly believe it myself. So, what brings you to Arioth?"

"Nathaniel suggested I visit you while he is away. He said he needed time alone to puzzle through something on his mind."

"My enigmatic friend has not changed since he married. Nathaniel often seeks places for solitude. I cannot tell you how many times I would find him in the fields alone, or even in our royal library," said Jared.

"I think he learned that from Michael. He was a solitary learner as well. They were very close friends and often their personalities ran in one direction," replied Nafaria.

"I am glad you mentioned your brother. We had a most unusual conversation about something he called 'transcendence'. It was an interesting conversation, but it seemed he was trying to warn me. He gave me a letter for you. Since you are here, it saves me the task of finding a courier." Jared ducked back into the carriage and returned with a small roll of paper sealed with hardened wax.

"Thank you, your highness. I wonder what he is up to now," Nafaria looked at the roll in her hand.

"Why not take some time to read it while we get settled? Perhaps that letter will shed some light on his conversation with me," replied Jared.

"That is a good idea. I need to rest, anyway. I feel a little drowsy," said Ephratha.

"Coleman found a guest room for me near your room. I will be there," replied Nafaria.

Moving away from the carriage, Nafaria broke the seal and unrolled the letter. His opening line made her smile.

Dearest little one,

I know you are quite grown, but in my mind you will always be my little one. I trust you and Nathaniel are enjoying your life in North Agea. Lillia sends her love, she is due any time now. I will send news when our child arrives.

Lord Reinard came to me a few days ago about a most peculiar matter that occurred along the Anenderes River. You may hear or experience things yourself. We are making careful study of the stars and found we are heading into what the ancients referred to as "transcendence". At this time, you may encounter visions or dreams. It is a time when the dead speak even more clearly than if you see faces in the river. I have copied our great grandfather's findings about transcendence for you. Be aware of these things as you come near or cross the river. Take great care, as I have no idea what to expect from the days to come. Always yours,

Michael

Nafaria looked at the accompanying pages. One was a chart with dots appearing to align almost perfectly. The other pages were copied notes. She knew her great grandfather grew up enchanted by the Anenderes River. Why would Michael write this to her? The whispered warning she heard played in her mind once more.

⋅⋅⋅✦✦✦✦✦⋅⋅⋅

Nafaria found Ephratha and Jared on the terrace overlooking Queen Clara's rose garden.

"What a lovely view," she said as she approached them.

"When mother moved here, Aunt Susanna suggested they both build a garden together. It was identical to remind each of the other. Mother says it helps her feel closer to her sister," said Jared.

"What did Michael say in his letter?" asked Ephratha.

"He sent me information about my great grandfather who studied the Anenderes River as a youth. When he took over the vineyard, he continued his study, but he never left Denholm Glen after his father died. Michael sent me information that Donovan recorded about transcendence and the Anenderes. It is fascinating."

"Perhaps I could read his letter while you are here? It would be a rare privilege to see how your brother thinks," said Jared.

"You may," said Nafaria.

Ephratha smiled. "Perhaps it will also take your mind off your cousin's ill mannerisms."

"Why is it you dislike Andrew so much?" asked Nafaria.

"I have always disliked my cousin. I have absolutely no respect for him," replied Jared.

"Why?" she asked in reply.

Jared took a breath before he spoke. "When we were younger, I traveled with my mother when she visited Aunt Susanna. I remember when we were either eight or nine years old. I came upon Andrew berating a young servant girl, who was a little older than us. Her mother was one of the housekeepers and this young girl worked with her. She loved her mother so much she gave up her free time to help her. I heard what Andrew said as I walked into the room. The girl burst into tears and ran out.

'Why would you say such horrible things to her?' I asked.

'If I am to rule as king, I must make my subjects fear me,' he replied.

'Your subjects will only fear you to your face. If you treat people with cruelty, they will treat you in kind. The only difference is they will do it when your back is turned.'

After that, I refused to go to Nereheim with my mother. I would only go at my father's strongest insistence. Andrew has only become more ridiculous and boorish over time. It is a shame, because I am sure there is brilliance buried in that heart somewhere. There must be kindness as well, or Nina would never have fallen in love with him. She is not the kind of person to marry only for station in life."

"Perhaps she will help him see what you tried to tell him so long ago," replied Nafaria. "People can change."

"You are right, of course. I wonder what Andrew will become. I fear he will only grow worse."

CHAPTER 4

Nathaniel's horse moved through the fields at a steady pace. The rainfall from the previous day made the air cooler. He put the hood up on his cloak for warmth. The mountains loomed in the distance.

He threw himself into constant study and begged YAHWEH for the answer to his conundrum. He struggled, cried out in anguish, but no answer came. The only word that seeped into the recesses of his mind was a name: Oberman.

He looked across the field. Three x-shaped crosses stood in the center of a hill with flames surrounding them. Nathaniel blinked his eyes and looked again. The field was empty. Halting his horse, he forced himself to breathe. A distant memory came forth.

Nathaniel and his father made their way across Nereheim after leaving Denholm Glen at Reinard's warning. As he rode with his father, his thoughts kept returning to Nafaria. Would Reinard be able to give her his letter? Would she keep it? Would Jason heed the warning and leave? Would they ever see each other again? He stirred from the barrage of questions with a sharp cry from his father. "Nathaniel, stop!"

His father pointed to a hill. Three young girls were each tied to a cross, their cries drowned out by loud shouts from a gathering of people. Three men held another thrashing about, trying to break free. Nathaniel and Malcom jumped from their horses and ran toward the crowd. Malcom drew his dagger from its sheath. Nathaniel pulled out his hunting knife.

Malcom jumped on the cluster of men, pulling one up from the ground. He put the dagger's blade to the man's neck and cried out, "Stay this madness, you fools! Who would kill innocent girls?"

"Father!" cried Nathaniel.

Malcom saw torches were thrown at the base of the crosses. Flames shot instantly through the dry kindling and screams of terror filled the air. The wood continued to burn.

"NO!" One man cried out as he struggled toward the crosses. Malcom and Nathaniel grabbed him, holding him fast.

"Come friend, there is nothing that can be done for them now." He looked at Malcom, then back at the girls who still screamed in agony. The air turned acrid as their bodies burned. He sank to his knees, crying in anguish.

"There is nothing left for me in Nereheim now."

The stranger rode with them for a while before he spoke. "My name is Roderick, and once upon a time I was the happiest man in the world. I am of the Craft, as was my wife. We were married five years before my grief began. My wife was pregnant, but died giving birth to the last of my three girls. As the midwives pulled the last baby from her, she cried out and breathed her last.

The townspeople were grieved that Sophia was dead, and each of the women helped me with the girls. I made the decision long ago not to train my daughters in the Craft. Sophia supported that decision. We hoped ignorance of their birthright would save them from persecution should it come to back to Nereheim as in the time of the Coe massacre. We planned to betroth them to others of the Craft as many families did with their daughters. This way YAHWEH'S power would continue.

I heard of what happened in Illith and Denholm Glen, but I thought we were safe. This morning the men of the village invaded my home and dragged my daughters away. I tried to stop them, but there were too many. They beat me and dragged me behind my daughters to the hill."

"My son and I are crossing the Anenderes into North Agea. You are welcome to join us," said Malcom.

"Thank you for the invitation. Ignorance and treachery have poisoned Nereheim. I care not to dwell within its borders," replied Roderick.

Malcom saw Nathaniel riding ahead of them. He sped up the pace of his horse. "What is on your mind, my son?"

Nathaniel faced his father with tears on his cheeks. "Those girls were so young and ignorant of their heritage. They knew nothing! They did not understand the madness happening around them! What if Nafaria—" Nathaniel could not finish his sentence.

"Have courage, Nathaniel. Jason will protect his family. Trust YAHWEH, you will see her again."

Nathaniel shook off the memory as he approached the mountains. A worn path beginning at the piedmont snaked its way up the side. Trees made the path dark and foreboding.

The setting sun caused a great shadow to engulf him. Nathaniel's heartbeat quickened. Something cold and strange reached out to him. His eyes darted from one section of trees to another, looking for any sign of life. A shriek made Nathaniel cry out. A raven sat in a tree to his left. He sighed and breathed deeply. He needed composure if he was going to meet this Oberman. What made him think this old hermit truly existed? Nathaniel moved his horse further into the woods.

"Maybe I am going insane," he said aloud.

"And what is insanity, but another pocket of the mind, ill explored for fear of what we will find?" A strange voice penetrated the air. Looking from tree to tree, he saw no one. His heart raced.

"Who is there?" shouted Nathaniel. His voice was sharp— eyes scanning the woods.

A black cloak emerged from the trees. The figure stood straight but remained hooded. He lifted his hand toward Nathaniel. A long bony finger, white with age, protruded from the cloak sleeve and pointed at Nathaniel.

"What is it you seek?"

"I was told to seek Oberman." Nathaniel was unsure what was being asked of him.

"A man is what you seek? Why ride all this distance to meet an old man forgotten and discarded by his countrymen?" The cloak turned away from Nathaniel.

"I seek power!" Nathaniel blurted out. "I wish to force justice on those who would destroy my family—my friends. I seek vengeance for the atrocities I have seen. I wish to protect those I love."

The hooded figure stopped, keeping his back turned to Nathaniel. "I have waited many long years for you, Nathaniel Stone. I was told you would decide the fate of kings. If power is your quest; follow, or perish with dreams of what might have been." The hooded figure walked away.

"You are Oberman?"

The figure stopped, and faced Nathaniel. "I am. You shall do greater things than I." Oberman continued into the woods. Nathaniel dismounted his horse and followed the cloak as it disappeared into the forest.

They came to a clearing in the trees where a small cottage stood.

"There is a hut around the back for your horse. You will find oats and water as well," said Oberman.

Nathaniel walked to the back of the house. The hut stood tall and dark as the house beside it. He shivered as he led the animal to the dark space. The horse ate the oats and drank water with such enthusiasm that Nathaniel felt hunger gnaw his stomach. He tied the animal to a pole and patted its head, then went back out front.

Oberman sat on a stool, adding twigs and sticks to a fire. The flames grew larger and brighter. The gleam in the old man's eyes made Nathaniel ill at ease. He motioned to a stump of tree next to his stool.

"Sit by the fire with me. Once the sun disappears, these woods are cold."

Nathaniel sat on the stump and watched the flames dance in the darkness.

"You have been restless over the years, enduring grief for the people of the Craft. Do you seek power at any cost?" Oberman's question lingered like smoke from the fire.

Nathaniel never considered the question before. What would he give up for the power to bring justice to the innocent?

"What is it you ask of me?" Nathaniel's wariness grew as he sat in the dark.

"The master has foreseen your house will be very powerful. The young woman of the Craft you married has power she does not realize flowing in her blood. You must be willing to train your first-born child whether male or female in the knowledge you inherit from me. Do you swear it?" demanded Oberman.

So, this was the price Nathaniel must pay—his children. He felt honored to pass such power through his line. "Why the firstborn?"

"He requires the first from your body. Are you willing to forsake YAHWEH and embrace this power?"

Nathaniel's mind returned to Nafaria and all the terrible things she witnessed: the burned out home in Wildemere, how she was forced to build a pyre to burn her father's body. Next he saw Joel holding a poisoned dagger at her throat, and Analia's hanging so many years ago. His blood burned as he thought of the pain she endured. Where was YAHWEH when Nereheim ravaged the people sworn to protect its mortals? Where was the creator when the created murdered the wise ones? Most were of too gentle a nature to fight. They cried out to their father who ignored them. Finally, one stepped from the shadows with an answer. He would take this opportunity and be the answer those of the Craft needed.

"I am willing," said Nathaniel sternly.

Oberman held out a knife. "Swear by your blood. Cut your hand and drip the blood into the fire."

Nathaniel took the knife. It was cool against his skin. He sliced his palm, barely feeling pain from the cut. His eyes followed the blood into the fire. The flames roared and met the dark liquid. "By my blood, I swear to embrace this power and leave behind the creator who allowed my suffering," said Nathaniel.

The flames shot above their heads. Oberman bowed his head low as Nathaniel looked up at the figure in the flames. A loud voice thundered through the forest.

"I have waited long for the honor of revealing myself to you, Nathaniel Stone. I have seen what plagues your heart. Your first child shall be powerful and through me, you will wield that power on the world."

Nathaniel fell to his knees, his eyes fixed on the form in the flames. His head felt lighter as he gasped, "My mind, my heart, my soul. Show me your ways so I can avenge those who have lost their lives." Nathaniel fell down before the fire unconscious.

✦✦✦✦✦✦

"Nathaniel!" Nafaria screamed and sat up in bed, her body covered in sweat. Her heart raced as tears streamed from her eyes. After a moment, she opened her eyes and looked at the lavish surroundings of the room and remembered she was in the king's castle. Her body shook as she recalled the image of Nathaniel before a great fire, blood dripping from his hand.

"Is everything alright?" Ephratha asked as she opened the door. Her face held concern. "I heard you shouting."

"Did I wake you?"

Ephratha smiled as she sat on the bed. "No. I was taking a stroll. I was outside the door when you cried out."

"I saw Nathaniel kneeling before the flames of a great fire. It was just a dream."

"Nathaniel is a very capable man. A few days in the wild are sure to be of little consequence to him," said Ephratha.

Nafaria sighed. "Of course, you are right." She looked at Ephratha. "Are you feeling well?"

"I am fine. I just get restless at night. Walking through the castle is a good way to clear my head," replied Ephratha.

"It seems like only yesterday that you and Jared were married. Now you are going to be a mother."

"It does seem that way, though we have all been married almost two years." Ephratha saw Nafaria was still shaken. "Is there anything else on your mind?"

Nafaria leaned over and picked up a piece of paper from the table next to the bed.

"Before you and Jared returned, I was reading in the library. I heard my mother's voice whisper to me. This is what she said." Nafaria handed Ephratha the paper.

"Beware the dark master." She gave Nafaria a questioning glance.

"I do not understand it either. She whispered something else too. She told me to 'beware lest I fall victim to him.'"

"Are you sure of what you heard? These castle walls can play tricks on a person when they are in a secluded place like the library."

"I am certain I heard my mother's voice as clearly as I hear yours. Michael warned me about transcendence. I read the things he copied for me. It is possible my mother sent me a warning. Now I have this strange dream."

Ephratha saw her friend was puzzled, but one look told her Nafaria was quite lucid. She gave a yawn. "I think it is time I try to sleep." Ephratha gave her friend a hug. "I am glad you are here," she whispered.

Nafaria watched her leave. She settled back in bed and looked out the window into the darkness; but sleep refused to come.

CHAPTER 5

Nathaniel opened his eyes. The orange glow of the fire did not penetrate the woods surrounding them. A large animal roasted above the flames while Oberman carefully turned it over. He looked at the fresh bandage on his palm.

"The food is almost ready. You slept a long time. There are some who never awoke after meeting our master face to face. You have strength equal to your ambition," said Oberman.

Nathaniel's mouth was dry. "I could use some water."

Oberman dipped a ladle into a bucket and handed it to Nathaniel who hastily drank the cool water. When he was satisfied the meat was cooked, Oberman broke off a piece for Nathaniel. He then took one for himself. They ate in silence, staring at the firelight.

"What do you hope to accomplish here?" asked Oberman.

Nathaniel thought about the question. What could his new allies show him that his father could not? "I want power unequal to any other man. Those of the Craft have cowered in fear too long. It is time we reveal our true strength." His words came with great conviction.

Oberman smiled—his dark eyes fierce in the firelight. "That is a most excellent answer. You are not far from that power. Your father taught you well. You will learn to tap the darkness of your soul. The master will show you that. For tonight, there is something I can give you." He rose from his stool and went inside. Nathaniel wondered if he was supposed to follow. A few minutes later, Oberman emerged from his house with something in his hand.

He handed Nathaniel a dark velvet bag with a drawstring on top. Nathaniel opened the bag and pulled out a delicate silver bell, a little larger than the palm of his hand. The glyph of Capricorn was etched into it. There was also a silver hammer in the bag. Both the bell and the hammer shined in the firelight.

"Behold—the sacred bell of Herron," Oberman whispered. Nathaniel's eyes widened as he looked at the object in his hand.

"The bell exists? I thought it only a legend used to frighten children."

Oberman laughed. "There are legends that exist to frighten us, but this is not one of them. The Anenderes indeed holds power for those searching for wisdom from the faces in the water. If you travel many miles to the east along the river, the abandoned city of Herron lies on a cliff at the headwaters. It is forsaken by all since its destruction. Superstitious fools say the place holds a curse. I was your age when I set out to learn the secrets of that great city. In my quest, I acquired the bell. I now give it to you."

"How do you use it?" asked Nathaniel.

"Strike the bell with the hammer and see."

Nathaniel held the bell in front of him from the top with one hand and struck it with the hammer. The soft chime resonated.

The air turned colder, and a gust of wind circled them. Nathaniel saw transparent faces of men and women swirling around them. The wind died down and the spirits floated before Nathaniel, as if awaiting his instruction.

"They are yours to command," said Oberman. "They will answer questions if they can, and will do whatever you wish."

Nathaniel was taken off guard by this new power at his disposal. He waved his hand. "Go. I will call again when I need you." The spirits disappeared into the night.

"The bell holds the power to call a great number of spirits at one time. Spirits of great armies can possess the souls of the living. When this happens, the soldiers are no longer in control of their bodies. An army that is relentless in its march forward is a fearsome sight to behold."

"How do you call forth so many spirits?" asked Nathaniel.

"You say exactly what you want. If it is soldiers you require, you call forth military spirits. They will be ruthless to be sure."

"Ruthless?"

"There is something legend does not get quite right. Only the darkest spirits hear the bell's ring and answer."

"Who crafted the bell?" Even as Nathaniel finished the question, he knew the answer.

"You know the answer. Our master showed me great things in my lifetime. He will show you more. You will become greater, I will become less[5]. That is the way of things," replied Oberman.

As Nathaniel held the exquisite bell, he could not help but wonder if he had gone too far.

⊹⊹⊹⊹⊹

Nafaria saw the bright sunshine through her window. She smiled and sat up. At that moment, the room swirled. She leaned over the side of the bed and vomited into a large shallow pan that waited for her. She sat up again, slower. Beads of sweat glistened on her forehead. She picked up a pitcher from the small table next to the bed and poured a glass of water. As she sipped, the queasiness in her stomach lessened.

---

[5]   John 3:30

"Nafaria, are you awake?" called Ephratha as she walked into the room. She looked at the pan and saw Nafaria with a glass in her hand. "Are you alright?"

"Yes. I just got sick a few minutes ago. It is nothing serious."

"You do not look well. Did you sleep?"

"Yes, but I am worried about Nathaniel. It was so important that he go on this trip alone, but he never said why. I am afraid he has found trouble he did not count on."

"Should we look for him?" asked Ephratha.

"No. I do not want him to think I am meddling in his affairs."

"Is it meddling if you are concerned for your husband?"

"Love always trusts[6]. That is what we are told. Many times those of the Craft need time alone to sharpen their skill. My parents pursued things alone as well as together."

"You know best what to do." Ephratha hugged her. "I just want you to be happy. Once you are dressed, come out on the terrace for tea."

"I will be there shortly," said Nafaria

Ephratha walked into her room while Jared dressed. He pulled a loose tunic over his muscular build. She watched as the fabric floated down to conceal his light skin.

He turned and saw her standing in doorway. "Is something wrong?" he asked with a smile.

---

[6]   1 Corinthians 13:7

"I am simply taking a moment to admire the view from my bedroom door." Ephratha moved closer and wrapped her arms around him.

"Are you sure nothing is wrong?"

"I am worried for Nafaria, but she assures me everything is fine. Something is not right. She is afraid for Nathaniel; yet she will not try to find him. I know those of the Craft are different, but something seems wrong with Nathaniel being alone somewhere in North Agea."

"If Nafaria really thought there was danger she would look for him."

"I think Nafaria is getting sick. I have known her for eight years, she is never sick."

"You cannot break your friend's trust, even for her own good. Your friendship will never be the same. If she says to leave Nathaniel alone, you must do it." Jared's words were gentle, but unwavering.

"Perhaps you are right. I am not as schooled in relationships as you are. The only people I ever really interacted with growing up were my mother, my father and Nafaria."

"It is a credit to you that you worry for your friend." Jared caressed her hair. "If she continues to be ill, we will send for Malcom. He might know something about her that may help us see this a little clearer."

"I do not want Nafaria to leave Arioth until she is well, and Nathaniel is found."

"We should leave Nathaniel to his quest. He will return when he is ready." Jared's confidence reassured Ephratha.

"If it were you, could you leave me alone for an indefinite period of time?"

"It would have to be a dire emergency to call me away for any length of time, especially since you are going to bear my child."

"Do you suppose Nafaria may be with child?"

"Anything is possible. Perhaps your midwife could see her. That will put your mind at ease."

"I will see to it at once."

"Good." Jared placed a kiss on her forehead and left the room. Ephratha went to find her midwife.

———————

Jared followed the Colonnade past the rose garden. The sound of horse's hooves filled the air as he spied a carriage.

His eyes brightened for he recognized it at once. When the driver opened the door, his face lit up.

"Aunt Susanna! What a wonderful surprise! What are you doing here?" Jared wrapped his arms around his aunt and hugged her tight.

"Even as queen of a country, I can sneak across the border every so often to visit my sister," replied Susanna.

"I am sure Uncle Rohn would not allow you to travel alone."

"That was a concern, so I have brought two passengers." Jared's face dropped as his cousin stepped out of the carriage. He then helped his wife out.

"We meet again, cousin," said Andrew.

"It is nice to see you again, Andrew." Jared's tone reflected he felt otherwise.

"You remember Nina?" said Susanna as she regarded the two princes.

Jared smiled and reached out his hand to her. "It is lovely to see you again, your highness."

"I have heard much about the splendor of Arioth. The queen has told me great things about North Agea," said Nina.

"That is another reason we have come. Nina has never been here before," said Susanna.

"I hope you enjoy your stay," replied Jared.

The four walked toward the palace. Jared walked beside his aunt, while Andrew led Nina up the colonnade. "Is there a reason why you chose to bring Andrew, or are you determined to make me miserable in my home?"

"Jared, you and Andrew will have to learn to get along with each other. One day, you will be on the throne at the same time. I hope he will earn your respect before then." Susanna sighed. "Besides, I thought it would be nice for Ephratha to spend time with Nina."

"She seems quite nice. When did he meet her?"

"They met the day of the riot in Wildemere. He saved her in the market square."

"That was the day I left with Nafaria and Ephratha for North Agea. She must have been the girl who came back with Andrew."

"Nina is genuinely taken with him. In my opinion, Andrew is quite lucky. He is a little full of himself, but she still managed to charm him."

"I am sure Ephratha will love to spend time with Nina. Nafaria is here on an unexpected visit. You will enjoy her company as well."

"How is Nafaria doing here in North Agea?"

"She is getting along quite well. Her reputation as a healer is almost as well-known as Malcom Stone's."

"I look forward to spending time with her and Ephratha."

They walked into the castle and made their way to the throne room.

"Mother, we have unexpected guests," said Jared with a smile.

The queen jumped from her throne and hurried toward them. "Susanna! What a lovely surprise! Why did you not tell me you were coming? I would have arranged a grand welcome."

"There is no grander welcome than a hug from my baby sister, Clara. I trust you are well?"

"Yes. This must be the season of untimely visits. Ephratha's friend is also here."

"Jared mentioned that. I am looking forward to spending time with her."

"She is a lovely young woman. It is a shame about her parents."

"Yes, Rohn still misses Jason."

"Does anyone in Wildemere know anything else about what happened that day?" asked Jared.

"No. The only person who unmasked himself in the market was Joel Blackstone. No one else with him could be identified," said Susanna with a sigh.

"The laws that protect those of the Craft also protect those behind the masks. We simply cannot find them," replied Andrew darkly. "No one in Wildemere can even give an inkling of who Joel Blackstone had with him that day."

"How would you know?" asked Jared. "What have you done about bringing Lord Jason's and Lady Thena's killers to justice?"

Andrew walked over to Jared. He stood inches from him. "All that the laws of Nereheim allow," he said quietly, and then left the room. Nina watched him leave. She approached Jared, her eyes blazing.

"How dare you?" she demanded. Her demeanor completely changed and caught Jared off guard. His gaze dropped to the floor while she continued. "Andrew has searched intently for any news or sighting of Joel Blackstone and the rabble rousers that were with him. It is as if they vanished within the confusion of the riot that day. I myself could have been lost or God alone knows what in that chaos. I realize you and Andrew do not get along, but until you have walked a mile in his shoes or lived twenty-four hours of his day, you have no right to judge him." Nina turned and went after Andrew.

"I do not believe I could have said it better myself," said Susanna. "Andrew has looked all over Wildemere for Joel. After he was seen here at Arioth, who is to say he ever returned to Nereheim?"

"You think he is still in North Agea?" asked Jared.

"It is quite possible. Have you noticed him here?"

"I have not thought to look. Everything settled down since Nafaria and Nathaniel married. I confess I left the matter alone."

"Then perhaps you should not judge Andrew so harshly. Even Michael Mauldon told Andrew to let the matter lie. He would not seek vengeance for his parents' deaths. Though Michael gave that advice, Andrew keeps looking."

Jared looked at the floor. He saw that his cousin was not as self-centered as he believed. "I think perhaps I owe Andrew an apology. Please excuse me." Jared left the two sisters in the room alone.

"I guess now is a good time to get you settled," said Clara. "I do hope this visit does not continue to be as awkward as its beginning."

"Things will sort themselves out. Jared may finally understand his cousin has a heart after all," said Susanna. The sisters exited the room together.

***

Andrew left the throne room and headed down the main hall. His feet moved with swiftness, past the paintings of the kings of North Agea, but he did not stop to look at them. He had no idea where he was going. He just wanted to be alone. Before long, he was in the library. He sat down at the table and put his head in his hands with his back to the door. He closed his eyes to shut out tears threatening to come.

He pondered Jason and Thena's deaths once again as he had in the past months. Why did he care so much for these people? He thought through various conversations with Thena. He remembered advice Jason gave his father as friend to friend. Both treated him with genuine kindness and respect. They were not hypocritical with their kindness as others were. Because of this, he could not accept Michael's wish to leave their deaths the mystery they became. Andrew felt that in order for Wildmere to heal from the riot caused by their murders, Joel Blackstone should at least be brought to justice. Jared's question only made Andrew more frustrated. It caused him to ask another: how do you bring someone to justice who has disappeared from the face of the earth? His thoughts were interrupted with one word.

"Andrew."

Andrew sighed. The voice belonged to the last person in the castle he wished to see. Jared stood in the doorway.

"How did you find me?" Andrew lifted his head to face the wall.

Jared walked into the room standing a short distance from him. "Books were always your greatest comfort. Whenever you disappeared, you were always in the library."

"What do you want Jared?" asked Andrew crisply. He wished his cousin would state his business and leave him alone.

Jared looked down at the floor. "I wanted to apologize for my behavior just now. I have no right to judge a matter I know nothing about."

Andrew was still. The last thing he expected to hear was Jared apologizing to him. He almost did not believe his ears.

"I heard someone say Raphael and a few of Coleman's scouts went out on a hunt. Dinner is sure to be spectacular." Jared came closer to Andrew. "In your search, you might question Lord Robert Stowe. Nafaria recognized him as one of the men she saw burn their manor after Jason was killed." He turned and left Andrew in the library.

———— ✦✦✦ ————

Ephratha and Nafaria were sitting on the terrace when Nina exited the castle. Their conversation cut off as she came toward them.

"Ephratha, did you see Andrew come through here?" she asked.

"No, I did not. Come join us. You look upset," replied Ephratha. She reached for a cup and poured some tea and extended it to Nina who sighed and sat down. She took the cup and after a sip felt more relaxed. "You look very well, Ephratha. Royalty agrees with you."

Ephratha laughed. "Thank you, princess, as it does you."

Nina looked at Nafaria. She recognized her from the apothecary shop the Mauldon family owned and operated. "You are Nafaria Mauldon?"

"Nafaria Stone. I have since married," replied Nafaria.

"Is it true Joel Blackstone killed your father and mother for revenge?" she asked.

Nafaria nodded her head. "Leanna had an accident and my mother did everything she could to save her. There is something men do not understand about power. It is for YAHWEH to grant who has it, and to what degree. My mother's skill was never meant to circumvent death in any way. I do not know why Leanna had to die. I do not know why my mother was not given the power to save her life. I only know that I must guard my heart so I will not lash out at YAHWEH for my ignorance of his design." Nafaria rose from the table. "Excuse me, please."

Nina rose as well and gently put her hand on her arm. "Please wait. I was only curious about what happened; I do not judge. No matter the circumstances, the loss of your parents is a tragic loss for Nereheim. Your father was a good and just man. He never once lost composure in all the times I saw him in his shop, or anywhere else in Wildemere. I followed your mother all over the city whenever possible just to watch her walk from place to place. She was a graceful woman. I am very sorry for your loss."

Nafaria looked at Nina. Her eyes seemed so naïve and innocent. She was like a child caught in a woman's world, yet was genuine. She might make a good queen in Nereheim.

"You have a good heart, Nina. Choose to see past a person's appearance and station in life, and you will see much."

"I hope to learn much while I am here."

Nafaria took her hand and gently squeezed it. "Remember you are a princess. Hold up your head and act confident. In time, it will be natural."

"I can see how Ephratha managed so well, with you as such a trusted advisor!" replied Nina with a laugh. The three young women carried on their tea and conversation.

—————— ✦✦✦✦ ——————

Nina wandered through Queen Clara's rose garden. The late afternoon sun was bright as she moved from flower to flower at a leisurely pace. The garden was enchanting and exactly the same as Queen Susanna's in Nereheim. She noted certain varieties of roses were in the same places. The paths winding through the garden even ended at a cobblestone patio with a table of wrought iron and four chairs sitting in the middle, exactly the same as in Nereheim. Nina knew this because she and the queen took tea twice a day together: once in the morning before breakfast, and once in the evening before bed. Morning tea was in the rose garden, weather permitting. Nina cherished these times with her mother-in-law because Susanna was unlike any other woman she ever knew.

Her thoughts were interrupted by a rustle of bushes. Susanna moved down the path toward her. "Nina, I have finally found you. Andrew wondered where you were."

"I was walking here among the roses, your majesty. This garden is exquisite, and if I am not mistaken; exactly like your rose garden in Wildemere. I feel as though I am at home."

Susanna looked at her daughter in law fondly. "Nina, how many times have I told you to call me either Susanna or mother?"

"I believe the count leaves me at three dozen. It seems odd to address someone of your rank with such familiarity."

"Familiarity is your right by marriage." After she spoke, Susanna gave her a questioning look. "Have you actually kept track of such a thing?"

"I retain odd pieces of information at random intervals. It is either a gift or an abnormality. Sometimes I cannot decide."

Susanna laughed. "Well, you are correct. This garden we are in now is an exact copy of the one in Wildemere. Would you care to know why?"

Nina caught the mischievous sparkle in Susanna's eye and smiled. "I would, mother."

Susanna laughed and grabbed Nina by the hand. They hurried past the clusters of maiden's blush roses, damask roses, and moss roses to the castle wall. She climbed the steps still holding Nina's hand.

At the top, the sentry turned and was surprised by their presence. "Your majesty, your highness; it is a pleasure," he said as he bowed.

Susanna smiled instantly to put the sentry at ease. "Could I borrow your lookout glass for a moment?"

"Yes, your majesty." He took the glass from his belt and gave it to her.

Susanna took the glass, raised it to her eye, facing to her right. "It still stands, after all this time." She handed Nina the glass. "Look out through the glass to our right."

Nina put the glass to her eye. Gently, Susanna moved it until a large stone manor came into view across the fields. The sides were covered with green vines trimmed to reveal the windows.

"That is where I grew up." Nina started at this information about her mother-in-law. The sentry also seemed surprised.

"This is where Clara and I lived. Our father owned all the fields you see between here and that manor. He was considered nobility because he owned land, but we were by no means rich. Mother and father provided for us well enough. We were given education, but were to balance indoor activities with work outside. Father would not allow us in the fields among the male laborers, but mother put us to use, keeping the plants and tending the rose garden by the house. Roses were her favorite flower. We learned to plant and harvest them; how to construct a trellis for the flowers to climb and populate, and how to arrange them in exquisite fashion. We sold our flowers in the market once a week. That is how I first met Rohn when he visited North Agea with his father.

Eventually we married, and I moved to Nereheim. Lian married Clara shortly after. A few months after their wedding, mother took ill and passed away. I wanted some way to comfort Clara, so I started a little rose garden with some of the maiden's blush roses you see when you first enter the garden. I took them from home. I returned and took the same roses to Clara. We planted them together. I told her it would be a way to remember each other as much as our mother.

Every year, I added something new to the garden and told Clara to do the same. Lian helped design and construct the arbors and the cobblestone area in the center. As time went on, the garden grew. It is amazing how a simple project became as vast as it is today. Just as I am amazed the manor house I grew up in is still tended and cared for so many years after my father passed away."

"Lord Rowen Cade was handpicked by King Lian to purchase the land. He is a meticulous man with a passion for plants and flowers." On hearing the voice, the women turned around and saw Coleman standing behind them.

"You know him?" asked Susanna.

"He is my father. When I made my intention known to join the royal army, he waited until I was stationed at the castle. He approached the king with an offer to buy the land. They were good friends, so the king knew of my father's meticulous nature, and that the manor would be kept in proper shape. He took a tour with my father and questioned him about the different flowers and plants on the grounds. Father was able to answer any questions and provide advice for their care in case he was not granted sale of the land. The king was impressed and sold him the land. Every year he sent a stipend to ensure its upkeep. Every year so far, my father sent it back with a letter stating it was not needed. The land provided for itself quite admirably. The sale of the roses in the market as well as other crops, including lavender, has been prosperous. I only hope it continues."

"I never realized Lian took such care with our old home," said Susanna.

"It is for the Queen's sake, your majesty. She could never bear it if her homestead fell into disrepair."

"You speak as though something is wrong with the Queen," said Nina.

"Clara is very sensitive to everything around her. She is not clairvoyant, as we are not of the Craft, but she has a strong intuition. Just as you sense something deep inside a person that puts you on your guard, Nina, so does my sister. However, your intuition makes you stronger and sharpens your focus. Her sensitivity weakens her. She often takes ill as a result," said Susanna.

"That is why you are so protective of her," said Nina.

"It is one of many reasons. I believe if something happened to me, Clara would be the first to know."

"Thank you for this time, mother," said Nina.

The Queen and Princess thanked the soldiers and left them to their duties.

✦✦✦✦✦

Jared stood on the terrace off the dining hall gazing at the late evening sky. He loved the pictures in the sky. They never changed; giving the corsairs a way to guide their ships over the seas. His perusal was interrupted.

"Do you have time to talk, cousin?"

Jared faced Andrew. "What is on your mind?"

"It is no secret you despise me. I just wanted to thank you for the kindness you and Ephratha have shown Nina. She feels a part of things here, for which I am grateful. I want her to feel like she has a friend in the family."

"Nina is a delightful young woman. You are lucky to have found her."

Andrew considered his cousin's words. "You do not think it lucky she found me, do you? What is it about me that you despise?"

Jared decided it was time to be candid with his cousin. "We are told in the sacred writings that man has a numbered set of years to live on this earth[7]. Our life is a mist[8]. War and pestilence claim even more of our allotted time. What are you doing with it? You are a prince. Your father will not live forever. Are you preparing for the day you will take the throne? What reforms will you make in Nereheim to protect its subjects? What will you do to make sure no other atrocities are committed against those of the Craft? To rule with wisdom, you must start by exercising it in your daily life. How can you rule such a great land if you cannot rule yourself?"

Andrew looked down at the floor.   "Perhaps you are right. I still have a lot of growing up to do." He left Jared to his stargazing.

After leaving his cousin, Andrew wandered the castle grounds. The fact that Jared was honorable and spoke his mind directly made it hard for Andrew to accept his words. Jared possessed tact, so his accusations were much less severe than those he overheard from the guards or other nobles. He heard himself described as arrogant, foolish, boastful, and boorish. He never heard one good thing about himself unless it came from his mother or as of late, Nina.

He remembered the ball that was thrown so he might find himself a suitable wife. Ephratha was there, and he might have met her, had he not acted so childish. Jared captured her heart instead. Andrew was too caught up in himself to be gracious. He enjoyed debasing the young women at court. When he thought about that night, his actions were insulting. He was wasting himself with these little jokes that were no longer funny, if indeed they ever were. "I am such a wasteful pig," he whispered.

The day he met Nina, he felt reborn. She was so fresh and innocent to the ways of court. Gentle and observant, she never pretended to know something she did not, but was eager to learn. She loved him genuinely for the man he was, not his crown. When they met in the market square, he

---

7 Psalm 90:10

8 James 4:14

dared not hope she would love him back. Yet she had. He never thought of what others would think. She made him proud to be a man.

"How will I protect her?" he whispered aloud. A cool breeze rustled his hair. He needed wisdom, but felt there was no time to gain it.

One glimpse around him and Andrew realized he was in the hall of kings, outside the throne room. The great oils hung on the walls down the corridor. These proud, stoic men represented generations of wisdom. They were mortal kings like he would be one day. Who did they trust?

Andrew spun around as a loud clang interrupted his thoughts. King Lian emerged from the throne room. He looked just as surprised to see Andrew.

"Andrew, I thought you would be out with Jared."

"Not at the moment. I was taking a walk to clear my head." Andrew glanced at the oils.

"Is something on your mind?" asked Lian.

"I was looking at these paintings. These kings were all great men. How did they come upon their wisdom?" asked Andrew quietly.

Lian looked at his nephew thoughtfully. Andrew never showed an interest in such things before. "There is an old proverb that says 'For lack of guidance a nation falls, but many advisors make victory sure[9].' These kings learned wisdom by watching others, and making mistakes as they ruled. They also had people they trusted to help them make wise decisions. Running a country and tending its subjects is a grave responsibility. Never be afraid to ask for help."

"That is where I must begin. Thank you for your advice, uncle."

Lian embraced his nephew. "I am always willing to give advice to those who will listen." They walked together down the hallway.

---

[9]   Proverbs 11:14

CHAPTER 6

The cold night breeze chilled Oberman's tiny house. As Nathaniel slept, he dreamed of Nafaria.

She ran through the fields near their house. Her breathing was rapid; panic on her face. She was searching for something she lost. She called out, but he could not hear her. On she ran, until finally he heard his name—*Nathaniel!*

"Nathaniel, wake. The time is now." Oberman's raspy voice was barely audible, as he shook Nathaniel. He looked out the window. The moon was a sliver, the darkness thick.

"Blood must be shed before the night is over," said Oberman.

"Blood?" asked Nathaniel. Oberman turned his head, his eyes hidden by the shadow of his hood. Nathaniel rose and followed the old man outside.

"You shall see." Oberman faced the direction he was walking as Nathaniel followed.

The fire roared before them. Its light cut the blackness like a sharp blade. Before the fire was a short stone bench. "Kneel," said Oberman. Nathaniel obeyed. The old man knelt beside him. He produced an athame and cup from his cloak. He reached under the bench and pulled up a large book that immediately caught Nathaniel's interest.

"Behold: the Grimoire Macabre." Oberman's voice was just above a whisper. He placed his hands reverently on the cover.

"The book of death," whispered Nathaniel.

"You have heard of it?"

"I thought it was only a legend. It is said to hold diabolical secrets."

"Like the sacred bell of Herron, this book holds great power. In it is wisdom from the dawn of time until now, power to wield great destruction on those who would scoff at the power of the Craft. This is what you seek."

"Where did it come from?" Nathaniel's heart beat faster.

Oberman looked at him. "You already know. Our master is pleased with your effort and careful study. You are to wield the book next. You will learn its terrifying secrets, and guard this book."

Oberman took Nathaniel's hand and sliced the palm with the athame. He moved the hand over the cup allowing blood to flow into it. Then he sliced the palm of his own hand and did the same. He stirred the blood with the athame and poured it on the cover of the book. Nathaniel watched as the cover absorbed the blood.

"The book is now yours to command. Use it, protect it." Oberman walked into the house. Nathaniel sat before the fire. His heart hammered within his chest. He remembered the cut on his palm. He tore a piece of cloth from his shirt, wrapping it around his hand. He opened the book of death.

⁘⁘

Ephratha was roused by a shriek down the hall. She bolted straight up in bed. Jared sat up as well. "What was that?" he asked.

Ephratha did not answer. She threw off the quilts covering her and ran down the hall. She found Nafaria sitting on the bed with tears streaming down her face as she wailed.

"Nafaria, wake up! It is only a dream!" shouted Ephratha, jumping on the bed and shaking her. "Nafaria, please wake up!"

Ephratha was aware of light in the room. She saw Jared holding a candlestick. Behind him, Nina and Andrew stood. Nafaria stopped thrashing. Her screams slowly became sobs. Ephratha held her as she cried.

"It was only a dream, everything is fine," said Ephratha.

"I saw Nathaniel kneeling before a book. He cut himself, and the book opened. My heart felt as if it was ripped apart!" Ephratha rocked Nafaria.

"Ephratha, her hair," whispered Jared. She heard the nervousness in his voice. Ephratha failed to notice what made Jared so unsteady. She looked down and reached a hand to touch one side of Nafaria's hair. A large white lock stood out against her black hair.

"Nafaria, your hair has turned white." Nafaria looked down at the lock of hair Ephratha held in her hand. She looked back at her with a mixture of horror and wonder on her tear-stained face.

⋅⋅◆◆◆⋅⋅

Nathaniel heard a rustle in the trees above him. The sky was a dark purple, instead of the coal black it was a few hours ago. A raven sat in the branches staring at him. He got up and rushed in the house.

"Oberman!" he shouted as he burst through the door. The old man lay on the floor in the middle of the room. Nathaniel walked across the floor, went to his knees, and rolled him over. There was no heartbeat. Oberman was now a corpse.

"Burn the old man; begin your quest for justice. Your wife is with child, go to her." Nathaniel spun around the room. He heard the strange whisper, but was alone. Outside, the fire blazed. *"Do not waver on your promise, and I shall make you great."* Nathaniel carried the corpse outside and threw it on the fire where the flames consumed it.

"So, this is the sum of our lives? We are to live, and be put on the fire to be reduced to dust and ash. What will be left of us when it is all over?" Nathaniel whispered as he watched the flames.

"The name you make for yourself as you live and breathe on this earth. Let that name be terrible indeed," the voice thundered from the fire. Nathaniel stared into the flames.

"Yes master." He got up from the fire, picked up the book and went to get his horse. He realized more than anything, he wanted to see Nafaria.

The sun pulled itself above the horizon when Nafaria finally went back to sleep. Ephratha came back to her room and found Jared on the balcony looking at the sky. He turned as she came toward him.

"How is she?"

"She fell asleep a few moments ago."

"You need sleep as well."

"Is something else on your mind?"

"Nafaria said something about Nathaniel and a book. I am not sure what it means, but Nathaniel may be in danger he does not realize. We need to find him."

"How will we do that? Not even Nafaria knew where he was going."

"Perhaps Malcom will know where to look for him, or we can send out scouts to search in the direction he went. He might be in the mountains."

"Nafaria was adamant we leave him alone, and you also suggested we follow her wish."

"Nathaniel needs to know what happened to his wife! She is with child and distraught. He would forgive an imposition on his solitude!" replied Jared sharply.

The look on Ephratha's face made Jared regret his outburst. He came to her, pulling her into his arms. "Forgive me. It is unfair to take my frustration out on you. Perhaps we should give Nathaniel another day. If he does not come to Arioth, we will look for him."

"You are afraid of something?"

"Nafaria described a book that opened when Nathaniel's blood touched it. I am very afraid."

The sun shined over Nathaniel's shoulder as the door swung open to his empty cottage. Everything was as he and Nafaria left it a few days before. He walked inside and stood in the middle of the room when he heard a rough voice behind him.

"Nathaniel, is that you?" Silas stood in the doorway.

"I just stopped in for a moment before riding on to Arioth. I will meet Nafaria there."

Silas chuckled. "I understand. I thought you might be gone longer, but a beautiful woman is hard to be apart from. I will refresh your horse while you get ready."

"Thank you." Silas left as Nathaniel readied himself for the trip to Arioth.

After his horse had water and food, Nathaniel rode for the king's castle. The cool wind refreshed his skin, though the sun was bright and warm. Summer was passing, giving way to autumn. Soon snow would blanket North Agea and the days would be cold. He looked forward to winter and time alone with Nafaria.

"Your wife is with child," the voice told him. She was likely unaware of the child she carried.

"She is fine and healthy. There is nothing to fear," said Nathaniel aloud. Concern gripped his heart all the same.

After a few hours, he spied the castle in the distance. Spurring his horse, he willed it to move faster. The fields blurred as he pictured Nafaria in his mind.

He saw her in the meadow in Denholm Glen. The sun was bright over a sea of red. Nafaria's eyes shined as she looked across the field of beautiful ripe strawberries. She ran toward them, down the hill until she came to the plants. She tested the first berry and a look of contentment washed over her face. Her eyes were closed as she savored the tasty berry bites. She then ate with great relish.

The sky overhead turned dark, and the expression on Nafaria's face turned to pain. She cried out, bending over at her waist. Looking down, her eyes grew wide as she held up the berries in her hand. Instead of the delta shape of the strawberry, she saw a branch with pointed leaves and three red berries on it. She looked around and saw the field was not of strawberries, but elderberries. Another sharp pain hit. She cried out, fell to the ground, writhing among the plants that were poison to her.

"NO!" shouted Nathaniel. He spurred the horse harder. He rode to the castle, his eyes ablaze.

Jared sat before the light of a single twisted candle in the heart of the castle. Here, there were no windows, and the servants rarely lit the fireplace. This was the royal library, housing the annals of North Agea's past kings. Volumes of history sat along one shelf while other shelves held books these rulers found intriguing. Many books pertaining to the Craft, including a copy of the Sacred Writings themselves, were housed here. One of these miscellaneous volumes sat before Jared. It was the diary of a young man named Marcellus—one of the Craft. He wrote in his journal of a certain tome…

The book was black and bulky with age. Indeed, it looked as though it should fall apart at the slightest touch, yet it remained intact all these long ages. The Grimoire Macabre is given from the god of blood to one he deems worthy of its secrets. It can only be opened once the chosen one has dripped his blood mixed with the blood of his predecessor on it. May YAHWEH forgive me, I witnessed this act…

Jared pushed the book away from him. Whispers of a sacred book of evil circulated among those of the Craft whose knowledge was deep, their memory long. This diary was over one hundred years old. He knew the story from servants who chose to tell a chilling tale to frighten him as a child. Marcellus came to his great, great, great, great, grandfather half-mad and terrified. He begged the king to read his diary and save it to warn others of evil that lurked in North Agea. In the annals of the kings, it was recorded that the king listened with patience to Marcellus and his lunatic ravings. He made Marcellus welcome in his court and bid him stay until he finished reading the diary himself. He took the king's offer of hospitality, but that night threw himself off the roof of the castle. The next morning, the servants found his body crushed from the fall, and the birds already feasting on the carcass.

Did he see this same book of evil those of the Craft feared? Did the god of blood create a book to deceive members of the Craft into following him? The sacred writings say he masquerades as an angel of light[10]. No one can know the heart but YAHWEH, and Nathaniel was difficult to judge. Was he chosen by this god of blood? If so, he chose a formidable ally. Jared needed to be on his guard around him, not only for his own sake, but every citizen of North Agea.

---

[10]   2 Corinthians 11:14

As he stared at the candle's flame, tears rolled down his face. He said aloud, "YAHWEH, I beg you to hear me. I am not of the Craft, but I have listened to your wisdom since I was a child. Indeed, I am still a child, and need to learn many things. However, I beg you, protect my family. Protect Nafaria as she may be in danger she is unaware of. Help me to have perfect love to drive away all fear[11]. For only you know the things that must come to pass that are for your good. Let my child grow to see a better future for the sister kingdoms. For this I ask, creator of all things." Jared closed the books in front of him and returned them to their proper shelves. He hoped YAHWEH heard his prayer, for if his fears were correct, only he had the power to save them.

⟶ ·⊹⊹⊹· ⟵

Coleman stood on the castle wall with his sentry. He looked at the vine covered manor his father owned. Though his eyes barely revealed activity, he knew his father kept his farmhands and gardeners busy. The manor was active before sunrise. Rowen Cade looked upon his lordship as one of great responsibility: first to his own workers and servants, next to the people in the village nearby, and lastly to his good friend, the king. Coleman learned from his father to take any responsibility he was given with great seriousness.

As he stood on the wall, he felt something was wrong. It was not the intuition Lord Bryant Saintclaire was famous for; just a twitch in his mind causing him to look at everything with greater than normal caution. The sentry noted this.

"Captain, you seem especially guarded today. What troubles you?"

Coleman shook his head. "I have no idea. Something in the back of my mind makes me uneasy. The air we breathe feels permeated with it. I wish to see the enemy before he strikes."

"Perhaps there is no enemy to be seen."

---

[11]   1 John 4:18

"Something is out there." Coleman turned to the sentry. "Keep sharp and focused." He descended the steps, leaving the sentry to his duty.

Coleman walked the grounds, slowly making his way to the castle. His sentry was correct, all seemed well. However, the young captain remembered Nafaria's shrieks that woke most everyone from their sleep. He heard Jared and Ephratha say a lock of her beautiful dark hair went completely white. He shuddered at what could have frightened her to make such a thing happen.

Jared was also different this morning. Worry furrowed his brow as if he carried the weight of the world. Jared was the most capable young man Coleman ever knew. He preferred to handle problems as they presented themselves, always seeking advice from those around him to solve what he could not. He knew if he could not solve a problem, worry would not give him the solution. Coleman was concerned for his friend.

At the heart of all this tension was Nathaniel Stone. Since the day he first met Nathaniel, he was wary of him. He never confided in him and kept him close enough to watch his every move, but never trust him. Coleman respected his father, Malcom, greatly. Since the day Malcom Stone walked into Arioth and opened his apothecary shop, he and Nathaniel worked hard to help the people around them at whatever they could. However, Nathaniel was different from his father. He was focused, driven, and did not tolerate a slight of any kind. He gave the harshest lessons to any bully he encountered with the severest possible consequence. The result was the bully repented of his sin and became gentle as a dove. Somehow Nathaniel learned early in life that the end product justified the means to get there. He certainly did not learn that from his father.

He continued his walk along the colonnade toward the terrace. Ephratha and Nina were out enjoying tea. Ephratha spotted him and waved.

"Coleman, come join us if you have a moment to spare," said Ephratha.

"I always have time for two lovely young ladies; especially when they could order me executed for disobedience." Coleman gave a forced smile. Ephratha laughed.

"The captain of the guard has a sense of humor after all."

"Never tell anyone. They would not believe you."

"I see why you get along with Jared so well. Both of you can be terrible pragmatics when the occasion calls for it. He told me before you take long walks when you are concerned with something. What is on your mind?"

"Something is not right. Nafaria has been agitated and anxious since she arrived here. She hears whispers when she is alone, and has had terrible dreams. I wish to be ready in case we are visited by unknown demons."

"You believe in being prepared: an admirable quality for the captain of the guard to possess," said Nina.

"That is my post; but how do you prepare for shadows and invisible whispers?"

"I see why you are concerned," said Ephratha. She understood that if they faced something as deadly as some kind of black demon, they would be powerless against it.

"Who is that?" asked Nina. Her gaze followed a young man walking swiftly toward the castle.

"That would be Nathaniel Stone," Coleman replied grimly. He quickly walked toward the colonnade to intercept him. Ephratha rose and followed him.

Coleman met Nathaniel a few feet before the end of the Colonnade. "Nathaniel, you have returned from your planned sabbatical."

"I am looking for Nafaria."

"The princess ordered that no one see her until she wakes." Coleman stood squarely in front of him.

"I am sure that order does not apply to me." Nathaniel took a step forward, but Coleman held him back.

"These orders were not given lightly. We are relieved you are here, but you need to let her rest." Coleman looked down and saw the bandage on Nathaniel's hand.

"What happened to your hand?"

Nathaniel looked Coleman square in the eye. "I cut myself while hunting."

"Why were you hunting?"

"A man needs to eat." There was distinct coldness in Nathaniel's voice. He grew impatient with Coleman's questions.

"Nathaniel, thank the creator you are here," said Ephratha as she came up to the two men. Nina walked with her, but stood behind Ephratha and Coleman. She shifted her gaze from Nathaniel to the ground.

"The captain tells me he has orders that no one is to see my wife."

"That is correct. When Nafaria arrived here, she began hearing whispers in the castle. Last night, she awoke shrieking from a nightmare and did not calm down. I ordered that she be left to wake on her own. She needs rest."

"Thank you for your concern, Princess, but I think she would want to see me."

"She will, but you must understand, something happened to her." Ephratha's voice took on a slight agitation.

Jared continued his walk outside, drawn to the commotion. He saw Nathaniel facing off with Coleman and Ephratha. Nina stood behind them, carefully watching Nathaniel as they argued.

"I must see my wife!" Nathaniel shouted.

"We are not keeping you from her! She needs her rest right now!" shouted Ephratha in return.

"Nathaniel! I am relieved you are here. Let us talk before you see Nafaria," said Jared as he approached them.

"Jared, thank goodness you are here," replied Ephratha. Nathaniel looked at Jared and saw worry on his face. He bowed his head. When he spoke again, it was with a quieter tone.

"Is Nafaria all right?"

Jared winced as he looked at his friend. The weary look in Nathaniel's eyes would match his own if the situation was reversed.

"She is resting. She was in good spirits when she first arrived, but has become distraught. My midwife confirmed she is with child, and is well physically. Her dreams have given her some very long nights," said Ephratha.

"Thank you for your hospitality and care you have shown her. I am sorry to have put this burden on you. I had no idea this would happen," replied Nathaniel.

Jared put a hand on his shoulders. "There is nothing to be sorry for. We are happy she is here. Now that you have returned, she will be more at ease."

"There is something else you should know. Last night, she had a nightmare that affected her greatly. A lock of her hair turned white," said Ephratha.

"I need to see her," whispered Nathaniel.

Jared turned to Ephratha. "Let us see if Nafaria is awake. She will be relieved to see her husband."

"I will return to duty." Coleman bowed to Jared and continued down the colonnade.

"I think I will go find Andrew," said Nina. She went into the castle from the terrace.

Jared and Ephratha took Nathaniel to Nafaria's room. She was sleeping. Her black hair had one large lock of sheer white, near her face. It was the only thing different about her. He knelt down beside the bed, his face next to hers. She looked so peaceful. Jared motioned for Ephratha to follow him out of the room. He led her down the hallway.

"I will not allow Nafaria to leave Arioth on horseback. When they are ready to leave, we will have Solomon and James escort them home in the royal carriage," said Jared.

"I wish she could stay here with us," replied Ephratha.

Jared smiled and hugged her. "I know you do, but she has her own home. She must be allowed to return to it if she chooses."

"Of course, I understand, but I will worry about her."

———— ·++◆++· ————

It was sometime later when Jared and Ephratha came back. Nathaniel sat on the bed, holding Nafaria. She was giggling about something he said when he saw them.

"Thank you again for everything you have done, Jared."

"You would have done the same for Ephratha."

"Indeed, our home is humble, but always open."

At that moment, Andrew and Nina entered the room. Andrew saw the newcomer and apologized. "We wanted to check on Nafaria. She had a rough night," said Andrew.

"Everything is fine, Andrew. I would like you to meet Nafaria's husband, Nathaniel Stone," said Jared. "Nathaniel, this is my cousin Andrew Catalane and his wife Nina. They are visiting with my Aunt Susanna, from Nereheim."

Nathaniel rose from the bed and put out his hand to Andrew. "You are the king of Nereheim's son? I have heard much about you."

"I am afraid I have not garnered a handsome reputation for myself." Andrew shook Nathaniel's hand.

"I am not interested in the foolish babbling of court officials. I make no judgment of someone until I know them myself."

Nathaniel turned to Nina. He gave her a slight bow. "It is a pleasure to meet you, Princess."

The princess's demeanor seemed natural to Jared, but was that fear he saw shadow her expression?

Nina smiled. "It is nice to finally meet you as well."

Jared respected Nina instantly. She remained calm in the midst of her fears.

"Nathaniel, you must stay the evening. In the morning, Solomon and James will accompany you to your home with the royal carriage. For today, enjoy the hospitality of Arioth," said Jared.

"That would be a pleasure," replied Nathaniel.

Nina and Andrew left the room with Ephratha and Jared. Each couple sensed the need for Nathaniel and Nafaria to be alone.

------- ·+++·+·+· -------

As they walked down the hall, Ephratha felt a tug at her arm. She looked over and saw Nina looking at her intently. She said nothing, but led Nina through the grand ballroom and outside into the queen's rose garden. The scent of fresh roses surrounded them.

"Is something wrong Nina?"

"I am afraid of him, Ephratha. I feel we may be in grave danger."

"Do you mean Nathaniel? That is silly, Nina. Nathaniel is a trusted friend." Ephratha's reassuring smile faded when she saw the expression on Nina's face.

"Is it so silly? This young man is a trusted friend of your husband, and is of the Craft. You do not know what he has been doing these past days, and Nafaria had terrible dreams regarding him. What she said about the blood—"

"Stop this foolishness, Nina. Nathaniel would never hurt us, and he would certainly never hurt Nafaria. He saved her life on the night of my wedding! You have nothing to fear from him."

"I understand he has shown himself to be a trusted friend. I can see how much you love Nafaria, and you are grateful he saved your friend's life. I would be too, if I were in your position. Ephratha, I have always respected you, and I have come to be very fond of you. I beg you to look objectively at this man. It may be nothing. But could you live with yourself if something disastrous happened and you could have prevented it if only you had been prepared?"

Ephratha regarded her new relation, with thoughtfulness. Nina was seeing the whole affair from the side of a stranger. Perhaps she saw something Ephratha could not. Her mother would tell her to ponder such things and not dismiss them as rash foolishness. If she was going to be wise, she must begin by acting prudently.

"You make a good point. Just this morning, Jared was concerned that we find Nathaniel. He may have noticed something is different about him as well. I will ask him about it and think about what you said."

"That is all I ask. After all, it could be nothing more than strange tales creeping in on me while visiting a new place." Ephratha hugged her as they walked out of the rose garden.

The late afternoon sky held large pillow-like clouds dotted across an azure field. A warm sun shone on Andrew while he sat under a tree a short distance from the castle. He saw the magnificent structure clearly. Many people came and went from its gate. It was a busy place, just like his home. Being royalty brought with it the responsibility of hospitality, along with governing the people. Running a kingdom was hard work, as Jared would say. Andrew wondered where these new epiphanies would take him. How would he manage Nereheim if it were up to him? His uncle gave him a clue where to start. Trustworthy advisers would be worth their weight in gold, if he knew how to choose them.

Andrew remembered stories of the days when Nereheim had Nathaniel's father, Malcom Stone as Court Adviser. He was the only one of the Craft his father trusted. He was skilled in YAHWEH'S wisdom and gracious with people. Malcom saw through political entanglements and was able to advise a better way. Is the time right for Nereheim to have one of the Craft in this position again? How would he choose that person? It could be exactly what was needed to bring unity to his country.

Andrew's thoughts were interrupted when he heard his name shouted. He saw Nathaniel walking toward him.

"Nina has been looking for you." Andrew made no motion to stand, so Nathaniel sat on the grass next to him.

"I needed a quiet place to think," replied Andrew.

"What is it you contemplate?"

"How to run a kingdom; I realize what a fool I have been."

"It is always better to learn that lesson as early in life as possible."

"I feel as though I have been given a new life—a chance to learn what I have not spent time to master. I want to be more like Jared. He has watched the business of his father while I have been enjoying my father's power. I was fortunate enough to find a wife as beautiful as she is prudent. She will make a wise queen one day. I cannot say whether I will be a wise king. I have so much to learn."

"The sacred writings encourage us to follow the examples of wisdom we see around us. We do well to learn from those we come in contact with. However, we cannot let our examples and mentors tear us in opposite directions. Somewhere in the valley of decision, you must trust yourself."

"Perhaps in time I may be able to do so. For now, I must be the student."

"You must also be a husband. Go find Nina before she becomes upset at your absence."

Andrew smiled. "Is that advice from experience?"

"Yes, very recent experience. I will not be taking any more sabbaticals for a while."

Andrew rose from his place under the tree. "I will find my wife, and contemplate the conundrum of a kingdom tomorrow." He and Nathaniel walked back to the castle together.

CHAPTER 7

The afternoon sun was bright and hot as Joel worked a piece of iron into a horseshoe. The thud of his mallet meeting the hot metal melded with his heartbeat. He looked intently at the piece before him, making sure the shape was precise. When he was finished, he laid the shoe on the workbench to cool.

He walked over to the entrance of the shop where he worked and looked outside the door. The cerulean sky had a wisp of white stretched through it like thin strands of cotton. Leanna would have said this day was a gift from God.

A mist threatened to grow in Joel's eyes. He missed Leanna with every breath he took, and he felt the futility of his oath to kill Jason's daughter. He became a murderer to vindicate Leanna's death. She never would have wanted that. She would want the man who enjoyed metalworking and caring for horses. She would want him to find peace with the tragedy that claimed her life and be grateful for the life he had left to live.

"The sky is beautiful today." Joel heard a voice at his side. He looked over and smiled at Enoch. He was kind and willing to help anyone who had need. The old man hired Joel one day when he went from business to business seeking work so he could stay in North Agea.

Joel nodded his head. "Yes, it is." In his heart he felt it was time to give up his oath and let Jason's family live out their lives in peace. It was time to return home.

He looked back out the door at the center of the market square. The royal city attracted merchants like magnets. His home of Wildemere was the same. People did not change with location. There was nothing new under the sun[12].

---

[12]   Ecclesiastes 1:9

He noticed Prince Jared out with his new wife at his side. They seemed in good spirits. Joel knew Ephratha very well. Robert Stowe was a trusted acquaintance. He was also with Prince Andrew and a young woman he did not recognize was on his arm. Then he saw Nafaria. She was very beautiful, with that sweet innocent smile he remembered.

Joel sighed and thought about his return home. He knew he would face severe consequences for Jason and Thena's deaths. Jason was a trusted friend of King Catalane. While he pondered this, he noticed the man with Nafaria. He came to her aid the night of Jared's wedding and foiled Joel's murderous plan. Suddenly, as if he could read Joel's mind, he turned and looked directly at him. Joel shuddered. He walked to the rear of the shop and resumed his work.

⸻⸻

Nathaniel was restless as they walked through the market. He felt he was being watched. He looked carefully from shop to shop. A man stared at him from a blacksmith's shop doorway. Nathaniel stared back until he went into the shop.

"Do not dismiss him so quickly. It is whom you seek. You must use him for your own ends." Nathaniel contemplated this as he walked through the market. Jared noticed his divided attention.

"You are very quiet, Nathaniel," said Jared. Nafaria looked at him.

"Something just occurred to me. We passed a shop I would like to go back to." Nathaniel touched Nafaria's cheek. "I will not be gone long." He turned and his black cloak was lost in the crowd.

Nathaniel reached the blacksmith shop quickly. He stood among a crop of trees so as not to be seen. A man was fitting a horse with shoes. He was careful, but his quickness showed he was skilled at his work. He stood up and patted the horse.

Nathaniel recognized him. He tried to kill Nafaria the night of Jared's wedding. Ephratha and Nafaria said he lived in Wildemere. Why was he in Arioth? Was he still pursuing Nafaria?

Nathaniel slipped away from the shop. He did not want this man to see him. He would decide what to do about him later.

Nathaniel returned to the group carrying a package wrapped in cloth and tied with string.

"What did you find?" asked Nafaria. "It looks like a book."

"A handsome one," replied Nathaniel. He untied the string, opened the package and handed her a book about ten inches tall, as well as wide. Nafaria opened the cover and saw the clean parchment pages. She looked at Nathaniel.

"Our child will need a diary one day."

"Is there more than one?"

"I hope we will need more than the two I was able to find."

"Now that we are together again, I suggest we head back to the castle. Dinner will be soon," said Jared. The group headed toward the castle.

The sun was setting as they strolled back through the castle gate. The sister queens sat on the terrace, watching the sunset.

They both waved as they walked by.

"Pieces fall to the ground—the jigsaw takes form." Nathaniel considered the words as he waved back at the queens.

The night was quiet. A breeze wafted through the doorway leading to the terrace. Nafaria's breath was heavy as she slept. Everything about the night was tranquil; but sleep eluded Nathaniel. It slipped through his fingers like sand.

He looked out the doorway at the crescent moon. He felt no peace, nor rest. He closed his eyes once more.

"Nathaniel." A familiar harsh rasp whispered his name in the darkness. *"Nathaniel!"* It was more insistent this time. He rose from the bed and walked onto the terrace.

The cool air added a pink blush to his cheeks. He looked at the ground and saw a robed figure on the lawn. Nathaniel hurried out of the room, grabbing his cloak as he went.

⁕⁕⁕⁕⁕

Two guards made their rounds about the castle in the third watch of the night. King Lian commanded his royal guards to be vigilant, and the captain took the task seriously. They heard the sound of footsteps in the corridor above them. One guard signaled the other. Nathaniel Stone came into view. He was putting on a cloak as he walked down the steps to the main foyer of the castle. Before they were seen, the guard grabbed his partner and moved into the shadows behind a large statue. Nathaniel passed by, unaware of their presence.

When he was outside, the guard whispered, "Tolliver, finish the round and report back to the captain. I want to follow him."

"We should go together, Sheill," replied Tolliver.

"I want to find out why Nathaniel Stone is out so late. If we both follow, he might see us. If I go alone, I have a better chance of staying hidden," replied Sheill.

"We should stay together. If the captain does not trust him, he is surely dangerous."

"I am only following him. I do not wish to tangle with anyone of the Craft; especially if he turns out to be a mad wizard." Sheill darted outside before Tolliver could reply.

———— ·++++·· ————

Sheill followed as Nathaniel walked past the end of the colonnade and disappeared into the wood after a hooded figure. His heart beat faster. Who was this other person? He trailed after them, careful not to make any noise as they entered the wood.

The starry night vanished as they went deeper among the trees. The branches cut off the light of the moon and stars. The figure halted amid a clearing and picked up a branch from the ground. Touching the tip, it burst into flame. He looked at Nathaniel who dropped to his knees and bowed his head.

"Master, you honor me with your presence," said Nathaniel, his eyes on the ground. The figure came closer to him and touched his head.

"Rise, Nathaniel. I chose to visit you because of your great potential. You will indeed drive nations to their knees. I have come to help you sort out the thoughts in your mind," said the stranger.

Nathaniel obeyed and rose to his feet. "The whispers I hear give me strange thoughts."

"You must protect your family, Nathaniel. The man you saw will kill Nafaria if he is allowed to live. You wish to bring justice for those of the Craft who have lost their lives through the silence of the king of Nereheim. Your own life was shaken to its foundation when you left your home behind as a youth. Your father was wise to move to a safe place. You have learned much since then. Use the power of the bell to possess the man who seeks your wife's blood. He will commit more evil than he could ever imagine."

"Joel would have a spirit reside in him who will kill one of my choosing." Sheill watched as Nathaniel slowly paced the clearing, as he spoke. "How would this avenge those of the Craft in Nereheim?"

"Even now, the king of Nereheim is on the fence of decision. He wishes to appoint another Court Adviser, but his choice has declined the commission. He is a wise king, but his emotions cloud his judgment. If he lost his queen, he will become rash and easily manipulated. He will see your potential the same way he saw your father's potential," replied the figure.

"The jigsaw," answered Nathaniel.

"It is no small thing when a royal is murdered. The king will agonize over the loss of his queen. Send him to kill her," replied the figure.

"This could send the sister kingdoms to war," replied Nathaniel.

"The king will be easily managed without his queen to help him see through his emotions. Then you will be able to direct his affairs. Go into the annals of North Agea. Pick a ruthless killer from its past. This will seal Nereheim's fate."

The loud snap of a branch sounded in the wood. Nathaniel looked around them.

"We are not alone," said the figure. "You were followed."

Horrified at being discovered, Sheill turned to run and suddenly burst into flame. His screams were swallowed by the rustle of birds in the air.

The light went out. Nathaniel headed back toward the castle, past the pile of ashes that was Sheill.

⋅⋅⊰⊱⋅⋅

Nafaria dreamed as the night went on, making her sleep less peaceful. She stood before an exquisite painting. The workmanship of the frame was as intricate as it was delicate. It drew one from across the room to see its extraordinary contents. The rich purples, blues and reds of the painting complemented the brown hair and dark eyes of a pensive looking man. It was a portrait of her beloved husband.

She appreciated the way the artist captured the flash and depth of his eyes. There was nothing in her soul that hid from his gaze. Even staring at this replica, her secrets came to light. It saw her as he did, with the intention of knowing her fully.

Her hand quivered as she reached out and touched his cheek. The painting melted under her finger. The colors ran together like hot wax spilling down the side of a candle. She touched it again. The eyes and mouth drooped. Tears streamed down her face as she screamed Nathaniel's name.

"Nafaria, what is it?" shouted Nathaniel. He shook her until her eyes finally opened. She saw his face come into focus and then burst into tears.

"I had such a horrible dream."

"It was only a dream. I am right here. I will always be here."

"Do you promise?"

"I will be here for as long as you will have me."

His smile reassured Nafaria. "It was only a dream," she repeated and snuggled closer to him and drifted back to sleep.

⋅⋅⊹⋅⋅

Nathaniel caressed Nafaria's hair while he thought back to another moonlit evening. He sat with Oberman before the great fire burning outside his house in the woods. The cluster of trees overhead blocked the moon from view. The old man stirred the fire with a branch. Sparks rose in the air. They sat a long time before Oberman spoke.

"After all you have seen, heard and partaken of, do you consider yourself loyal to our master?"

"I do." Nathaniel spoke with conviction.

"Your allegiance must be absolute. It cannot waver between two different worlds. Your greatest test of allegiance was not when you cut your hand and poured your blood into the fire before him, nor when you swore the blood of your firstborn. It was not even when you mixed your blood with mine to claim the secrets of the Grimoire Macabre. It will be when you are with your wife and friends again. That fellowship has the strength of iron. You must not allow your resolve to weaken. Our master is jealous and demands absolute allegiance. You will have days when you doubt your decision. During those times say aloud, 'I will not be moved.' Say it now."

"I will not be moved." Nathaniel felt the power of those words.

"Remember them when you doubt. Say it again," said Oberman.

"I will not be moved," repeated Nathaniel.

"When you are faced with fears, and decisions you made cost the lives of those around you. Say it again."

"I will not be moved." replied Nathaniel with a sternness that caused Oberman to look at him. He saw the glare in Nathaniel's eyes and nodded. "The Master demands complete allegiance. Never waver in your resolve to fulfill your devotion to him."

Nathaniel looked at him with complete resolution. "I will not be moved."

Nathaniel stared at the ceiling above him. "I will not be moved," he whispered.

He rose out of bed and crept across the room. He grabbed his cloak and pulled it on as he walked out, leaving Nafaria to her slumbers.

Coleman continued in silence as he walked the corridors with one of his newest subordinates. He did not often take the night watch, but tonight he was especially vigilant. Nafaria's bold young husband returned from his sabbatical and Coleman did not trust him. He understood enough about people to see that Andrew's new wife was of the same mind. She was pleasant but never let her guard down near him. "Keep your friends close and your enemies closer," Coleman thought to himself. This was something he could learn by watching Nina. She did not trust Nathaniel any more than he did. Perhaps there was more to his worries than petty jealousy after all.

The great stone hallway was dimly lit with torches set about twenty feet apart from each other. They were kept burning by the royal guard as they made their rounds. Nathaniel had no idea when the evening guard would pass again.

"Master I call on your power, let me walk unseen through this hour," Nathaniel whispered. He continued down the hall, becoming a shadow as he went.

The corridors were silent as he made his way to the royal library. He remembered every turn and doorway perfectly. He came within sight of the great door when he heard footsteps in the passage opposite him. He sank into the closest wall and did not breathe as Coleman and another soldier passed him. The captain paused a moment and looked behind them.

"Is there something wrong, captain?" asked the soldier.

"No," replied Coleman. After a moment, he turned and continued down the hall.

Nathaniel waited until the sound of footsteps was gone. He moved toward the door, letting himself into the library. He snapped his finger and a bright flame shot from his fingertip. He walked over to a table and lit a candlestick that was left behind. The light from the candle lit the room enough to see the books by. He picked up the candlestick and walked over to a shelf with a set of books marked by an embossed gold crown. Each volume had a name and a year beneath it. They were thick volumes with a handsome leather binding. Nathaniel picked one off the shelf, curious as to its contents.

He opened the book and smiled. He was staring at a volume of the annals of the kings of North Agea. He looked at the binding and saw the year. This book was written almost sixty years ago. This would suit his purpose. Nathaniel took the book to the table and sat down.

He glanced through it until he found something very interesting. In the time of this king, there was a murderer who was caught and hanged. The king himself gave the order to execute this man named Michalis. He was a cruel man who killed many women and young girls, by stabbing them multiple times with a dagger that was found on him when he was captured. He was covered in the blood of his latest victim when he was caught.

"This is what you seek," Nathaniel heard a whisper. He read the account, put the book back on the shelf, and blew out the candle. He made his way to Nafaria before dawn.

· ·+·+·+·· ·

The sunshine was bright as Susanna stepped onto the balcony of her room. She breathed the clean air deeply. She closed her eyes and smiled as she felt the heat of the sun and the cool autumn breeze on her cheeks at the same time. It was a fine day.

She sat outside, enjoying the tea that was brought up for her. Clara knew Susanna loved a hot cup of tea in the morning and always made sure the servants had it to her early.

A knock on the door interrupted her thoughts. Andrew walked onto the terrace. "I was told you wanted to see me, mother."

"I am going back to Nereheim tomorrow. It has been a pleasant visit, but I think I have stayed long enough. However, you should stay longer. It makes me happy to see you and Jared getting along so well. Spend time with your cousin. I think Nina would also enjoy the time with Ephratha."

"I have enjoyed this visit. I found I have much to learn. I would be happy to spend more time with Jared." Andrew looked at the courtyard. Susanna noticed his brow stitched together at his words.

"Is something on your mind?"

"I have squandered so much time when I could have been learning and building good character like Jared has. I fear I will never be ready to be king."

Susanna walked over to him and gently pulled him close to her. "That you recognize your failings while you are young is a good thing. You have time to grow into a man of noble character. You will be a good king one day if you begin making wise choices now. Find those you can trust to guide you. There is still time."

Andrew felt tears well up and spill from his eyes as he clung to his mother. "I love you so much mother. You have been a constant voice of encouragement, even when I have been the most stubborn of fools. I hope to make you proud one day."

"You already do. Help your father govern Nereheim justly."

"I have thought about that over the past few days. I need advisers I can trust."

"I am certain your father will see to it Nereheim no longer persecutes those of the Craft."

Andrew nodded his head in agreement. "I will check on Nina and let her know we are staying longer. She will love the time with Ephratha and Nafaria."

"I will leave early tomorrow." Susanna returned to her study of the clouds from the balcony.

———— ·+++++· ————

Tolliver briskly walked through the castle checking every room as he went. It was now after sunrise, and he could not find Sheill anywhere. He cursed himself as he looked, for he feared something dangerous happened to his partner, and he was a party to it. When he finished on the main floor of the castle, he sighed. There was nothing left to do, but find the captain and tell him what happened. He went outside and climbed to the top of the castle wall. He saw the captain standing alone, facing out toward Lord Cade's lands. "Captain, I need to tell you something," he said quietly.

Coleman continued to look out. "What is it?"

"Sheill and I were taking our rounds in the castle during the third watch. We saw Nathaniel Stone leave the castle. Sheill told me to continue the round while he followed him. I have not seen him since."

"Why did you not go with him?" The sternness in the captain's voice showed his annoyance.

"He said if we both follow him, Nathaniel would see us. I am afraid something happened to him."

"Where did Nathaniel go?"

"I only saw him start down the colonnade. I have no idea after that."

"Perhaps he went into the woods. Follow me, soldier. We will see if we can find your missing partner." They left the castle wall and headed for the colonnade.

They spread out once they came to the end of the colonnade and made a careful search of the grounds. "The only place left is the woods," said Coleman.

"Yes captain."

They headed into the woods, keeping their eyes to the ground. They did not go far, when Coleman spotted a queer pile of dust on the forest floor. He crouched down, touched it and shuddered. It was ash. He put his fingers further into the ash and picked out a silver ring.

Tolliver crouched down next to the captain and looked at the ring. "That is the ring Sheill always wears. He keeps his mother's wedding ring as a good luck charm." They rose and exited the wood.

"The pile of ash you found the ring in—was that Sheill?" asked Tolliver.

Coleman nodded. "Sheill is dead. I do not know how, but it appears he was completely burned. Speak of this to no one. I do not want our discovery to get back to Nathaniel."

"What do we tell the others?"

"He asked to visit his mother. We all know he was homesick when he first arrived. That will be a plausible story for now."

"Yes captain." Tolliver looked down at the ground.

Coleman put a hand on his shoulder. "If you had been there, you would have met the same end, and I would be looking for two soldiers." They were silent as they returned to the castle.

<hr>

Nathaniel headed outside to join Nafaria, Nina and Ephratha while they enjoyed tea. He turned a corner quickly, and nearly ran into Susanna.

"I beg your pardon, your majesty. I was going to join my wife for tea."

"It is quite alright, Nathaniel. I was hoping to speak to you before I left."

"You are leaving?"

"One cannot stay away from home forever. I will return to Nereheim tomorrow morning. Andrew and Nina will remain here a while longer. The six of you seem to be getting along so well."

"Nafaria has enjoyed meeting Nina," replied Nathaniel.

"Andrew continues to need support from peers such as yourself and Jared. I am so pleased he and Jared are finally in agreement with each other. I love my son, but as of late, I am proud of decisions he is making for the better," said Susanna.

"Andrew has a good heart; he will make a good king one day."

"I think so too. Your father was one of the wisest men of Nereheim. Andrew wishes to make sure those of the Craft are no longer persecuted. Help him, if you can."

Nathaniel looked at Susanna. Her eyes held great passion as well as warmth. He saw how much she hurt for those of the Craft. She took his hand and gave it a gentle squeeze. Nathaniel felt his breath catch.

"I am very sorry about Lord Jason and his wife Thena. No greater injustice was done in Wildemere than their murders."

Nathaniel's eyes narrowed. His blood went cold at the mention of Nafaria's parents. His resolve flooded back into his heart as he looked at Susanna.

"Thank you, your majesty. The sacred writings tell us there is a time and season for everything that happens under heaven[13]. You can be assured

---

[13]   Ecclesiastes 3:1

YAHWEH will call what is past into account.[14]" Nathaniel bowed and continued down the corridor more determined than ever to carry out his master's task.

⋅⋅✦✦✦✦⋅⋅

Joel tossed in his bed, staring at the ceiling when he turned on his back. A light breeze ruffled the trees outside Enoch's shop. No matter what position he chose, sleep eluded him.

Though he felt calm in leaving his vendetta behind; he feared what he intended to do. Fulfilling his oath would never bring Leanna back to him. He no longer wished to be a killer. He wanted to be the blacksmith he trained to be.

A sound outside the shop brought Joel from his thoughts. He sat up and listened. He heard it again, only louder this time. He rose from his bed and pulled a shirt over his head. He put on his boots and cloak and went outside.

In the moonlight, he scanned the woods behind the shop. A lone figure stood amid a cluster of maple trees. Joel became nervous as seconds passed and the stranger did not move. He finally took a few steps forward.

"Friend, come closer so we can talk. What business cannot wait until sunrise?" he called out.

A low unsettling laugh came from the stranger as he pushed down his hood. "I am no friend, Joel. An evil moon hangs above us this night."

Joel remembered his encounter with this man at Jared's wedding. He would have died, if not for Nafaria's intervention.

"You should have gone back to Nereheim. My wife convinced me to spare your life. Your quest for revenge has brought you to an evil end."

---

[14]　Ecclesiastes 3:15

Joel stood still. He remembered this man's power and knew he was dead any time he willed it.

"Killing me will only make you a fugitive in your homeland. It will not right any wrong I have done," said Joel quietly.

"I was driven from my home when I was a boy for the knowledge and power I possess. Nobles fear what they cannot control; royals plot to use me as a pawn. There is no sanctuary for me," he replied.

Joel realized this young man was originally from Nereheim. It was likely his family fled persecution and sought anonymity in North Agea when he was just a boy. "You are one of the exiles," whispered Joel.

He remembered what Jason told him about those of the Craft who fled Nereheim during persecution. Many uprooted their families and left their businesses to become citizens in other countries, hoping to live respectable lives again.

"What will you do?"

"What I do will pay for the wrong you did to Jason and Thena Mauldon. They were magnificent people. You will become a walking nightmare to serve my purpose."

He pulled a small silver bell and hammer from his cloak. Joel focused on the bell, for it was crafted beautifully. It looked so light and delicate— such a beautiful piece of silver. When the stranger struck the bell with the hammer, a soft note echoed in the night.

At once, their cloaks whipped around them, and a cold wind surrounded them. Joel stood across from this young man whose face was twisted into an evil smile. "Michalis come forth," said the stranger. Joel took a step away. He looked at Joel and said, "You will stay."

Joel's feet seized in their place while a mist engulfed him. The stranger spoke to the air. "I have read your deeds, and know of your infamy. I have called you forth for a special task. You alone possess the desire and skill for this endeavor. As I summoned you with the bell, I now command you to enter the body of this man." The stranger pointed at Joel.

Joel trembled at what he heard. Wind rushed through his mouth and cold air filled his lungs. He tried to cry out, but only uttered a loud gasp. He crumpled to the ground as the cold coursed through his blood. There was something inside him. His body rose from the ground, though he never willed himself to move.

"What, what is happening?" shouted Joel. His mouth did not move. "What is this? What have you done?" shouted Joel again. Joel felt his feet move easily, as his body came closer to the stranger.

This being, Michalis, now controlled him. His body was a mere vessel for another spirit. Joel could only listen to them.

"You have brought me from death, Necromancer. What is it you wish of me?" asked Michalis.

"Tomorrow morning, Queen Susanna will be returning to Nereheim. She will be in a carriage that will bear the figure of the Eagle, the royal crest of Nereheim. You are to kill the Queen and all who are with her." The stranger produced an ordinary hunting knife. It was polished to a high sheen. Joel saw his hand raise as Michalis took the knife and looked at it carefully.

"The act must be done in North Agea. Follow the main road out of Arioth. Find a secluded area so that you have sufficient time to kill those you find in the carriage. Your soul will return to your grave at midnight tomorrow."

"I never had the opportunity to violate royalty," said Michalis.

"The details are unimportant to me. Kill the queen and those with her."

Joel listened in horror as he heard the order. He was about to kill Queen Susanna. He now understood the terrible price he would pay for his vengeance.

Michael sat on the rooftop of Reinard's manor. It was nearing the middle of the fourth watch and was cold as it was black. The moon lowered itself in degrees. Dawn would soon follow. His fingers curled around a polished brass mug holding a steaming liquid. The mulled wine held hints of cinnamon, cloves and even orange flavor. Lillia was becoming exceptional in her cooking skills. She still had not mastered yeast rolls, but Maia was as patient a teacher as she was free with her cooking secrets. He sniffed the spices residing in the aroma as he took a long sip.

Reinard stood a few feet from him, gazing through his glass. A lantern was hidden in a corner so as not to obstruct his view of the sky. His chart lay next to it so he could easily record the positions the stars were taking.

"The transcendence is nearly complete," said Reinard as he gazed through the glass. "Is there anything Donovan wrote about how long these periods last?"

"He writes about strange stories like the one he encountered for one year after the stars align. Once the stars align, there are accounts that coincide with each full moon for that year. The effects of transcendence last longer than the event itself," replied Michael.

"So, we can expect these occurrences to end in early September."

"It has been a long time since 1305. Who knows what we can truly expect?"

Reinard wrote on his chart after looking into his glass once again. "I wonder what this time of transcendence holds for us."

Michael pondered his father in law's query as he looked at the sky. "Look—the moon," he said quietly. Reinard lowered his glass as he looked at the moon. It was red as scarlet as it stood in the night.

"A blood moon is a bad omen. Some evil has been wrought this night," said Michael with a shudder. Both men stared at the moon, a sense of dread settling over them.

——— ·+++·· ———

The early morning sun was veiled in white mist. The fog that rose up in the night refused to burn off. The whole of Arioth seemed to be shrouded in its milky white grip.

Susanna stepped out of the castle with Clara and embraced her. Clara seemed uncertain about the weather.

"The mist is very peculiar for Arioth. Normally this type of fog is seen around the Anenderes, but it dissipates well before it gets here," said Clara with concern. The more she looked at the thick white mist; the greater her uneasiness. "Why not stay a little longer and see if it burns off?"

Susanna smiled at her sister. Clara tended to worry and fret very often. "Clara, we both have traveled the roads from Arioth to Wildemere many times. Even with so thick a fog, there is no danger. I have my escorts with me. I miss Rohn, which means it is time for me to go. Remind Andrew that I expect him and Nina to leave at the end of the week."

"Yes mother," replied Andrew as he and Nina stepped to her side.

Susanna was startled when they appeared in the mist. "Andrew, I did not expect you up this early."

"I wanted to see you off, no matter how early you choose to go." Andrew stepped forward and kissed her cheek. "Have a safe trip back, mother." He wrapped his arms around her and breathed her jasmine scent.

"We will head back to Wildemere at the end of the week," replied Nina as she hugged Susanna.

"Have fun while you are here," said Susanna with a wink and a smile. She climbed into the carriage.

"Wait, Aunt Susanna!" called Jared. He and Ephratha rushed up to the carriage.

"What are you two doing up this early?" asked Susanna.

"I know of your fondness for slipping away at an early hour. I made sure we were up to see you off," said Jared. He climbed into the carriage and gave her a hug.

"Keep a close watch on Andrew," whispered Susanna.

Jared smiled. "As often as I can. I hope that when we are each on the throne, the sister kingdoms will continue to have good relations." Jared stepped down, and Ephratha stepped up.

"It has been a pleasure to see you again, your majesty," she said as she hugged Susanna.

"Ephratha, call me Aunt Susanna when we are not in court. That is what I am, after all," said Susanna.

"Yes, Aunt Susanna," replied Ephratha with a smile.

"Remember to use the wisdom your mother passed on to you. It will show you much in this life." Ephratha nodded as she stepped from the carriage.

"Have a good trip, Susanna," said Clara.

᛫᛫✦✦✦✦᛫᛫

Susanna waved as the carriage pulled away from the castle. Soon, the sound of the horses' hooves and the jingling bells on the harnesses was the only thing she heard. She looked out the window, disappointed that the fog covered the countryside.

One of the king's guards from Wildemere rode in the carriage with her, as well as the one accompanying the driver. This was to satisfy her husband's worry about her traveling unprotected. Today she felt glad for the escort.

"Is something on your mind, your majesty?" asked the guard.

"I guess the fog is a little more unsettling than I thought it would be," said Susanna after a moment.

"We can always go back," replied the guard.

"No, it is nothing. I would like to get back to Wildemere."

The carriage drove on for another hour before Susanna looked out again. The fog lifted a little. She saw a lone figure at the side of the road walking in the direction they drove. When the figure heard the carriage, it moved over.

"Tell the driver to stop," said Susanna.

The guard leaned out the window and shouted the command to the driver. They stopped next to a man in a black cloak with the hood covering his head. Susanna made out his chin with the beginning growth of an auburn colored beard. The guard opened the carriage door.

"It is a dismal morning to be out walking. Let us give you a ride to your destination," called Susanna to the stranger.

The man turned his gaze and looked at Susanna. He smiled and said, "That is very kind of you, my lady." The stranger climbed into the carriage.

CHAPTER 8

By midday, the fog covering North Agea disappeared. Lord Rowen Cade traveled on horseback with two servants who rode next to him. Another was driving a cart pulled by two more horses. Their spirits lifted and they felt more at ease on their journey back to the estate.

"The sun finally reveals itself," said Rowen.

"What is that up ahead?" asked the servant who rode next to him.

"We shall see soon enough," replied Rowen.

Rowen gasped when they saw the blood-stained door of a carriage off the road. He stared at the eagle on the door. Three horses stood nearby, as if waiting to start again. He hopped down from his horse, strode to the carriage and opened the door. He sighed heavily as he peered inside.

"My lord, two men are next to the carriage with their throats cut," said one of the servants.

"Dear God," Rowen whispered as he shut the carriage door. He looked at his servants. "Two of you stay with this carriage. Do not go inside, and let no one disturb it until I return."

"Where are you going, my lord?" asked one of the servants.

"I will report this to the captain of the royal guard. A great treachery has happened and the king must know about it." Rowen mounted his horse and rode for Arioth with one of his servants.

"What happened back there?" his servant asked him.

"The queen of Nereheim has been murdered," replied Rowen grimly.

------ ·✦✦✦· ------

Clara stood on the terrace overlooking the winding road out of Arioth toward the Anenderes River, the same road Susanna departed on a few hours earlier.

The fog lifted by degrees all morning, but her heart was troubled. She was convinced an irrevocable evil occurred in those early morning hours.

She looked at the china doll in her arms. Over the years, Clara had taken to holding the doll when she was distressed with fear she did not understand. It was a gift from Susanna on her wedding day.

Clara loved dolls. She was fascinated by the craftsmanship that went into the tiny faces, the hair, or the little dresses they wore. China dolls were her favorite. Their faces were so shiny and white, attributes of beauty and purity.

She recalled the day Susanna gave her this doll. She stood before a full-length mirror, anxious at the thought of becoming a queen. She knew her husband to be loved her very much, but she did not know if she were as equal to the task of queen as her older sister was.

"You look perfect." She watched Susanna step into view so that she stood beside Clara in the mirror.

"I do not feel perfect, sister. I am afraid I will not be equal to the task of queen," said Clara.

"I remember that feeling well. You will face your fear, and conquer it." Susanna held up a silk bundle. "This is a gift for you. I hope you like it."

Clara smiled as she opened the silk and saw the china doll. It was dressed in a pink chiffon gown that went down to her feet. "It is beautiful."

"So are you, my sister. You always will be," Susanna whispered as she hugged her.

That day, Clara walked confidently down the aisle toward her husband with the doll tucked firmly in her arms.

Her thoughts were interrupted by the sound of footsteps. Ephratha walked onto the terrace.

"Jared wanted to let you know we are going into the market today with Nina, Andrew, Nathaniel and Nafaria." Ephratha saw Clara's expression and noted the doll in her hands. A look of concern crossed her face. "Is everything alright?"

"I do not know. The day has turned lovely, but I feel a terrible price has been paid for it."

The sound of horse's hooves interrupted the conversation. Ephratha and Clara looked down as two riders entered the castle grounds.

Rowen looked at the terrace and saw Queen Clara with the new princess. The blank look on Clara's face told him she was not well. She held something in her arms, but he was unable to make out what it was. They hopped down from their horses as Solomon approached them.

"Lord Cade, this is an unexpected surprise," said Solomon in greeting. His smile disappeared when he saw the grim expression on the noble's face.

"I need to see the king on an urgent matter. Where is my son?" Rowen glanced once more at the queen and princess.

"The king is in his throne room," said Solomon.

"I will wait until whatever business he has is concluded. Find Coleman; tell him I wish to see him in the throne room." Rowen turned to his companion. "Stay with the horses." He walked into the castle while Solomon searched for Coleman.

Rowen was no stranger to the castle. He easily found his destination. As he hoped, Lian was alone. He did not wish to be overheard by others. When the king saw his friend, he brightened. He rose from his throne to greet him.

"Lord Rowen Cade, what a surprise. What business keeps you from the market today?" asked the king as they clasped hands.

"An evil business your majesty," replied Rowen as he bowed.

The king waved off his bow. "You are my friend. There is no need to bow to me."

"Your majesty, a leader is only a leader if he commands the respect of his servants. If I do not show proper respect to you, what will your subordinates think?"

"Your point is warranted. I will heed it in the future. Now, tell me why you are here."

"I was coming home after delivering some roses and other plants to another village. We came across Queen Susanna's carriage. It was on the side of the road, and everyone was dead. I did not go inside, but I saw a knife stuck into her chest."

Lian's features darkened. His wife's sister, the queen of Nereheim, was murdered in North Agea while heading home. Solomon and Coleman entered the room.

"Solomon, find my son and Prince Andrew. Bring them here immediately," said Lian. His voice was barely audible.

"What has happened father?" asked Coleman. Rowen shook his head and looked back at Lian.

A few moments after Solomon left the room, Lian saw his wife enter with Ephratha following behind her. He noticed the blank expression on Clara's face. She was absently playing with the blond curls of the doll's hair.

"Susanna?" said Clara tonelessly.

Tears formed in Lian's eyes, but he could not answer. Clara fell backward in a faint as Ephratha managed to catch her.

Jared entered the room with Andrew and Nathaniel and saw Ephratha on the ground with his mother in her arms. "Mother!" exclaimed Jared. Nafaria and Nina followed behind them. "Father, what happened?" asked Jared as he kneeled beside Ephratha.

The king ignored his son's question and walked over to Andrew. "I was given news of a great treachery. Let us see this thing that has come to pass." Lian left the room. Jared followed his father, with Rowen and Coleman following after them.

Andrew looked at Nathaniel. "Please come with me," said Andrew as he left the room.

"Stay here with Ephratha. Something is wrong, and if there is danger, I want you away from it," said Nathaniel to Nafaria.

"Be careful," whispered Nafaria. She watched him leave. The girls were alone with the fainted queen.

"What happened?" asked Nafaria. She knelt down to Ephratha, who sat on the floor holding Clara.

"I do not know," whispered Ephratha.

The men followed Rowen down the country road. Coleman rode close beside his father. Andrew followed with Nathaniel and Jared. Two more guards rode in the rear.

The green countryside spread out before them under the blue sky. The road wound into a crop of trees. Rowen slowed his horse and trotted through the wood until a carriage came in view. Rowen saw his servants perched on their horses, each one looking the opposite direction, ready to hurry curious onlookers past the spectacle.

Andrew saw his father's carriage. He jumped from his horse and ran toward it.

"Mother?" he shouted. He stopped suddenly when he saw the blood stains on the door.

"Andrew, wait!" shouted Jared. He caught up to his cousin and grabbed him in a bear hug to hold him back.

"Let go of me!" shouted Andrew. He wrestled Jared away and plunged toward the carriage, yanking the door open.

Susanna's lifeless eyes met Andrew as he stood before the open carriage. A knife was buried in her chest. He covered his face with his hands and cried out. Tears flowed from his eyes and his body was wracked with sobs.

Nathaniel stepped forward and gently laid a hand on his shoulder. "Andrew, there is nothing more you can do for her," he said softly.

Andrew wiped his eyes. "I should have been here."

"If you had been, you would be dead as well," replied Nathaniel. "Have courage. Follow me."

Andrew slowly backed away from the carriage. Lian embraced his nephew and let tears fall freely as they stood in silence.

"Coleman, drive the carriage back to Arioth," said Lian.

Coleman hooked his horse next to the lead horse and the party made their way back to the castle.

⋅⋅✦✦✦✦⋅⋅

Lian set aside an area in the stable for the carriage. Susanna's body was prepared for the trip back to Nereheim. He had no idea what to say to his brother in law to convey his heart in the matter. He sat in the garden, staring at the flowers and shrubs, lost in thought. He could not even face his wife to comfort her. How would he explain this murder that happened nearly under his nose? He sent Solomon and James to Nereheim when they got back to Arioth to bring word to Rohn. Was the whole world suddenly mad? How was such a tragedy visited, and no one around as witness? Lian closed his eyes and felt the sunlight on his face. He hoped answers would soon come.

Coleman made the afternoon round in the castle. He was unnerved at finding Queen Susanna, but did not want talk about it. He was also uneasy that his father found the carriage. He could have easily been hurt, even though he was with companions. Queen Susanna had a royal escort, and none of them survived.

He continued down the passageway, checking the torches and looking carefully into dark corners. He thought through the matter carefully. In his heart, he could not believe this was a coincidence. The queen's death felt like the foundation of a clever plan, but whose? What end did it accomplish? These questions crowded his mind as he went on his task.

He stopped at the preparation room the king set aside. He opened the door and saw an old man with white hair looking at him. He gave Coleman a grimace.

"Cornelius, have you shed any light on the matter?" asked Coleman.

"Captain, I have found something. I must speak to the king alone," replied Cornelius.

"I was hoping there was an answer to this madness."

"I am afraid the answer may be as perplexing as the incident itself."

They moved closer to the queen's body. It was covered with a sheet, but blood still soaked through it in some places. Her clothes and other articles lay on another table. Coleman walked over to the polished steel hunting knife that caught his attention.

"This is the knife that killed the queen?"

"I pulled it from her chest when she was brought here," replied Cornelius.

"I will tell the king." Coleman left the room.

•••••••

Cornelius continued to study Susanna's body. The door opened a few minutes later and Lian entered the chamber, followed by Coleman.

"You found something?"

"Yes, your majesty. However, I am at a loss as to what it means."

Cornelius lifted the sheet and revealed Susanna's left leg. Halfway between the knee and the hip, a crude star was carved: four lines intersecting each other to form the pattern.

"The star that fell[15]," whispered Lian. "What can this possibly mean?"

"I cannot imagine. Susanna was loved by many in Arioth. No one loyal to North Agea would have done this," said Cornelius as he covered the body again.

"The symbol is most unsettling. The killer would have to have a long memory to know its significance. That evil was done a generation ago," replied Lian.

---

[15]   Luke 10:18

"The symbol is the only clue to her murderer, yet it makes no sense. One cannot simply rise from the grave to kill again," replied Cornelius.

"I must think on the matter. Rohn will arrive soon and I have no idea what to tell him."

Lian turned to Coleman and spoke in a barely audible voice. "I need to speak to Jared at once. He is to meet me alone in the royal library. Do not tell him, write it down."

"Your majesty, you can trust your family—" began Coleman.

Lian cut him off. "I am afraid this is the season for testing trust."

———— ·⊹✦⊹· ————

Jared stood in the meadow, a few yards from the edge of the woods. He faced the trees, as if trying to see something. The birds came and went from the woods, but everything else was quiet. Hearing a faint rustle, he turned and saw Coleman coming toward him.

"You should not be out here alone," said Coleman.

"I intended to go to the garden, but I continued walking until I stopped here. I have never been out here before," said Jared.

"Is there something on your mind?" asked Coleman.

"I suspect Aunt Susanna's death is no coincidence. What do you think?" replied Jared.

"There is a clever game of chess being played, but I cannot guess who is moving the pieces. We must be cautious," said Coleman. After a moment he continued. "Your father wishes to see you." Coleman handed him a piece of paper. Jared took the paper, an unspoken question on his face.

"There is something else you should know, your highness. One of our guards went missing on his round during the third watch last night. I found a keepsake of his amid a pile of ash just inside those woods. I do not want you out here for any reason."

"You do not wish to tell me more?"

"You must know as little as possible about the situation. It is to save your life."

They walked back to the castle in silence. Coleman excused himself and headed for the sentry.

⊹⊹⊹⊹⊹

Jared unfolded the paper. The words, *royal library*, were written in Coleman's careful script. Jared threw the paper into one of the torches and continued through the castle.

He entered the library and closed the door behind him. Lian motioned for his son to sit next to him at the table in the middle of the room.

"You wished to speak to me father?"

"No one knows you are here?"

"Coleman knows."

The expression on the king's face was grim. "Has Cornelius found something?" he asked.

"Cornelius has found something indeed." Lian turned a book lying on the table toward Jared. It was open to the middle. "Read."

The book was open to the account of a murderer named Michalis. Jared was already familiar with the account as he was familiar with the annals of North Agea's past kings. However, he read it again, for if it was important enough for his father to command him to read, it was worth another examination. Jared read the account again and looked at his father.

"This was written by my great grandfather himself. Michalis was a diabolical man. Before he turned to murder, he was said to have violated many young women. However, nothing was ever proven, and North Agea's justice acquitted him. It was whispered Michalis was protected through a blood oath he made with a demon. As time went on, he became demented and was finally seen in broad daylight murdering a young woman in the most gruesome way. He carved a figure into her upper thigh that was also found on other murdered women. My great grandfather believed this figure to be proof of killing the other women as well. He ordered Michalis executed. Before Michalis was hanged, his final words were *'I am the star that fell.'*"

Jared looked down at the picture of the figure that was found on all Michalis' victims. His father pointed at the figure.

"Cornelius found this same figure on your Aunt Susanna's body, in the exact same place."

"I have heard the elderly whisper of this treachery, father. Michalis was executed sixty years ago. How can this be?"

"I do not know, Jared. I have no idea why someone would commit a murder in such a fashion that it resembled a killer from sixty years ago. Perhaps an evil not bound by natural law is upon us. If this is true, you must be very careful. You are my only child and I love you dearly. You must be prepared for whatever this evil is."

Jared put down the book and put his arms around his father. "This is merely a time of testing, father. The sky always becomes black before a storm. The sun will appear once it has passed."

"I fear we may not survive the storm," replied his father.

⋅⋅⋅✦✦✦✦⋅⋅⋅

Jared emerged with his father from the library full of thought. A clank echoed down the hall as his father closed the door behind them.

A powerful traitor, walked among them. He sighed as he suspected Nathaniel was that traitor.

The question not resolved in his mind was *how*. Jared knew Nathaniel's father, Malcom, was not powerful enough to raise a person from the dead. He suspected this is what happened.

There was also the matter of the missing guard that Coleman mentioned. He would not say more, for his protection. Did Coleman suspect Nathaniel was responsible for that as well?

Jared felt his heart race as he thought once more about the Grimoire Macabre. If a book of evil existed that those of the Craft refused to speak of, were there not other tools just as sinister? Would there be secrets within this legendary book that could raise a person from the dead? Were there other tools for this purpose? Jared thought about the possibility of an evil presence in their midst. Their ignorance shielded them so far. He must act as though he suspected nothing.

"YAHWEH, calm my heart in the face of the monster," Jared whispered as he walked down the hall with his father.

⁕⁕⁕⁕⁕

Solomon and James escorted Rohn and a company of his royal guard on horseback to Arioth. The king was silent. The only indication Solomon had that the monarch was indeed human were the tears that periodically fell from his eyes while they rode.

As they passed Lord Cade's estate, the king slowed to a stop before the worn pathway leading to the noble's land. The king stared at the path.

"Is there something wrong, your majesty?" asked Solomon.

"I wish to see this place," said Rohn quietly. He did not wait for a reply, but continued toward the manor. As they drew closer to the house, they were approached by a man who looked to be sixty years old. Though his auburn hair was graying, his eyes were sharp. He recognized his visitors. He bowed his head before Rohn could dismount. "What does his majesty require?"

"Do we know each other?" asked Rohn.

"We have met on occasion. You are King Rohn Catalane of Nereheim. I am Lord Rowen Cade, and I am at a loss as to why you would visit me."

"These are your lands?"

"Yes, your majesty. I was allowed to purchase the land with the requirement that I keep the manor and its grounds in their original beauty."

"Who gave you this order?" Rohn was surprised such a requirement was part of a land transaction.

"King Lian Saint Marc. We made the arrangement when my son Coleman joined the royal guard. I wanted my son as close to me as possible."

Rowen looked at the king. The noble could see his eyes were puffed and filled with sadness. "Your majesty, would you like to tour the manor?"

"I would like to see the rose garden."

"Yes, your majesty."

They walked to the back of the large house. Rohn walked almost reverently to the entrance he knew so well. He was overwhelmed with grief. He felt Susanna's presence among these precious flowers.

At the cluster of maiden's blush roses, he paused and touched their soft petals. "Susanna," he whispered. All at once, he dropped to his knees.

"Susanna!" he shouted as he clutched the flowers in his hands, tears streaming from his eyes once again. Rowen, Solomon, and the rest of the company stood at the edge of the garden as the king grieved for his wife.

<hr>

They arrived at the castle a short while later. Rohn was stone faced as he followed Solomon down the colonnade. Jared saw them arrive and greeted his uncle.

"Uncle Rohn," said Jared politely.

"Jared," replied Rohn. He pulled his nephew into an embrace. After a moment he said, "Take me to her."

"Follow me."

Jared led his uncle to the chamber holding Susanna's body. Jared nodded to the guard posted outside the chamber, and he opened the door. Rohn went inside followed by Jared.

Andrew sat next to the body. He stood immediately as his father came to him.

"Father," Andrew began to speak, but his voice cracked. Rohn wrapped his arms around his son.

"I am thankful you are still alive. How is it you were not with your mother?"

"Mother asked us to stay until the end of the week. She was pleased that Jared and I were getting along. I feel like I should have been there."

"You and Nina would have been killed if you were there. The blame is not yours to take. It belongs to another." Rohn let his son free after a moment.

"Jared and Nathaniel told me that also, but I feel guilt all the same."

"Nathaniel?"

"Nathaniel Stone. He is the son of the apothecary here in Arioth and Nafaria Mauldon's husband."

"Jared, will you find this Nathaniel? I wish to meet my nephew," said Rohn softly as he looked at Jared.

"Yes uncle." Jared left the chamber.

Rohn looked at the white sheet covering his wife's body. He did not have the heart to lift it yet. He laid his hand on her head for a moment. He saw the table set up next to her body. He walked over to it and examined the various items on it.

"What are these?"

"They were found on mother when her body was removed from the carriage."

"This knife was found on your mother?"

"It was buried in her chest when we found her."

"A hunting dagger," whispered Rohn. He looked at the instrument that killed his wife. More than a thousand men in both North Agea and Nereheim owned such a weapon.

"Does Lian have any idea who the murderer might be?"

"A man named Cornelius inspected mother when we arrived back here. He sent for uncle right away. He seemed agitated about something." After a moment Andrew asked, "Father, why did you call Nathaniel Stone your nephew?"

"Nathaniel Stone is the son of Malcom Stone."

Andrew sucked in a breath. Even with his self-centered attitude and self-indulgent living, he knew that name. Malcom Stone was last Court Adviser of Nereheim.

"Mother said he was your last Court Adviser. Because of him, you never considered another until you met Jason Mauldon."

"Malcom was married to my younger sister, Sasha. She died in a plague that broke out after Nathaniel was born. We had a very strong disagreement. Malcom took Nathaniel and left Wildemere. Eventually he settled in North Agea. Jason used to speak of his son Michael's friendship with Nathaniel. He said they were alike in wisdom and drive. I want to see what Jason meant."

"Why was I never told I had another cousin?"

"I never thought it important."

When Nathaniel entered the chamber with Jared, Rohn's eyes fell on him. "Jared said you wished to see me your majesty." Nathaniel bowed his head.

Nathaniel looked into the strong gaze of Rohn Catalane. He saw that father and son had many similarities in their gaze. Andrew looked like his mother, but his confidence and steadiness came from his father.

"I see a man I once knew in the eyes before me. You are indeed the son of Malcom Stone."

"I am."

"Your father was one of two men of the Craft I trusted. Tell me, did he ever mention his life as Court Adviser of Nereheim?"

"I only remember growing up in Denholm Glen, your majesty. Father mentioned his time in court as if it were a part of his life he wished to forget."

"When your mother died, he was appalled at the thought of raising you in Wildemere. We differed greatly on the use of power, even while your mother was still alive. When she died, Malcom chose a quiet life of obscurity," replied Rohn with a note of disdain in his voice.

"Power is a great responsibility. It should be used in service to all men. However, if those who possess power refuse to wield it, the corrupt are allowed to go unchecked," said Nathaniel.

Andrew looked at Nathaniel. He was not sure, but it sounded like Nathaniel believed himself right to use the power he was given as he saw fit, rather than to protect mankind as he was told those of the Craft believed. If that was true, who determined who was corrupt? Andrew thought about this as he listened. Rohn nodded his head in recognition of Nathaniel's statement.

"We seem to be in agreement. Andrew is your cousin, Nathaniel. Your mother was my younger sister."

"Father told me about mother once when we still lived in Denholm Glen."

"Perhaps the time has come for you to return to Nereheim. Would you be willing to come to Nereheim as my Court Adviser?"

"Yes, your majesty. I would like the opportunity to influence Nereheim for the good of all men."

Lian waited in the throne room for his brother-in-law. Solomon wasted no time reporting to him that he arrived. He drew in a deep breath as he saw Rohn enter the throne room, his eyes puffed and red. Andrew and Jared followed behind him. Lian stood and walked toward his brother-in-law, hand extended.

"Rohn, it is truly a black time that brings us together. No words can express the sincere grief I feel for you."

"No words can express, so none will be given. My wife and her guards were murdered within a few miles of the estate where she grew up. Do you have a clue as to who the murderer is?"

Lian looked at his brother-in-law grimly. "No."

"My wife was found on your soil with a hunting dagger buried in her chest. Someone saw an opportunity to cripple Nereheim by murdering its queen," replied Rohn.

"We do not know who did this. The knife could have been used by anyone; even someone from Nereheim," said Jared carefully. He spoke loud enough to be heard, but his voice held calm and reason. Rohn was silent at his nephew's rebuff.

"I admit this is a perplexing matter. The temptation to place blame on anyone we can attach it to is great. Jared is right. We cannot unjustly accuse our citizens for the sake of a common weapon used here in North Agea," said Lian.

"The peace between our nations rests in your ability to find the killer. Until then, we have no peace. I will not step foot on this soil until you bring me my wife's killer." Rohn walked out of the throne room.

Andrew's eyes went to Jared. He felt pain and confusion in his heart as he understood the meaning of his father's words. *No peace.* He would be separated from his cousin he only just came to respect and wish to emulate. Jared looked at Andrew as well and whispered one word, *"please."* Andrew shook his head and walked out of the throne room after his father.

"Andrew!" Jared shouted as he rushed down the hallway to his cousin. Andrew paused and looked back at him.

"Andrew, listen to me. These last days I feel as though I have only begun to know you and I have enjoyed this time. Do not let this tragedy pull us apart. Very soon, our nations will depend on our brotherhood. Do not leave in haste."

Andrew closed his eyes as he listened to his cousin. Hot tears formed, even as he tried to shut them out. He was silent for a moment. He did not trust himself to speak. Finally, he opened his eyes again.

"I have learned much by being here. I am glad Nina had this chance to be with Ephratha. You may never know how much I truly respect you, Jared." Tears rolled down Andrew's face. "She was my mother Jared! There is nothing we can do to bring her back. Even if the one responsible is found, how am I to look upon the people of this country? My mother is dead! You cannot tell me there is a purpose to this, some higher reason YAHWEH would have for taking her from me—"

"She was also my aunt, and I loved her very much. There is pain now, but all will show itself in the end. There is a reason, for even this."

"Keep your reason, Jared." Andrew's reply was bitter as he walked away from his cousin.

"Your answer must be yes." Nathaniel heard the whisper in his mind again as he searched for Nafaria. He heard the command, and spoke his answer. He would simply tell Nafaria they were going back to Nereheim.

He found her with Nina and Ephratha on the terrace. "Ladies, I am sorry to interrupt you, but I must speak with my wife." Nafaria saw a shadow cloud Nathaniel's face. She looked at the others.

"Well, go on, Nafaria. It is not right to keep a husband waiting," said Ephratha with a smile.

"Especially not one of the Craft," said Nina.

"I will be back in a few minutes." Nafaria rose and followed him.

Nathaniel led her to the colonnade. When they were away from the others, Nafaria asked, "Is something wrong?"

Her eyes held the confused gaze of a child that does not understand something difficult. Her trust was shown as she patiently waited for him to give her the news. How would Nafaria feel about returning to the place her father and mother were murdered? He had not anticipated this to be difficult. He knew Nafaria would follow him anywhere. Was he asking too much of her to follow him back to Wildemere? He stepped closer and touched her chin. It felt soft to his touch. Her long, dark hair was the first thing he remembered falling in love with as a child. He took a deep breath and looked into her eyes.

"I was handed an opportunity by King Rohn," said Nathaniel quietly.

"You spoke to him?"

"He remembered me."

Nafaria looked at Nathaniel questioningly. Nathaniel went on. "I am not sure you ever knew this, but my father was the last adviser to the royal court of Nereheim. He was also the king's brother-in-law."

"He was?"

Nathaniel went on to tell her about his association with king Rohn. "Now my uncle has offered me what father refused to hold on to: the opportunity as the next adviser to the court of Nereheim. I said I would take it."

The color drained from Nafaria's face when she heard his news. They were returning to the city where her parents were killed. "How could you do this without asking me first? After Joel killed my parents, I swore I would never return there. I will be having your child and now you tell me that I have to raise our baby in the same place my parents were murdered? Could you not even discuss this with me first before you gave your decision to the king?"

"The king is leaving with Andrew and Nina soon. I had no time to consult you. I feel a great purpose lies in this opportunity. Perhaps it is

YAHWEH's decision that I should be used as an instrument to bring peace and justice to Nereheim again."

"I cannot return there! Do not make me go!" shouted Nafaria. She ran down the colonnade away from Nathaniel.

<hr>

Nafaria continued down the colonnade away from everyone. Her only thought was that Nathaniel was taking her from her new home, one filled with hope for the future, back to her old one, a place filled with despair. The path came to an end, and she slowly sank down on the steps facing a meadow of wildflowers mixed into green grass. She closed her eyes and thought back to that infamous day two years ago.

Joel came with his marauders, bent on revenge. They left her father for dead, and took her mother to be killed. She blinked back tears, remembered the knife in his back as she came upon him lying on the ground. Screams of the servants filled the air from the broken windows of her home. Her father's final words to her: find Malcom and Nathaniel. What would he say today? Was she to blindly follow her husband back to Nereheim? Why would Nathaniel choose to go back to a place he knew would cause her so much pain? What could she accomplish in Wildemere beyond facing her past?

Nafaria was so lost in her thoughts; she jumped when she felt a light tough on her shoulder. Expecting Nathaniel, she was surprised to see Nina.

She sat down on the steps next to Nafaria. "I do not know what made you run away, so I cannot begin to imagine what you are feeling."

"We are returning to Wildemere. I am sure there is nothing to fear, but I am afraid for my life just the same," replied Nafaria.

Nina looked at Nafaria. "That is certainly natural. I would be afraid as well if I were in your place," replied Nina.

"I keep picturing my father dying in my arms. How can I go back there?"

Nina put an arm around Nafaria. "You are not alone. I will be there with you and I need you. I need your gentle optimism to help me keep my own fears at bay."

Nafaria sighed as she looked at Nina. "If it will help you be strong, I will face my fears and be strong too."

Nina smiled and hugged her tight. "Let us take this step together." She stood up and held out her hand to Nafaria.

"We will take this step together," she repeated. Nafaria took the hand in front of her, and allowed Nina to help her stand. They walked back up the colonnade together.

***

Nafaria walked up to Nathaniel and looked into his eyes. She crossed her arms, trying to calm herself. "I am afraid to go. However, I am your wife and I will follow you to whatever end." Nathaniel approached her and put his arms around her. After a moment, they walked back to Ephratha and Jared on the terrace.

Jared sat next to Ephratha when they approached. A look of concern crossed his face when he saw Nina and Nafaria's expressions. Nathaniel spoke. "I have been asked to accompany King Rohn back to Nereheim. There I will serve as Court Adviser."

Ephratha looked at Jared who stood up instantly. Nina stayed silent.

"Nathaniel, may I have a word with you?" asked Jared. He rose and walked away from the women, while Nathaniel followed.

"Nathaniel, you are one of my closest friends and I hold a great deal of respect for you. I cannot stop you in this decision, but is this best for

Nafaria? She lost her mother and father there. So much injustice has been done to those of the Craft."

"Yes, it has. Too many times people raised their hands against the wise ones in anger or greed. That will change." Nathaniel's voice had an edge to it.

"You cannot repay evil for evil. It has never worked that way."

"I do not wish to repay evil for evil. My wish is for those of the Craft to be respected. We will no longer hide the power YAHWEH entrusted us with. I will help the king enforce the laws protecting *all* men. The nobles will learn a healthy fear of those who hold great knowledge and power."

"There will be tension between our nations when you go back. We may not see each other again for a while. I hoped we would raise our children together," said Jared.

"Perhaps our children will heal our nations. You have been a good friend, Jared. We will bring peace to the sister kingdoms once again."

Jared sighed. "I certainly hope so."

At that moment, Solomon approached them. He bowed to Jared. "Your highness, I was told to inform you that King Catalane will be leaving early tomorrow morning. He instructs all who are leaving with him to be ready at first light."

"It seems I have preparations to make." Nathaniel bowed to Jared and went back to the others.

He watched Nathaniel leave the terrace with Nafaria and Nina. "A new chapter begins for the sister kingdoms," he whispered.

⁜

Malcom looked up when the bell of his shop door sounded its subtle tinkle. He smiled when Coleman and his father entered.

"Coleman, Lord Cade; to what do I owe a visit from two distinguished gentlemen as yourselves?" asked Malcom cheerfully. He held out his hand to Rowen first, then to Coleman.

"The king requests your presence at the castle," replied Coleman.

Malcom looked around the shop. It was empty at the moment, but large bundles of various herbs and plants sat on the counter. "I cannot leave the shop unattended today," replied Malcom.

"That is why I am here," replied Rowen. "The king needs you."

The look on Rowen's face gave Malcom pause. Lord Cade would not be offering to tend his shop if it were not important. He nodded his assent. "I will leave it to you, Lord Cade. You know my shop as well as Nathaniel and Nafaria."

"I will be fine. Take whatever time you need," replied Rowen.

⋅⋅✦✦✦⋅⋅

Coleman led Malcom to the castle and into the royal rose garden. "I take my leave," he said, leaving Malcom alone with the king.

Rohn turned and faced him. "It has been a very long time, Malcom."

"Your majesty." Malcom bowed slightly. "I had no idea you were here in North Agea."

"I was afraid you would not come if you knew."

Malcom stepped forward, arms outstretched.

Rohn heartily embraced him. "It has taken me a very long time and the death of Jason Mauldon to realize how much I missed you. My pride has cost us much." He drew back and looked at Malcom with sadness in his eyes. "Susanna is dead— murdered. She was found in her carriage by Lord Cade and his men on her way home from her visit with Clara."

Malcom stared at the king, his eyes growing moist. Queen Susanna had been killed in her own birth country? He could not believe that anyone in North Agea would do such a thing. "I am so sorry for your loss. You know I loved Susanna very much."

"And she loved you— missed you greatly after your departure." Rohn paused with a sigh. "I have met with your son. He has grown into an excellent young man, on par with his friend Michael Mauldon. I wished to speak with you because I have offered him the position of Court Adviser. I wanted to know how you felt about that."

"Nathaniel is certainly old enough to make his own decisions. If he desires the position, I will give my blessing." Even as he said the words, Malcom worried that Nathaniel and Rohn were too much alike in their views about the use of power and arcane knowledge.

"I am confident Nathaniel will grow into his position quickly," Rohn said. "He has great conviction for one as young as he is."

Malcom forced a smile. "Only encourage him to come visit me from time to time."

"We shall see." Rohn embraced him again. "We leave at first light tomorrow."

"Well, then," Malcom said. "I suppose I should go see my son and daughter-in-law so that I may say goodbye."

As he and Rohn walked toward the castle, Malcom contemplated what this new development would mean for his family.

———— ✦ ————

First light of morning came quickly. The sun appeared over the horizon bringing its golden hue to the land by inches. Only the posted sentries saw the morning. Everyone else in the castle was busy readying king Catalane for his return home.

Nina and Nafaria stood with Ephratha. The three were in a giant embrace. Neither could bear to let the other go. "I will miss you both," said Ephratha.

"I will miss you as well," said Nina.

The women finally tore themselves from each other. Nina backed away, but Nafaria stood still. She looked at Ephratha. "You are my greatest friend. I cannot imagine Wildemere without you."

Tears rolled down Ephratha's face as she nodded toward Nina. "However, I am not your only friend. Watch over Nina and give her the same wise counsel you gave me. She will need someone she can trust."

Nafaria smiled through her tears. "Nina's trust comes at a great price for those who seek it. She may be the one watching out for me."

Jared approached Andrew. He held out his hand to his cousin. "Andrew, your visit has been a pleasure. This is the first time I can say those words with sincerity. It pains me to think that it may also be the last."

Andrew looked at his cousin's hand. He shook his head and embraced him. "This situation was not created by us, so it will not affect us. Though I am angry about mother's death, I will not let it come between us. You have been most kind to me, when I have not deserved it. I will miss you greatly." After a moment, he let go of Jared and turned to Ephratha to say goodbye.

Nathaniel embraced Jared next. "I will miss you, Jared. You will be a wise ruler one day."

"If that is so, it is largely due to the wisdom your father has shown over the years. I pray we will see you again on this side of the Anenderes," replied Jared.

Malcom came up to Nathaniel and embraced him. "Trust in YAHWEH to give you the strength and courage you need to help your uncle make wise decisions. He will lead you where Nereheim needs to go."

"Thank you, father."

Malcom then turned to Nafaria and gave her a hug. "Take care of yourself and my grandchild."

"I will." Nafaria gave him a gentle smile when they parted.

Lian stood with Clara and watched everyone as they said their various and tear-filled goodbyes. He felt as though his heart might break at the thought of such deep friendships changing like this. Rohn continued his stoic gaze.

Lian approached his brother-in-law. "Rohn, may I make a suggestion?"

"Yes?"

"Please keep in touch. Andrew is my nephew and I wish to know how he fares."

Rohn considered his words. "Agreed, after all, Jared is my nephew as well."

He walked over to the wagon holding Susanna's coffin. A few moments later, the carriage and wagon pulled away from Arioth. Jared held Ephratha as she sobbed. She would not take her eyes off the road even after the carriage was out of sight.

"Come Ephratha. We have our own lives to live," said Jared in a quiet voice. She said nothing, but followed him into the castle.

⊹ ✦✦✦ ⊹

Coleman found Jared at dusk, with the sentry. His gaze was fixed on the road leading to the Anenderes River.

"Permission to speak, your highness."

"Coleman, you are my friend. Say whatever is on your mind."

"I fear for the safety of Andrew, Nina, and Nafaria. Nathaniel Stone is not to be trusted." Though his words sounded harsh, he knew no other way to speak plainly. "When Sheill disappeared, he was following Nathaniel."

"That is what you did not want to tell me before?"

"Yes."

"Nathaniel is as much a friend to me as you are, Coleman. However, I fear he is not the man he used to be. Something happened in those mountains when he disappeared." He looked at Coleman. "I must ask you to keep what I say to yourself. It will worry Ephratha too much if she heard it. Also, you must promise that if anything happens to me, you will be there to protect Nafaria, Nina, and Ephratha. I lay this charge to you as my friend and captain of the royal guard."

"You know I will accept. What do you fear?"

"My days may be numbered." Jared looked back out toward the road but said nothing more.

CHAPTER 9

Sunshine faded into pink and purple as the first stars of twilight made their grand appearance. Joel glanced at the sky and noted the coming darkness.

He rode through the day, since the dreadful act in which he was forced to partake. He remembered the intrusion Nafaria's husband brought upon him: vileness both cold and bitter. There was no remorse, only desire for unscrupulous acts that are whispered in secret to be done in broad daylight. Joel shuddered at the memory. It was worse than physical rape of the body, where emotions are also torn. His soul felt the violation of evil, forcing him to kill the queen of his land. He now understood why a maiden cries when she is torn by a vagabond's lust. He would never again allow such a thing to happen if he were there to prevent it. No rape deserves a place on the face of the earth— physical or otherwise.

His keen ears picked up the call of the gulls and the waters of the Anenderes came into view. Its waves rolled; carrying the faces he now knew were more than legend to be told by bards and minstrels. Truth was its own mystery and often stranger than the machinations of mortal man. Joel finally understood that. "Jason was right," he whispered. "Vengeance is folly for a man to claim."

The dirt road gave way to cobblestone and he heard the myriad noises of a city. The sound of horses passing him roused Joel from his thoughts. He left the horse he rode at a stable of an inn. He knew he could not take care of such a majestic beast in his state. He continued on foot to the quay, looking across the river. He felt in his pocket and found three gold pieces. He took one out and held it in his hand. He put the coins in his pocket and wrote a short note of thanks to Enoch before he left Arioth. The evil demon was inside him but Joel found he was able to control his own body enough to perform menial tasks. Joel knew he would not be able to circumvent the deed Michalis would commit. So, he grabbed the coins to be able to disappear quickly. Would this man come looking for him again? He suspected not. Nathaniel Stone was done with him.

Joel paid the fare with his gold coin and slowly moved onto the ferry. His destination was Nereheim, but he would not go to Wildemere. There were other things to seek before his return. He stood on the boat and watched the shore of North Agea disappear in the twilight. "A new chapter waits," he whispered.

Joel did not cower in the hold of the barge, or cringe along the cabin walls as he journeyed across the river. He stood at the side, willing the faces to reveal themselves. However, there were none to be seen. The faces, it seemed, had other places to be. "It is just as well. What counsel would they give that I have not already foolishly disdained?" he thought. Joel was left with his question of what to do next. When the boat docked, he wandered off, safe inside his own country once again.

The next morning Joel started out of the city of Burnea, along the shore of the Anenderes. His mind recalled happier times with Leanna. The country was greeting him with fond memories of his wife's smile. Even the rustling leaves of trees in the breeze reminded him of her. He drank it all in, as a particular brand of ale he cherished. Soon the city was far behind him. The path he was on wound away from the river's edge and cut west. He followed the path, deciding it would take him to his new life. There were many parts of Nereheim Joel never encountered. Perhaps he would visit his country before settling down.

"Joel." He stopped on the road and looked up. Leanna's voice whispered his name. He took a deep breath. There was nothing to hear but the wind. He continued on.

"Joel." The whisper was sharper this time, and to his right. He looked in that direction and saw two paths cross each other. Though both were visible, neither path was marked. His path was well worn and bare ground was seen. The other path was visible, but grown over with moss: easily missed if riding a horse or in a carriage. He considered the moss path when he heard a carriage approach. It pulled to a stop before him. A young woman leaned out the window.

"Sir, need you a ride to your destination? I am traveling this road many miles." She smiled at him as she spoke.

Joel was too stunned to answer. It was as if the fateful day of Queen Susanna's death were trying to replay itself. With the way the woman wore her hair and the good-natured flash in her eyes, she could be the queen herself. Joel blinked, but said nothing.

"Sir?"

Joel roused himself after a moment. "Thank you for your kindness, my lady. The day is fair, and my destination will surely be there when I arrive on foot. However, could you tell me where this path leads?" He pointed to the moss-grown path to his right.

Her smile faded. "It leads to the wasteland. Legend says it was a road that led to Herron, the city that housed the fabled silver bell that will call the dead."

"Call the dead?" Joel never heard of this legend.

"It is only a story meant to frighten children. However, that path is dangerous. Many outlaws travel the wasteland. Do not go there."

"Joel." Leanna's voice was sharp again. It pulled his eyes back to the path.

"Can you tell me more about the bell?"

She shook her head. "It was only a tale I heard once from my great grandmother one dark evening. She believed it as truth, but I never heard it again since."

'Thank you for your counsel, my lady. I believe my journey begins here."

Her brow furrowed slightly but her reply was pleasant. "Good day sir." She watched him walk toward the moss-grown path.

Joel discovered though the ancient path was moss-grown, it was far from grown over. Easily two feet wide, the turns were placed strategically to accommodate any kind of travel. It cut back to the river's edge; the waves a hypnotic drone as he walked.

Why was he on this road? The question implanted itself in his mind. He should be on his way back to his home in Wildemere, not wandering lost roads searching for—what? In search of a sacred object that would call the dead? That was only a legend. It was ludicrous, yet Joel could not dismiss the fascination of such a claim.

"Power is dangerous," Jason once told him. It strengthened the noble and wise, but corrupted the weak and foolish. Joel saw in his own life what the power of conviction in the hands of the foolish reaped. He nearly destroyed a noble family that loved him. Jason's children survived, but everything else he built in Wildemere was moss grown or destroyed. The only thing left of Jason Mauldon was his good name and what people remembered of his character. He swore a blood oath over his wife's grave, but now he saw the folly of his decision. He wanted Jason and Thena to die, so he killed them. He knew it was wrong, but he was blinded by vengeance and pain. He used his conviction to persuade others to help him. The single-mindedness of conviction was so enticing it sent him after Nafaria as well. It was not until his part in Queen Susanna's death that he considered his oath to be in vain. As Nafaria's husband said, it brought him to an evil end. There was nothing else left to do. He would find the city of the dead and strike the bell. If luck was with him, he would become another face in the water.

The path made a gradual climb. The river was to his right, but the path wound uphill into a low cliff. In the sunlight he saw the outline of buildings. All was quiet. The buildings were abandoned—mere shells speaking of lives that once inhabited the place.

It was past midday and the shadows were long when Joel reached the top of the cliff. Here his feet found broken stone for a path. Moss grew between the cracks of the ancient road that wound past crumbled buildings. Bugs and wild animals peeked out from the ruins.

He looked over to the edge of the cliff and saw what looked like a walkway extending past it about thirty feet. A large stone object sat at the end. The river rolled below him.

This curious structure was made of wood. Its style was very old, however the wood seemed sturdy. Curiously, there were no rotting boards or weathering of any kind. Joel stepped out, putting his full weight on it. There was no groan or creak. The only sound was the noise his footfalls made as he cautiously walked toward the stone.

It was a very delicately carved pedestal. A hook protruded from the surface. Joel read aloud the words on a plaque beneath the hook. "Caution to the one who stands ready to strike the bell. Though ready for the secrets of the world, are you ready for the secrets of your soul?" Joel stood still. If there was a bell to strike, here was a clear warning perhaps he should not. A shiver ran through his body. The city of the dead made a peculiar claim on his heart.

"Joel." Joel flinched when he heard a voice speak his name. He recognized it as strong, yet compassionate, wise and full of concern.

He turned around and faced Jason Mauldon.   "Jason," Joel whispered. His breathing became shallow as he stared at what he believed a ghost of the friend he betrayed.

"Why have you come here?" asked Jason.

This was a question Joel could not answer as he stood at the stone. What did he hope to accomplish? His wife's voice led him here. However, he could never be with her. She was dead, and he was here in a ruined wasteland.

"I came to call the dead, but there is no bell."

"The bell was taken. Why else have you come?"

Joel thought about Leanna all day. He thought about how she looked, the way she laughed, even how her voice seemed to be filled with song when she spoke. He missed her. All the evil he was party to had not filled the pit of ache in his heart for the woman he loved. He tried vengeance and found it unsatisfying. He found no peace. There was only one choice left to him.

"I wish to join my wife. You gave so much wise counsel in the short years we knew each other, yet I practiced none of it. I listened too late. I am sorry for what I have done to you, Thena, and Queen Susanna. I wish to leave this world and go be with Leanna. Even if it is only to wander as faces in the Anenderes, I wish to do it together."

"You cannot go where you are not bidden, Joel. Your time is not at hand. Your heart is strong and good remains in it. There is much you can do to heal this land. You must ask forgiveness for the death of Queen Susanna, for me, and Thena. You cannot bring Leanna back and it is not for you to join her yet. You will only find peace when you seek mercy. Perhaps you will find it in Wildemere."

"I cannot!" cried Joel. "There is nothing left for me. I wish to die!" He shouted as he ran to the cliff's edge and jumped.

He awoke drenched in water. Sitting up quickly, he looked around. He was at the water's edge, on a soft beach. Looking up, the pedestal was far above him. Joel staggered to his feet. Seeing the sun peeking over the horizon, he was finally aware it was *rising*. He must have slept through the night. His first thoughts were of his conversation with Jason. Was it just a dream? Joel looked down at the sand beneath his feet. It was not a dream. Written in the sand was a single word: CONFESS.

⋯✦✦✦⋯

Joel walked along the water's edge as far as there was sand. His conversation with Jason was no dream; the word in the sand convinced him of that. He was not ready to return to Wildemere. He feared the king's wrath to be sure, but also felt there was something greater he must do. Whatever that task was, it would not come to fruition if he swung from the gallows.

Climbing the riverbank, he found the moss-grown path once again. The gnawing in his stomach announced his need for food. He filled his flask with water. He would have to be content with that until other nourishment was found. He exhaled deeply. He was the only living soul out here. He would have to keep moving.

Once on the path, Joel heard a sound like a horse's neigh. He looked out and saw a brown horse on a hill; standing still as if waiting for its master. He was quiet as he crept up to it. Joel recognized it as a mare, with its bridle attached. He stepped carefully and put his hand on the animal, speaking in a low soothing voice.

"Shhhh, my lady. You are quite a sight in this desolate area. How have you come to be here?" he asked the horse as he petted it. Rising smoke from the bottom of the hillside caught his attention. He mounted the horse and rode to it.

Joel found dead men, and tents burned to the ground—the remains of a nomadic shepherd camp. He heard stories of vagabonds who overtook these camps and raided them for women and livestock. He heard faint shouts and screams as he jumped down from the horse. He spotted a large axe lying on the ground next to a dead body. Grabbing it, he mounted the horse again, taking off after the noise.

Women and young children were herded like cattle. The marauders were on horseback, lashing them with whips. He counted eight men. The closer he rode, Joel could see panic in the eyes of those being whipped. Rage burned deep inside him. The sight of these helpless people who lost so much already gripped his heart. Joel whispered words he never thought he would utter. "YAHWEH, I am not worthy to call on your name. Please give me strength to right this terrible wrong." He raised the axe in the air and spurred the horse's sides. The creature took off after the marauders with Joel screaming as loud as he could.

At the sound of Joel's shouts, the oppressed looked up and saw him racing from the hills, wielding a large axe high above his head. His eyes blazed as he took off the head of the first man he came in contact with.

The children screamed and ran about as he went after the men with the strength of a heard of wild boars. The women wasted no time gathering them and moving out of harm's way.

Suddenly a mist rose up around the marauders who circled around to face Joel. They shouted to one another, but were cut off in the fog. Joel was as perplexed about the fog as his adversaries, but he used it to his advantage. His axe skillfully cut through the haze and found its mark. One by one, each man's voice vanished in the milky haze.

When the fog lifted, Joel was the only man on horseback left. He sat there panting, exhausted even further from his escapade. He closed his eyes and whispered, "Thanks be to YAHWEH for giving me this victory."

The women and children looked at him in wide-eyed amazement as he jumped down from his horse. He walked to the closest one. "Are you all accounted for?" he asked.

The woman looked at him for a moment. Her stare finally broke when she realized what he asked her. She looked around the group. "No, one is missing. Where is Carissa?" asked the woman as she looked at the other women. The group quickly looked around themselves. The young woman in question was not there.

"I will find her. Go back to your camp and bury your dead," shouted Joel as he mounted his horse and rode off.

Joel moved quickly, keeping his ears tuned for any sound that gave a clue as to which direction to go.

"Joel." He pulled up quickly. He heard Leanna's voice again. He moved in its direction and heard a piercing scream. He tugged on the reins and went after it.

————— ·+++++· —————

A young woman let out another ear-piercing scream in a last effort to ward off the man who had taken her. He shoved her to the ground and threw himself on top of her. She thrashed and screamed, pulling his hair and kicking as hard as she could. His cheek bled where she scratched him.

"Silence, gypsy; there is no one to come to your aid!" he shouted.

The sound of horse's hooves filled the air and caught the villain off guard. Joel jumped from the horse, and without hesitation, buried his axe into the man's back. He stared at the girl as he slumped to the ground, dead.

Joel looked at the young woman who stared up at him. The sandy brown hair that fell to her shoulders framed her face in light wisps. Her blue eyes like little orbs trained on him. His breath caught. She looked so much like Leanna.

"Have mercy, sir. If you intend to kill me, do it quickly," she said. Joel offered her his hand. After a moment, she took it and he pulled her gently to her feet.

"You are Carissa?" asked Joel.

"Yes."

"Come, your people are waiting for your return."

Joel guided her to his horse. She climbed up at his insistence and he climbed up behind her. They rode back the way he came in silence.

When they reached the camp, Joel found the women gathering the dead into a pile and others salvaging what they could from the burned tents. Some busied themselves preparing a meal as the group worked. Carissa jumped down from the horse and ran to one of the women.

"Carissa, you are safe!" cried the woman as she threw her arms around her.

"Yes mother, thanks to this man." Carissa turned to Joel. "You must be starving, please stay for dinner."

"I am a long way from starvation, my lady, but I would welcome a hot meal," replied Joel.

"A hot meal and rest at a fire for the evening are things we can still provide," replied an older woman.

Joel helped the women gather their dead. The children gathered sticks and other types of kindling, and threw them around the pile they created. He asked Carissa about this.

"We burn our dead on a pyre as a matter of tradition. Out here in the wasteland, it is also practical," she replied.

"You are of the Craft?" Joel felt his face flush.

"Yes." Carissa offered no more on the subject, and Joel was silent as they worked.

The pyre burned, as the sun set. Each woman and child sat in silence around the cooking fire as they ate their meal. Joel counted twenty in all. Carissa's mother looked at Joel as he ate his meal.

"You came to us in our greatest distress. Thank you for saving us," she said.

"I cannot abide the sight of evil men whipping women and children into submission. You owe me no thanks," replied Joel.

"Gratitude must always be shown, no matter what the circumstance. We lost so much by coming into the wasteland at all. Now we lose our men as well. YAHWEH'S time of testing is equal to that of the Coe massacre," said Carissa's mother.

"You are of the Craft, yet your men did not have the power to defeat such villains? Why did you come into the wasteland at all if you could not protect yourselves?" asked Joel.

"We all have different gifts bestowed to us. We know much about herbs and healing, but not all possess supernatural force. Very few are given such ability," replied Carissa.

"We were ostracized by our villages after the riot in Wildemere. We heard a woman was burned in the market square. Some say she was a witch," said Carissa's mother.

Joel felt pain in his heart at the news as he realized they were talking about Thena's death. Shame welled inside him. He was responsible for the peril these people faced. His rash actions of killing Jason and making a public spectacle of Thena as he killed her led to the riot in Wildemere. He rode out of the city in search of Nafaria to end his quest for vengeance. He never thought of what others might do after he set events in motion.

He saw Carissa watching him from across the fire. Joel saw wisdom in her eyes, but much innocence as well. What would her life have been if Leanna lived and he had not killed Jason and Thena? Would she be married? What life would she live? Jason said once that those of the Craft acquire various types of knowledge and are responsible for passing it on. One who has been given knowledge must be faithful with that knowledge, no matter how insignificant it seemed.[16] What would she have passed on? He rose from his place and walked away from the group as they finished their meal.

Joel heard footsteps behind him and saw Carissa approach.

"Is there something you wish to say?" asked Joel as he turned his back on her.

"You looked as though you have something you wish to say sir." She saw Joel shake his head slowly, but he kept his back turned.

"I am an evil man. I do not belong among such people."

"Evil men repent, and go on to be used for something greater."

---

[16]   1 Corinthians 4:2

Joel cringed at her words. Her voice was soft and very soothing. He felt tears roll from his eyes even before he knew they formed. "I have done great evil to you, my lady," he whispered.

"I barely know you sir. What is this evil that is so great that it cannot be forgiven?" Joel faced her with tears in his eyes. He shook his head.

"If I am to tell my story, it will be in the presence of all I have wronged."

They walked back to the fire and Joel resumed his seat. Carissa called everyone and sat beside him. She took his hand in hers, refusing to let Joel pull it away. He let his hand go limp as she said gently, "Tell us what has brought you here."

Joel looked around the campfire. He took a deep breath and began his story.

CHAPTER 10

The carriage transporting Rohn and his entourage arrived at the edge of the river. He spied a boat and spoke quickly to his companions. "Nathaniel and Andrew, take the women aboard the ferry. The servants will stay with the carriage and watch our belongings."

"Yes father."

As everyone boarded, the carriage was moved onto the boat. Nafaria watched Rohn stop at the edge of the river. He turned and looked back the way they came. Though her body was boarded on the ferry, did Rohn wonder if Susanna's presence chose to stay in North Agea—with her sister? His eyes moistened as he whispered, "Goodbye Susanna, I will love only you." He turned and boarded the ferry with a stride befitting a king. Such character and stature he possessed; yet she never witnessed this side of him before. She felt privileged to see such emotion, for Rohn struck her as one who did not let his guard down. She wondered what charm Susanna possessed to make such a man love her so much.

He walked past Nafaria and Nina without even a sideways glance. She looked at Nina and wondered if she witnessed the same event. Nina nodded her head slightly and moved toward her, putting her arm around Nafaria as they both looked back at the road they traveled. It led to Arioth and her best friend. How would she live without Ephratha's gentleness in her life?

"Our destiny waits in a new place," said Nina in a broken voice.

She looked at Nina and saw tears in her eyes. The princess made no attempt to hide her sadness—she would miss Ephratha as well. Nafaria nodded her head and looked out across the water, tears rolling down her face.

⋅⋅◆⋅⋅

165

The rose color of the sunset gave way to purple twilight as the ferry glided across the Anenderes. Nina looked at Nafaria's long dark hair billowing in the breeze. She glanced at Nina, then at the water again. At that moment, Nina was struck with how much Nafaria resembled Thena. That same gentle smile Nina remembered was forever shadowed with sadness she never really grasped. What secrets did the mother of this extraordinary young woman hold that made her feel this way? Nina feared though Nafaria went through much sorrow; she would go through more still. She feared they all would.

"The first time I crossed the Anenderes, I cried because I lost my father and mother. Now, as I cross the Anenderes again, I feel as though I have lost my best friend. These waters are a symbol of loss for me," said Nafaria softly.

"Jared and Ephratha are not lost completely to us. The awkwardness of this event will reverse itself in time. The king will not let his grief separate him from his family for long." Nina spoke the words with a confidence she did not altogether possess.

"Whatever happens, I look forward to the time the two of us will have together," replied Nafaria.

"Perhaps our friendship will be the sunshine behind these coming storms," replied Nina.

The carriage left Burnea early the next morning after Andrew insisted they stop and rest for the evening. Rohn insisted that only the weak stopped when Andrew reminded him the horses needed adequate rest. When he heard not only the sense of his son's words but the gentle insistence in his voice, he relented. The exchange was uncomfortable to the others, but Nina gained a new respect for her husband. She never saw him take a stand on anything before. Jared took a stand plenty of times in the week they were at Arioth. She felt she was seeing a new person emerging from the superficial husk of a man she heard many officials mock behind Andrew's back. "It may only be over horses, but it is a beginning," thought Nina. This beginning could change the future of the sister kingdoms.

Nafaria watched the green countryside on their journey back to Wildemere. She wondered if the royal city would be as she remembered it. What would Elias Wheaton be doing within the walls of his antiquarian library? It was a place of comfort for her brother when they lived here. She thought she might visit him when they settled in again.

As they neared the city, the road widened and was busier. Nafaria looked out the window and tensed. She gripped Nathaniel's hand tight, her gaze fixed on the entrance of the long path that led to the manor she spent part of her life in. Nathaniel pulled her close and put his arm around her while she worked to keep her emotions guarded. The king sighed as they passed the entrance but said nothing. Andrew gave her a sympathetic look. He knew she must miss her father and mother very much, for he missed them as well. Now he had his own pain to deal with. He felt a gentle nudge at his side. He looked down and saw Nina looking at him with a questioning glance. He gave her a gentle smile and pulled her close to him as they continued to the castle.

⁘⁘⁘⁘⁘

The next morning, Nafaria woke as the sun shone through the window. Nathaniel was already gone from their bed. She reached her hand over to the side where he lay the night before. The sheets were cold. He must have risen very early to start his day. She sighed and rose from her place and dressed quietly.

There was very little activity in the castle and the passageway was dim. King Rohn did not burn torches the way Lian did in the castle. Nafaria found it difficult to keep her footing as she moved down the great hall toward the only light she could see. She descended the stone staircase and walked out to the courtyard.

She stepped into the sunlight and continued to Queen Susanna's rose garden. It was just like the rose garden in Arioth. Susanna must have thought the flowers in that garden breathtaking to have copied the arrangement so completely. Or was it Clara who copied her older sister? Such familiarity immediately put her at ease in her new surroundings.

"Good morning Nafaria. Did you sleep well?" Nina spoke from the table where she sat, drinking a cup of tea.

Nafaria sat down next to her. "Yes. I was exhausted when I went to bed."

Nina put down her cup and picked up another. She filled it with tea, added a sprig and held it out to Nafaria. "This is Roman Chamomile with a sprig of lemon balm—truly the best way to wake up."

Nina looked out at the flowers in the garden surrounding them. "Queen Susanna and I started our day together with a cup of tea every morning and ended it with a cup every night. In the morning she would use lemon balm. In the evening, she would use mint. It must stagger the imagination of the angels in heaven; the things we remember." A few tears dropped from Nina's eyes.

Nafaria reached for Nina's hand and gave it a gentle squeeze. "Through this whole ordeal, we have all shed a wide range of emotions. I wondered when your turn would come."

"Time and chance do not always allow for such trivialities as a show of emotions. I cannot say how many times I have heard Rohn utter those very words," replied Nina with a weak smile.

"The sacred writings tell us the heart is the wellspring of life[17]. My father used to say that a man who cannot reveal his emotions lives but a shadow of his true self."

"Tell me more about your father," said Nina.

---

[17]   Proverbs 4:23

"He was blessed with great wisdom for a young age. He never stopped encouraging us in the Craft. He was very proud of each of us for the different paths we chose. Philip has become horse master and teacher to Count Lucerne. Michael always sought some kind of new learning. He kept the schoolmasters in Denholm Glen very busy when he was younger. I am sure he is pursuing another strange knowledge quest while he is married to his childhood love. As for me, mother made sure a love of plants and their healing properties became my calling. While we are of the Craft, we each have our separate paths to follow. Father was a good leader. He let us choose our passion, and directed us in it."

"Indeed, he was a wise man, then. How many men in this world force their opinions and desires on their children, all in the name of carrying on their legacy? I shudder to think how many men have taken their own lives because they could not live up to the monumental task their fathers carved out for them." Nina looked out around the garden once more. "I think it is time to reacquaint you with Wildemere. A day in the market will be a treat for both of us."

"That sounds perfect. I want to see Elias Wheaton if possible," said Nafaria.

"Then we shall see it done," replied Nina with a smile.

Nafaria walked with Nina through the market square. It was as busy and full of life as she remembered. Children ran from vendor to vendor curious about what each little cart held. The Grand Cathedral in the center of Wildemere was at the market's edge. The great dome rose above the other buildings, drawing attention to its multi-colored roof.

They passed the abandoned apothecary shop. Nafaria stopped and looked through what was left of the shop window. She thought it strange the space was unoccupied.

"No one will buy the shop," said Nina.

"Why is that?" asked Nafaria.

"No one has stepped forward to inquire about the property. It, like your estate, holds a shadow over Wildemere. People understand what happened to your parents was wrong. Perhaps they fear retribution from God."

Nafaria thought about what Nina said as they walked into the antiquarian library. She smiled when she heard the familiar tinkle of the bell. She stood in the doorway with Nina and looked around the room. The rich mahogany shelves were polished and gave it warmth that could only be found in a library. She heard a throat clear and saw Elias Wheaton standing at his desk as he did many years ago.

"You still have that same look of innocence you had in your eyes when you first walked through my library door." Elias came to her as Nafaria held out her arms and gave the old man a hug.

"It has been a long time, Elias," said Nafaria.

"It has, child. I am truly sorry for what happened to your parents." Elias looked at her for a moment. "How is Michael?"

"He is happy and living in Denholm Glen with his wife at our vineyard. If he ever comes to visit, I will make sure to bring him to see you."

"That would be a pleasure," replied Elias.

"Why has no one occupied the shop my family owned? The space is in a very good location in the market, yet no one has taken it," said Nafaria.

"Perhaps merchants fear retribution for past sins. Who can say for sure? My son's estate lay dormant a long time before your father came and inquired of the king about it."

"So, once again, the manor as well as our shop has become something of legend," replied Nafaria.

"So, it would seem," said Elias.

"It was good to see you again, Elias. I will try and visit more often now that I live here again," said Nafaria.

"I would enjoy that," he replied.

<hr>

Nafaria thought about the librarian's words as they continued walking. Soon they were in the center of the market. They stood before the grove of trees she once admired as a child. Part of the grove was missing. One of the benches was also missing.

"Perhaps we should go," said Nina quietly as she tugged on Nafaria's arm. Nafaria stood where she was, refusing to take her eyes from the place.

"Did you see it happen?"

"Yes."

"Tell me about it."

"I am sure Ephratha and Jared told you what happened—" began Nina, but Nafaria interrupted her.

"Tell me what you saw that day." Nafaria looked at the trees and waited for Nina to speak.

Nina took a breath and exhaled. "I remember wandering the market alone that day. I saw Ephratha and Jared together, and I thought she was so fortunate to have found a man as respectable as Jared. There are things you know about a person just by observing them. He was gentle, and patient. His eyes brightened every time he looked at Ephratha. In a world where so many noble women are betrothed, I thought Ephratha lucky to be found by one who captured her attention so completely. I was lost in thought as I watched them, but my thoughts were interrupted when Joel and the others, rode into the market square shouting wildly.

He pulled your mother off his horse like she was nothing more than a sack of potatoes. She was such a gentle woman; I did not understand why Joel treated her so harshly.

I listened to the accusations from the back of the crowd, and was horrified when I realized what was coming. Ephratha cried out against Joel; Jared desperate to contain her so she would not get hurt.

I cried when Thena was hung, but I was also afraid for Ephratha and Jared as they were in the middle of the whole ordeal. Everything happened so fast. A mob formed and terrorized the market. Joel rode off, but he left pandemonium in his wake. Then I fainted. When I came to, I looked to my right, and saw Andrew sitting next to me. He was dazzlingly handsome, but what took me off guard was the gentle concern in his eyes. I was speechless for the moment.

He introduced himself to me and asked me my name. After that, we sat in the Cathedral and talked while the riot continued outside. He saw me faint and was concerned for me. Andrew saved me from being trampled. He refused to let me out of his sight. For some reason, I captured his attention that day. Looking back on it, I remember thinking it strange that a day beginning so tragically, ended with such hope."

Nafaria smiled at Nina. She was such a warm and tender person. Her spirit was as refreshing as a spring breeze.

"Indeed, it seems that love and good fortune can be found in any tragedy," replied Nafaria.

At that moment, a slight pain in her stomach caught Nafaria off guard, and she double over.

"What is it?" asked Nina, alarmed. She helped Nafaria to one of the benches next to the trees. Nafaria had a smile on her face.

"I felt the baby kick!" Nafaria gave Nina a hug. There in the market, hope rose from the ashes of a scene of great loss.

PART 2

CHAPTER 11

Dark storm clouds hung over Wildemere accompanied by loud thunder in the royal city. Lightning lit the sky at intervals. It was as if nature was in protest of a significant event going on within the palace walls.

Nafaria's cries echoed through the gloomy halls. A loud roar issued from a room where firelight peeked out from its doorway. A series of short gasps and groans precede another howl of pain. A high pitched squeal sounds in the room in answer to these agonizing groans.

The midwife cleans the child, and then presents it to Nathaniel as he holds Nafaria in his arms. "It is a girl," he whispered. She strained her neck to look at the child as the midwife hands it to her. She was perfectly formed: light, delicate features were her makeup; light colored eyes with perhaps a hint of green, fair skin, and possibly the whitest wisps of hair she ever saw. She smiled—and then another gasp. Her task was not finished.

"She is still in labor," said the midwife. Nafaria groaned again. The latest thunderclap masked her cry.

"What is happening?" asked Nina. She sat holding one of her hands, a look of concern on her face. She glanced at the child in the arms of one of the midwives as Nathaniel held Nafaria while she gasped again. "I see the head of another child," said the midwife.

Nafaria gasped and a smile crossed her face in between grimaces of pain. A few moments later, another child's cry fills the room.

"Another girl," said the midwife.

Nathaniel's face was blank as he looked at the second beautiful child to come from his wife's body. Her features were as dark as the first was light; eyes of the deepest sapphire, hair as black as midnight, but her skin was pure white with a pinkish glow to the face. She was also enchanting in her own way.

Nafaria beamed at him as he drew her closer. "They are both beautiful," whispered Nathaniel as he kissed her gently on the forehead.   "I will leave you alone to rest. You had a long night."

"Are you pleased?" Nafaria's question held a note of concern.

"Our children are both beautiful and healthy. Of course, I am pleased. We shall raise two beautiful women in the Craft."

Nafaria smiled at his reassurance and fell into the pillows on her bed. She was the mother of twin girls. She drifted off to sleep content to contemplate raising them when she awoke.

·•+++•·

Nathaniel descended the stone staircase that took him to the lower level of the castle. He stopped at the doorway leading to the courtyard. The rain continued to batter the ground, digging little puddles and trenches into loose earth. The sky raged with loud thunder and white lightning. He could not remember the last time he saw such a storm. He felt as if he were gazing upon the beginnings of what old Noah might have seen were he not shut in his ark surrounded by his family and the wild kingdom he was entrusted with.

He turned and descended another set of steps. Here, torches were kept lit for ease of passage. This staircase was open to all who resided within the castle but few dared go. As his footsteps clicked on the stone, Nathaniel thought his father must have come here many times. Here was where the royal library of Nereheim was kept. The wisdom of the country was held on this floor. Now that he assumed the position his father abandoned, the library was at his disposal. However, this was not his destination. He continued past the library to the end of the corridor. He grabbed a torch from its sconce and opened a large door, stepping through to an even more somber place. The door closed with a clang, the torch—Nathaniel's only light.

He continued down the steps until his feet touched soft earth. Nathaniel passed the royal crypt area, a network of chambers designated for burial of the royal families of Nereheim. Beyond the crypt, he followed a tunnel in the caverns. A cave exited off the tunnel he entered. Walking to the center of the cave, he threw the torch into a ring of stones on the ground and whispered, "Master, come forth, so I may be in your presence."

The torch's flame grew into a great fire and rose above Nathaniel's head, its voice as terrible as the thunder outside.

"Nathaniel."

Nathaniel knelt before the fire, bowing his head. "Nafaria has given birth, master. We have twin girls."

"I have seen. You are not pleased?"

"People respect men more than women, regardless of how much wisdom they have—men are considered stronger. How can my firstborn be of use to you?" Nathaniel's voice was tinged with regret.

"A man is only thought to be more powerful because men assume they are stronger than women."

"I have seen how rash emotion destroyed women of the Craft. They either become victims of their own rage and jealousy, or fall victim to the folly of another," replied Nathaniel.

"I do not deny what you say, for I have seen it many times. However, a woman brought up in the Craft and taught to control her emotion is more powerful than you could possibly imagine."

"How is that possible?"

"Men think themselves superior to women because they foolishly think themselves in control of their senses. Most men do not practice the temperance it takes to learn wisdom. Men of the Craft are taught to check their emotion with humility and let YAHWEH guide them with greater knowledge. You know of what I speak. Your father had the calm and steady repose of a man who calculates. Nafaria's father was a man who put reason first above all. Do you think this teaching is only for men? A female can be taught to be as calculating and reasonable as any man. Great wisdom can flow from her mind as well. You have a great task ahead as teacher, but the power will be immense."

"A woman will never be accepted as a Court Adviser."

"Men still have not learned that power shows no favoritism."

Nathaniel remained silent. The idea was so simple he was surprised he never thought of it before. He could bring up his daughter to be just as wise and powerful as a son. His master broke his thoughts.

"Even now, the princess of Nereheim is carrying a child she does not realize. The child will be a male. A kingdom is dependent upon a king to govern it. You have something more powerful than a sorcerer to advise a king. You have a sorceress to seduce him. Use your influence. Infiltrate the future king."

The fire diminished to the small flame from the torch and once again the tunnel was silent. Nathaniel contemplated his master's last words as he picked up the torch. His task was clear. He will raise his firstborn daughter in the way of the Grimoire Macabre to make her a sorceress. Nathaniel knew she would be powerful indeed.

He traveled back through the crypt, lost in thought. He opened the door and stepped through the walkway; replacing the torch in its place. Continuing down the hall, he was approached by a castle guard.

"Your presence is requested by your wife," said the guard.

Nathaniel smiled at the soldier. "I was just on my way to see her."

The guard bowed his head and considered his duty done when he delivered the message. He let Nathaniel pass, watching him as he continued down the corridor. He shuddered. The new adviser to the royal court of Nereheim, made him uneasy. He was merely a soldier, but even he knew there was something ominous about this young man of the Craft. This was not the first time he was found wandering the corridors leading to the library and the crypt. What business brought him here so often? The guard took a deep breath and pushed uneasy thoughts from his mind as he continued on his round of the castle.

Nathaniel found Nafaria holding the dark haired child to her breast. Nina held the light colored child in her arms. Nathaniel remembered the fair haired child was the firstborn. He walked over to Nina and held out his arms. "May I?"

"I was holding her so Nafaria could feed the other." Nina smiled and handed Nathaniel the child in her arms. Nafaria beamed with delight.

"I thought of names for them." She looked at the child in Nathaniel's arms. "The one you are holding is Fiona." Then she looked down at the child on her breast. "This one is Leona."

Nathaniel looked at the child in his arms. "Fiona," he whispered.

"Do you like the names?" she asked.

Nathaniel looked at her. "They are perfect names. I could not have come up with better."

Nathaniel looked down at the sleeping child in his arms. He breathed her sweet scent and placed a kiss on her forehead. He walked toward the window and whispered, "You will be a powerful sorceress and your hand will decide the fate of kingdoms."

CHAPTER 12

Michael,

I hope this letter finds you and Lillia as happy as when I last saw you. I have grand news. You are once again an uncle as Nathaniel and I have been blessed by YAHWEH with our first children. The twins were born on my birthday, Midsummer Day. Nathaniel is very proud to have beautiful twin daughters. He has taken to Fiona especially. Please come to Wildemere quickly to share in our joy.

With my love,

Nafaria

Nafaria dipped wax into the candle flame that sat on her desk. She sealed her letter and laid it on the table. Her head felt a little fuzzy. She took a deep breath and waited for the moment to pass. This was a frequent occurrence during the past few days, but her midwife assured her things of that nature would happen; especially if nursing twins. Soon this would pass, and she would be back to taking long walks about the castle grounds again.

She was happy Nathaniel was so proud of the girls. She thought he would be disappointed at not having a boy. She smiled as she thought of how quickly he took to Fiona. It was as if an intense bond formed from the moment he first held her. He was not dismissive of Leona, but his clear favorite was Fiona.

Nafaria took the letter and headed downstairs to the informal dining room where Nina took her tea when it rained. She looked out one of the great windows into the gloomy morning sky while the rain created a steady thrum as it hit the ground.

Nina sat at the small dining table sipping her tea. She smiled when Nafaria walked into the room. "Good morning, Nafaria. Did you manage any sleep last night?"

"Yes, for a few hours. I came to give you a letter before the girls were awake."

"For your brother?"

"Yes. You said you were sending a note to Lord Reinard Sallen in Denholm Glen. He is Michael's father-in-law." Nafaria handed Nina the letter.

"I will make sure he gives it to Michael."

Nafaria sat in a chair next to Nina. "How is it you are acquainted with him?"

"He is my great uncle. I saw him quite often growing up. I send news of the happenings in the castle every so often. He is very dear to me. I am sending my letter today, so Michael will receive this within the next three days. Do you think he will come to visit?"

"I am certain he will try. He has not come yet, but that is no surprise. Michael tends to forget how quickly time passes outside his library."

Nina laughed. "It is healthy to be curious, I suppose."

"I better go. When the girls wake up, they are usually very hungry."

"I will find you later." Nina gave Nafaria's hand a gentle squeeze as she left the room.

✦✦✦✦✦✦

Reinard walked up the cobblestone path of Mauldon manor. This path once again became a welcome friend leading him to people he dearly loved.

He entered through the side door, knowing he was welcome to do so. Michael caught a glimpse of him and came to meet him.

"Father, this is an unexpected surprise!" Michael embraced his father-in-law. "Lillia is still asleep. William kept her up late again."

"It is you I seek. Princess Nina sent me a letter filled with her adventures in Wildemere. She also sent a letter for you from Nafaria," He handed Michael a roll of paper sealed with wax.

"As you worry about Nina, I worry for my baby sister. She may be too gentle to be the wife of the Court Adviser. Let us hear her news." Michael broke the seal and opened the letter.

As he scanned the letter, his eyebrows rose. A smile crossed his face. "Nafaria had twins! Both girls, they were born on her birthday, Midsummer Day. She wants me to visit."

"Nafaria was born on Midsummer Day?"

"Yes."

"What an enchanting time of year; especially for one of the Craft," said Reinard. Nafaria's daughters being born on such a day unsettled him.

"I will see if Lillia is up to coming with me. She has had many sleepless nights, and her strength is sapped."

"If she stays behind, I can check on her while you are away. Get ready to meet your nieces."

⁕⁕⁕⁕⁕

Michael found Lillia in their bedroom. She held William in her arms as she looked out the window. Her face brightened when she saw him. She lifted a finger to her lips; a warning their son was sleeping.

He crept up to her and took the child from her arms. He gently kissed his forehead and placed him in the cradle. When William did not stir,

Michael led Lillia out of the bedroom. As they walked down the hall, one of the servants passed them.

"Maria, please sit with William while he sleeps. I need Lillia for a few moments." The servant nodded, and went to their room.

"How is it whenever you move him, he stays asleep? No one else can do that."

"Perhaps I have my father's touch when it comes to babies. My mother told me about it from time to time when I was younger."

"What is it you wished to talk about?"

"I received a letter from Nafaria. She gave birth to twin girls on Midsummer Day. She asked me to visit. I would like to go, as I have not seen her since she returned to Nereheim. What concerns me is that you may not be well enough to travel," said Michael.

"That is wonderful news, Michael! I want to go. The last time I was in Wildemere, Alana Deveraux saved my life. Do you think it safe to travel with William?"

"I am more concerned for you. Do you feel able to make the trip?"

"I should be fine, as long as we take the carriage. I am not ready for horseback yet."

"I am happy we do not need to have that argument."

"It is good we have this opportunity. You need to spend time with Nathaniel."

"I will find Maia and let her know we are leaving. She will oversee the manor while we are away. She can call your father if there is any trouble. We will take another with us to drive the carriage. I want to be able to enjoy the countryside with you."

Lillia kissed him on the nose. "What a lovely adventure we shall have."

Michael and Lillia left Denholm Glen the next morning under bright sunshine. William was in good spirits, comfortably snuggled in Lillia's arms. Michael watched the countryside as he pondered Nafaria's new life as wife of the Court Adviser who was his best friend and brother-in-law. Would his life have to change because of his relation to Nathaniel and Nafaria? His life in Denholm Glen was exactly as he hoped it would be. He had no greater ambition than to be a good husband and carry on his family name with the vineyard. However, a dark sensation crept upon him. Would he be called to do something else? Only time would tell. Until then, he would continue his study to protect his family; wherever they were. A tap on his shoulder brought him from his reverie. He looked at Lillia.

"Will we try to ride through the night?"

"No. Rowall is a good place to stop for the night. It is never wise to fatigue your animals needlessly. That is one lesson I remember from Lord Saintclaire." Michael fell silent as he looked back out the window.

The next morning they continued on. Michael hoped to reach the royal city by twilight, but he was content with their steady pace across the countryside.

He considered the ramifications of the twins being born on Midsummer Day. Nafaria had such a gentle nature that any supernatural power, however latent she possessed, would never come to light by her insistence. Only if Nathaniel wished to nurture it, could this power be dangerous. In the past, only men were trained in this manner. Outside his father, Michael never knew anyone who had visible supernatural ability. Jason never trained the boys to be powerful enough to take people by this type of force. It was to protect mankind, and Jason believed there were other ways to accomplish this goal.

"Good intentions do not keep the bearers of such power free from harm," Michael thought. He remembered the cruel way his parents died. Jason trusted no one lightly, and in the end he was still betrayed. Who could say what Nathaniel might be willing to do if forced to make such a choice?

Did his concerns have any foundation? Nathaniel was his childhood friend, Michael knew him. There was mischief in his heart, but no malice. Nathaniel was never tempted with greed as a child. He wanted nothing he would not ask or work for, and was honest in his approach. He was only cruel to Dominic Cavanaugh, and only to protect Nafaria. Time and circumstance have a way of changing a heart, but even at their wedding, Nathaniel looked as though he possessed the world when he took Nafaria for a wife. He was proud as any king to have a quiet life.

The carriage slowed to a stop. He leaned out the window. "Is there something wrong, Peter?"

"We should let the horses drink in the creek beside the road. A short rest for them is in order," replied Peter.

"Good idea. I think we will take a few moments to stretch as well."

Michael caught sight of the creek that ran parallel to the road when he and Lillia stepped out of the carriage. She held William and wandered along the road, content with the breeze in the afternoon air.

He stretched as the horses drank from the creek, a smile on his face. He saw a large rock and moved toward it to sit down. When he touched the rock, a flash of light blinded him for a moment and faded. He looked at the countryside once again and saw the hills covered with people.

Two great armies rushed toward each other. One marched steadily on, never wavering from its goal. The crest of the eagle was emblazoned on a banner that flapped in the breeze.

The other army advanced slower, and much less steadily. Michael saw terror in the eyes of the men moving forward. "Why are they so afraid?" he thought to himself.

As if in answer to his thought, another flash came and the faces of the Nereheim soldiers became visible. Their eyes were soulless—they advanced like walking corpses toward their goal. In the distance, a beautiful young woman with brilliant green eyes took in the scene before her. Her hands held a delicate silver bell and hammer; a cruel smile twisted her face.

"The bell of Herron," he whispered. After another flash, Michael dropped to his knees in the creek. He gulped a few deep breaths and splashed his face with water, looking around him once again. All was quiet and they were alone on the road. Lillia stood wide eyed looking at him from the road. He climbed up from the creek, shaking from his vision.

"Michael, what is wrong? You look as though you have seen a ghost," said Lillia.

"You would not be far from the truth." Michael watched as Peter hitched the horses to the carriage. "Do you remember I told you I had dreams and premonitions of the future?"

Lillia nodded her head. "You said you saw your father's death."

"Now I have seen much more. I am not sure what it means, but it was important enough to see in full daylight. Let us get on our way again. It is too quiet out here," said Michael as he looked around. They quickly settled inside as the carriage started moving again.

Before, Michael only saw premonitions from dreams. Never had he been awake and seen a vision. What message needed to be conveyed that did not wait for nightfall? Was the countryside to be the scene of some great future battle? Would this young woman lead the charge, using the bell of Herron? The bell was supposed a myth, but no longer to Michael. He was certain the vision showed him the sacred relic that called the dead. It was too precisely and delicately made to be anything fashioned by man.

The faces of the soldiers were vacant and devoid of emotion; empty vessels filled with dead spirits to ensure victory. What other dark secrets did this young woman possess? Who was she? These questions played on his mind as they continued to the royal city.

"Peter, there's a cobblestone pathway coming up on the right, surrounded by trees. Turn onto that path," said Michael as he leaned out the window.

"Yes, my lord," Peter replied.

Michael looked out the window and saw the remains of his old house. It still stood, though portions were burned. The remains of his father's pyre were visible next to the house. It was as if Jason were still holding on to this world. The manor was deserted once again. Were there whispers in the city about that black day?

"This is where you lived while you were here. We visited this place when I was here with father," said Lillia.

"My father had to gain permission from the king just to see the place. We dispelled an old rumor in order to be able to buy the property. I fear once again, this place has become a thing of evil to everyone in Wildemere." Michael called to Peter. "Thank you for stopping. We need to move on to the castle." Peter started the horses down the path and into the main road leading to Wildemere.

"What do you think will happen to that property? I remember you said it was quite valuable," said Lillia.

"It is, and right within walking distance of the city. A spring flows beneath it, and the woods behind the estate are full of wild flowers, herbs and plants. Nafaria collected the herbs we used and sold in the apothecary from those woods. Philip hunted in them nearly every day. I wonder if

Nathaniel and Nafaria have even considered what to do with it," replied Michael.

The carriage continued through the city and reached the castle. As they rode up the path, Michael felt a strange sensation encroach upon him. He recalled words his father-in-law spoke to him when he began training in alchemy… *"There is a presence all around us. It lingers in the air we breathe, and in all we feel. Awareness of this presence will lead us away from danger. Choose to ignore it, and you will find yourself in the very clutches of darkness. Evil often masquerades as an emissary of light*[18]*. It also manifests itself in shadows. Be on your guard, and you will save yourself."*

Michael felt a powerful force at work. He looked warily at the castle. William stirred in Lillia's arms and began to cry. She cuddled him closer to soothe him, but he would not be comforted. Finally, she looked at Michael. "I cannot seem to get him to stop crying. Will you try?"

Michael took William in his arms and held him close. The child calmed by degrees and his wail became a quiet whimper. They stepped out of the carriage and were greeted by a guard with a grim expression.

"What business brings you to the royal court?"

"I am Michael Mauldon. This is my wife Lillia, my son William, and Peter is one of my servants. I am here to see my sister, Nafaria Stone." Michael's gaze never wavered. The guard glanced away from him for a moment.

"Follow me." After Peter left the carriage with the stable hands, the guard led them toward the castle. "The Court Adviser does not receive many visitors," he said.

"I am sure he is very busy for the king. I have not seen him in a long time," Michael replied.

---

[18]   2 Corinthians 11:14

After a short walk, they came to the terrace. "I will leave you in the care of your sister. She is with the princess taking tea."

"Michael!" Nafaria shouted. She jumped from her seat and made her way down the steps to join him. Michael's eyes widened when she drew near. He gave William to Lillia and turned back to Nafaria. She stopped in front of him. "What is the matter?" He touched the shock of white in her hair.

"What happened to your hair?"

"Oh, it is nothing. Ephratha's midwife said it was likely caused by stress when I was in Arioth." He looked at her face. Her eyes were as youthful and vibrant as he remembered. Her skin was still the soft cream color it always was. Nothing else was different but the streak of white in her hair. He finally smiled and said, "You look well, little sister."

"Thank you. The girls are sleeping, so I took a moment to have tea with Nina." Nafaria looked at Lillia and smiled. "Who is this little one?" She peered at the little bundle in Lillia's arms. The child looked at her and cuddled closer to Lillia.

"This is your nephew, William. He is usually a quiet baby, but for some reason he is agitated at the moment," replied Michael.

"I am glad all of you are here." Nafaria gave Lillia a hug.

"I am glad to be able to make the trip. Since William's birth, I need more rest than usual," said Lillia with a smile.

Nina came up to them as they spoke. She held out her hand to Michael. "It is a pleasure to finally meet you."

"For me as well, your highness—Lord Sallen sends his greetings," Michael bowed his head slightly.

"I am sure he has expressed his concern for me?"

"He has. However, I see it is misplaced." Michael noted that while Nina had a very gentle demeanor, her presence was definite; almost as if she chose to be visible at will.

"Nathaniel will be excited to see you," said Nafaria.

She led them through the castle, with Nina following, watching him carefully. He saw right away nothing passed without her knowledge. It would be a clever individual that would take her by surprise. Nafaria opened a door leading into a room lined floor to ceiling with books. Nathaniel sat at a table bent over a book with a single candle next to him. He looked up when they entered and a smile brightened his face. He quickly rose from his seat.

"Michael! I was hoping to hear from you soon!" Nathaniel gave his old friend a strong embrace. He then looked at Lillia.

"It is good to see you again as well, Lillia," said Nathaniel as he gave her a hug. "Is this William?" he asked. He looked closely at the child. William stirred and cuddled closer to Lillia.

"Yes. He is usually an easy going baby, but for some reason he is restless," replied Michael. He ran his hand across William's forehead to calm him. Michael furrowed his brow.

"What is the matter?" asked Lillia quietly.

"His forehead feels warm," said Michael.

"Perhaps the journey has upset him," replied Nafaria.

"That is a possibility. He may settle down in a while," said Lillia.

"Let us see if the girls are awake," replied Nafaria. The group exited the library.

"I will go find Andrew," said Nina. She left them and headed down another passageway.

"You look well, Nathaniel. Apparently, the life of Court Adviser agrees with you," said Michael.

"I am merely the giver of advice. Though this takes insight and diplomacy at times, Rohn and Andrew have the harder task. They must make decisions based on that advice."

"Is there a place I can nurse William after we see the girls?" asked Lillia.

"There is a guest room near us where you can settle in," said Nafaria.

The nursery was still quiet when they entered. Michael and Lillia crept up to the two cradles that were in the corner. Both girls were still, breathing contentedly in slumber.

Michael smiled as he looked at their delicate heads peeking out from the blankets they were tucked under. One had a thick head of black wavy hair. Her skin was porcelain white with just a little pink in her cheeks. He saw instantly that she took after Nafaria.

The other, was more flesh toned, with light brown hair. She took after Nathaniel, but the hair color also reminded Michael of his father. The longer he looked at her; a shadow grew over his face. This child veiled his heart with dread. Nafaria touched his shoulder. They all crept out of the room again.

"They are precious, Nafaria," said Michael. "Which was first?"

"The fair haired one, Fiona was first. The dark haired one, Leona, came a few minutes later."

As they entered the guest room, Michael thought about Fiona. What concern could he have about her? His senses pricked at him to be on his guard.

Nathaniel stopped at the entrance to their room.   "Michael, come with me. The king will be happy you are here. He is very fond of you," said Nathaniel.

"I will be happy to see him as well," said Michael. He turned to Lillia. "Take William and see if he will nurse. He may just be hungry." said Michael.

"I will see you again at dinner," said Nafaria. She stepped to Michael and quickly planted a kiss on his cheek. Nafaria left as well to give Lillia privacy.

<hr>

Michael followed Nathaniel down the steps and turned down a long corridor. The paintings of various men stared back as they passed. The depth of the wisdom in their eyes was matched only by the richness of the colors that captured them on canvas. Michael remembered this famed hall. This was the hallway leading to the throne room, where portraits of past Court Advisers hung. He stopped at one of the paintings. The stoic features and pensive look of Malcom Stone stared back at him.

"I often forget your father was once Court Adviser."

"It is a world he rarely spoke of, and one he does not miss."

Nathaniel opened the large doors leading to the throne room. Rohn sat on his throne, watching the darkening sky.

"Your majesty, I bring a guest. Michael Mauldon has come from Denholm Glen," said Nathaniel.

Rohn's expression brightened. "Welcome, Michael. It is good to see you once again." Rohn came toward them, his hand extended.

Michael embraced the king.   "Thank you, your majesty. My wife and son have joined me."

"We will have a wonderful visit. Where are they?"

"Lillia is nursing William. He seemed agitated when we arrived. I wanted to see if he would calm before dinner."

"No doubt it is the long trip," replied Rohn.

"I believe so, your majesty. This would mark his first adventure."

"I hope he fares well here in Wildemere. How old is he?"

"Six months, your majesty."

"I look forward to seeing Lillia once again and meeting this little one."

"Your majesty, I wish to convey my condolences for your loss. There was no one I loved more in Wildemere than Queen Susanna. She was a remarkable woman."

"Thank you. I know she was very fond of your family as well. She mourned the loss of your parents greatly."

Just then a servant appeared to announce that dinner would be served shortly. "I better go see to Lillia."

"We will see you in a few minutes," replied Nathaniel.

Michael left the throne room and headed up the stairwell toward the nursery, where he first saw the girls. He peeked into the room and saw Nafaria sitting in a chair on the far side of the room. One glance and he could see she was nursing. He glanced down at the floor as Nafaria looked up. She smiled and said, "Lillia is in the next room."

"Thank you. I will see you at dinner."

Michael heard William wailing before he entered the room. There he found Lillia pacing the floor, trying desperately to comfort William. His face was red as she looked over at Michael. Her expression was one of alarm.

"He has not stopped crying since a few minutes after Nafaria led me here. I have tried everything; I cannot get him to stop."

Michael took William in his arms and he quieted by degrees. Finally, his wail became a soft whimper as he nestled closer to Michael's chest. Michael looked down at him with concern. "Something is wrong. William has never been like this. Come here and feel his chest."

Lillia came over to them and put her hand over his chest. "His heart is beating fast. What do you suppose it could be?"

Michael looked at her. She had a right to know what was on his mind, especially since it would help her understand what William was going through. However, he was at a loss to explain what he felt.

"I am not certain. I feel something here, some foreboding presence. Perhaps William senses it too. Dinner was just announced, but I will stay here until you are ready to go. The king would like to see you and William."

"I still need to nurse William." Lillia went to take William back, but he became restless again. She sighed. "I cannot nurse him if he will not leave you."

Michael looked at the child, and then looked down at the obsidian stone he wore around his neck. He handed William to her. He then took off the necklace and put it around the baby's neck. He remained quiet. She smiled with relief and sat in a chair in the corner. "Now let us see if hunger is what you face," she whispered. After a few moments, William settled down and began to nurse.

"That was a good idea with the necklace." Lillia glanced up at Michael.

"It seems so. I wonder why he does not feel calm with you."

"If he senses what you do, perhaps he also senses who is stronger of the two of us. He feels safer with you."

"You may be right. I will take William when we go to dinner. I do not wish to be a bother while we are guests."

Michael carried William and Lillia followed as they walked into the dining chamber. Andrew and Nina greeted them.

Andrew held out his hand. "It is good to see you again, Michael."

"You as well, your highness." Michael shook his hand as gracefully as he could with William in his arms. Nina peeked over Andrew's shoulder.

"He is absolutely precious."

"He looks like his father already," said Lillia.

"You think so? I think he looks like mother," said Michael.

"That is because you resemble your mother so," replied Lillia.

"Only someone who grew up with you would know that," said Nina.

Rohn entered the room, followed by Nathaniel and Nafaria. Each was carrying a child.

"It seems the nursery has come to dinner tonight. It is good to see everyone so happy," said Rohn. He came over to Michael. "This must be William."

"Yes, your majesty."

"He is a handsome child. I am sure he takes after his father."

"Thank you, your majesty. Lillia was just saying she felt that William and I take after my mother."

"May he take after you, your mother and your father," replied Rohn. From then on, dinner was relaxed and jovial. However, there was still something about the affair that kept Michael on guard.

After dinner, Nina offered to take Lillia and Michael about the castle grounds. Both were delighted with the idea. They wandered through the courtyard, to the rose garden. The many different roses and their colors captured Lillia's attention. Her fondness for plants and nature were a comfort over the years she and Michael were apart. Michael was amazed at the things she learned and appreciated. In nature, Lillia saw every drama of human life portrayed. She saw fierce anger in violent storms. A calm quiet evening, reminded her of love. A bright morning whispered peace and hope. "This place is enchanting," said Lillia as she stopped at the cluster of maiden's blush roses in the center of the garden.

While they walked, Michael felt the dread sensation once again. While he considered this agitated state, Nina looked around them. When she was certain no one else was near, she looked at Michael. "I wondered if I might have a word with you," said Nina.

"We are your guests. What would you like to talk about?" asked Michael.

"I was hoping to speak to you alone, Michael."

"There is nothing you cannot say in front Lillia, no matter how strange it may seem. She understands more than you realize."

Nina hesitated. She looked around once again. "There is something wrong here, can you feel it?" asked Nina quietly. Her voice was barely above a whisper. Michael and Lillia looked at each other.

"We were discussing that earlier. When I first arrived, I felt an intense uneasiness—something foreboding in the air."

"I have felt the same since we arrived back from North Agea. At first, I told myself it was melancholy due to Queen Susanna's death. However, the birth of Nafaria's twins has not made this feeling dissipate." Nina looked at both of them. "How well do you know Nathaniel?"

"We grew up with him. The three of us are the same age," replied Michael.

"Is he the same as you remember?"

Michael hesitated. In many ways, Nathaniel was as quick witted and headstrong as always, but there was something Michael noticed that he never saw before. His eyes were darker; his expression wore a harder edge than before. It was subtle, but Nathaniel's demeanor was different. Was he really the same person Michael grew up with?

"It seems as though something has changed," he replied quietly.

Relief washed over Nina like a flood; as if his acknowledgment was a verdict pronouncing her sane. "There were disquieting things that happened at Arioth when Andrew and I went with the queen to visit Jared and Ephratha. Nafaria had bad dreams involving Nathaniel. One in particular, she awoke screaming his name, and the lock of white you see in her hair appeared. I met him for the first time when he came to the castle after his sabbatical. I have been wary of him ever since."

"Nathaniel took a sabbatical?"

"Yes. Apparently, he was gone a week when Nafaria was having these dreams."

"Have you talked about this to anyone?"

"I mentioned it to Ephratha, but she was quick to reply that I was misjudging Nathaniel. I thought perhaps I was a little jumpy. Arioth can be an imposing place when visited for the first time."

"It is not nearly as imposing as this place has become," replied Michael quietly. Nina nodded in agreement.

"Keep your fears secret, Nina. There may be nothing to what we are sensing. However, innocence is often the best defense and naiveté can protect one," said Michael.

"I will say nothing, but keep an open eye to what goes on around me."

"I have a feeling you have been doing that for quite some time," said Michael.

Nina smiled. "What is it the sacred writings say? Be as shrewd as snakes and innocent as doves[19]. There can be no better advice than that."

"Indeed, there is not," replied Michael.

———— ·++++·· ————

It was midnight when Michael sat up in bed, drenched in sweat. His heart was beating fast as he looked around the room. There was nothing wrong or even out of the ordinary to startle him. Lillia lay next to him with William in her arms. The baby's eyes were closed, but his breathing was faster than normal. "There is nothing to fear," he whispered. He lay back down and closed his eyes.

"Michael." His eyes snapped open when he heard his name. It sounded like his mother's whisper. Looking around, he yawned. "It must be the wind." Michael closed his eyes.

"Michael." The voice was more insistent this time—cross. He sat up in the bed. There was nothing, once again.

He slowly threw back the blanket he was under. He crept out of bed, and grabbed his cloak. "Perhaps a short walk will ease my mind," he thought as he walked out of the room.

A light caught his eye as he walked in the dimly lit hall. He stepped into the shadows the passage afforded and watched it. A hooded figure carried a torch. Michael recognized Nathaniel's cloak.

"Do not let yourself be seen." Michael heard the command as clearly as he heard his name whispered. He followed at a safe distance.

---

[19]   Matthew 10:16

They descended the stairs and continued into the lowest level of the castle; past the royal crypt into a cavern. He sensed Nathaniel made this walk quite often. The uneven ground seemed to be anticipated as he moved. Nathaniel turned into a room, toward a ring of stones. Michael stood outside the room and looked inside. He said to himself, "Spirit of YAHWEH, hear my plea; let me walk unseen to the powers that be." He took a deep breath and entered.

Nathaniel set the torch inside the ring and waved his hands over it. The flames from the torch burst into a fire lighting up the room. A large book lay on a shelf that was hewn from stone. He carefully crossed the room and glimpsed the cover. It was leather and completely black. There was no writing to give a clue to its contents; a skull was embossed in the bottom right hand corner.

"Master," whispered Nathaniel as he stared at the fire.

The flames rose above their heads and a hooded face appeared out of the top of the flames. Michael cringed as he realized what Nathaniel was doing. The apparition spoke.

"The king of Nereheim is losing the willpower to be gracious to North Agea. He wants blood in return for the blood of his queen. However, he also wishes to maintain amiable relations with his brother-in-law. In order to bring the new king, you must replace the old. Make Rohn think the king of North Agea is personally responsible. He will seek vengeance for his queen's blood. Make your child ready. She will only be as strong as you train her to be. Seek your answers in the Grimoire. When the time for war comes, you will build an unstoppable army with the bell. You have much in common with Rohn. You seek vengeance for the many wrongs you witnessed in Nereheim as a child. You seek justice for your wife's family."

"Joel disappeared since Susanna's death. I cannot find him."

"Others were present the day Jason Mauldon was killed. Do you think one of the Craft as clever and powerful as Jason could be destroyed so easily? He was mentored by your father. You know he was trained well. Joel had help."

"Accomplices."

"Nafaria recognized Lord Robert Stowe, the princess of North Agea's father, as one of the men present when Joel killed Jason. The others created a diversion so Joel could attack from behind. It was clever enough for mortals, if not predictable. Execute Robert Stowe and take his land. Your vengeance for Jason Mauldon will be partially complete."

"Thank you, master."

Nathaniel walked over to the book, close to where Michael stood. He opened the book and slowly turned the pages. Each one was written in an obscure runic language. From what Michael could understand, he saw very black rituals and incantations. His mouth went dry.

"The Grimoire Macabre," thought Michael. His stomach tightened as he realized who Nathaniel was now. He backed away from the scene and out of the room.

Michael hurried as quickly as he could through the passages back to his room. He heard William's cries as he entered. Lillia was pacing the floor in an effort to calm him. She gave Michael a worried look.

"He just started crying a few minutes ago. When I awoke, you were not here. Where did you go?" asked Lillia. Her question was more of a demand than she intended. Michael came over to her and put his arms around her and the baby. Instantly William quieted to a whimper once again. He leaned over his wife and whispered in her ear.

"Lillia, listen to me carefully. I cannot explain anything to you until we leave Wildemere, and we cannot stay here. Evil lives in this place, it is all around us. You must act as though you suspect nothing. I will speak to Nafaria and Nathaniel in the morning, and we will leave shortly after. Do you understand?"

She looked into Michael's eyes. They held an intensity that showed his seriousness. She nodded her head and said nothing. They got back into bed with Michael holding William. Michael lay in bed shaking as he thought about what Nathaniel sold himself to. Why had Nathaniel betrayed his entire family and all he believed to serve the god of blood? It made no sense to him. Hot tears formed in his eyes as he felt the loss of his childhood friend.

CHAPTER 13

The eastern sky was turning pink. Michael stood on the balcony outside his room looking toward Denholm Glen. He inhaled the morning air. There was much to be said as quickly and diplomatically as possible to keep Nathaniel's suspicion at bay. It was good fortune that William's demeanor provided them with the perfect excuse to leave. Michael was guardian of a terrible truth; he must protect his family at all costs.

Though it would disappoint Nafaria, he knew she would understand. William's cries were not lost on her. She knew the child was not at ease. Nina suspected something terrible right from the beginning. She must be told the truth to keep her from looking closer. He grabbed his cloak as he walked through the room and into the hall.

Michael headed for the terrace garden. Nafaria mentioned Nina's morning and evening tea ritual. He found her sitting at a table with a cup in her hand. Her eyes were closed, the cup just under her nose. She savored the scent before she drank. Her eyes snapped open as he approached.

"Good morning, your highness."

"Good morning, Michael. I thought I was the only early riser."

"I am fond of an early start to my day." He sat down next to Nina.

She looked at him carefully. "Will you be leaving?"

"Yes. William did not sleep well at all. Lillia is very worried, and I think it would be best to get him home where he is at ease. However, I wanted to speak with you before I left."

Nina carefully put her cup down. "Is it as we feared?" She gave Michael a penetrating look.

"I am afraid it is much worse, your highness. You must be brave and innocent at the same time. Andrew will need you."

"You will not tell me what you discovered, will you?"

"If you knew, it would only endanger you and Andrew. The only thing I can tell you is that you must watch out for the king. He may become a danger to himself and others."

Nina sighed. "I need to be careful for the sake of our child as well. Nafaria's midwife confirmed my suspicions before you arrived. It is early, but I am with child."

Michael started at the news. "Be brave, Nina. YAHWEH will protect us in the end."

Nina smiled weakly. "Perhaps our children were born to help our nations through the darkness to come."

Michael smiled in return as he left her to her tea.

———————

Nafaria smiled when she saw Michael coming toward her from the terrace outside. "You are up early. I suppose I should not be surprised."

He gave her a hug and planted a kiss on her forehead. "I am afraid I must leave this morning. William did not sleep well last night. He has been ill at ease since we arrived. I am worried for him."

Nafaria sighed. "I understand. I was afraid he would not settle down and you would have to leave."

"Perhaps when you are up to it, you could come visit us in Denholm Glen. It might do you some good to visit the vineyard." Michael leaned closer. "Be patient with Nathaniel. He has a lot of work to do here."

"You must say goodbye to him before you leave. He will be disappointed if you do not."

"I wish to see him as well." He looked at her again. "Do you still have the letter I sent you around the time Nina and Andrew were married?"

"You mean the letter about transcendence?"

"Yes."

"I do. It was a lot of information."

"The occurrence may show itself to you, as you are very close to the Anenderes River here. I thought you should know about it."

"Jared was interested in it as well."

"I suppose I should not be surprised at that. Where is Nathaniel now?"

"I am here." Michael and Nafaria turned as Nathaniel descended the stairs. Nafaria kissed Michael once more and gave him a hug. "Be safe," she whispered.

"Be careful," Michael whispered. She held him tight for a moment before excusing herself. Michael turned to Nathaniel.

"I am afraid we need to return home. William did not sleep well at all, and Lillia barely slept as a result."

Nathaniel sighed. "I am sorry William has not settled down enough for you to stay. Perhaps we can visit another time. Thank you for taking the time to see your new nieces and visit with us; brief as it was." Nathaniel embraced him.

A chill raced through Michael's body, causing his heartbeat to increase. He willed himself to stay calm and relaxed. "Make good choices for Nereheim."

"Have a safe journey home," replied Nathaniel.

Nathaniel's eyes followed Michael for a moment. He considered the reason his brother-in -law gave for the departure. Was there another reason besides a child's hardship in the night?

"He suspects you." The thought came as a whisper through the hall. Nathaniel's heart quickened. Michael was wise in the Craft, but he could not judge a heart. Did he know his dark secret? Nathaniel headed toward the lower levels of the castle where he could decide in solitude what to do next.

As he moved into the crypt, his thoughts found a voice.

"How could he suspect anything?" asked Nathaniel as he walked. The answer whispered in the dark cavern.

"Perhaps he sees what others do not."

"What does it matter? Michael has always kept to himself. He would not interfere."

"He might to save his sister. He might to save North Agea."

"Perhaps he could be swayed," said Nathaniel. As he walked into the chamber, his master awaited him in the fire.

"The house of Jason Mauldon will not be swayed from its path," was his master's dark reply. *"Use the bell; send spirits to destroy Denholm Glen and Illith."*

Nathaniel felt his pulse quicken. "Illith?"

"Count Deveraux controls the region containing the village of Illith. Exact your vengeance on the Count for his wrong against Raymond and Analia Bernard. The Saintclaire Manor is being rebuilt. Those who still fear and respect the Craft are there. They might align themselves with the Mauldon family."

"He is my brother-in-law. Surely there is another way," replied Nathaniel quietly.

"There is no other way. You must destroy him."

<hr>

As the carriage moved away from the castle, Lillia felt William relax in her arms. Michael's necklace was still around his neck, and his breathing returned to normal. Michael stared out the carriage window as they left the royal city behind.

She sighed. "William is breathing normally again."

Michael glanced down at William and kissed him on his forehead. Then he leaned closer and kissed her as well. She felt relief in the touch of his lips.

"You said you needed to tell me something," said Lillia.

Michael sighed. "I have something very important to tell you. However, before I do, I want you to answer one question for me if you can."

"What is it?"

"Does Nathaniel seem different to you?"

She considered his question. They did not have time to notice much, but Nathaniel seemed more ominous than she remembered him. His intense stare and dark demeanor was almost menacing. The look the guards held when they first arrived at the castle was another tell-tale sign. They were clearly afraid of him.

"Remember when we were children and Dominic Cavanaugh tried to bully Nafaria? When everyone in the village found out what happened, Nathaniel became someone to be feared. Until you left, no one bothered Nafaria again as a result. I remember many stayed away from Nathaniel for fear that he would do the same or worse to them. Now, he seems more focused; even sinister," said Lillia.

"He is more focused. I think William sensed it before I realized it. The gift YAHWEH bestowed on our son may be the same sensitivity Lord Saintclaire was known for. People whispered that he knew the future, but he was not clairvoyant. He sensed things, and prepared himself for what was coming. It is like the wise man in the sacred writings who built his house on a rock.[20] Lord Saintclaire was the same way. He protected those around him and provided for them in the end. William sensed the evil in that castle, and he was afraid," replied Michael.

"Evil?"

"Nina told me she knew something was wrong from the moment they arrived back at Wildemere after Susanna's death. She said from the moment she first met Nathaniel, she was afraid of him. When she first arrived at Arioth with Andrew, Nafaria was there for a surprise visit. Nathaniel took a sabbatical and was gone for a week. She had terrible dreams and from one of them, she received that lock of pure white hair she now has. She tried to talk to Ephratha about her concerns, but Ephratha trusts Nathaniel, so she did not see the threat."

"I can see how that would be unnerving, but evil?"

"Last night, I could not sleep. I heard my mother's voice calling my name. At first, I thought it was only the wind, so I ignored it. When I heard it again, it was with the same tone she used when she was cross or impatient. I took a walk to clear my head. I saw Nathaniel in one of the corridors and I followed him. Under the castle in the catacombs near the royal crypt, he went into a cave. There he summoned the god of blood. He is in possession of the Grimoire Macabre, a book thought only to be a dark legend among those of the Craft. Many did not believe it truly existed.

Nina mentioned in one of Nafaria's nightmares, Nathaniel dripped blood on the book. According to legend, only the keeper of the book can

---

[20]   Matthew 7:24-25

open it, and only after it has been passed from one successor to another by blood. I think when Nathaniel went on his sabbatical; he met someone who passed this book to him. He now serves the god of blood. I cannot begin to understand why."

Lillia was quiet as she digested Michael's story. "Nathaniel was always driven by use of knowledge as power. He was always very clever, as in the situation with Dominic Cavanaugh. With you as a friend, and under his father's influence, he used his knowledge to help and protect people. I believe he truly wanted to do this. On the day of Analia's death, I saw he was visibly angry about Count Deveraux's decision to execute Analia along with Lya. You all left so quickly, it is hard to be certain, but suppose he began to pursue more arcane knowledge of the Craft in a quest for power? You certainly have. Some of the books you possess might lead one to think you are some kind of sorcerer. Do you suppose Nathaniel sold himself for the knowledge and power to take vengeance the way he could not when we were young?"

"That is possible. Perhaps the confrontation with Joel when he was reunited with Nafaria made him pursue such power. Or such power pursued him," replied Michael grimly.

Lillia looked down at the sleeping baby in her arms. He was so tiny and vulnerable. "What will become of William?" she asked quietly.

"He will have a much greater task. He will have to carry on with study so that he can fight evil in his generation, as I have tried to prepare myself for ours. He needs to develop his acute sensitivity into intuition the way Lord Saintclaire did. That is truly a gift sent from YAHWEH to give hope in such a dark time," said Michael.

"I wonder if he will fight alone, or will he have allies?" asked Lillia.

"Only time will tell." Michael thought of Leona as the carriage drifted across the countryside.

⸻ ⸙ ⸻

Michael awoke in his bed after midnight. Looking around the little room of the inn they stopped at he saw everything was the same as when he went to sleep. He rubbed his eyes and looked over at the window. Bright light shone from the waxing moon outside. He carefully threw off the quilt covering him. There was no reason he could point to that would rouse him from his dreams. He felt a tug at the very back of his mind as if something was trying to reach out to him.

He walked over to the window and glanced at the moon. The light cast a strange glow on the grass and trees. A lone figure stood outside below, looking up at him. The figure raised a hand beckoning him.

Michael turned and saw Lillia and William asleep on the bed. He grabbed his cloak and left the room. He rushed outside. The figure lowered his hood and Michael recognized his father.

"*Michael,*" he spoke.

"Father, is it really you?" Michael whispered as he stepped closer to the figure.

"*Hello my son. I bring you a warning. I am afraid you will live to see evil times come and go from Nereheim. You must not only take courage, but be wise as well. You have prepared your whole life for what you will face. You will be tested, and the sister kingdoms will hang in the balance.*"

Michael was silent as he listened to his father's words.

"Nathaniel has sold himself to evil and betrayed us all," said Michael.

Jason nodded his head. "*You must protect yourself and your family. You will be no good to Nafaria or anyone else if you are dead. The villages of Illith and Denholm Glen will be destroyed unless you act quickly.*"

"What must I do?"

"Remember the sacred writings. Remember the blood that saved the ancients the night death came[21]. Protect yourself with the blood. Be careful my son. You are far too valuable to join me in an early grave."

"Father, how are you here?"

"You know the answer."

"It is because of the transcendence."

Jason nodded again. *"The dead are warning those they left behind. The times to come will be the darkest the sister kingdoms have ever faced. Be careful my son."*

Michael blinked and was alone. He looked at the tree his father stood under for a few moments before he made his way back to the room. As he took off his cloak, Lillia woke up.

"What is it?" asked Lillia. She saw his grim expression by the moonlight coming from the window.

"My father appeared to me. He warned me Nathaniel will soon try to destroy us. He told me to protect myself with the blood."

Lillia's eyebrows furrowed. "Blood?"

Michael began to gather their things together.

"What are you doing?" she asked.

"There is no time to wait. We must head home now. There is much to do. Get ready and meet us downstairs." Michael grabbed his cloak and left the room again. Jason's words played on his mind as he went to wake Peter to ready the horses for their journey home.

• • •

---

[21]   Exodus 11-12

The carriage moved swiftly with the rising sun. Peter willed the horses to an almost breakneck speed. Michael recalled the story of the blood and was thinking through each detail so he knew what to do when they arrived home. He must talk to his father-in-law as quickly as possible. Reinard would be able to help him ready the village for whatever was coming.

The warning went through his mind once again. His father said Illith and Denholm Glen would be destroyed. Why would Nathaniel destroy both villages? Illith was the home of Lord Saintclaire. He remembered King Rohn pardoned Count Deveraux and set him as Count in Illith. Was that why Nathaniel would destroy it as well? Lillia said he was visibly angry the day Analia was hanged. He recalled his friend's bitterness as well. Would Nathaniel destroy an entire village to exact his vengeance on the Count? He did not want to find out.

Why would Nathaniel choose murder to keep his secret? For that he had no answer, but he would take no chances. He would not risk his life and put Lillia through the hell of sorrow accompanied with losing a husband if he could prevent it. He loved her and vowed to protect her. No power of the Craft would save them if he did not heed his father's warning. For the first time in his life, Michael felt the urgency to live for this life and make sure he and Lillia grew old together. If Nathaniel tried to eliminate him, Michael would have his answer as to how much his old friend had changed.

His heart pounded as they finally arrived home. Stephen was coming from the field when he saw them.

"Stephen, find Lord Reinard and tell him to come here at once. I must speak to him," said Michael. "Peter, see me in the barn when you take care of the horses." Both servants went about their orders as Michael ran to where the animals were kept.

Reinard arrived with Stephen twenty minutes later. Michael and Peter carried two lambs from the rest of the livestock. "I came as soon as Stephen found me. Is something wrong?" asked Reinard.

"Yes," Michael replied. He turned to Peter. "I need both these lambs bled, then skinned and prepared for dinner this evening."

Peter nodded as he looked at his young master. This was by far the most gruesome task Michael ever asked of him, but one look told Peter he was quite serious. He took both the lambs and walked away to carry out the order.

"Let us go to the terrace; there is much to tell." Michael motioned to the stone steps leading to where he and Lillia preferred to take their tea. They settled at the table.

"What do you remember about Nathaniel?" asked Michael.

Reinard was silent as he considered Michael's question. "Both you and Nathaniel were very meticulous boys for your age. At thirteen years old, which is when I last saw Nathaniel, you were calculating and methodical. You were born to be great men of the Craft, and were walking that path. You have become as great in your learning as your father hoped. You are a very calculating and precise student of alchemy as well. I imagine Nathaniel is just as calculating and precise."

"I encountered strange things on our trip. When we arrived in Wildemere to visit Nafaria, I felt a presence that masked everything about the castle in a dark film. William must have sensed the same thing, because he was visibly upset the entire time we were there. He would not stop crying, he could barely eat. His temperature at times was higher than normal and I almost thought he had a fever coming on. He was only calm when I was with him. Even the princess, who is not of the Craft, noticed things were not right. She gave Lillia and me a tour of the rose garden to talk to us about it. I have confirmed that Nathaniel is in possession of the Grimoire Macabre and is in the grip of the god of blood."

Reinard's face lost all expression. "Does Nafaria know?"

"I am sure she does not. It is best for her not to know at this point. Nathaniel loves her and would never harm her."

"What of their children?" asked Reinard.

"They are another reason I do not want Nafaria to know. She will teach the girls what my mother taught her. They are not a threat to him. If they were to leave, Nathaniel may harm them. It is best to see what happens. Also, there is Nina and Andrew to consider. She is pregnant."

Reinard gave a look of surprise. Michael went on. "When I was in the castle, I followed Nathaniel and overheard him speaking to the flames of a great fire. This fire must be how the god of blood reveals himself. He gave Nathaniel instruction to make Rohn believe Lian was personally responsible for Susanna's death. I told Nina to be careful and make sure she and Andrew watch out for Rohn."

"It seems there is much to think on," replied Reinard.

"There is still more. My father visited me last night. He told me to protect myself and help Nafaria when the time came. He said I 'will live to see evil times come and go from Nereheim'. He insinuated I will be needed in the future. We need to ready Denholm Glen and Illith for a catastrophe that is coming."

"What kind of catastrophe?" asked Reinard.

"I do not know for certain. My father gave me a clue as to how to protect ourselves from Nathaniel. The ancients used a blood ritual where they sacrificed a lamb and spread its blood over the doorposts of their homes to make the death angel pass by. He alluded to this ritual. We must spread blood over the doorposts of our homes. We need to convince everyone in the village to do the same," said Michael.

"You are sure you saw the Grimoire Macabre?" asked Reinard.

"Nathaniel had a book the flames referred to as the 'Grimoire'. It contained the blackest rituals and incantations I have ever seen. What else could it be?" replied Michael.

Reinard sighed and shook his head. "The Grimoire Macabre was only supposed to be a dark legend. Many of the Craft have never even heard of it. What other icons are out there if it exists?"

"Perhaps these legends of the Craft exist because those icons once existed, or still do. I am sure the sacred bell of Herron is somewhere as well. We must get ready. Go home, select some male lambs and slaughter them. Drain the blood and cover your doorposts with it. We must convince each of the villagers to do the same. It seems Denholm Glen will have lamb for dinner tonight."

"I will send out my servants to take care of the villagers. Do not worry Michael. YAHWEH has kept you safe this long. He will not fail us now," said Reinard as he pulled his son in law into his arms.

"We must leave for Illith to warn Count Deveraux. My father would not have warned me about Illith if Nathaniel were not planning on destroying that village as well," said Michael.

"Why destroy Illith? Many of the villagers are openly distrustful of the Craft after the whole affair with Lord and Lady Saintclaire. Count Deveraux has only strengthened their resolve," said Reinard.

"Perhaps there are people there who will listen," said Michael.

"In order for us to cover everything, we must enlist the aid of the other village elders. I will speak with Lord Luxton and tell him about the message you received. He already suspected that transcendence would bring times like this to Nereheim. He will embrace such a grim message and make sure the village responds appropriately. When I return, I suggest you and I ride as hard as we can to Illith and try to convince Count Deveraux calamity is coming," said Reinard.

"I hope we are able to convince someone there. We will not make it there and back. We will have to spend the night. I suggest we bring a flask of blood with us just in case of emergency," said Michael.

"That is the very thing the son of Jason Mauldon would think of. We should bring two; one for each of us to carry. We will leave as soon as I return." Reinard made his way to his horse and took off toward the village. Michael went to find Lillia and tell her their plan.

He found her in the bedroom unpacking from the trip. William lay in his cradle gurgling contentedly. He crept up to her and lightly touched her shoulder. She turned and looked at him. He reached out and gently wiped her cheek where a few teardrops fell. Smiling, he pulled her toward him. "Your father and I will need to go soon," said Michael. He saw her curious expression and explained. "We need to ride to Illith to try and convince Count Deveraux of what is about to happen and to prepare the village and the outlying landowners in his district."

"I understand why it needs to be you. Perhaps the Count will listen to the one man the message was given to," said Lillia with a sigh.

"That is my hope. However, I am not blind to the fact the people of Illith still distrust those of the Craft after what happened with the Saintclaire family and Count Vedan. There are still those that believe the lie Vedan shouted out when he accused Lady Cassandra. There is no way she would have done such a thing, but some people will believe anything," said Michael quietly.

"Some people will never see reason. That is what I am afraid of. You and father will kill yourselves riding out to convince people who will never listen to you, and risk your lives if you stay overnight and no one takes you in," said Lillia.

"I have faith YAHWEH will provide a contingency. There is always at least one person willing to listen. Those rebuilding the Saintclaire manor may heed the warning," replied Michael.

"I hope so. At any rate, be careful. Remember you have a young wife and son that need you desperately." Lillia kissed his cheek. He kissed her back.

"How could I forget?" he asked. He looked down and put his hand on William's cheek. The child responded with a giggle and reached for his fingers. Michael reached into his pocket and pulled out a satin sack with a drawstring on the top.

"When we were in Rowall, I found something for you," Michael handed her the sack.

Lillia opened it and pulled out an amethyst crystal two inches long and an inch thick. It was set in a delicate gold chain.

"This crystal is amethyst, your birthstone. I would like you to wear it at all times, Lillia. Never take it off. It will hide you from those seeking you by the Craft." Michael produced another cloth sack and opened it and pulled out a diamond crystal. "This stone is diamond, William's birthstone. He also must wear this."

Michael put the chain gently around his neck and tucked the crystal into William's shirt. She pulled the crystal over her head and let it drop to her chest. It was a lovely piece of jewelry. She looked at Michael and asked, "What about you?"

Michael pulled a crystal from his shirt. It was a rich blue color. Lillia recognized it as sapphire. "My father gave me this crystal when I turned ten years old. However, as you well know, I have not worn it constantly." Michael winked at her.

"Thank you. It is beautiful. I will always wear it." Lillia put her arms around him and kissed him gently.

"I am off. Your father will be here soon," said Michael as he left the room. Lillia sighed and went back to her task at hand.

Reinard rode to Lord Luxton's manor and was shown to the great room. Bennett entered moments later with a book in his hand.

"Lord Sallen, I was told you were waiting for me. To what do I owe the pleasure of your visit?" asked Bennett in greeting. He asked his question calmly, for it seemed Reinard was agitated and in a hurry.

"Michael Mauldon went to visit his sister Nafaria and her husband Nathaniel Stone in Wildemere two days ago. He took Lillia and little William with him, as he planned a longer visit. While he was there, William was so upset he did nothing but cry. They headed home the next morning. While they stayed overnight in Rowall, Michael was visited by his father with a warning that Denholm Glen and Illith will be destroyed. I have kept a careful record of the stars for this year, and last night was a night of transcendence. The stories I have heard only occurred along the Anenderes River. This is the first time I know of that someone saw a person they knew was deceased so far from the river," said Reinard.

"Perhaps during certain phases of transcendence one can appear to whoever they wish, wherever they may be. Or maybe there is another reason for Jason to be able to appear to Michael," replied Bennett. His brows knitted into the pensive look he wore when thinking on a puzzle that was hard to decipher.

"Jason instructed Michael on how to protect the villages from a coming disaster," said Reinard.

"What disaster?" asked Bennett.

"Jason did not say. He may not have known exactly what was going to happen and was warning his son to protect him," replied Reinard. He went on with the instructions Michael gave him. "Michael said this ritual was used in the sacred writings of the Craft. You must spread the word here. Michael and I are riding to Illith to warn Count Deveraux."

"So, you believe this warning should be taken seriously," said Bennett. There was no mockery in his question.

"In life, when have you known Jason Mauldon to be wrong? If he found a way to rise from the dead and give warning that might save our lives, how foolish would we be to spurn it?" There was a distinct edge to Reinard's voice.

"Your point is well made. I will do what you say. If nothing happens, it will merely look as though we are senile old men running after a ghost story. However, if something happened, I would feel even more a fool for not listening," replied Bennett.

"That is my thought as well. It may be a fool's errand to run to Count Deveraux to warn him. However, Jason specifically included Illith. There must be a reason why," said Reinard.

"Go quickly. I will handle things here." Bennett sighed. "If only Sebastian Cavanaugh were here to help."

"I am sure Ian Keller will rise to the occasion," said Reinard as he left the house, leaving the care of the village to Bennett.

⁺⁺⁺⁺⁺⁺

When Reinard returned, Michael mounted his horse and turned to Peter. "Make sure the blood covers all entrances to the manor and the stable areas. When you finish, round up all the servants and make them come in for the day. No one is to be out at night for the next three days. Keep replenishing the blood over the doors until the catastrophe has passed. Remind Lord Luxton and the other villagers to do the same."

"When will you return?" asked Peter.

"We are only staying the night in Illith. We will be back tomorrow before sunset," replied Michael.

"The God who watches over you will bring you safely home," replied Peter. He took a leather bag and carefully strapped the pack to the horse

Michael sat upon. "Maia wanted to make sure you had a supply of wild turkey and cheese for dinner—and of course, yeast rolls."

"Tell her we are grateful for her thoughtfulness," said Michael.

Michael's eyes moistened as he touched the pack. The last time he left this home in haste, Nafaria was given yeast rolls by Sylvia for the family. Before another painful memory played in his mind, He pricked the sides of his horse and started down the pathway at a steady gait, with Reinard following behind.

CHAPTER 14

Bennett went to the barn where he found one of his servants feeding the sheep and goats. He sighed as he watched the care his servant took with his task.

"Jacob, please come here." Jacob turned and smiled as he walked toward Bennett.

"Yes, my lord. What do you require?" asked Jacob.

"I have a gruesome task that needs to be done by sunset tonight." Bennett quickly outlined the instructions Reinard left with him. Jacob's eyes widened as he listened, but then simply bowed his head when his master finished speaking.

"Yes, my lord," replied Jacob.

"It is a very earnest task, for a very earnest time." Bennett sighed. "I need to find Ian Keller, so I will be gone quite a while. Please have everything ready by sunset."

"It will be done before you return," replied Jacob with confidence.

"Thank you, Jacob. If anyone asks what you are doing, tell them to spread the word and have everyone in the village do the same."

"My lord, what is coming?"

"Something I cannot begin to explain," replied Bennett grimly as he retrieved his horse and rode for the village.

⸻ ✦ ⸻

Bennett was grateful the Kellers showed up when they did to take over the apothecary shop after Malcom and Nathaniel left. Though not of the Craft, Julia was very knowledgeable with the herbs and plants they harvested and sold to the villagers. She was especially skilled with lavender, one of the most popular plants in the area. Ian was hard working and aided as village messenger when needed. He filled the void Sebastian Cavanaugh left behind when he and Alana Deveraux left Denholm Glen. He slowed his horse and pulled the reins around a post in front of the shop and went inside.

Ian turned when he heard the door open and smiled brightly. He put the bottles in his hand on a shelf. "Lord Luxton, what can I do for you today?" he asked.

Bennett smiled in return. "I have a very important task I need help with that needs to be done by sunset."

"What is it you need?" Bennett heard Julia's voice as she walked into the room, carrying a bundle of Rosemary plants.

"Good day, Julia. I need to borrow your husband for a while."

"Oh? He seems to find his way out of daily shop duties whenever you stop by," she said with a smile.

"It is an important task. Lord Sallen visited me less than an hour ago with the most amazing story. I have no doubt it is true. We must ready the village by sunset for a great catastrophe."

"That does not leave us much time," said Ian.

"No, it does not," agreed Bennett.

"What do we need to do?" asked Julia.

Bennett repeated the instructions he was given. He looked at the couple carefully. "Attention to this instruction is well warranted. We have been given an urgent message from the most arcane place. We must heed it."

"Where would that be?" asked Ian. He was respectful, but dubious as to the instructions.

"I will tell you only because you were in Lord Saintclaire's employ, and I daresay you knew him to give you some almost eccentric commands. However, when you saw the wisdom in his instructions, you learned to trust his intuition. Trust this the exact same way. I understand it takes a lot of faith to believe it. However, Jason Mauldon would not have sent a message from beyond the grave if it were not important," said Bennett.

Ian flinched at the mention of Jason's name and nodded his head. "I agree," he finally said. He turned to Julia. "Select a lamb from the village market and take care of things here. I will help Lord Luxton convince the other villagers to do the same."

Julia nodded in assent. "It is a gruesome task, but I will get it done. I will also help spread the word when I finish."

"Thank you both for your efforts here. You two have been witness to some of the darkest times of this village's history. I would not blame you if you decided to leave after today." said Bennett.

"We are thankful to have a home here, and will do what it takes to protect it," replied Ian.

✦✦✦✦✦

Bennett returned home two hours later. There were two lambs hanging over basins filled with blood, each one large enough for the entire household. Jacob squatted over the basins evaluating his progress.

Bennett looked at the blood pooling in the basins. He grimaced at the inky dark liquid. He did not doubt Michael's word, but wished there were a less barbaric means of protection. Why did YAHWEH require blood? Reinard insisted: it must be blood; it must come from a lamb, and the best of the flock. Perhaps that was standard knowledge among those of the Craft, but he could not fathom why it was necessary. Bennett would follow the advice he was given; to the letter of the law Michael Mauldon held sacred.

"This should be more than enough for the manor, Jacob. Take the lambs to the cook, and cover the doors and windows while the meal is prepared. When you finish, call the servants in for the evening," said Bennett.

"Yes, my lord," replied Jacob. Bennett turned to leave, but Jacob spoke again. "My lord?"

"Yes Jacob?"

"Will the rest of Denholm Glen be safe?" Jacob looked up from the ground where he squatted.

"I expect so. I have confidence in Michael's instructions. As long as we follow them, we will be fine."

"How have the villagers responded to this news? Will they go along with it?"

Bennett remembered reading a story once about another old man who was placed in this very position. He was given a simple task and told to warn the people of coming disaster. In the end, only his family was saved[22]. Was history doomed to repeat itself? What could he say to convince people this would save their lives?

"My lord?"

Bennett looked at his servant and finally shook his head. "There is nothing I can say that will convince anyone. I can only provide the information, and follow the instructions myself. In the end, the choice for redemption is theirs."

"What of Count Deveraux?" Jacob was only twelve years old when Ana was poisoned by Lya, but as he grew older, he knew the Count distrusted those of the Craft.

---

[22]   Genesis 6-7

"We must trust that Lord Sallen and Michael Mauldon can convince the Count to believe what they have to say," replied Bennett as he looked into the afternoon sky.

--------++++++--------

Reinard and Michael rode hard for Illith. The countryside flattened into open fields as the village drew near. Michael focused ahead, glancing at the advancing sun, willing it to stop in its tracks. He read once in the sacred writings about how the sun was stopped for a whole day[23]. If only YAHWEH would do that again. He prayed silently that the sun would halt its path across the sky, but it moved onward, marching to its destination—the horizon. His heart beat fast as he followed Reinard to Count Deveraux's manor. It looked the size of his estate in Denholm Glen, surrounded by fields. The stained glass windows reminded him of the Grand Cathedral in Wildemere. They rode up a stone path and quickly dismounted their horses. Reinard grabbed the flask that held the blood from his horse as Michael followed him to the entrance. A servant greeted them right away.

"Gentlemen, to what does Count Deveraux owe the honor of your visit?" he asked.

"We need to speak to the Count immediately on an urgent matter," said Reinard.

The young servant regarded the pensive look on both men. "Please follow me."

They followed the young servant into the study. The Count sat at his desk with a parchment in his hand. He looked up as Reinard and Michael entered the room. If he was surprised to see his two visitors, he held it carefully in check. He rose and stood behind his desk.

"Lord Reinard Sallen," said the Count. He glanced at Michael but did not address him. "To what do I owe this visit?" The question was more of a demand.

---

[23]   Joshua 10:12-14

"Count Deveraux, we have reason to believe a great catastrophe is coming to Illith," said Reinard. "We have a strange but urgent request."

"What is it?" he asked.

"Please allow us to spread this blood over the doorposts and windows of your manor." Reinard's tone was matter of fact—his facial expression serious.

"Is this some kind of dark ritual designed by those of the Craft?" There was suspicion in the Count's voice.

"Yes. It is a blood ritual designed to protect those who live within its perimeters. Please instruct each member of the village to do the same," said Reinard.

"What do we need protection from? We live a simple life here in Illith; we are a threat to no one."

"We do not know exactly what, but it is meant to save us," replied Reinard.

The Count did not try to hide the skeptical look on his face "Lord Reinard, surely you must understand how ridiculous and barbaric this request is. Why would I take blood and do this thing? You cannot even tell me what is coming!" demanded the Count.

"This information was given from someone I trust. Evil is coming and we may not survive the night. Please, for once, put your disdain of the Craft aside and let the people in your district be saved!" pleaded Reinard.

"I will not be saved by any design that claimed the life of my daughter! Take your blood and spill it elsewhere!" The Count's voice turned to an angry roar. Michael saw rage showing on his father in law's face. He stepped toward the Count.

"Count Deveraux, listen to reason. Something terrible is coming to Illith. It will be a darkness that you cannot prevent without this blood. Do not let the past cloud your responsibility to the future. If you do not do this, you will die." Michael's calm demeanor silenced both men. Reinard noted how much he sounded like Jason.

"I have heard enough, go now!" The Count raised his arm and pointed to the door of his study.

Reinard bowed his head and sighed. "We cannot force you to make the choice. If you will still be so stubborn, you will destroy your entire household along with this village tonight." He turned and walked out of the room with Michael following after.

⸺⸺⸺ ·‹‹‹‹‹› ⸺⸺⸺

The servant followed them to their horses. "Lord Sallen, is what you say true? Will Illith be destroyed?" he asked.

"Yes," said Reinard with a sigh.

The young man looked at the large house. His whole life and livelihood was tied to every brick and piece of wood. The sun glinted off the stained glass windows. His father came to work for Count Vedan when he was a little boy. His entire boyhood was spent on this property doing one task or another. He chose to stay after Count Deveraux arrived. He knew the Count distrusted those of the Craft; many in Illith did. However, he felt the earnestness and sanity of the two men before him.

"People in the village are whispering about the caretaker of the Saintclaire manor. He bled lambs for the past three days and is doing what you suggest. What must I do?"

"The Count made it clear he does not wish to follow our instruction. If you defy him, you will need new employment."

"If I do nothing, then I will die. I need to try." The young man looked at Reinard—determined in the midst of his fear.

"What is your name?" asked Reinard.

"Jonathan, sir."

Reinard gave him the flask. "I cannot bear the thought of innocent people dying for one man's foolishness. I have known the Count for many years, and when his mind is made up, it is vanity to try and change it. We will go into the village to warn others. Follow my instructions; save as many as you can."

"I have heard the Countess speak of another daughter. What of the Viscountess Alana?"

Reinard remembered Alana Deveraux. If not for her, Lillia might not be alive today. "What of her?"

"She and her companion, Sebastian Cavanaugh, are traveling abroad. What if she returns in the night?"

"We can only pray she does not return until tomorrow." replied Reinard quietly.

"What is coming, sir?" asked Jonathan.

"A great and terrible storm," replied Reinard as they mounted their horses and rode toward Illith.

⊹⊱•⊰⊹

Jonathan watched the two men ride toward the village. He looked at the flask in his hands. He did not know either of them, but Count Deveraux evidently did. They seemed to be practical men. It may be a gruesome task, but Jonathan trusted his instincts. If these men said covering the door and window frames of their homes with blood would save them, it probably would.

He went to the stable and sat down on a bench. He put the flask down next to him, putting his hands in his head. He was about to defy his master. However, this was not what weighed on his mind. The question he faced was how to complete the task without the Count's knowledge. His response to their suggestion was obviously one these men expected. They did not spend time trying to convince him of the truth to their claim. They simply stated their business, asked him to consider it, and moved on.

He wondered about this new Count and the circumstances surrounding his arrival. He only knew that originally Count Deveraux oversaw the district that held Denholm Glen, and that a tragedy took the life of his older daughter, Ana. He heard the Countess speak of another daughter, Alana, frequently. However, she never appeared. When asked, the Countess simply said Alana chose to travel abroad, taking her studies from cities and villages all over Nereheim. He suspected not even the Countess knew where her own daughter was.

Jonathan remembered when Count Vedan was taken into custody and later executed for conspiring against Lord and Lady Saintclaire. Even this action from the king himself was not enough to make the villagers understand they made a mistake in stoning the horse master and his wife. It was as if there was a pact between the villagers and the Count to forget the past, and never trust anyone of the Craft.

It was time to get to work. He would be faithful to this task, but wise as well. He rose and went inside the stable and found a smaller bucket. He dumped out some water the bucket held and went back outside. He carefully poured some of the blood into the bucket and hid the flask under the bench. Finding a rag in the stable, he took the other bucket and walked back to the house.

⋅⋅✦✦✦✦⋅⋅

The Count came out of the house as Jonathan was covering the windowpanes with the blood. He stood stock still, taking in the scene. "Jonathan! What is the meaning of this?" he shouted.

The Count marched over to Jonathan and grabbed the blood-soaked rag from his hand. Finally, Jonathan looked at him. He noted the seething expression on the Count's face.

"I specifically told Lord Sallen I wanted no part of this madness. Why would you defy my wish?"

"Lord Sallen left this blood as a means of protection for us. I am trying to protect you. Do you not want to see your daughter again?" asked Jonathan.

"My daughter is dead because of the Craft!" shouted the Count in reply.

"I was referring to the Viscountess Alana, my lord. She could return any time from her travels. Have you so easily forgotten your other daughter?"

The Count became mute. In his rage, he completely forgot about his youngest daughter. Alana certainly made it easy for him to. She rode out of his life after defying him in public with the son of a trusted noble in Denholm Glen and was barely heard from. God alone knew where she was.

"When I see Alana again, it will not be on account of some barbaric ritual claiming to stand between my life and some unnamed evil Lord Sallen fears. Get some water and wash this abomination from my house."

"I will not." Jonathan's tone was steady and full of conviction.

"You dare defy my direct command?"

"I will do whatever it takes to protect your life, my lord. If you want this blood washed from your house, have someone else do it." Jonathan turned and walked away.

"You will find employment elsewhere in the morning, Jonathan."

Jonathan hunched his shoulders, but kept walking toward the stable. "I suppose I shall, my lord."

The Count turned and stormed into the manor to find another servant.

⊹⊹⊹

Jonathan walked along a path behind the stable next to a stream running through the Count's fields. He squatted down and washed his hands in the water. It felt cool to his touch and was clear as glass. The only color the water held was the tinge of red where he washed his hands.

The only way left to protect the household was to cover the stable with the blood that was left. He would wait until the end of the day to do it. He would talk to each servant privately and tell them about the two strangers and their warning. The servants would have to make their own choice whether they would live or die. As he let the water run over his fingers, Jonathan became convinced there was no other way.

He rose from his place by the stream and walked to the stable. Christina walked toward him. "Count Deveraux is furious with you, Jonathan. Is it true you will be leaving in the morning? What is this business of the blood on the doorposts?" she asked. Her questions came one after another, but Jonathan grabbed her arm and ignored all of them.

"Christina, we must talk. The Count has disregarded an urgent request from two nobles who rode here from Denholm Glen meant to save our lives," said Jonathan.

"What do you mean?" He heard suspicion in her voice.

"They say something terrible will happen to Illith this night. Lord Sallen gave me the blood and instructions. I suspected the Count would be angry about covering the manor with it, so I kept some aside and will cover the stable doorposts and window panes around sunset. I need you to help me warn the other servants to go into the stable before dark so they will be saved. We need to gather anyone willing to come. I thought we could at least save the horses as well."

Christina looked at the empty bucket in Jonathan's hand. She saw the dried blood beginning to flake on the sides. "You are asking me to go against the Count's wishes and defy him as you did." She looked him in the eye. "I have lived my whole life in this manor, Jonathan. If not for the Countess and her kindness, I would have been turned out when

Count Vedan was taken by the royal guard. How can you ask me to do such a thing?"

"I have lived my whole life on this land as well Christina! Count Deveraux may be rash in his judgment of those of the Craft, but I still care about what happens to him! I could never live with myself if people die some horrible death when I could have prevented it. I will fight Count Deveraux for his life if I have to. Lord Sallen and Michael Mauldon are certain this is the only way to survive. Please, help me get the servants to see reason and come into the stable tonight."

Christina saw earnestness in Jonathan's eyes. "You believe what they say? Is it the only way to survive?" she asked.

Jonathan nodded his head. "These men were earnest, and reasonable. There is no reason for them to make up such a story. If they believe this is the only way, then surely something terrible is coming."

"I was not here when these men came to Count Deveraux, but I trust you. I will help you. Perhaps even the Countess can be made to see reason. However, she asked me to run an errand in the village. I was coming to get a horse. I will help as soon as I return." Christina went to the stable and mounted one of the horses. Jonathan watched her ride for the village and then headed to the field in search of the other laborers.

At the edge of the field, he saw the particular cluster of men he was looking for. They saw him before he greeted them.

"Jonathan, what are you doing out here?" asked one of the laborers. He stood up straight, with his hoe at his side. He looked to be the oldest of the group.

"Good afternoon, Samuel. There is no easy way to say this, so I will come right to the point. Count Deveraux was visited today by Lord Sallen and Michael Mauldon with an urgent request that we spread blood over the manor to protect us from an unknown evil that is coming. The Count refused, so I told Lord Sallen I would see it done. The Count found me after I was done, and was furious. He ordered the blood to be washed off the manor, and I may be looking for a new place to live in the morning."

The laborers looked at each other with questioning glances.

"Why would you do such a thing, Jonathan?" asked Samuel. "You know the Count holds special disdain for those of the Craft. Why would you jeopardize your life and livelihood?"

"I am doing this to protect the Count, his manor, and everyone under his care. I promised Lord Sallen I would try. I saved some of the blood and hid it. When it is near sunset, I will cover the doorposts and windowpanes of the stable and will spend my last night there. I am asking any servants that wish to join me to come into the stable before dark tonight. I do not know what else to do," replied Jonathan.

"You are asking us all to defy the Count. What if these men are wrong? Then we will be unemployed as well," replied one of the younger farmhands.

"I have heard the village elders speak of Michael Mauldon. He is known for his wisdom and study of arcane knowledge. If he says something terrible will happen, I believe him. This is to save our lives! If you will not listen, you will die the same way the Count will," replied Jonathan.

Instinctively, the others turned to Samuel. He was the oldest of the field laborers, and everyone looked to him for guidance. He leaned against his hoe and was quiet for a few moments.

"I came with Count Deveraux from Denholm Glen. I remember when the Viscountess Ana was killed. My Uncle Jerome overheard Lya Bernard and Ana in the garden and reported to the Count what he heard after Ana was poisoned. Lord Sallen was afraid persecution against those of the Craft would break out, so he warned the Mauldon family and Malcom Stone to leave. Lord Sallen was not wrong then," said Samuel.

"Then you will come tonight?" asked Jonathan.

"I will, and so will my wife," replied Samuel. The others looked at Samuel.

"I will heed the warning," replied Samuel as they looked at him. "If Lord Sallen is wrong, then I will also be looking for new employment in the morning."

"I must keep spreading the word. I hope to see you all after sunset," said Jonathan.

The group watched him as he walked back toward the manor. "Samuel, are you mad? If the Count finds out we plotted against him, we will all be looking for other employment," said one of the younger laborers.

"David, did you not hear what Jonathan said? Lord Sallen provided the blood for this himself. He knows something we do not, and is trying to protect us. My wife has heard talk of the people in Denholm Glen doing the same thing. The caretaker at the Saintclaire manor has been bleeding lambs as well. These men may not know exactly what will happen, but they are trying to help us. It may be that we will have to save the Count from himself," said Samuel.

"I have never known the Count to be wrong either," replied David. "I will stay silent about this, for your sake, Samuel. However, I do not think anything is coming. What could possibly happen in Illith?"

"That is exactly what I said when Analia Bernard was hanged and Lord and Lady Saintclaire were stoned," replied Samuel. He walked away from the group with his hoe in his hand.

"Where are you going?" asked David.

"I am going to find my wife. If evil is coming, I want to spend the last few hours of sunlight with her." Samuel headed toward the manor.

⋯⋯✦✦✦⋯⋯

Michael and Reinard rode into the village. They stopped before a great stone fountain in the village square. It was much like any stone piece set in a village or on an estate. It was there to give water as much as to provide aesthetic beauty. This was the scene of Lord and Lady Saintclaire's last moments together. Michael gave a shudder.

"Stay with our horses. I will go speak with the magistrate. Perhaps he will see reason in our fantastic tale," said Reinard. Michael nodded as they both dismounted their horses. He watched Reinard as he walked toward a distinguished stone structure covered with ivy. It reminded him of Elias Wheaton's antiquarian library in Wildemere. Michael sighed and sat down on the edge of the fountain. What could Reinard say to convince the magistrate to believe them?

"You have not yet resisted to the point of shedding your blood[24]", a voice whispered. Michael saw a flash and Lord and Lady Saintclaire huddled together while villagers pummeled them with stones.

Tears rolled down his face as the grisly scene played before him. Lady Saintclaire was accused of a vicious crime she never dreamed of. Lord Saintclaire died for the love of his wife. Though these people were responsible for the deaths of two people he loved, he could not stand in the middle of the village and let them go on about their daily lives when he knew disaster was coming.

Michael climbed on the edge of the fountain and called out, "People of Illith listen to me!"

Some of the villagers stopped their activities to hear his shout at the fountain. Michael went on. "You are in danger! This village will be destroyed if you do not cover your door posts and window panes with the blood of an unblemished lamb! Protect yourselves—cover your dwellings with the blood!"

A group gathered as he continued his warning. At the mention of blood, they became angry. A woman bent down to pick up a rock at her

---

[24] Hebrews 12:4

feet. "We do not wish to hear of the gruesome rituals of those of the Craft! We have suffered enough due to witchcraft and sorcery! Leave us!" she shouted as she threw the rock. It hit Michael square in the chest. Other villagers did the same.

✦✦✦✦✦

Christina rode into the village, and saw a young man standing on the edge of the fountain. A group was throwing rocks at him. She heard his shouts about blood and pleas for the crowd to listen. He looked to be about her age. "So, this must be Michael Mauldon," she thought. Her errand for the Countess would wait. She shook her head and rode into the crowd. She positioned her horse in front of Michael.

"Stay this madness! Will you have innocent blood on your hands the way your elders did? Go back to your duties, leave this man alone!" she shouted as she gave the sternest look she could muster. As the crowd dissipated, she hopped down from her horse. Grabbing Michael by his cloak, she pulled him off the edge of the fountain. He barely landed on the ground with both feet under him. "What on earth do you think you are doing?" Christina demanded.

"I was trying to warn these people of a coming disaster. You need to hear my warning as well," replied Michael.

"I have heard the warning already. You are Michael Mauldon the son of Jason Mauldon, correct?" she asked.

"Yes."

"You are well known all over western Nereheim for your wisdom. It is said to be unmatched against any with the possible exception of the new Court Adviser to King Catalane. Where is the wisdom I have heard so much about at this moment?" she demanded.

"Along with prudence, it seems to have taken a sabbatical." Michael heard the disapproving tone of his father-in-law. Christina turned around and faced Reinard. He bowed slightly to her. "I thank you for your wisdom in grabbing my son in law before he could be stoned the way his predecessors were." He looked at Michael. "What were you trying to accomplish?"

Michael sighed. He thought he was being bold, but in light of such rebuke, he shrugged his shoulders. "I had a vision of Lord and Lady Saintclaire. It was the day they were stoned, in front of this fountain. I guess I was just overcome with emotion. I want these people to listen—and be saved."

"I do not wish to go home and explain to my daughter that her husband was stoned to death because he was overcome with grief for the people he tried to warn. The magistrate is unyielding as well. We need to find another way," replied Reinard.

"These people will not listen. You do not live here, and you are already distrusted by Count Deveraux. The Count's distrust is matched only by those here in Illith. They care nothing for greater wisdom. Those of the Craft have been spurned here for the last ten years. The people who will listen are busy at this moment, doing what you suggested to the Count. It may not seem like much, but some will be spared in Illith if the doom you speak of comes to pass," said Christina. She climbed back on her horse. "Please follow me. I will take you to a safe place for the evening."

Christina rode out of the village with Reinard and Michael following. The countryside was flat and there were fewer clusters of trees. A brook flowed parallel to the road. A large structure loomed in the distance.

Michael remembered this area. He was only here for one summer, but he never forgot the Saintclaire manor. Christina turned down the path, moving toward the half-finished structure. A great production lay before them. Men were covering three different buildings with a dark liquid. After a moment, Michael realized it was blood.

"Before you came to Count Deveraux, I heard servants whispering about the caretaker of Saintclaire manor covering the whole place with blood. I see now that was embellished a bit. He seems to only be concerned with the doorposts and windowpanes of each building," said Christina as she looked at the structures before them.

"Who is this caretaker?" asked Reinard.

"His name is Samson. The older villagers remember him as one of Lord Saintclaire's trusted tenants. He was thought to be living in the mountains of the West, but he came forward the past autumn to petition Count Deveraux for the task of rebuilding the manor. I am sure it was a great relief for the Count, for he was commissioned for the task by the king. However, until Samson came along, no one in the village would have any part of the project. It was almost as if the village thought the whole place was cursed," said Christina.

"What of you? Will you not be shunned for your willingness to help us?" asked Michael.

"I care not what people think of me. My mother taught me to do what was right no matter the cost. Doing what is right often falls on the same side as great wisdom and discernment. I would rather be known for those things than for cowardice," replied Christina.

As she spoke, a large man with dark hair and even darker eyes came toward them. He moved with purpose, determined to meet a deadline. He looked puzzled at the sight of strangers on his land. He greeted Christina.

"Good day Christina. What have you here?" he asked.

"Good day Samson. I have brought you two strangers who came to Count Deveraux to convince him to take on the very task that keeps you busy," said Christina. Michael and Reinard came down off their horses.

Samson looked carefully at Michael. After a moment, he laughed and clapped him on his back. "You are Michael Mauldon, son of Jason Mauldon of Denholm Glen! So, it seems the question I have always pondered has been answered. You did learn to ride!" He pulled Michael toward him in a hearty embrace.

"It is good to see you, Samson. When I first returned to Denholm Glen, Ian told me you took up permanent residence in the mountains. What exactly is going on here?" asked Michael.

"Many things," replied Samson. He looked at Reinard. Michael quickly introduced them.

"I do not know if you ever met my father-in-law, Lord Reinard Sallen," said Michael.

"I have not, but Ian told me a fantastic tale about you, your daughter, and the Viscountess Alana Deveraux." Samson put out his hand.

"Fantastic as it may sound, every word is true. Lillia is alive today because Alana had the courage to defy her father and save her," replied Reinard as he shook Samson's hand.

"Let us take your horses to the stable master, and I will tell you how I came to be here," said Samson.

"Gentlemen, thank you for your endeavor here. I must go," said Christina. Michael grabbed her horse's reins before she could leave.

"Where will you go?" he asked.

"If this is to be my last day on earth, I wish to spend it with the man I love. I promised Jonathan I would help him after I returned from my errand for the Countess Deveraux."

"May YAHWEH keep you all safe tonight," said Michael.

"May he also keep you safe," said Christina as Michael let go of the reins. "Good luck gentlemen!" She called out as she rode toward the main road.

"Christina is one of the few villagers left in Illith who truly respect those of the Craft. Rhea Calloway was one of her closest friends, but she refused to believe Count Vedan's accusations against Lady Cassandra. She ran from the village in tears while they stoned her," said Samson as they walked toward the stable.

"So, how are you here?" Michael could not wait to hear Samson's story.

"In early September of last year, I had a vision of Lord Saintclaire when I was in the mountains. He told me to come back to Illith and rebuild the manor. He said it needed to be ready if ever Nadia wished to return," said Samson.

"Early September? Would you say it was the fifth of September?" asked Michael. Reinard looked at him.

"Yes, I would say so," said Samson. "Does that mean something?"

"What are you thinking?" asked Reinard.

"In Donovan's journal about the Anenderes River and transcendence, he mentions that he spoke to people visiting Denholm Glen when he returned. He wrote down new information as he received it. It seems the dead are not tethered to the Anenderes River to deliver messages to the living during transcendence. He also concluded that a period of transcendence, when it began, would end in one year," said Michael.

"So, we can expect these strange occurrences to happen anywhere until September fifth of this year?" asked Reinard.

Michael nodded. "It makes sense. Nafaria claims she heard whispers that sounded like mother before she was aware she was pregnant. One evening, before Queen Susanna's murder, Nafaria claimed mother whispered a warning to her about her children. Others have continued to tell strange tales as they journey through Denholm Glen. I have heard some; the innkeeper has heard many more. Three days ago, I was visited by my father with his warning," said Michael.

"Three days ago?" asked Samson.

"Yes," replied Michael.

"That was the other part of this strange tale I had for you. Lord Saintclaire appeared to me again three days ago, during the fullest moon I have ever seen. He warned me of a disaster that would follow. He did not say when, he only gave instructions and told me to be ready," said Samson.

"Did you warn the Count?" asked Michael.

"I have not had the time to test my patience in such a foolish venture. I instructed the servants to pass on the warning, but no one has believed them. They have treated it as vain babblings from hired hands having nothing better to do than spread gossip," said Samson.

"The Count regarded it as foolishness," said Reinard.

"It is just as well. The Count believes himself to be wiser than the God you serve, Michael. Tomorrow we shall see who is the fool," replied Samson grimly.

⋅⋅✦✦✦⋅⋅

Nathaniel's black cloak swayed in the passageways of the castle as he descended toward the royal crypt. Most knew he kept strange hours, driven by his insight and knowledge. Because of his focus, one would find him in the royal library at odd times, deep in study. The guards and servants alike knew his station as Court Adviser made him one to be feared. When they caught a glimpse of him, people often turned back in the direction they came—just to avoid that black cloak turning in their direction.

He followed the caverns into the open air. One of the caves led to a field that ended at the edge of a very old cemetery. He walked among this resting place many times. He noticed each one buried there had one thing in common: they were all ruthless criminals of Wildemere's past. He found their names listed in the annals of Nereheim's history. They would respond quickly to the bell.

Nathaniel felt cool air on his face. The last glimpse of the sun was seen as it sunk below the horizon. One by one, the brightest stars popped out like little pinpricks in the purple sky.

He shuddered as he opened the gate and stood among the graves. Was this what he truly wanted? Michael was not just his brother-in-law; he was his greatest friend. He was the only person Nathaniel connected with besides Jared. Michael was filled with great knowledge, but in his wisdom he never debased himself by flaunting it. He was a man who lived above reproach. Was this truly the only way?

His mind filled with the image of those three young girls once again. He thought of Jason and Thena and how they were betrayed. He remembered the man who tried to kill Nafaria. Michael would stand in his way of making the mortals of Nereheim pay for their crimes. He would tell Nathaniel vengeance belonged to YAHWEH alone. Those of the Craft were not to seek it on their own.

Nathaniel tightened his fist and quickened his pace. Michael would never see things his way. "Vengeance is not the same as justice. I am here to exact justice," whispered Nathaniel. His resolve held him at the heart of the cemetery.

The moon was bright in the growing darkness. He took an athame from his cloak. With the blade, he carefully cut the palm of his hand. He exhaled sharply while blood trickled from the wound. He counted on his blood to bring forth the worst of the spirits in the cemetery. He took the bell from his cloak and struck it once with the hammer. The chime was soft and hung in the air. A moment later, white wisps swirled toward him. Soon he was surrounded by the mist; he could hear strange whispers and shrieks. Distorted faces appeared before him. They were different from the faces seen on the waves of the Anenderes River. The wind surrounded Nathaniel, whipping his cloak around him. He stood unmoving in the center as he spoke. "Spirits of Nereheim, I call you forth to seek out the villages of Denholm Glen and Illith. Destroy all who live within their borders. Leave no one alive by morning." The swirling wind rose into the sky heading west.

The sun was setting when Lillia looked out the broad window of her bedroom. William lay in his cradle next to the bed. She sat in a chair in the corner with her sketchbook in her lap, a candle burned on a table next to her. Any stranger looking in on her from outside would assume she was in deep thought.

The book was aged not only because it was old; use had worn the life out of its tender binding. Its ink, though fading, was still sharp enough to read. Lillia felt confident the book would outlast her.

It was open to nearly the beginning. She looked at each sketch and read each entry in Michael's careful script once again. She treasured this book even more than the book he wrote for her and gave her on their wedding day. It was the first thing they created together. It comforted her when she was growing up while they were apart. His writing was beautiful, even when they were younger. When most boys were running outside to play, Michael spent his time perfecting his penmanship to match her skill as an artist. When he first discovered her sketching different plants and flowers in the village, he suggested that he provide details about each plant so she could learn more about them. This book was how they became friends.

She glanced outside and drew a deep breath. She was so afraid of what would happen tonight. She had confidence that her home would be safe from all harm. She trusted Michael's words to be true. Ian Keller spent the afternoon going from place to place giving the villagers Lord Luxton's warning, and helping them follow the instructions if they were willing. As far as she knew, everyone heeded the warning, and blood was on every doorpost and windowpane in the village. The villagers also did not allow strangers wandering about at sunset. They were invited to stay for the evening at the closest house that could take them. She did not know what strangers thought of this behavior. She hoped they listened and took advantage of the invitation.

Michael feared a new death angel would be sent by Nathaniel. She hoped the blood would protect them the way it protected the ancients.

Had Nathaniel really changed so much as to destroy the village? Lillia wanted to find it hard to believe, but she remembered her conversation with Michael on the way home from Wildemere. If they had stayed longer, Lillia was certain she would see that Michael was right. He was the brightest young man she ever knew. He surpassed everyone in his knowledge. In her eyes, Michael was sent by YAHWEH himself, and the world was not worthy of him[25].

"Michael is right," Lillia said out loud. Her confidence brought trepidation, for Lillia knew Count Deveraux would not listen. She feared her husband and father would be lost running a fool's errand to save a man who would not see a reason to trust such fantastic instructions from its mysterious source. Count Deveraux lacked the faith needed to believe such a tale.

She heard a soft whimper from the cradle where William lay. She went to the tiny bed and found him stirring from his sleep. His eyes stayed closed, but his whimper grew. She picked him up and nestled him against her chest while massaging his back. He became quiet again, but he clung to her tightly. She kissed him on his forehead and rocked him in her arms.

There was a rustling outside. She looked out the window and saw dark shadows rushing by the window at great speed. She moved closer for a better view. William whimpered once again.

The sky was filled with birds of all kinds. There were large black crows, and even smaller bluebirds and cardinals, all flying in the direction of the mountains. The animals from the stable were restless as well. Their brays and yelps were loud. "It begins," she whispered. She closed her eyes and prayed for them all.

+++++++

The sounds of the birds were not lost on village residents. A blacksmith came to the window and looked outside as the birds flew overhead. A deer passed by the window. "What on earth is going on out there?" he asked.

25   Hebrews 11:38

"What is wrong?" His wife joined him at the window.

"I just saw a deer pass by our window," replied the blacksmith.

"Here in the village square?" she asked.

"I have lived here my entire life. I have never seen a deer come through the center of the village," he replied. A moving figure caught his attention.

"Stay inside."

He ran outside toward a man on horseback.

"Sir, have you a place to stay for the evening?" asked the blacksmith. The rider looked at him.

"I have been traveling all day and was looking for an inn. Is there somewhere close by?" asked the stranger. The blacksmith shook his head.

"The only inn is completely full. Come and stay with my wife and I. Tonight is not a night to be out," replied the blacksmith.

"I would be most grateful, sir," replied the stranger. He climbed off his horse and followed the blacksmith to his home.

"We will take your horse to the stable first and get it settled," said the blacksmith.

The stranger followed his host to the stable. He grimaced as he noted the thick stains on the doorposts, but said nothing.

"I appreciate your hospitality. Normally, it would not bother me to ride late into the evening, but the behavior of the animals has me a little nervous," replied the stranger.

"What kind of behavior?" he asked.

"All the animals seem to be fleeing this area. Rabbits and squirrels are scurrying every which way, and the deer are running toward the mountains. You must have heard the birds just a few minutes ago. They were flying overhead as if to be gone quickly. That was when I decided it was wise to stop for the night."

"I think a storm is coming," replied the blacksmith. They both walked into the house. While his wife saw to the stranger, he went to the window and peered outside once again.

The sun was setting as Jonathan grabbed the bucket from under the bench where he left it. He dipped a piece of cloth into the blood and began covering the doorposts with it. The air was calm, but the moon could be seen. He was thankful for the fading light to see the progress of his task. He willed his hand to be steady. Every minute counted. When the birds took flight, he knew he was running out of time. The animals inside the stable also grew restless. The horses stamped their feet. It would be a long night.

From the corner of his eye, Jonathan caught the yellow light of a torch. Samuel and his wife walked toward him. Relief spread over his face. "Samuel, you startled me. Where are the others?" asked Jonathan.

"I suspect some will be along shortly. I do not know how many. The household is divided over what they should do," replied Samuel.

"The strange behavior of the animals should help them decide," replied Jonathan.

Samuel nodded his head. "Nature knows something for sure. Can you use some help?"

Jonathan held up the bucket. "If you can find a cloth, help me cover the window panes."

Samuel took a corner of his shirt and ripped off a piece. He walked over to Jonathan, dipped the cloth in the bucket, and set to work on the window panes.

The sky was black as Christina stood in front of the great window in the Countess's bedroom. The stars were out, and all was quiet. A shudder ran through her body. She saw the faint glow of light from the stable. Jonathan was already there with whatever servants dared to show up, settling in the animals for the night.

She drew the curtain in front of the window. "You are quiet this evening, Christina," said the Countess. She was in her favorite cotton gown that fell past her knees. Christina held the end of the curtain for a moment in her hands. The rich silk was soft in her fingers.

"There is something in the air, my lady, can you not feel it?" asked Christina, her voice quivering. She took a deep breath to compose herself. The slight falter in her voice was not lost on the Countess.

"Child; is there something wrong?"

Christina came close to her and looked earnestly into her eyes. "Something wicked is coming, my lady. It threatens everyone in Illith. People have talked of nothing else today, in whispers so low as to not wake the dead."

"I heard something of it from the other servants. This idle chatter; is this what you refer to?"

"My lady, it is not idle chatter. Lord Reinard Sallen and Michael Mauldon came today, entreating the Count to follow his instructions about the blood. Have you not heard?"

"I was unaware of their visit. What about the blood?"

"They came this afternoon, asking the Count to perform a blood ritual to save us. When he refused, Jonathan took the blood from Lord Sallen. At first, he spread it across the manor, but the Count saw him and was furious. Even now, Jonathan has spread the blood over the doorposts and window panes of the stable. Some of the servants are gathering there. Please come with me."

The Countess looked at Christina. "There is nothing to fear, Christina. What could destroy our village that a mere splatter of blood can withstand?" She meant to sound confident, but her words were hollow.

"You know Michael Mauldon is no fool, my lady. If he expects this to save us, I believe it will," Christina became agitated. She knew the Countess did not loathe those of the Craft the way her husband did. Would she take shelter under the blood?

Christina grabbed the Countess's arm and rushed onto the balcony, through the doors that were left open. They stood outside in the late night air. Finally, the Countess spoke. "Christina, what is the meaning of this?"

"Can you not hear it, my lady?" Christina's voice quivered again.

The Countess paused; then shook her head. "I hear nothing."

"That is because there is nothing to hear! There are no crickets, not a sound from the owls, even the wind is silent! My lady, something terrible is coming and all nature knows it! Please, before it is too late, come with me!"

"Christina, you are being unreasonable. You are letting the servants' fears and a quiet evening unnerve you. Why, there is nothing to be afraid of. Let us speak with the Count. You will see there is nothing to fear."

"I beg your pardon, my lady, but if Lord Sallen and Michael Mauldon could not persuade the Count, no one can."

The Countess looked into her servant's wide and imploring eyes. Tears formed in the corners, threatening to splash down her cheeks.

Christina was a sensible girl, not given over to wild fantasies of any kind. She was skilled and quick-witted. She was not someone who listened to gossip and certainly did not entertain it. She was truly frightened.

"My lady, the sun is gone. We do not know when to expect this catastrophe to come upon us. Please do not delay or I am afraid we shall not see each other after this night." Christina rushed to the Countess and embraced her tightly. "Please come." Then she withdrew and quickly left the room.

Jonathan stood in the stable stroking his favorite horse. He owned no horses, but he secretly claimed this beautiful chestnut mare as his own. He took the time himself to feed and water her, to brush her properly and show her special attention. Few women in the world could look this beautiful. The stable door opened, and Christina entered. He quickly walked over to her and hugged her.

"Christina, I was worried about you."

"I tried to convince the Countess to come." Christina looked around the stable at the other servants. The same apprehension was on their faces she knew was on her own.

"Do you really think it will happen?"

Jonathan nodded his head. "I do. We are in for a very long night."

"Then Count Deveraux is truly a fool." Christina moved over to a window facing the manor and looked out. She hoped the Countess would come.

The Countess found her husband in his study. He sat at his desk with a book open and a candle burning next to him.

"Some of the servants have gathered in the stable for the night. They believe danger is coming that we cannot withstand without the blood Lord Sallen brought you today. Why did you not tell me of his visit?"

The Count balled his hands into fists and exhaled deeply. "There was nothing to tell. Lord Sallen came to me with a silly request that I refused."

"He thinks it will save our lives! Have you learned nothing from our tragedies? Ana was murdered by a jealous young woman. Alana chooses to live as far away from you as possible. We lost one daughter to evil, the other to your stubborn pride!" shouted the Countess. Her eyes held a steadiness in them that was as strong as her voice. She took a breath and calmed herself. "Please, come with me to the stable. Let us start tomorrow by building a life with the daughter we have left when she comes to us. I miss Alana. I want her to be a part of our lives again."

The Count looked at his wife. She was a sensible woman, and very loyal to him. He knew it was his fault Alana did not return home. She was pardoned by the king for thwarting Lillia Sallen's execution years ago. While he despised the knowledge of the Craft, she revered it. When she left, they were two wild dogs fighting each other. He knew she did what she thought was right. In the end, he was glad she intervened. However, he could not forgive Lya Bernard for taking Ana from him. That act left him distrustful of the Craft.

"I cannot forgive the treachery that took Ana from us so easily."

The Countess looked at him sadly. "Then you will never know what it is like to be healed and set free. You will never know peace."

At that moment, an intense wind outside was all they could hear. The Countess rushed over to the window.

The trees swayed in the wind and threatened to uproot them. There was no thunder or lightning, or anything else that accompanied a storm. Her eyes grew wide as she realized what this wind was. She turned and faced her husband. "Come, we must get to the stable at once. What Lord Sallen feared, has come!"

The Count rose from his seat and hurried to the window. He saw how the wind circled around them. It looked as if it were trying to force itself inside; an unwanted guest bringing disaster in its wake.

They rushed through the house, to the front door. As they opened it, a swirling mass of white mist rushed in. The Countess hurried outside to the stable. The Count tried to follow her, but the mist became a wall of white so thick he could not see two paces before him. The shrieks and screams in the air disoriented him.

He moved forward, bumping into walls and furniture as he tried to find his way out of the house. He was alone in this loud and terrifying mist. Shrieks and laughter grew around him. This was not a natural storm with wind and rain. It was one filled with spirits and ghosts and things that haunted a person. He believed himself safe from any disaster. He covered his face and sank to his knees— lost to this strange mist. Once again he would suffer by one of the Craft, for only they could bring this terrible fate. Cold chills wrapped around his body like fingers with nails digging deep into his skin, scratching it to pieces. His cries of terror and pain were drowned by the shrieks of the spirits descending upon them.

The Countess ran into the small courtyard between the house and the stable. Her white gown blended with the mist. She held her hands over her eyes so she could see through the wind swirling around her.

Christina watched from the window, and saw the white gown coming toward them. "Countess?" She whispered as she ran to the stable door to open it.

"Christina, have you lost your mind? What are you doing?" demanded Jonathan as he rushed to the door to stop her.

"The Countess is coming, we must help her!"

"We cannot go out there! This wind is what Lord Sallen feared!" replied Jonathan.

"We must try to help her!" Christina forced open the door but stayed inside the stable.

"Countess, come this way, to your right! The stable is to your right!" she shouted as loud as she could.

The Countess heard a shout coming from her right. She followed the path in that direction when she suddenly stopped. She listened carefully to a soft voice calling her. The wind began to die down by degrees, so she heard it better.

"Mother, please come! I miss you!" The voice was gentle. The Countess recognized it as Ana's.

"Ana?" the Countess called. She turned and went back the way she came.

"No Countess! You must come toward the stable!" shouted Christina. Samuel and the rest of the servants stood in the doorway with Christina and Jonathan. They watched the figure in the middle of the courtyard.

The Countess stood still. She heard voices shouting her name, but she waited to hear her daughter's voice.

"Ana?" whispered the Countess again. Her eyes filled with tears of longing to see her daughter once again.

In reply to the Countess, the wind swirled around her. She felt it pricking her skin and ripping her gown as if hands ripped the material off her back. Blood on her arms came from long gashes the wind left behind. She screamed in pain, sinking to the stones on the pathway. Christina cried out as they watched her body ravaged by the wind.

"We must go out to her!" shouted Christina.

"We cannot go out there! We will be dead as well. There is nothing more we can do," shouted Samuel.

Jonathan closed the stable door. Christina sank to the ground in front of it and cried as the spirits shrieked in the darkness.

The winds and shrieks lifted by the fourth watch of the night. Christina sat looking out into the darkness. The animals finally calmed down. The servants slept on the floor. Only Christina and Jonathan were awake. He refused to close his eyes until she did. He sat beside her, wrapping her hand in his. She was sapped of vibrancy. Her eyes were dull, her hair in complete disarray. To Jonathan, she was still the most beautiful woman in the world.

He knew where she fixed her gaze. She was staring at the courtyard between the stable and the house. Christina's focus was in the direction she assumed her deceased mistress lay.

"Yesterday, she asked me to go into the village and see if there was any lavender oil at the general store. That was the errand she asked me to go on. When I got to the village square, I was distracted with the people trying to stone Michael Mauldon. I completely forgot what I was doing there. I only just now remembered. Who knew it was to be her last wish?" Tears ran down her cheeks at intervals.

"No one knew it would be like this. I do not even think Lord Sallen and Michael Mauldon really knew. I was still holding out hope the Count would change his mind. You see what became of that."

"Love always hopes[26], Jonathan. That is what those of the Craft say. You may not have known him long, but you loved him. You loved his fairness and sense of justice. We all did. It was a breath of fresh air after Count Vedan's shrewd and unfair dealings. What will happen to us now?"

---

[26]   1 Corinthians 13:7

"We do our best to rebuild Illith once again. It is our home. We have a right to remake it into one we are proud of."

"One that does not spurn those of the Craft," whispered Christina.

Jonathan put her head gently on his shoulder. "Close your eyes, if only for a moment. Worry about the future when you open them again," he whispered.

Christina closed her eyes and drifted to sleep as he held her close.

⸺ ✦✦✦ ⸺

Morning sunlight through the window woke Reinard. At his right Michael was lying on a blanket next to the hearth. There was nothing left of the fire but orange embers. Samson stood next to one of the windows looking around the room. The servants' cottage contained the various people he was responsible for. A sigh escaped his lips. He seemed grateful that everyone under his roof was still alive.

"It seems we live to see another day," said Samson quietly.

"I hope Jonathan was as fortunate as we were," replied Reinard.

"We should ride to Count Deveraux's estate and see if anyone is alive, as well as check the village square. Perhaps some fool eccentric heard Michael's warning and acted on it. Though I find it very unlikely," replied Samson.

"I will go with you, but first I need to wake Michael to let him know where we are going. We should let the others sleep. Everyone has had an exhausting night," said Reinard.

Reinard came over the Michael. He opened his eyes immediately. "What happened?" he asked.

"There is no cause for alarm. Samson and I are riding into the village and to Count Deveraux's property," said Reinard.

"I will go with you," replied Michael.

"There is no need, if you would rather stay," said Reinard.

"I want to go. I need to see what this incident cost Illith. I feel responsible," replied Michael.

"You are not responsible for another person's actions. Nathaniel has gone too far, and we now know we cannot trust him," said Reinard.

"This makes things difficult as he is my brother-in-law," replied Michael grimly. They headed to the stable, mounted their horses and rode for the village.

⁘

They slowed their horses and stopped in the village square. The entire place was completely destroyed. Each building looked as though it was ripped apart; the pieces thrown to the ground and smashed. Dead animals lay everywhere. The fountain was gone. Dead bodies littered the ground or were buried in rubble. Samson grimaced as he looked around.

"There is no one alive here. We should come back later and sort this out," said Samson.

"We need to ride to Count Deveraux's manor," said Reinard.

"What on earth for?" asked Samson.

"We need to see if Jonathan was able to follow my instructions," replied Reinard.

They rode up the pathway of Count Deveraux's estate and stopped in front of the house. Reinard looked at the remains of the beautiful manor he and Michael visited the day before. The windows were blown out and stained glass lay everywhere. The doors were torn off their hinges. He dismounted his horse and slowly walked to the entrance of the house. A body lay between the manor and the stable. As he came closer, he saw it was horribly mangled. The flesh was cut to ribbons and lying in a thick puddle of dried blood. The knotted and twisted auburn hair was the only clue the mutilated corpse was the Countess. He walked into the house and found Count Deveraux's body face down in the hallway, bathed in his own blood.

He went to the stable with Samson and Michael. The blood above the windows and doorposts made Michael sigh with relief. The stable door opened, and Jonathan looked outside.

"Is it over, Lord Sallen?" asked Jonathan.

Reinard came to the servant and embraced him. He looked up and saw others looking at them curiously. Christina stood up. Her eyes were red and puffed. She looked as though she spent the night crying.

"I believe so."

"Is the Count dead?" asked one of the servants.

"Yes."

"What is to become of the manor?" asked Jonathan. Reinard looked at the young man carefully. He then turned to Samson.

"I think perhaps the scope of your duty has widened, Samson. You need to oversee these people until the Viscountess returns," said Reinard.

"Who is to say the Viscountess will return?" asked Samson.

"Who can say for sure, but she is the rightful heir to the Count's lands and his responsibilities until the king appoints another Count for this district," said Reinard.

"The king needs to know what happened here and in Denholm Glen. I will ride back with you and then on to Wildemere," said Samson. He looked at Jonathan. Samuel stood behind him.

"Jonathan and Samuel: both of you have shown yourselves capable of leadership and following instructions. Jonathan you are younger and full of energy; Samuel you are older and full of experience. Both of you will take care of the duties here in Illith until my return. If the Viscountess returns in my absence, inform her of what has happened and of her new responsibility. When I return from Wildemere, I will have more to say to her," said Samson.

"What of the bodies?" asked Jonathan.

"We will take them back to Denholm Glen with us. It was always the Count's wish that the family be buried together. We will bury him and the Countess next to their daughter's grave," said Reinard.

"You will need a cart and driver," said Jonathan.

"Choose a driver for us, and that person will also accompany Samson to Wildemere. I think it would be prudent to travel with companions for a while," said Reinard.

"I agree," said Samson.

⊹ ✦✦✦ ⊹

An hour later Samson, Reinard, Michael, and a young stable hand named Levi rode to Denholm Glen. Samson looked around the group, then down the road. "The last time I was on this road, I was riding Saint trying to intercept Nadia to send her away from Illith. Now I am traveling to bring news of the village's destruction. It seems this road brings ill-fated tidings."

"Such is the way with troubled times. I am confident we will live to see better ones," replied Reinard.

Reinard noticed Michael's pensive look as they rode. It showed itself only when he was puzzling out the most intriguing questions. "You look as if you have something on your mind."

"I was just thinking this through. Lord Saintclaire visited Samson to warn him of coming danger. Father included Illith in his warning to me. Why did Nathaniel choose to destroy Illith?"

"Maybe whatever being he serves commanded him to do so. It is no secret the Saintclaire manor is being rebuilt. Maybe by destroying two places at once, it takes care of two problems that could become a thorn in his side," said Samson.

"When you go to Wildemere, you need to be very careful, Samson. I have no idea what you may encounter," said Michael.

"That thought crossed my mind as well. The suggestion to travel with companions is wise. This may be the season of very tragic 'accidents'," said Samson grimly.

The group fell silent as they continued their journey. Reinard considered Samson's last remark. He felt fortunate to have survived such a wicked storm. However, he could not shake the idea that another more powerful storm was yet to come.

CHAPTER 15

The day Michael and Lillia came to Wildemere to visit Nafaria, a young woman sat on a beautiful chestnut mare standing at the bank of the Anenderes River. Her dark hair flowed around her; gentle breezes lifting it like an afghan left on a line to dry.

Her blue eyes took in various scenes. People bustled along the riverbank, from one place to another. Others boarded the ferry for North Agea. Some carefully waded into the depths of the river on horseback, only to turn back to the shore after moments in the water. One would have to be a desperate soul or a great fool to try and cross the Anenderes River without the ferry. Though calm, it was too vast to traverse on horseback. One never knew when the faces of the dead would appear to bring warning or wisdom; often spooking the horses with their presence.

Alana Deveraux contemplated the skill it would take to cross the river with her horse alone. She trusted her ability as a rider, but she thought not even Lord Saintclaire would have done such a foolhardy thing. He would not risk putting such a noble beast through that duress. She stood in water pooling at the horse's knees, looking out at the expanse that divided the sister kingdoms.

She thought about her father. She respected his judgment and wisdom; however, she was at odds with him on a deeper issue that drove a wedge between them and sent her in search of a life worth living.

She took a deep breath and exhaled. The fresh air near water always invigorated her. If she were not set on crossing the river, she might settle in a cottage outside Burnea, close to the river. Here, the waves could charm her to sleep every evening with promises of fresh beginnings for each new day. As she gently nudged the horse deeper into the water, she heard her name.

"Alana, what are you doing?"

A young man, somewhere in his mid-twenties called her. His medium build was muscle riddled from riding horseback for the past ten years. His hair framed a boyish face, but his eyes showed wisdom beyond his years. While lost in thought, Alana forgot her companion. Sebastian Cavanaugh was a man worth doing well for. He believed in doing what was right and helping any he could along the way. This was why he accompanied her.

"Surely you do not intend to cross the river?" he asked.

"My travels and learning have finally led me here, Sebastian. I have seen all I can in Nereheim, with the notable exception of Herron. It is time to move on to North Agea."

"Viscountess, if you are so troubled by the things you have witnessed that brought you here, I wonder why you do not use your great learning, and status in Nereheim to help change what is. The king now has a Court Adviser who is of the Craft, as it was in the past. Perhaps you can help turn the tide against the wave of bigotry that put you on this road in the first place."

"I am no match for the wits of the nobles. I cannot change what goes on, if others more powerful than I cannot. I wish to lead a quiet life away from such malicious behavior."

Sebastian looked her in the eye as he moved his horse closer to her. "Your wit would be more of a test to the nobles than you think, Alana. Do not forget the king's pardon. You are free to return to Denholm Glen any time you like."

"I did not ask you to follow me to the ends of the earth, Sebastian. Your service ends here. You need not follow me any longer."

"My service ends when I say it ends. I will follow you to the ends of the earth and beyond, as I have done so until now, Alana. Think of your mother. How long will you make her worry?"

Alana sighed. "That is a wicked card to play, Sebastian. She is the reason I have not gone sooner. I still do not know if this is the right choice."

"If you do not know, perhaps you need to wait a while longer."

Alana stared into the clear blue water. The day was perfect. The air was warm and breezy. The river rolled in gentle waves, as if it had nothing else better to do than meander downstream. If ever there was a day to attempt to cross the Anenderes on horseback, this was it. The horse bent her head to drink from the water where she stood.

Alana gasped—she recognized a face in the water. There was no mistaking her sister Ana. She concentrated her gaze on it until she caught the words that face was mouthing: go home. She stared at the water until Ana's face disappeared.

"Perhaps you are right, Sebastian. A visit home may be prudent." Alana's voice gave away that she was visibly shaken. She turned the horse around and climbed up the riverbank. Sebastian followed, wondering what so suddenly changed her mind.

⸻ ✦ ⸻

From the moment she saw her sister's face in the water, dread shrouded Alana's soul. She felt something terrible was coming, but did not understand what. Her heart told her to get home quickly, but there was nothing to indicate anything was wrong. Life in Denholm Glen would always be the same. The execution of Lya Bernard, the exodus of the Mauldon family and Malcom Stone, and of course the intention of executing Lillia Sallen were the only events that were ever different in the village. They traveled at a steady pace, her need to be home increasing.

The blue sky above with its clouds like pillows dotting the air showed pure contentment in the sunshine. The countryside was the vivid green she was fond of. She ignored the fresh air as she spurred her horse, daring Sebastian to keep stride with her almost reckless pace. Why did she feel this way? Was it the shock of seeing Ana's face in the water attaching greater significance to those two words? For not everyone who came to the river's edge or even crossing the Anenderes saw faces in the water. Indeed, there were days that went by before someone would speak of them.

"Perhaps I am going mad," whispered Alana as she crouched lower; willing her horse to go faster.

Sebastian called out. "Alana, we have ridden hard these last few hours. We must take a rest and find lodging for the night."

"No, we must get home!" she shouted in return. Time seemed of the essence now.

The sun crept its way to the west as they moved across the countryside. The mare's breathing was heavy now. Alana knew she must rest the horse soon.

"Alana, there is nothing more for you to do. Tomorrow must begin a new day." Alana slowed her horse, her face blank. She came to a stop and looked around the deserted road, bewildered. She heard Ana's voice. She knew this was impossible, but who spoke? She heard a female voice, but no one was around except Sebastian.

"Did you say something?" she asked.

"No." Sebastian looked at her warily. She averted her gaze to her horse.

"I thought I heard a whisper." After a moment Alana shook her head. "No matter, we cannot go further today. We should lodge in Rowall for the night and continue on in the morning."

"Alana, what brought this haste to return home?"

"Back at the river's edge, I saw Ana's face in the water. She mouthed the words 'go home'. I fear something terrible is about to happen."

"There has been no news from any travelers we crossed to show that Denholm Glen is any different from when we left." Sebastian spoke with confidence, but Alana's concern made him feel ill at ease.

"Things change," replied Alana in a worried tone. She tugged her horse and continued toward Rowall.

———— ·⊱✦⊰· ————

After midnight, Sebastian awoke to a shrill scream. It was loud and piercing, resonating through his mind. There was something familiar about the sound. His eyes snapped open when he realized it was Alana who screamed.

He ran out of the room, wearing only the light pants he frequently slept in. He rushed over to the next door and found it locked. "Alana, open the door!" shouted Sebastian beating his fist on the door.

The innkeeper was at his side with a set of keys. People poked their heads into the hall to see what the commotion was about. "Let me get this for you," said the innkeeper. "I am sure the lady is having a frightful dream."

"Thank you," replied Sebastian. He did not bother to tell the innkeeper Alana was not given to frightful dreams.

Alana sat up in her bed; screaming with her eyes squeezed shut. Her hands clutched her head.

"Alana, wake up!" shouted Sebastian. Her screams continued. He jumped on the bed and grabbed her hands.

"Alana, wake up! You had a bad dream!" He shook her, shouting her name over and over until she finally opened her eyes and saw him sitting on his knees in front of her. She started to cry.

"It was just a dream, Alana. You are safe now." His voice was soothing. He pulled her close to him and let her cry.

"I saw her! Mother was running in the dark; then she just stopped. All of a sudden, she was screaming and cuts appeared on her! Like a giant knife was cutting her over and over while she screamed and bled! The windows…the windows of the manor were completely gone and the glass was on the ground everywhere!"

After a few minutes, Alana wiped her eyes. "We must go."

"Go where? It is the middle of the night! We ran the horses hard yesterday. They need a full night's rest."

Alana got out of bed and paced the floor. "Then we must go in the morning. Denholm Glen is less than a day's ride, if we do not tarry along the way."

Sebastian nodded his head. He knew this firm resolution in his companion. It meant she understood the reason in his words, but she still determined to do things her own way. He loved and hated this quality in her. Often, it was at the same time. "You must get some sleep."

"I cannot sleep."

"You must try," replied Sebastian firmly.

Alana knew this firm tone very well. It meant Sebastian would not tolerate disobedience from her. Usually, it was for her good. She sighed heavily. "Perhaps some tea by the fire in the common room will soothe me enough to sleep."

Sebastian followed Alana downstairs to the common room where they found the fire newly stoked. A tray containing a teapot, two cups, and a pot of honey sat on a table near the fire. The innkeeper sat in one of the chairs sipping a tall mug of ale.

"I took the liberty of preparing tea. I thought it might help the lady sleep," said the innkeeper.

"Thank you," replied Alana wearily. The adrenaline from the nightmare was wearing off, and she started to feel tired. She walked over to the tray and picked up a cup. Carefully, she poured the tea, and sat in another chair by the fire.

"Is it late to be drinking ale?" asked Sebastian as he sat down.

"I need something to calm my nerves," replied the innkeeper.

Alana sighed. "I am sorry. I am not given to dreams of any sort, but this was so vivid. It felt like I was standing right there watching the whole thing. It was horrible."

"I am sure it is nothing. When we get to Denholm Glen, you will see all is well," replied Sebastian.

"Denholm Glen, did you say?" asked the innkeeper.

"Yes. We are traveling home after being on a long journey," replied Sebastian carefully. He was always kind with strangers, but careful to never say too much.

"I have heard strange tales from travelers as they passed through today. They said something queer is going on in Denholm Glen and even out in Illith," replied the innkeeper.

"What kind of things?" Sebastian asked.

"There were people rushing about making preparations. No one really knows. Travelers were bid to stay the night, or leave the village by sunset. There was also mention of blood," replied the innkeeper.

"Blood?" asked Sebastian.

"Yes. The villagers were busy spreading it over the doorposts and windowpanes of their homes. Travelers left because they feared a mania settled over the village," replied the innkeeper.

"Mania?" Sebastian could not hide his alarm.

"That is merely suggested. However, I fear it may be something else," said the innkeeper in a hushed tone.

"What do you think it could be?" asked Alana.

"It is hard to say for certain. However, blood is not chosen lightly, my lady. I believe it is an unnamed evil those villages face."

Alana looked at Sebastian and found the same expression of concern on his face she knew was on hers. "You are right, Sebastian. I must try to sleep. However, we leave after breakfast tomorrow."

"Very well," he replied. They rose from their seats and went back upstairs, leaving the innkeeper to his ale and suspicions.

The morning sun was bright when they left Rowall. Their steady pace was not overpowering in any way. Alana continued a steady gallop moving them slowly along the countryside. She told herself she needed to give their horses a break, but after their conversation with the innkeeper the night before, she was fearful that something was amiss in their home village.

Her dream was not just a haunt in the night. Ana's appearance to her at the Anenderes convinced Alana of that. She was sure the blood-soaked vision of her mother came to pass. She did not wish to arrive home and confirm that as fact.

She looked up and moved off the road to the shallow brook nearby and let the horse drink.

"What are you doing?" asked Sebastian.

"We need to stop and water the horses. They are strong, but even they have their limits." Alana looked at him with apprehension in her eyes.

As they continued home, memories haunted Alana like daylight specters. Her thoughts drifted to a sunny afternoon, when she was eleven or maybe twelve. She was in the woods on the other side of the stream beyond the apple grove. The sun was bright and warm. It felt good on her skin, as she followed a bluebird couple while they went from tree to tree. Their songs were bright and cheerful, like the color that covered their bodies. On she went through the woods until she looked down and found herself in the middle of a pile of buzzing dust. A moment later, bees swirled up from the ground. Alana ran as fast as she could toward home. Dozens of bees swarmed around her as she ran, screaming in pain and fright. Her mother ran outside and took in the scene. Grabbing a pail of water from the fountain, she doused Alana with it. Alana collapsed in her arms screaming and thrashing about wildly.

"Alana, Calm down! They are gone now!" shouted her mother. Alana thrashed about until she opened her eyes and saw she was in her mother's arms, and the bees were gone.

"They are gone?" asked Alana.

"Yes, what happened?" asked her mother.

"I was following some bluebirds in the woods when I stepped on a patch of dirt. The bees came up from the ground and started chasing me."

Her mother gave her a weak smile. "You stepped on a wild beehive, child. When you are out in the woods, you need to take care where you put your feet. How would you like it if some large wild thing came and stomped on our house?"

"I would be very afraid," replied Alana.

"The bees were just as afraid, so they protected themselves. You must learn to have respect for everything around you. It is said you must respect even the air you breathe," said her mother.

"How do I do that?" asked Alana.

"You start, by watching where you put your feet," her mother replied.

Her mother rubbed aloe on her skin to soothe the beestings. Alana never forgot the lesson of the bees. From that time forward, she was mindful of where she stepped in the forest.

A cool breeze cut through the late afternoon heat. The rustle of leaves caused Alana to look to her right. They were passing an apple orchard about a mile long. She saw a young man in the trees picking apples and putting them into a sack. She stopped her horse.

"Sir, could you spare a few apples for us to eat on our way home?" asked Alana.

The man looked down from his perch in the tree. "Yes miss, can you catch?" he asked as he tossed four apples her way. Alana was already on the ground and caught each apple in quick succession. He laughed as he exclaimed, "It seems you can!"

"Thank you, sir," she replied. Alana tossed two Sebastian's way and fed one to her horse. She looked at the apple's bright red color. The piece of fruit felt hard and was without blemish. She was sure when she bit into it; she would hear a loud crunch and feel sweet juice flood her mouth. "Just like home," she whispered.

She sank to her knees. She no longer controlled the tears that flowed. Sebastian sat down next to her.

"What is wrong?" asked Sebastian in a gentle voice.

"I do not want to go home!" cried Alana. "I know I must, but I am afraid of what I will find. I do not wish to go!" Alana leaned into Sebastian's arms and continued to cry.

"It was only a dream, Alana. The sooner we return home, the sooner we will know what happened. We must not borrow trouble for ourselves on the way."

"Trouble seems to be the only thing we find."

Sebastian had no reply to comfort her. "Come, let us continue home."

Alana sighed and let him pull her to her feet. He put a hand to her chin and gently tilted it up so she looked into his eyes as he smiled.

She felt the strength his smile gave as she smiled and nodded her head. "Let us go home."

Tears rolled down her cheeks as Alana thought of her mother and all the things she stood for. She was life, vitality, and tenderness. She was a genuine person who did not pretend to be something she was not. She did not possess any supernatural wisdom or skill of the Craft, but she was not afraid. Alana loved her mother so much. When they came upon Denholm Glen, her eyes were completely dry. She had no more tears left to cry.

⋅⋅✦✦✦⋅⋅

Michael was quiet as the rest of the group traveled to Denholm Glen. The flat ground gave way to rolling hills the closer they came to the village. They approached the familiar meadow where he and Lillia spent so much time as children—the place they eventually shared their sacred vows to each other. Surrounded by so much pain, he willed himself to smile at happier times.

He saw the vineyard in the distance. "I need to check on Lillia and William," he said aloud.

"Meet us at Count Deveraux's property. We need to bury the bodies and report to Lord Luxton what happened to Illith," replied Reinard.

"I will be there as soon as possible." Michael spurred his horse and headed to the vineyard, leaving the others on the road to the village.

⋅⋅✦✦✦⋅⋅

Lillia saw him in the distance as he came closer. To another villager, Michael probably looked like any other man on horseback. However, Lillia was fine tuned to his steady but careful gait. It was a trait he never grew out of. Michael loved to ride, but his childhood insecurities about horses and riding rode with him, even now. If Lord Saintclaire had any fault, it was this: Michael never forgot his last words to him as his trainer, so he was careful not to hurt himself or his steed. Lord Saintclaire made Michael understand he would never truly master a horse. It was the only disagreement she would ever have with him.

With William in her arms, she walked toward Michael as he rode to her. He smiled a broad grin and his eyes brightened at the sight of them. He slowed the horse and jumped down to the ground.

"Lillia, thank goodness you are safe," he whispered as he drew her and William into his arms.

"I am more relieved that you are safe. Were you able to convince the Count?"

Michael shook his head. "The Count and Countess are dead. He would not listen to us. However, one of his servants did. The workers and animals on his property were saved."

"Where did you stay?"

"We found an old friend. Samson, one of Lord Saintclaire's horsemen, is rebuilding Saintclaire manor. He claims to have received instruction the way I did—in a vision from Lord Saintclaire himself. We stayed with him last night. Illith is completely wiped out. The destruction was terrible."

She kissed him gently. "You are safe now. Where is father?"

"He, Samson, and a worker named Levi are on their way to Count Deveraux's property to bury the bodies next to Ana's grave. I need to go meet them. When we are finished, we need to speak to Lord Luxton and let him know what happened." He looked down at William. "How did he sleep?"

"He was a little restless when the birds flew overhead, so I picked him up from his cradle. He immediately calmed down. I held him the entire night, for fear he would cry, but he slept through the storm."

"He knew he was safe. Intuition is what we need to focus on with him. I wish I had greater insight as to how to nurture that."

"Perhaps, when all settles down again, you can look through your father's diary. I will read the family annals to see if anything is written that can help." She kissed him again. "Go, there are many things to be done."

Michael kissed her and William and climbed back on his horse. "I will be home before nightfall."

⸺⸻⸺

At midday, Joseph sat with another servant outside near the lilac bushes at the front of the house. Queen Susanna may have preferred roses, but the Countess loved lilacs. Their freshness cleansed the air around them.

Joseph started his morning welcoming the sun. Its yellow glow flooded his world. Curses could not hold out against such brilliance. He was employed by Count Deveraux as he entered adulthood. He saw everything that happened with Ana, and how Alana retaliated against her father to save Lillia Sallen's life. The Count was a fair man, but when Ana died, he had no trust left for those of the Craft. Indeed, the trust that was there while she lived was barely a thread. He elected to stay behind and care for the Count's land until it sold. As chief caretaker, he traveled to Illith once a year to give a report of the manor the Count left behind, and how it prospered in his absence.

Joseph spent the morning digging graves for the Count and his wife. He hoped he was wrong—that the Count somehow survived. When Lord Sallen and Michael Mauldon returned from Illith, they would have more important duties to attend. The last thing they needed to be doing was menial work. So, he prepared for the worst.

Now as he breathed in the freshness of the lilacs, Joseph heard the sound of horses coming up the pathway. He rose and came to the side of the manor where he found Lord Sallen with another on horseback. Another man drove a horse and cart.

He sighed when he saw the cart. He tried to hold back tears, but they welled in his eyes. His voice was quiet as he asked, "Did the Count and Countess not survive?"

Reinard sighed. "No."

Joseph sank to his knees as his tears rolled down his face. Reinard climbed down from his horse and put his hand on the young man's shoulders as he kneeled down to him.

"Come, let us lay your master to rest," said Reinard gently.

Samson and Levi lifted the bodies out of the cart and the men proceeded to the apple grove, a solemn quiet in the air.

————— ⦙⦙⦙⦙ —————

Bennett looked over his fields as the laborers went about their work in the late afternoon sun. The terrors of the previous night seemed lost in the familiarity of routine.

He envied the men their toil. It proved a welcome distraction to any ill tidings the day may offer. There seemed to be only one casualty in the night. Bennett's long time mentor and friend, Lord Whitmore, died peacefully in his sleep. "Rest well, my friend," he whispered as he watched his workers' progress.

The sound of horse's hooves roused Bennett from his thoughts. He walked over to the edge of the terrace. Ian Keller rode toward him.

"Good afternoon, Lord Luxton. I checked all the homes in the village. With the exception of Lord Whitmore, everyone survived the night. The innkeeper is quite busy with his extra guests."

"I am sure he is," replied Bennett. "Your news is welcome, Ian. Thank you."

"Lord Sallen and Michael Mauldon have returned from Illith. Lord Sallen is at the Count's manor," said Ian.

"Let us go meet him. I am sure they have much to tell us," replied Bennett. He went to the stable for his horse and together they rode to Count Deveraux's property.

———— ·++++·+· ————

Michael trotted through the village on his way to Count Deveraux's manor. People went about their daily tasks, but a solemn quiet permeated the air. He spied various dead animals. Squirrels, birds, and rabbits littered the side of the road like so much rubbish in need of collection. When he came nearer the village, he saw men around fires throwing the carcasses into the flames to consume them. No one kept the animals for eating. He did not blame them. These unfortunate creatures were victims of the night before. No one was interested in anything death touched.

When he neared the Count's property, he saw two riders coming toward him; a man and woman. Both looked young but travel worn. He continued toward them.

"Is that you Viscountess?" he asked.

The woman regarded the young man who rode up to them. He was fair haired with a light complexion. He seemed accustomed to indoor activities, but was also given to being outside on occasion. He looked younger than she was, and his gaze held a certain steadiness.

"Michael Mauldon, would that be your name?" she asked.

"Yes, Viscountess," he replied.

"You came back to Denholm Glen." She gave him a soft smile. "I have no doubt Lillia Sallen is well?"

"Lillia Mauldon is her name now, Viscountess. Yes, we are all doing well."

"Can you tell us what happened here? Sebastian and I have passed a lot of dead animals on the road as we neared the village. We were told by an innkeeper in Rowall the villagers were putting blood over their doors and windows. I see now, he was not exaggerating," she said.

"Come; let us go to your residence and sort everything out there," said Michael quietly.

"Can you tell me how my mother is?" she asked as they rode.

Michael's shoulders stiffened for a moment at her request, but he remained quiet as they rode up the path to her old home. They stopped in front of the house, and Alana took a long look at it. The windowpanes and doorposts were covered in blood, as was every other building they passed in Denholm Glen. Alana focused on the blood. After a moment, she looked at Michael.

"My father would never have agreed to advice given to him by any of the Craft, especially not one that looks as barbaric as this. Where are my parents?" she asked.

Michael was silent as he looked down at the ground between them. Alana's heart sank. She was weary from her long journey and the heartache she was feeling at its end slowly crushed her spirit.

"Michael, where are my parents?" Her voice was barely above a whisper.

"Viscountess, perhaps—" he began, but Alana interrupted him.

"Where are they?" she demanded.

Michael sighed as he looked at her. "You will find them with Ana."

Alana dismounted and followed the path leading to her father's apple orchard. Sebastian jumped from his horse and followed her. Michael dismounted, grabbed the reins of their horses and tied them to the nearest tree. He followed behind them.

Alana knew the orchard well. It was a place she and Ana spent many days running through and hiding in. Her father and mother always preferred they play in the garden close to the house, but the girls gained strength and character by climbing trees and running among the vast root system the orchard afforded. Alana grew to be swift and light-footed when they were about their chores, or running errands in the village. It was better than the garden, even with its dangers.

She walked slowly, with Sebastian at her side, toward the end of the orchard where Ana's grave was. The Count could not bear to have her buried in the village burial garden with other villagers. He left instruction for the family to be buried together, so in death, they would rest in peace together.

The sun gave off just enough light to see two fresh headstones, no doubt hastily carved and put in place by the servants who buried them. Alana sank to her knees before her mother's grave.

"Oh mother! Why did it have to be you? There must have been warning given; why did you not listen? You have always taught me to seek wisdom, why did you not heed it yourself?" A fresh wave of tears overtook her.

She looked to the left and saw her father's grave on the other side of Ana's. She scrambled over to the other headstone. "You!" she snarled as she looked at it. "You always believed you were better than they were—simply because you had the king's favor and were appointed over them. Look what your power and foolishness brought you now! Why did you have to take mother with you? Why could you not die in torment and leave her here to live a full life?" Alana yelled as loud as she could. "You were not happy when your favorite died, so you ignored wise counsel and followed her! Why could you not leave mother behind for me?"

Alana crawled over the freshly dug soil and with another loud yell, pulled up the stone marking her father's grave. Sebastian and Michael watched wide eyed as she hurled it from where she sat on the ground. She sat on the fresh dirt as Sebastian wrapped his arms around her and cried once again for her deceased family.

CHAPTER 16

Alana sat in the great room of her home, with Sebastian next to her. She looked around at the faces surrounding her: Lord Luxton, Ian and Julia Keller, Lord Sallen, a man named Samson, and Michael Mauldon. They patiently waited for her to collect her thoughts.

She would grieve for her mother later, distracting herself with whatever task was now at hand. She pressed her index fingers to her lips and closed her eyes. She was ready to concentrate.

"Someone—tell me what happened after we left Denholm Glen ten years ago."

Everyone looked at Reinard. He cleared his throat. "When we parted: Ian, Julia, Lillia and I rode to Wildemere to report to the king Lillia's foiled execution. The king already knew about her. Jason Mauldon came to him in a panic begging him to send the royal guard to Denholm Glen to stop the execution. We advised the king that your father was only guilty of making a rash judgment."

"A rash judgment?" interrupted Alana. "Your daughter was almost killed."

"I remember well, Alana. However, your father was grieving and while I did not like his accusation, other Counts did far worse. We appealed to the king to spare your father's life. The king agreed, but he was not left in Denholm Glen.

Ian and Julia knew the details surrounding the deaths of Lord and Lady Saintclaire. Julia overheard Count Vedan's plot to blackmail Lady Cassandra. The king was outraged by Vedan's actions. Jason pleaded with the king to send him to prison. He was executed instead. Your father took over lordship of Count Vedan's estate and governance of his district including the village of Illith. He left me to oversee this property until it sold or you returned. The property is now yours."

"Mine," she repeated quietly.

Reinard nodded his head and sighed. "There is something else that you must know. You are now Countess over your father's district. Until the king appoints another, it is your responsibility to carry on his duties."

"That is an awful lot to lay on someone the moment they return to find their family deceased, Lord Sallen," said Sebastian. His tone suggested Reinard was cold and unfeeling.

Alana looked at Sebastian and touched his hand. "No, he is correct. It is my duty. I need to go to Illith and begin where my father left off."

"That is easier said than done. The entire village is destroyed, as well as the Count's manor. The municipal building holds the important papers and work your father was doing, but there is nothing left of it," said Michael. Alana looked at him.

"Illith was left without one stone on top of another. I am traveling to Wildemere to inform the king of the destruction, and the Count's demise," said Samson.

"No, I will go to the king. It is my responsibility as my father's only heir. I will also request to take over my father's district," said Alana.

"You need not make a decision right away, Alana. You should think this through," said Sebastian.

She looked at Sebastian. "Before we headed back here, you told me I should use my influence to change what I do not like in Nereheim. I wish to do what is right and help those of the Craft. We need them. They need protection. If this will help, I will do it."

Sebastian saw the determination and steadiness in her eyes as she spoke. He shrugged his shoulders. "It seems we are going back to Wildemere."

"There is something else I would like an explanation for." Everyone turned their heads to Lord Luxton. "Why is it you returned so quickly from your visit with your sister, Michael?"

Michael took a deep breath. "I will answer your question, but I ask that what I am about to say does not leave this room." Michael paused and looked at everyone. When he saw he could trust his audience, he related everything that happened in Wildemere.

"That is quite a tale. So, you believe Nathaniel is doing the bidding of some devil?" asked Samson.

Michael nodded his head. "Somehow, Nathaniel gave his allegiance to this dark lord. He is now keeper of the Grimoire Macabre, a book that was thought to be a dark legend of the Craft. I also believe he possesses the bell of Herron."

"The same bell said to be at the head of the Anenderes River?" asked Alana.

"Yes," replied Michael.

"How would he come in possession of it?" asked Sebastian.

"It was whispered for generations that a man named Oberman, who was possessed by evil, went to Herron and stole the bell from its resting place. No one knows how. Many believed the bell to be a myth. No one goes to Herron, so no one has ever confirmed the story, or even if the bell existed in the first place. The wasteland that lies near it is too dangerous to travel alone. Many people have been robbed, killed, or disappeared when they journey near there," said Michael. "A man named Joseph Wheaton tried to call this being for power. He failed in his attempt, and his family was killed. This scandal haunted Wildemere for a generation."

"What is this Grimoire Macabre?" asked Alana, concentrating on Michael's words.

"It is a book of dark rituals said to be written by the god of blood himself. Those of the Craft searching for power often go in search of the legend. Many of the Craft did not believe it existed. I myself thought it a myth until that night.

Before leaving, I warned the princess to be careful around Nathaniel. She understands tact and will keep her and Andrew far from suspicion. I also told her to let me know if the king's behavior changes."

"What kind of change?" asked Samson.

"Nathaniel was told to drive the king insane. It will be very subtle. However, if he succeeds, there is no telling what the king may do to himself or someone else." Michael looked at Alana. "When you go before the king, it is very important you do not draw Nathaniel's suspicion. You returned home at a very unfortunate moment, but the timing is uncanny. You at least know what is happening. Someone else may not realize the danger until very late in Nathaniel's plans and could be used as a pawn simply because his guard is down."

"What if Nathaniel does not accept me? He is the royal Court Adviser. He might advise the king against me," said Alana.

"I do not believe Nathaniel will perceive a woman as a threat," replied Bennett. Alana looked at the village elder as Sebastian glared at him. Michael quickly came to his defense.

"No one is saying Alana is incapable of carrying out her duties should she be appointed by the king. She is actually perfect, because she is a woman. Nathaniel will see her as inferior to himself. He may dismiss her so that he does not have to think about what to do with the Count's district. You must keep yourself humble and diplomatic in his presence. Look to the princess for guidance. She shrouds her sharpness in ignorance and silence and does not attract attention to herself. Simply state your business, and be gone before any suspicion is raised. Pay attention to the king. Does he give command, or only follow advice given by Nathaniel? That interests me most. King Rohn listens to advice but makes his own decisions. How quickly he agrees with Nathaniel will tell you how real the danger is that we face," said Michael.

Alana nodded her head as she thought through Michael's words. She looked over at Sebastian. "It seems we are to become diplomats to the royal city." She turned her head to Michael again. "Do you have any other instruction?"

Michael shook his head. "That should be everything you need to know. If the princess approaches you, do not be alarmed. She may want to send a note to Lord Reinard through you, as he is her great uncle."

"We will head to Wildemere tomorrow and report what happened in Illith. I will state my interest in the matter, and await the king's decision. When I return, I will let you know what I find," said Alana.

"We will be setting things in order while you are away. There are men already in Illith organizing what is left," said Samson.

"Tomorrow looks to be a busy day," replied Bennett as he sat in his seat. Everyone was quiet while they thought about what waited in the royal city.

CHAPTER 17

Shadows fell across the castle wall as Rohn felt a shadow over his heart. Another day was coming to a close. He breathed in—and slowly let it out. Life during the past months was reduced to a series of breaths. Each one turned seconds to minutes. The minutes turned to hours which in turn granted him another day. What was another day? He was lost in a sea of breaths, always hoping to wake from this nightmare. He would find his queen sleeping beside him, her golden hair spilling around her so he could reach out and take those long tresses into his fingers. Then he would know there was a God in heaven once again. He would not allow his heart to understand: Susanna, the most beautiful thing in his life—was dead. His eyes welled with tears. He wiped them, rose from his seat, and walked out of the throne room.

Rohn received subjects who needed him since his return from North Agea with Susanna's body. She was laid to rest, and he tried his best to mourn in silence and be the king she always knew him to be. He did not feel up to the task these days. It was too hard to breathe, let alone govern as king. For this reason he found himself grateful for the presence of Nathaniel Stone. The young Court Adviser settled into his new position and put Rohn's mind at ease. He did not want to think that his loved ones were being stripped from him one by one. For Andrew and Nina would be next. He could not bear to lose his only son.

Lately Andrew changed to be more like Susanna. He used more grace and gentleness than he did before. He was less arrogant and more humble. He asked more questions and gave less opinion. Andrew was becoming a future king. Rohn could not be more proud. He only wished Susanna were alive to witness the transformation. She always said he had the potential, he just needed a catalyst. Susanna's death broke through to him and helped him be the man Nina said she always knew was there.

"You would be so proud, Susanna," he said quietly as he made his way through the castle. He headed toward her most cherished place inside the castle. He stopped a moment before a tiny room that sparkled from the doorway. This was Susanna's crystal and blown glass collection. He carefully stepped into the tiny room, taking care not to bump a shelf or stand. He stopped before each piece, taking in the intricate beauty she found so fascinating. He thought back to why this room existed. When they first married, Susanna wanted to help the local artisans make their place in the market. "What better way to sell your wares than to say, 'I sold a piece just like this to the queen herself.'" She always thought of her subjects and how she could help them. If anyone used their influence in service to their fellow man, Susanna did. She was a bright light of hope to Nereheim from the day she set foot on this side of the Anenderes to call it her home.

He stopped in front of a crystal angel that sat on a shelf by itself. He stared at the beautiful features. "Susanna, how I miss you," he whispered.

"*Rohn.*" His breath caught. He thought he heard her whisper his name. He closed his eyes. His grief made him hear things that were not there.

"*Rohn.*" There was the whisper once again.

"Susanna?" he whispered as he looked around the tiny room.

"*Listen to Nathaniel. He will guide you.*"

"Susanna?" Rohn called out. Her voice was gone as quickly as it came.

———— ··✦✦✦·· ————

Nina stopped in front of the crystal and blown glass room. She heard Rohn calling out for his wife. This happened more often lately. She sighed as she thought of Michael Mauldon's warning. She hoped her father-in-law would not grow worse.

"Father?" she called as she entered the room.

Rohn looked at the entrance and saw Nina standing there.

"Is anything wrong?" she asked.

"Did you hear her?" Rohn's eyes were wide, as though he saw a specter.

"Hear who?"

Rohn shook his head. "I thought I heard Susanna speak to me." He looked at Nina fondly. "Do you need anything?"

"I was just looking for Andrew. Have you seen him?"

Rohn shook his head. "Perhaps he is with Nathaniel."

"You may be right. Perhaps they are with Nafaria." Nina walked out of the room, leaving Rohn to his thoughts.

Andrew was in good spirits when he awoke the next morning. He knew Nina to be an early riser, so he did not wonder when he found himself alone, with a lavender rose sitting atop a note. Nina could be playful as well as mysterious and everything else in between. She was not a woman of many moods; brooding one day and joyful another. Her demeanor was very appropriate for the occasion at hand. Yet, she used her mind to keep Andrew wondering what she was up to.

He was used to this behavior. His mother often left his father clues about the castle that led to a surprise. Only when he followed along with her game was the prize revealed. His father must have learned quickly to indulge this, for he never complained. He simply followed the clues and was often delighted at the end of the hunt. Andrew wondered if this was a secret his mother revealed to Nina.

He looked at the beautiful penmanship on the paper. *Meet me where our love began*, the note said. He smiled as he thought of the cathedral. One of the darkest days in his life ended with the greatest hope. The riot that spread into the market gave birth to the incident that brought Nina into

Andrew's life. His smile continued as he headed to the stable. He quickly mounted his horse and rode to the market area.

The cathedral's stained glass windows shone in the sunlight. He left his horse outside and made his way into the sanctuary. Nina sat in the first row, facing forward. She turned and smiled at him as he came down the aisle. He gently placed a kiss on her forehead as he sat down, then handed her the rose she left him.

"I found your token, princess," he whispered.

Nina took the rose and smiled. "Thank you. I was hoping the note was clear enough."

"You did fine. So, why are we here?"

Nina smiled, but Andrew saw concern in her eyes. Something important was on her mind.

"I needed to talk to you, but not at the castle. I have three important pieces of information for you, and I did not want to be overheard."

"Overheard?"

Nina nodded her head. "The first thing, we will announce right away. I am pregnant, Andrew. There will be more children than the twins in the castle next spring."

Andrew's eyes widened and his smile broadened. "You are with child? It seems so soon, but that is wonderful, Nina!" He pulled her to him and hugged her tight.

"What other news do you have for me?"

Her smile faded and she spoke in a quieter tone. "Your father is becoming unstable. I am sure you have noticed. It is very subtle now, but I fear it will grow worse. I was told to watch for it."

"Told?" Andrew's questioning look encouraged her to proceed quickly.

"That is part of the third thing I need to tell you. You must not repeat to this anyone, especially Nathaniel. When Michael Mauldon came to visit Nafaria, he said he followed Nathaniel the evening before he left. He gave his allegiance to a demon and is becoming consumed by evil. Nathaniel was commanded to drive your father mad. You must notice how distracted and distant your father has been. He relies more and more on Nathaniel to make even the simplest of diplomatic decisions. Michael warned me not to cross Nathaniel or raise suspicion around him. I beg you to do the same. We are only safe if we remain ignorant of his designs."

"Nathaniel is the only person besides you that believes in me! Are you saying he is purposely deceiving me?"

"We are pawns to him. Nathaniel is in the grip of a demon wishing to exploit him. He is dangerous and we must be careful." Though she was calm, he saw fear in her eyes.

"Why would he do such a thing?"

"There is no telling. Nafaria told me of how he protected her from a bully once, but he used a very harsh lesson to do so. That was when they were children. Perhaps the persecution that forced his father to move to North Agea also affected him. Then, there is the death of Jason and Thena Mauldon to consider. Nafaria said when Malcom and Nathaniel traveled to Wildemere to see Jason, they found the manor destroyed, and Jason's pyre next to the house. It was still smoking when they arrived. He may have sought this dark power to be able to protect what is his, the way Jason could not. Nathaniel's motive is noble; but he has given himself to a force he cannot control and it has mastered him. Can you not feel its presence in the castle?"

Andrew shook his head. "No. What makes you so certain your emotions are not running away with you? After all, you are pregnant. You may be susceptible to a delusion."

"I am not mad! I know what I am saying is true! Why do you think I wanted to meet you here? The castle walls now have ears. For the sake of our child, we must conduct ourselves with caution." Nina's tone was refined. Her eyes— were ablaze.

"I am sorry Nina. I just cannot believe something I have not witnessed for myself. I promise to be careful, but I need proof of what you say before I make up my mind about Nathaniel."

Nina sighed. "That is a noble answer that comes from a good heart. However, it is foolish if we all end up dead!" She rose and walked down the aisle toward the door of the sanctuary.

Andrew watched her leave. "Where are you going?"

"I will be in the market for a while. If you will not listen, I must think about what to do next." She opened the door and left the cathedral. He sighed as the door closed behind her.

⋅⋅⋅✦✦✦⋅⋅⋅

Andrew walked the corridors of the castle after he returned from the cathedral. His argument with Nina made him feel lost. His mind wandered and before he realized where his feet had taken him, he was in the royal crypt, where his mother's coffin rested. A bench was set in the middle of the small room. Andrew sat facing her coffin. Moments seemed to pass as hours. His voice found words and he spoke into the empty silence.

"Mother, I had my first argument with Nina today. She told me something I know she could never lie about, but I do not wish to believe it as true. I wish you were here to guide me." His last words ended in a whisper.

He finally put his head in his hands and spoke his thoughts aloud. "People say they have seen loved ones come back from the dead. I hoped that was more than just a fairy tale, because I need you now."

Andrew sat still and listened for something more than the silence he heard. He finally rose from his seat, grabbed the torch he left in the sconce near the door, and left the room.

He was about to turn to his right, when a flicker of light to his left caught his eye in the darkness. He turned toward it, curious as to what it could be when he heard a sharp voice. "Andrew, where are you going?"

Andrew turned and saw Nathaniel standing behind him, a torch in his hand. He looked at him suspiciously.

"I came here to sit with mother for a few minutes. When I left, I saw a light," said Andrew.

"What light?" asked Nathaniel.

Andrew turned and looked in the direction where he saw the light and frowned. There was only a dark hole where he could see the beginning of a tunnel with their torches. "I thought I saw a light down there." He turned and regarded Nathaniel with suspicion. "What are *you* doing down here, Nathaniel?"

"I was looking for you. I saw you head downstairs, but thought you were in the library. I kept looking until I found you here," replied Nathaniel. "Your father wanted to speak to you."

After a moment, Andrew relaxed somewhat. "Is he in the throne room?"

"Yes," replied Nathaniel.

"I will go see him," replied Andrew. As he walked past Nathaniel and headed up the steps, he asked, "Have you ever been down here before, Nathaniel?"

"Yes, many times." When Andrew turned to look at him, Nathaniel said, "I have inspected every area of this castle since we moved here. You will understand when you have children of your own."

Andrew smiled and said, "That time is coming. Nina told me this morning she is pregnant."

Nathaniel smiled as he said, "Congratulations. I wish you the best."

As they headed up the steps, Andrew's thoughts wandered back to Nathaniel's comment. Was he protecting his family through vigilance? Or was he hiding something in the darkness below the castle? He suspected he should believe Nina for the moment, and be wary of Nathaniel.

⸻ ⟩⟩⟩⟨⟨⟨ ⸻

Andrew made his way to the throne room. His father stayed there until dinner was served. It was his new way of life. He made himself accessible to his subjects six days a week. For even the creator rested on the seventh day. Or so he was always told.

When he entered the room, he saw his father on his throne. His eyes were distant, as if he were trying to recall something important that left him for the moment. He finally noticed Andrew.

"Andrew, what brings you here?" he asked. Andrew hid his surprise. Nathaniel told him his father was looking for him.

"I have news that could not wait. I believe congratulations are in order. Nina just told me she is pregnant. If all is well, we shall have our first child by early spring of next year."

Rohn's face lit up into a smile. "That is wonderful news!" he exclaimed.

After a moment Andrew spoke again. "I am concerned about Nina. Ever since mother died, I noticed a subtle change in her disposition. She is cheerful enough in public, but I fear she still grieves in secret. Tomorrow I am taking her out for the day."

"There is nothing happening that you need to be here for, Andrew. Enjoy the day with Nina. Soon, you will not have such times," said Rohn with a laugh.

"Thank you, father, I hope the weather will be pleasant." Andrew turned and left the room.

————— ·+◆+· —————

The afternoon sun was bright as Alana and Sebastian made their way through Wildemere's market and past the cathedral. When they were in front of the castle, Alana took a long look at the structure before her. From its turrets to its lowest level windows, nothing seemed unusual or sinister. The colonnade stretched from the stable area to the castle, providing a covered walkway easily traversed by the most delicate step. Panning across the other direction, she took in the manicured lawn and a large crop of color coming from rosebushes marking the entrance to Queen Susanna's famed rose garden. She sighed as she viewed the flowers. For Alana, Queen Susanna stood for so much that was good in Nereheim.

She had a good ethic, a beautiful heart for her kingdom, and she possessed wisdom to understand her place in Nereheim. Susanna's example showed Alana the kind of woman she hoped to be one day. The first step to becoming that woman was to claim her rightful title as Countess in her father's district.

Sebastian followed her gaze to the castle. "What are you thinking?"

"I was trying to sense what Michael Mauldon did when he came here. He said he felt a shadow over the place. I feel nothing."

"Michael is of the Craft and studies alchemy as well as any other arcane subject he can find. His awareness of things is probably much greater than ours."

"That is all the more reason to keep our guard up. If not for Michael's warning, we might have walked into a trap."

"Remember the princess. I think she would find a way to warn us."

"If she were able, I believe she would. We must be careful nonetheless. The walls have eyes in a place like this," replied Alana quietly. She got off her horse and led it to the stable.

"Good day. How may I help you?" asked the stable boy, when they darkened the entrance.

"We have come for an audience with King Rohn Catalane. Where should we keep our horses?" asked Alana.

"I will take care of them, my lady. Just follow the colonnade to the end. The main hall into the castle will take you to the throne room," replied the stable boy.

"Thank you," said Alana.

They followed the colonnade to an entrance opening into the hallway the stable boy described. There, the oils of past Court Advisers clung to the wall on one side, while the bottom floor of the castle opened to them on the other. A posted guard greeted them.

"State your business," he said in a tone that suggested he was not accustomed to foolishness of any sort. His gaze settled on Sebastian who was silent.

"We are here to see the king. We have news from the village of Illith," said Alana.

The guard looked down at her, but said nothing. She glanced at Sebastian who gave her a wink. He loved the looks people gave when Alana spoke with tact and always the correct amount of power. She smiled back and followed the guard when he turned and started down the hall, motioning for them to follow.

Alana knew of this famed hall. For who could be a citizen of Nereheim and not know of the royal tradition to hang a portrait of all the Court Advisers of the past? They served as a remembrance and a way to honor those of the Craft who came forward to help each king govern with wisdom. The regal oils floated past her as she walked with Sebastian.

The hall ended with the last two paintings. The one to her left, she recognized after a moment. She knew this man as much older. However, there was no mistaking the benevolent gaze in the eyes of Malcom Stone. Alana glanced at Sebastian whose eyes widened a little. She knew he recognized him as well. She never knew Malcom Stone, the man who was the apothecary of Denholm Glen, was once Court Adviser to the king. What other secrets did he hold behind his kindness? She looked at the last painting. He too was young, but there was no mistaking that firm conviction in his eyes, or the way his jaw was set. This was a painting of Nathaniel Stone. Once again, she remembered him as a youth, but his gaze was just as powerful as this painting captured.

"So, it is true," she whispered.

The guard looked at Alana. "Who may I ask wishes an audience with the king?" he asked.

"The Viscountess Alana Deveraux," she said carefully. Her tone came out evenly, a perfect mask for her nervousness. The guard disappeared through the doors. He returned a few moments later.

"The king will see you now."

Alana gave him a nod and slight smile. She and Sebastian followed him into the throne room. As they moved closer, she glanced around the room. Nathaniel stood next to the throne the king sat on. He focused completely on her as they approached the king.

"Viscountess Alana Deveraux. I am pleased to make your acquaintance after all these years," said the king. Nathaniel watched her as she looked at the king, a question in her eyes.

"To what do I owe such an honor, your majesty?" asked Alana as she bowed her head to him.

"It was your bravery that saved Lillia Sallen from an unjust execution ten years ago. I always wondered what kind of person would stand up against such terrible judgment, justified or not," replied the king.

"One who was taught to never tire of doing what is right[27], your majesty."

"What brings you before me?" asked the king.

"I bring news of a tragedy in Illith. The entire village has been destroyed in a terrible storm I was told came out of nowhere. Only a handful of people survive. I came home to Denholm Glen to find my father was given charge over Illith and that he and my mother both perished in this storm. Their estate in Illith is gone. Only the stable on their property stands, and the unfinished Saintclaire manor my father was charged to rebuild."

The king's face registered shock at the first mention of her news. Nathaniel seemed more composed than the king, as if expecting this report. His demeanor was not lost on Alana.

"So, Michael Mauldon was correct. It seems we have a snake in the royal court," thought Alana.

She looked at the king. "The shock of losing my family is great, but I was strongly encouraged by the villagers of Illith to come to you and state my wish to become Countess of my father's district. The people of Illith need someone to help them rebuild what was lost. I wish to do so."

The king looked at Alana thoughtfully. He seemed doubtful of her competence in such a position. After a moment, he finally spoke. "It is noble of you to desire to continue the duties of your father. Governing a district is a very delicate task. Your subjects may not be willing to take direction from someone they have never met, much less a woman."

"Your majesty, if I may," said Nathaniel as he moved closer to the throne. He stood between Alana and the king, his eyes on her. "I remember

---

27   2 Thessalonians 3:13

you. For years you and Philip Mauldon were as one in the woods. You are practical, intelligent, and sensible enough to know when and how to speak. These are all traits that are examined when considering someone for position of Count, are they not?" Nathaniel asked as he turned to face Rohn.

The king nodded his head slowly. "They are."

"If the Viscountess is willing to take on such an appointment, we should let her try. If she fails, we can replace her with someone else of our choosing. However, if she succeeds, who better than she to carry on her father's legacy?" said Nathaniel.

Alana watched the king's expression as he considered Nathaniel's words. He then gave his verdict with a nod of his head. "Then let it be so. I confer on you the title of Countess, Alana Deveraux, and give you the district your father governed. Bear it well," said the king. He nodded to Alana and Sebastian, then rose from his throne and left the room.

Nathaniel looked at Alana. "Please send me a report on the extent of the damage to the village and what is being done to re-establish it. I will send supplies in a week to help in your endeavor. Send me a monthly report after that so I may see how you are getting along. I will see you to the colonnade," said Nathaniel.

Alana and Sebastian followed Nathaniel down the great hallway they passed through minutes before. It seemed less than a quarter hour passed, and they were standing outside once again. Nathaniel looked carefully at Alana. "Use your best judgment when making decisions, Countess. I am sure you are equal to your task."

"Thank you for your confidence in me," said Alana. He nodded his head and without another word, turned and went back to the castle. They watched him as he left.

"Do you get the feeling that was a little too easy, Sebastian?"

"I was thinking the same thing, Countess. You must be wary in the future."

At that moment, they heard footsteps coming toward them from the opposite direction. They turned and saw a young woman with fair hair and bright eyes walking toward them. She stopped, and dipped her head to them. "Good day, I am Princess Nina Catalane. What brings you to the king's castle?"

Alana bowed her head to the princess. "I am Countess Alana Deveraux. This is Sebastian Cavanaugh. We have been with the king to give report of what happened to the village of Illith. We are heading back there now." Alana waited to see what the princess would say next.

"What happened to Illith?"

"It was destroyed. I was told not one stone stands upon another," replied Alana.

Nina's eyes widened at her words. She looked at the ground and then asked, "Are you, by chance, heading through Denholm Glen? I was hoping to find a courier just now to take a letter to my great uncle, Lord Reinard Sallen. However, no one can be found in the stable except the stable boy who cares for the horses. Would you take it?" She gazed at Alana intently as she held out a carefully rolled paper bound with a wax seal.

"It would be my pleasure." Alana took the paper from the princess.

"Take care as you return. There is much trouble on the roads these days." Nina smiled again and continued toward the castle. Alana spoke quietly when the princess was far enough away not to hear her.

"Three for three, Sebastian. Michael Mauldon called each play perfectly. We must get home quickly." They retrieved their horses and started out of the royal city.

<hr>

Nina sat in a quiet room near a low fire. She put a candlestick on the table next to her favorite reading chair. It was one of two such chairs in the room, but she would never sit in the other. It was Queen Susanna's favorite— Nina still missed her too much to think of using it.

This quiet space was the queen's private sitting room where she took her tea before bed. A bookshelf from floor to ceiling spanned the entirety of one wall. Susanna encouraged Nina to look through her personal library and read whatever she found of interest.

Now Nina sat with her own book in hand. It was a very old book of poetry she was finally able to purchase when she married Andrew. When Elias Wheaton procured the book for her, he remarked that more young women would do well to have such taste. "A keen mind trains the body," he told her.

Nina looked at the lines of poetry, but all she could think about was her earlier conversation with Andrew. She reached for the teacup sitting on a table next to her. Nafaria mentioned that while she was pregnant perhaps she might try mint tea. The flavor settled her stomach better, and was refreshing. She hoped Andrew would not be angry with her when they met for dinner. She did not wish to raise Nathaniel's suspicion. He would question any tension between them.

A flutter of movement at the door caught her attention. She smiled when Andrew walked in. He returned her smile and went down on one knee before her. He noted the teacup in her hand.

"Is everything alright?" Concern shadowed his face. She put down the cup and wrapped her arms around him.

"Everything is fine. I thought a cup of tea and a little poetry would be relaxing."

He kissed her hand then looked into her eyes. "I wanted to tell you that I trust you, and will believe what you tell me for now."

He shook his head when he saw the question in her eyes. "That is all I can say for now. I will tell you more tomorrow."

"I do not understand."

Andrew pointed to the book in her hand. "I thought we might have a picnic along the Anenderes; a chance for the two of us to be alone, away from the castle." He kissed her cheek as he rose from his place. "Let us get ready for dinner."

Nina smiled, put down her book and followed her husband out of the room.

⁃⁃⁃◆◆◆◆◆⁃⁃⁃

Michael sat in the library in his father's favorite chair by the fire. When he returned home from his life in Wildemere, he quickly realized though the chair was the softest leather and was firm enough to add comfort to the lower back, it was also situated in a place that captured the best light for reading and writing. This proved to him mere aesthetics can often hold great functionality. His father must have known this as well. He was reluctant to move any furniture in the house as a result.

He sat with a book he had not looked at in almost ten years. In some ways he feared it would have some uncanny effect on him that would drive him to commit some despicable act against his family. For though the book was a compilation of great knowledge and wisdom of one of the Craft; it ended in bloody tragedy. He regarded Joseph Wheaton's diary with caution and perhaps trepidation. Fear of what may happen often keeps one from straying off a dimly lit path into complete darkness. Now, Michael was faced with no other choice. He must look at Joseph's diary once again to see if there was something that would help him against Nathaniel.

He carefully turned the pages, reading each one slowly and thinking about how and what Joseph learned as he grew in the Craft. He remembered finding kinship with him as a youth. His study into esoteric and perhaps mystifying parts of the Craft earned Michael's respect quickly. For how could he fail to see the similarities he and Joseph held in common? Now that he was older, Michael was still impressed with this intricate knowledge and the detailed incantations he found written to call upon YAHWEH for greater knowledge, wisdom to handle that knowledge correctly, skill to heal with what was found in nature, and to fight evil in his generation. Joseph Wheaton served as a mentor to Michael as he pursued the darkest power imaginable to fight the even more insidious evil coming.

He turned the book near where he knew the writing stopped, and carefully looked at the last pages marking the end of Joseph's life. There was a page among them written in a complete runic language. Michael discovered early that Joseph jealously guarded his deepest secrets in symbols. Some incantations Joseph wrote in a rune language barely used anymore. If not for Lord Sallen's invitations for him to read books of alchemy from his private library, Michael never would have been able to read the message Joseph wrote on the wall of his estate when he was thirteen. Things of that nature were all over the book.

As he looked at the page again, his brows knitted together in puzzlement. He could not understand it at all. It was as if this one page was written in a language even more difficult to decipher. Why would Joseph disguise this page so carefully? What knowledge could be so important as to be completely hidden from everyone but Joseph himself? After peering at the page for almost a quarter hour, Michael looked at the opposite page. It held a date in early December, the words of Joseph himself explaining what he wrote:

All my study and careful planning brought me face to face with a man. Oberman approached me one morning as I walked in the woods behind my home. He looked ages old, but moved with the agility of one my own age. He knew of my desire for the power to protect Wildemere against the evil of the foolish and abusive and to protect others from the fate of the Coe family.

"What is this power you speak of?" I asked him.

"Show me you are worthy of such power and I will show you how to summon it," he replied.

I wrote this incantation and gave it to him. After reading it, he told me how to summon his master. I must be willing to follow the instruction completely, or else fail in my effort. YAHWEH has abandoned my pleas for wisdom. Though it cost all I have, I will do this thing…

The next page was the page written on 12-21— the details of the ritual. Now this made sense to Michael, where he did not comprehend it as a youth. Joseph became consumed with pursuit of power, so he followed the instructions of this man Oberman, and was betrayed. Was the incantation Joseph wrote among Oberman's secrets now? Joseph was used and betrayed by him for a small token of knowledge. Is that how the god of blood collected his secrets?

He copied the incantation on another sheet of paper and folded it up. There was one man who may have an answer as to the nature of these symbols. He would need to see Elias Wheaton.

PART 3

CHAPTER 18

Andrew waited for Nina's eyes to flutter open. She gave him a gentle smile when she saw him. "Good morning," he whispered as he kissed her cheek. He wrapped his arms around her. "If we are to be gone for the day, we need to get ready."

"I will pack lunch after breakfast," said Nina.

"I need to see to a few details before we leave," said Andrew as he rose out of bed and dressed.

"I will be ready soon," replied Nina as he left the room.

Andrew sought out Colin, who was next in rank below the captain. Of all the royal guard, he trusted Colin the most. He stayed busy for the captain, and never indulged in idle gossip. He was loyal to his father and wise for his age. Andrew counted on his discretion for the task he had in mind.

He found Colin on sentry duty, looking across the fields toward Burnea. His concentration held, even as Andrew approached him.

"Good morning, your highness. You are up early today," said Colin as he continued to look at the scene in front of him.

Andrew marveled that the guard knew who it was, for his eyes never left the countryside.

"How do you do that?" asked Andrew. "You did not turn your head, yet you knew I was coming."

"You have a specific stride that is heavier than others. I can hear you approach before you come into my peripheral vision. When on sentry duty, I focus on the horizon. Peripheral vision comes in handy," said Colin.

Andrew followed Colin's gaze. "I am taking Nina out for the day. I need a favor of you while we are gone."

"Ask anything, and I shall do it," replied Colin.

"Watch my father carefully. When I return, let me know if you notice any sign of delusion. It could be very subtle. Also, beware of Nathaniel. He must not know you are specifically watching the king."

"Yes, your highness." Colin continued to look at the scenery. "Do you fear something will happen while you are away?"

Andrew sighed. "I fear many things may happen while I am away. This trip is for me as much as for Nina. I need to be able to think outside the castle walls."

"Your father would be better served if Michael Mauldon would have accepted the position of Court Adviser when it was offered him."

Andrew was surprised at the guard's opinion. Most of the royal guard seemed indifferent but kept their distance from Nathaniel out of respect for his position. "Unless it is out of fear for their lives," he thought to himself.

"I understand he is the king's nephew, but I do not trust him."

"Why is that?"

"His eyes are quick, unreadable. When they are still, they seem cold and calculating," replied Colin. "It is as if he is constantly working out a riddle of one sort or another."

"His eyes?" asked Andrew.

"You can read a man's life in his eyes. Nathaniel Stone is dangerous," replied Colin.

"I have been told as much." Andrew turned and walked down the steps, leaving Colin to his duty.

———————

Andrew then hunted Nafaria. When he and Nina were last in Arioth, he remembered she received a letter from Michael that Jared was very interested in. He thought it wise to see what made his cousin so curious. He found her in the nursery with one of the twins. She was laying Leona back down to sleep when Andrew appeared in the doorway.

"I wonder if I could ask you something, Nafaria," whispered Andrew.

She turned around and faced him. She smiled as she crept into the hallway. "What is it?"

"When we were in Arioth, Jared gave you a letter from your brother. Do you still have it?"

Nafaria nodded her head. "It was a long letter. He copied much information from two sources of our family annals for me. He wanted me to have the information to answer questions I may have in the future."

"May I borrow it? I think I might find what he had to say quite interesting," replied Andrew.

"You may. Let me get it." He followed her down the hall to her private study. She disappeared for a moment, and returned with the roll of paper in her hands. It was larger than Andrew remembered.

"Thank you very much. I will return this at the end of the day. Nina and I are going out for a ride along the Anenderes River."

"If you are going out with Nina, are you sure you need this with you? It may prove to be very tedious reading," said Nafaria.

"Nina enjoys riddles of various kinds. I am sure we will both find this interesting," replied Andrew as he headed downstairs.

<hr>

Nina felt her heart lift as she rode with Andrew on the road along the Anenderes. She glanced at the river every so often and watched the sun glistening on the surface of the water. A gentle wind sent cool air to her skin, refreshing her from the warm sun. She glanced at Andrew every so often, who smiled back at her. Though he seemed distracted, he clearly enjoyed the ride. It was as if his mind drifted down the mighty river beside them.

It was nearly two hours before Andrew slowed and veered off the road. The grass near the river was soft, the area deserted. Andrew pulled a large blanket out of his saddle bag and spread it on the ground. She unfastened the bag on her horse and walked over to the blanket while Andrew tied the horses to a nearby tree. He then took out a thick roll and came over to the blanket and sat down next to her. She watched as he carefully unrolled the paper.

She looked out at the waves of the river. "You picked a pleasant day for an outing, Andrew. This place is quiet and peaceful."

"I am a very lucky man when it comes to the weather. It could easily have been cold and rainy, and we would not have this opportunity together." He looked intently at the paper in front of him.

"What is that?"

"A letter Jared carried back to Nafaria after our wedding. I remember seeing him and Michael speaking to each other and always wondered what it was about. I need answers for your concerns, and I fear leaving the castle to go to Denholm Glen."

"What is in Denholm Glen that you do not have here?"

"Michael Mauldon." Andrew continued to look at the letter. He turned the page and Nina saw a meticulous chart covered with various sized dots.

"It looks like a star chart." Andrew looked at her. Nina smiled at him. "Great Uncle studies the stars as closely as he studies alchemy. He even has a special place atop his manor for gazing at the sky."

"Michael told Nafaria this chart is something your great uncle and he are currently working on." Andrew turned the next page and found another chart that looked identical to the first one. He looked at a notation on the bottom of the page. It was a date from the year 1305. He narrowed his eyes as he studied both pages.

"What is it?"

"These pages are identical. Michael tells Nafaria their great grandfather made the same chart in the year 1305. Apparently, there is a time that occurs very rarely that affects the Anenderes River. When the stars align in this fashion, this is known as transcendence. Michael warned Nafaria in case she saw strange things or heard strange stories from people along the river in North Agea," said Andrew.

"Why is this of interest to you?" asked Nina.

"After you left the cathedral, I went back to the castle. I went to sit by mother's coffin. I have heard people whispering about these things, but she never appeared to me. I do not know what I hoped for. I guess I wanted a little wisdom to help me with our argument. Nathaniel found me instead. He told me father was looking for me, but when I went to the throne room, he did not seem as though he needed anything. That was a clue you were probably right. Nathaniel is hiding something," said Andrew as he continued reading. After a few moments he said, "According to Michael's notes, this transcendence will end around the fifth of September."

"So, whatever occurrence allowing the dead to appear along the river will be lost?" asked Nina.

"So it would seem. Nathaniel picked the right time to strike. People are already speaking of strange things. If father acts rash or foolishly, people will believe him when he says he sees mother. He could be seeing visions of her caused by Nathaniel, and we would never know," said Andrew.

"What of Nafaria? Do we tell her about this?" asked Nina.

"We cannot tell her anything. That would only make Nathaniel suspicious. If he has sold himself for greater power to protect his family and others he trusts or cares about, he will never harm her. There is only one thing that concerns me," said Andrew grimly.

"What is that?" asked Nina.

"If Nathaniel is in the grip of a dark lord, what if he continues to grow in power and his mind is clouded even further? Whatever this presence is, it reached out to Nathaniel because of his skill in the Craft. You have to admit he is an apt pupil. If he continues down this path, Nathaniel will change. That is the nature of darkness; it consumes all in its path. If he continues to gain greater power and higher knowledge, what can we do against him?" said Andrew.

"Perhaps that is not for us to be concerned with. Michael knows what is happening. He will not abandon us. We just need to watch out for your father as he asked us to," said Nina.

Andrew nodded. "That will be our focus. There are others that do not trust Nathaniel either. Before we left, I asked Colin to watch father as closely as possible without arousing suspicion. He confided in me that he does not trust Nathaniel."

"Do you know if Lian is any closer to finding the person who killed your mother?" asked Nina.

"I have not heard anything. I am sure if father had news of that sort, he would share it with me."

Nina's face held a black expression that was quickly replaced with fear. "Andrew, what if Nathaniel orchestrated your mother's death to become Court Adviser, and get closer to Rohn? The king is our monarch, but if he is deferring to Nathaniel, he is simply a puppet. Nathaniel holds all the power of the kingdom."

"Do you think he would go to that length?" he whispered.

Nina nodded her head. "Yes, I think he would. What is more, I think Michael might also confirm that suspicion."

"We must not entertain that thought when we return to the castle. We may become targets ourselves if we do," replied Andrew quietly.

Nina crawled into Andrew's arms. "I am so afraid right now."

"I am too. However, as you said, Michael knows what is happening. We are not alone." Andrew looked out at the river as he held her.

"I am looking for something that will help me hear and see from far off. Is there anything in the alchemical arts that will accomplish that?" asked Michael. They were in Reinard's study, busy over books laid out on a large oak desk. Reinard shook his head.

"Alchemy is not the same as supernatural power bestowed by YAHWEH, Michael." Reinard thought a moment. "Is there an incantation of the Craft that could send your consciousness to where you need it to go?"

"You speak of projection?" asked Michael. Reinard nodded his head.

"No. That is a specific gift from YAHWEH, not a learned skill," said Michael.

Reinard looked intently at his son in law. "Do you know that for sure?"

"I cannot say without a doubt, but I have never heard of anyone of the Craft achieving that type of power through mere study alone." Michael looked down at the books lying on the table. His eyes focused more at that moment. "However, there may be one other place I could look," he said quietly.

Reinard knew that tone of voice well. It was the one Michael used when he felt he may be on to something important. Their conversation was interrupted as Alana and Sebastian entered the room. Both Michael and Reinard looked up at them.

"You are both safely returned," said Reinard.

"How did it go?" asked Michael.

Alana handed Reinard the note from the princess. "Princess Nina asked me to deliver you this letter, Lord Sallen. We met her on the colonnade as we were leaving." She looked at Michael as she spoke.

"How is the king?" asked Michael.

"I think he is following Nathaniel's advice a bit too carefully," said Alana. "At first, the king was not sure that I should be given opportunity to take over my father's duties. Nathaniel convinced him to let me try. However, I felt the argument he used was a little weak. If I were the king, I am not sure I would hand over the district so easily to someone without proper experience. I have time to prove myself. If I fail, I will be replaced by another."

"The king agreed to this?" asked Michael.

"A little too heartily," said Sebastian.

"Michael, I have something for you." Reinard interrupted the conversation as he held out a piece of folded paper. "It was inside my letter."

Michael took the paper and unfolded it. He swallowed hard as he read aloud the two words that were clearly written: it begins.

Everyone looked at Michael. "What begins?" asked Sebastian. He was the quickest to find his tongue.

"I warned the princess that Nathaniel would drive the king insane. I told her to let me know when she noticed anything different about him," said Michael.

"How do you know Nathaniel would be the cause of any such difference? He just lost his queen, and the love of his life. He could be grieving," said Alana.

"I was there the night Nathaniel's master gave him the command to drive the king insane. It is the perfect opportunity, for no one would suspect an outside force to influence the king. Everyone knows how much Rohn loved Susanna. Her death would cause great sorrow for him. It could even bring on madness. Who knows how far this treachery goes? Susanna's death could have been orchestrated by Nathaniel for just this opportunity," said Michael.

"That would be a heavy stretch," said Sebastian. "There is no one around who can confirm such a thing. Who would ever know if it were true?"

"Someone always knows. That is what my father used to say. However, we cannot wait for that someone to appear to give us the answers we need. I know what I heard, and I know what Nathaniel's goal will be. He was commanded to drive the king insane, and he will. The only question is to what end?" said Michael.

"I think for now, we should busy ourselves with the obvious tasks before us. Sebastian and I will return to Illith and help Samson rebuild the village. Nathaniel expects a monthly report. He said he will send supplies and money by the end of the month to help the process along," said Alana.

"I have some things I need to research, and Lillia is reading my family annals for something that will help us train my son. Perhaps she will find something of use," said Michael.

"We will have to wait and see what comes next," said Sebastian. He and Alana walked to the door.

"Do you have a place to stay?" asked Reinard.

"We will stay at my family's manor here, and leave in the morning for Illith," replied Alana.

"I will see you both before you leave," said Reinard.

"Make sure you are early. I wish to leave after sunrise," said Alana. She and Sebastian left the room.

"Now it is more important than ever I find what I am looking for," said Michael as he also left the study.

"It seems these dark times are going to grow darker still," Reinard thought grimly.

CHAPTER 19

The next morning was warm and bright. Lord Robert Stowe stood at the window of his great room looking out. His eyes landed on a spot of color off to the left in the front yard. A trellis clustered with pink and white roses stood there. They were large and magnificently shaped, sure to be the envy of any visitor who stopped by. When Lydia was here, there were many visitors. Now there was no one but the servants to enjoy the flowers. Robert found he no longer wished to look at them.

He considered taking the trellis down and destroying the flowers forever. The only thing that stayed his hand was the hope that his wife would return to him. If she did, he did not wish her to see that he destroyed her most cherished home project.

He missed Lydia. Her musical laugh was sweet and filled the household with life. She was his partner in life; a wise and good manager of everything he owned. Because of this, they could afford to be one of the most benevolent families in Wildemere. The kitchen was always filled with people needing bread or a bowl of soup. Now, the kitchen was quiet. What once was a nuisance, Robert missed greatly. The servants could never make enough noise to compete with the memories of his wife.

He never thought she would stay away long. Every time he heard the sound of horses' hooves on the cobblestone path, he thought it was a carriage bringing her home. He anxiously awaited that sound every day, hoping Lydia would be coming up the path announcing she was home.

All at once, Robert heard horses' hooves on the path. His heart quickened as his eyes followed a team of horses. His face fell as he recognized the colors of the royal guard. However, instead of a carriage, a wagon pulled up behind them. His heart beat faster still. The wagon meant someone was to be imprisoned and brought before the king for trial. He rushed outside to discover why it was here.

"Captain, to what do I owe this early morning visit?" asked Robert.

The captain eyed him steadily as two soldiers jumped down from their horses. "Lord Robert Stowe, you are under arrest and required to appear before the king and the Court Adviser immediately."

Shock registered on Robert's face. "What are the charges?" he demanded.

"Conspiring in the murder of a noble man and his wife here in Wildemere," replied the captain.

"This is preposterous! Who is the man that I have conspired to murder?" Robert demanded.

"Jason Mauldon, the apothecary owner and his wife Thena," replied the captain.

Robert's face was ashen as the soldiers shackled his wrists and led him to the wagon. He was too stunned to resist as he was made to climb inside.

The royal city was teeming with activity in the market. Through a thin crack in one of the sides of the wagon, Robert saw children gathering and heard their sounds of laughter and sighs of wonder as they moved from place to place with parents or other children. He felt cut off from this world as the wagon went by. The sunlight that shined in the market refused to penetrate the darkness of the wagon.

He found another small crack in the back of the wagon and spied the antiquarian library the new princess was said to frequent. He never walked through the doors as it was owned by Elias Wheaton. He never trusted anyone of the Craft for anything, so he never gave the librarian the time of day.

The wagon continued slowly as the royal guard made its way through the bustle of people. The next building Robert noticed was the ruined apothecary shop Jason and Thena owned and operated. Their daughter also helped in the shop until the day it was destroyed.

For the first time, Robert wondered if he did the right thing. Was it his place to be a part of a murder to take vengeance on another? He was fueled by Joel's rage and when he realized these people who lived among them were of the Craft, he felt betrayed and fooled as well. His own distrust of those of the Craft melded with Joel's passion to create a force that swept through Wildemere causing so much pain and destruction. Now Joel was nowhere to be found, and Robert was to face the consequences of his actions alone. Were his actions truly what the Mauldon family deserved? He was left to explore that question as the wagon made its way through the rest of the royal city.

His shackles were firmly in place as he was led to the throne room. The sunshine outside was a stark contrast to the shadows of the castle interior. There was richness in the dark to be sure; Robert sensed it all around him. Mahogany made up the wooden tables and chairs he passed. Woven silk of gold and garnet hung on the walls in luxurious tapestries. He could enjoy none of it. The guards marched Robert by each wonder of royalty on their way to see the king.

A young woman walked down a corridor toward them. She stopped short as the entourage passed her. She looked at him as if she recognized him, but he could not place her at all. She could have been any number of young women he saw in Wildemere over the years. Her long golden hair reminded him of Ephratha. Robert pitied himself as he realized he may never see his daughter again.

⁘

Nina watched the royal guard pass by with Robert Stowe. Her eyes met his, but she knew there was nothing she could do for him. If Nathaniel had anything to do with his shackled presence, only one person may hold sway over him. She quickly headed upstairs in search of Nafaria.

She found Nafaria in the nursery dressing the girls. They wore matching light dresses. Fiona was in pink, while Leona wore lavender. Nafaria turned and saw her standing there.

"Good morning Nina. Did you sleep well?" asked Nafaria cheerfully. Her voice was like a song.

"Nafaria, leave the children with one of the servants. You must come with me quickly," said Nina.

Nafaria saw the worried expression on her face. She left the room and returned with one of the maids. "I must go with the princess for a few minutes. Please stay with the girls until I return."

The maid smiled and nodded as she walked over to the bed where the girls sat. Nina grabbed Nafaria's arm and quickly led her from the room.

"Nina, what is the meaning of this?" asked Nafaria.

Nina let go of her arm and slowed her pace so she and Nafaria walked side by side down the staircase toward the throne room. "I just passed the royal guard in the corridor as I was looking for Andrew. They led Robert Stowe to the throne room in shackles."

Nafaria stopped short. Robert was Ephratha's father. He was present the day Joel killed her father. She confronted him in Arioth before Ephratha's wedding. Her brother Philip wanted to kill him, but Nafaria stopped him. Now it seemed Nathaniel was bringing him to justice.

"Nafaria, you are the only one who can convince Nathaniel this is wrong. He will execute Robert unless you say something," said Nina.

Nafaria started walking again. "He must not execute him. Father forbade us from seeking vengeance for his death. Nathaniel is wrong, though he may not listen to me."

"We must try," said Nina. Together, they continued toward the throne room.

⁂

Andrew's eyes widened as the captain of the royal guard led Lord Robert before the throne. He stood, shackled—fear written on his face.

Even in his self-absorbed days before his mother's death, Andrew knew of Robert's vehemence for those of the Craft. Since he became more involved in the dealings of the royal court, Andrew watched as Nathaniel exacted punishment for those proven guilty or even accused of abusing members of the Craft. Many of the punishments were harsh considering the offense, but there were no executions yet. Now Robert stood before Nathaniel, and Andrew understood why. No matter how Robert would plea for his life; he would no doubt be executed.

Andrew looked at his father. The king stood staring at Robert with a coldness that was frightening. He would allow Nathaniel this treachery in the guise of justice to make up for the one Robert was a party to. He felt his heartbeat quicken as he waited for Nathaniel to speak.

Nathaniel walked up to Robert and stood inches from him. "Just how long did you think I would let you live when I learned of your part in the murders of Jason and Thena Mauldon?" he asked quietly.

Robert looked into the black eyes of the young Court Adviser. He suddenly feared for more than his life. He saw the prince standing next to the king. Was there sadness or compassion on his face? "I—I beg for the king to hear me," he pleaded.

Rohn's eyes narrowed to slits. His voice thundered through the room. "You can make your appeal to the God of Jason Mauldon! Although I hardly believe he will hear you."

Robert felt the gravity of his situation as he stood before the throne. He sank to his knees and bowed his head.

"You are here to answer for crimes committed by you and a group of others against my family. A man was murdered on his own property, and you were there, Lord Stowe. You could have prevented it, yet you did not," said Nathaniel.

"How do you know this?" whispered Robert.

"Do you deny it?" asked Nathaniel, ignoring the man's question. "My wife identified you as one of the men present while Joel Blackstone killed her father. Joel then took her mother, hanged her, and then burned her body. This action resulted in a riot that spread throughout Wildemere. I will find this man and punish him as well. Your part in this treachery is to be vindicated today, Lord Stowe. You will be hanged and your body burned in the same market square Lady Thena was hanged and burned at noon three days from today. Your land will be confiscated and sale from it will be added into the royal treasury."

"Nathaniel," said Andrew as he rose from his seat. He moved closer to the Court Adviser and lowered his voice. "This does not have to happen. Prove yourself to be the better of the evil that was done to your family. Show mercy."

"I will exact justice based on the gravity of the offense. This man has no respect for those of the Craft. He will be an example to any who disrespect those who possess greater wisdom," replied Nathaniel coldly. His gaze did not leave Robert's face.

"The sacred writings speak of justice. They speak of an eye for an eye[28]," said the king. It was the first time since his mother's death that his father quoted the sacred writings.

"The sacred writings also speak of mercy[29]. It is said to be a by-product of the grace YAHWEH extends. Do we disregard mercy for justice?" demanded Andrew.

The king looked at Andrew—an icy expression on his face. "If you are not in agreement with this proceeding, perhaps you should not be present."

---

[28]　Exodus 21:24
[29]　Hosea 6:6

Andrew averted his gaze to the floor and was silent. He looked at Nathaniel, the cold glare the Court Adviser was becoming known for, directed at him.

At that moment, Nina and Nafaria entered the room. Nafaria looked at Robert, her gaze focused on the shackles around his wrists. "Nathaniel, what is happening?" she asked.

"This man is to be executed for the death of your parents," replied Nathaniel.

A look of horror crossed her face. She stepped toward the shackled noble. "You cannot do this, Nathaniel. My father warned me not to take vengeance for his death. No shedding of blood can bring him back. It is not right!"

"It is just!" shouted Nathaniel. He looked at the guards. "Take this man to the dungeon to await his execution."

Nafaria looked at Robert. His eyes filled with tears as she whispered, "I am sorry." He could think of nothing to say in return as the guards dragged him away. Tears continued down her face as she watched him. There was a soft touch on her shoulders. Nina whispered, "Come Nafaria. We must go." Nina led Nafaria out of the room as she cried.

Nathaniel left a few moments later. Andrew followed him.

"Nathaniel," called Andrew.

Nathaniel turned and faced the prince.

"Is this truly right?" asked Andrew.

"According to the law of Nereheim, any man who is involved in the murder of another man pays the penalty of death. Lord Stowe is to pay that penalty," replied Nathaniel.

"Nafaria said it was not right. Her father himself insisted that she not seek vengeance for his murder. Why are you seeking what is against his wish?" asked Andrew.

"I will make an example of those who break the laws of this country so that it does not happen again. Many nobles think they are above the law. I will protect the citizens of Nereheim the best I can," replied Nathaniel.

"Is it the citizens of Nereheim you seek to protect, or those of the Craft?" asked Andrew.

"What do you mean?" asked Nathaniel.

"If you are seeking vengeance for your own kind, Nathaniel, it will only lead to greater tension," replied Andrew.

"I seek protection for all Nereheim's citizens. Some have deserved justice longer than others." Nathaniel stepped closer to Andrew. "Do not forget; my authority is given me by your father, the king. Perhaps you question his will?" Andrew looked down at his feet. "I thought not," Nathaniel replied as he turned and walked away. Only when the Court Adviser rounded the corridor and was out of sight, did Andrew breathe again. He inhaled deeply, wondering what would happen to him and Nina if he made an enemy of Nathaniel.

———————— ·•••••· ————————

Nathaniel found Nafaria in the nursery. She held both the girls in her lap while she sat on the floor. As the girls reached for random objects to grab at and feel between their fingers; she wiped tears from her eyes. She took turns gently stroking the soft tufts of hair on their heads. He stood in the doorway for a few moments watching them. Her heart was so good. He felt that overwhelming urge to protect them, all over again. If he ever doubted his decision for Robert Stowe's execution, watching Nafaria with their little girls reinforced it.

He finally spoke. "Why were you there?" Nathaniel meant to be gentle, but the question came out like a demand. It sounded harsher than he meant it to be.

Nafaria breathed a sigh and tried to compose herself. She sat quietly as he towered over her. "I came to tell you not to execute Lord Stowe for his crime. I wanted you to show mercy, not justice."

"He was involved in killing your parents. I swore if I came back to Nereheim, I would seek justice for those of the Craft."

Nafaria turned her head and looked up at him. "To what end?"

Her question caught him off guard. His focus was making those who persecuted members of the Craft pay for their offenses. He wanted to show that wealth and affluence did not make one above the law. The word was spreading throughout Nereheim that as Court Adviser, he was willing to bring justice to all who broke the law. Even now, each district and village reported less violent acts. However, Nathaniel felt it was not enough. Examples needed to be made to prove his sincerity. These examples would show people he was as serious as he was powerful.

Influence and wealth only went so far— anyone could attain both. The power to give and take life was as fearful as a mighty storm. He wanted to show himself master of such power.

"I must do what is just, Nafaria. He was responsible for your father's death, as if he used the blade himself. He must pay the price, just as Joel Blackstone must pay when I find him," replied Nathaniel evenly.

"He is Ephratha's father!" shouted Nafaria.

"Which is why he must die!" shouted Nathaniel in return. She stared back at him with wide eyes. "I cannot show favoritism," he said in a quieter tone.

"If we use this measure to mete out justice, it will be used against us. We cannot live life this way. Blood for blood, it does not work that way!" exclaimed Nafaria.

Nathaniel steeled himself. He took a deep breath before he spoke. He tried to think of a compelling argument, but no words came to mind. "Lord Robert Stowe will die at noon three days from today." He turned and stalked out of the nursery, leaving Nafaria to the children and her tears.

✦✦✦✦✦

Andrew walked out of the castle and down the colonnade. The sun was very bright. There were no clouds hiding the judgment that came to Lord Stowe. He needed to talk to Nina, but first he sought another. As it happened, Colin walked toward him with another guard who looked a little younger. He counted himself lucky to have found his quarry so quickly.

"May I have a word with you, Colin?" he asked as he stopped the guards. They looked at each other and then at him.

"Of course, your highness," said Colin.

"Do you trust the man standing next to you with your life?" asked Andrew.

"This is my cousin, Emil. I trust him with anything, your highness," replied Colin.

"Then follow me. I have an urgent message for you to bring to Jared at Arioth," replied Andrew.

The guards turned and walked with Andrew down the colonnade to the stable. The only person there was the stable master's son. He showed no surprise, as people came throughout the day.

"What is the message, your highness?" asked Colin.

"You are to speak to Jared and Ephratha directly. Let them know Ephratha's father, Lord Robert Stowe is to be executed at noon three days from now. The king has sentenced him to death for his part in the murder of Jason and Thena Mauldon," said Andrew.

Both guards stared at Andrew. Not since the king executed Count Vedan for the plot against Lord and Lady Saintclaire had there been an execution in Wildemere.

"Tell Jared the king did not come to this decision on his own. The Court Adviser pronounced this decision and my father agreed to it. He must be careful in the future. Things are taking a strange turn here. He needs to be on his guard," said Andrew.

"We will convey the message as quickly as possible, though there will be no time for appeal from King Lian," said Colin.

"It is enough that Ephratha knows her father is to be executed. I cannot make any other appeal on Lord Robert's behalf. I just wanted them to know," replied Andrew.

Colin bowed his head. "We will see it done." Colin turned to the young stable hand. Andrew looked at the young man as well. He completely forgot he was there.

"I am here to assist my father. I hear only the horses," he said.

"Well then, let us be off, so you will hear two less horses," replied Colin. He turned to Andrew. "Please let the captain know where we have gone."

"Of course," said Andrew. Both the guards quickly saddled, mounted their steeds and rode for their destination.

———— ✦✦✦✦✦ ————

His first task complete, Andrew followed the colonnade to the garden where he found Nina. She sat with her back to him, facing the roses. Andrew often found his mother this way; a teacup in hand, sorting through a latest puzzle or worry, looking for insight to manage the concerns that came with royalty. It was a different kind of drinking habit altogether—one that was not only healthier for the body, but for the soul and mind as well.

He sighed. He missed the calm confidence his mother possessed. Her laughter lit up the darkest corners of his heart when he was afraid. He was sure his father fell into the gloom of despair because he no longer felt her presence. If only he would take time to come to the garden. He would find her there.

It was uncanny how events turned his life upside down. He managed to meet Nina and marry her before his mother died. She had the rare opportunity to know the queen as a woman who cherished her last days with her and showed her everything she could, as if Nina were her own daughter. The creator knew his creation enough to know what void needed to be filled in each person's life. He packed the cracks of their lives with the love and tenderness like a mason fills in bricks with mortar.

YAHWEH knew he could never live without the qualities both his wife and mother possessed. Without them, Andrew was a ruined man. He smiled at the thought of the creator sitting in command above the earth[30] as the sacred writings said. Perhaps he was there for those outside the Craft as well as those within its ranks after all.

As if feeling his eyes upon her, Nina turned her head. She smiled when she saw him. Andrew sat down next to her.

"Were you looking for me?" Nina put down her cup, poured tea into another cup and handed it to Andrew. He took it and drew the cup to his face. He felt the steam on his upper lip as he gently sipped the liquid, a smile on his face.

"I have not taken time to enjoy a hot cup of tea since mother died," said Andrew quietly.

"I have found it to be a very calming ritual. It is a form of meditation that helps clear my mind of the poisons of life's worries. Your mother was truly a wise woman." Nina went on. "She once said to me, 'A cup of tea in the morning to prepare you for the day. A cup of tea in the evening to contemplate all you have encountered and put your mind to rest. A cup of tea throughout, if you feel you need extra strength

---

30   Isaiah 40:22

or special insight.' However, today feels like a day where there is no answer at the bottom of the cup." A tear dropped from her eyes and rested on her cheek.

Andrew was touched by her emotion. "Did you know him well?"

"I knew of Lord Stowe. He was very protective of his family and everything else he possessed. He was suspicious of anyone of the Craft. He was rich, but Lydia, through her wisdom made him richer. I remember my mother being jealous of Lydia's good fortune. However, as I grew up, I took notice of the way she lived. Robert's fortune was not doubled by her good luck. She worked hard for her husband and always chose the wisest path in any decision. It would not surprise me to find she sought special counsel from YAHWEH himself."

"I never knew anything about either of them. I never even met Ephratha before Jared introduced me to her, the day after the ball my parents held for me. She was there, and I never knew it. I was angry at Jared because he met her first. Of course, all that changed when I met you. At first all I saw was a beautiful girl in desperate need of aid. After being with you, I find you are everything I could have wanted and needed a wife to be. If it was YAHWEH's plan all along, I praise him for his wisdom." Looking into her eyes, Andrew reached for her hand and took it in both of his. "I cannot lose you, Nina, not ever. I am very afraid for all of us right now."

"Afraid?" asked Nina.

Andrew nodded his head. "You did something courageous today. You brought Nafaria to the throne room with the hope of convincing Nathaniel to show mercy to Lord Stowe and stay his execution. It was the right thing to do. However, I fear it has put Nathaniel on guard in his quest for power. He is wise for being so young, and his intelligence is matched only by Michael Mauldon. Jared is the only other man I know who has their quick wit and cleverness, but even he bows to their skill. We must be careful around him. If he perceives us a nuisance to his goal, he may strike out in ways unimaginable."

"What goal would that be?" Nina's eyes suddenly widened. He could tell she pieced it together.

"What ultimate goal could there possibly be than to rule a kingdom?" asked Andrew quietly.

"Nathaniel is not royalty," said Nina.

"He is my cousin, and Court Adviser. He shapes the policy of Nereheim with the king's approval. Remember our conversation the other day. If my father is deferring to Nathaniel, what might happen if he mentored the future king? This king would grow and mature under his influence. He would see Nathaniel's way as the only way to govern a kingdom. He would be worse than a puppet on a string," said Andrew.

"We cannot let that happen," said Nina.

"The die was cast when my father offered Nathaniel the position of Court Adviser. I believe this is why he did not hesitate to give his answer. Now, it is just a question of time. Our baby will be heir to the throne of Nereheim when I am gone. If it is a boy and he came to power as a young king, Nathaniel would mentor him. Perhaps he might even choose one of his daughters as his wife. After that, it will only be a matter of a well-placed set of unfortunate accidents to help events unfold for Nathaniel's ultimate purpose," said Andrew grimly.

"What do you suppose that is?" asked Nina.

"If one of his daughters married our son, an untimely death could make her the future queen," replied Andrew quietly.

Nina felt the tears spill out of her eyes and burn her face as she understood what Andrew was saying. There may be no growing old together. They were caught in a web so intricate that one move would strangle them.

"What can we do?" whispered Nina.

"You must be completely invisible. You cannot allow yourself to stand out in any way. Our baby will need you. Nafaria will need you. I may last ten years, I may last five days. I need you to be wise, so that you will be safe," said Andrew. He brushed a hand across her face and cupped her cheek.

"Nina, you are my most precious jewel. I cannot bear the thought of a world without you in it." Andrew leaned closer and kissed her lips.

"I love you so very much Andrew. You are my heart, and always will be." They sat in the garden amid the roses as the minutes of that tainted morning ticked away.

CHAPTER 20

Robert Stowe sat chained to the wall of the castle dungeon. After Nathaniel's pronouncement, the only appeal in his favor came from the one person who should have hated him most bitterly. The young Court Adviser's wife—the daughter of Jason and Thena Mauldon, was the only person who begged Nathaniel to show him mercy. This was the second time she pleaded to others for his life. He decided he would never understand those of the Craft.

He faced these and other thoughts as he felt the chill of the stone floor. He was locked in a room with the demons of his mind, and no way to escape them. Was this how prisoners went mad? Was this why execution was not immediate? The room he was locked in seemed to have one way out. It led to a path that took him on a journey to his past.

Robert was thirteen, when a distinguished older man made his way up the gravel drive to his home. The spring day was bright, with a refreshing breeze from the countryside. The first dandelions and violets sprang up all over the hillsides. He was contemplating an afternoon by the creek with his fishing pole after he completed his chores.

"Good morning to you, young master. Is Lord Stowe available today?" asked the stranger. He took off his hat and bowed to him. Robert was wary of the stranger. His eyes seemed a little too friendly, his voice too cheerful. However, he nodded politely. His father had many business dealings with people who made a show of treating Robert with such honors. They thought they were winning him with their charm, but Lord Stowe's only son was never taken with anyone.

"My father is in the stable. Follow me please," replied Robert. The man followed him down the path behind the house to a stone structure twenty feet away. He opened the door and led the stranger inside. His father was with his horse attendant.

"Father, this gentleman is here to speak with you," said Robert.

His father looked at the visitor, then to his son. "Thank you, Robert. Are your chores completed for the day?"

"I have yet to weed mother's flowers. It should not take long," replied Robert.

"There is no other work, after you are finished then," replied his father. Robert nodded and left the men to their business.

After he finished with the flowers, Robert gathered his pole. He told his mother he planned to fish in the creek. She wished him luck as he left the house and wandered down the road toward the woods and his favorite path to the creek. His father was walking to the front of the house with the stranger. He wore a thoughtful expression on his face.

"You cannot afford to pass on this opportunity, Lord Stowe. The land is good, come see for yourself," said the stranger.

"I have no need of more land. What I have provides well for my family. A man can overextend himself if he is not careful," replied his father.

"At least, see the land. Perhaps you will change your mind," replied the stranger.

Lord Stowe noticed his son walking toward the woods with his pole in his hands. He thought about the stranger's words. "Robert, come here," he called.

Robert obeyed. "Yes father?" he asked.

"I have the rare opportunity to acquire a parcel of land at a good price. What do you think of that?"

"Very often, rare opportunities disguise something less promising. I would expect you to at least survey the land before you make any decision," said Robert.

The stranger laughed heartily. "Those are wise words from one so young! You will be a shrewd businessman one day."

"He is now," replied Lord Stowe proudly. "He catches and cleans his own fish, and sells them in the village market."

"That is very industrious for a young man," said the stranger.

Lord Stowe looked carefully at his son. "Robert is right. Before I make any decision I must look at the land myself."

"Would now be a good time?" asked the stranger.

Robert's father looked at him. "Would you like to accompany me, Robert?"

"Yes father." Robert tried to sound as mature and businesslike as possible, but this was rare. He was never asked to come on a business venture.

They rode on horseback a few miles from their village. Robert had never been on this road before, and he wondered what land was for sale here. The stranger led them off the country road on a path ending in a meadow. The grass was green and smelled sweet; wildflowers and plants grew everywhere. He noted the wild strawberries growing among them. He jumped off his horse and reached out to pick one.

"What are you doing?" asked the stranger. His voice was low, but sharp.

Robert looked at the stranger. "I was just about to pick a berry. I wanted to see if it was ripe."

"You should not eat wild plants and berries. Poisonous berries and roots have been known to kill people who think they know better." The stranger's eyes seemed narrow and less friendly than before.

Lord Stowe was looking out over the pasture at the green grass. "You are right, sir. This land does seem to be very good for farming and as pasture for animals."

Robert looked at the stranger. Something did not seem right about the situation, but he was not sure what. Then he remembered. This was the wrong month for strawberries. The plants would be green, but not bearing fruit yet. "Father, may I have a word?" asked Robert.

"It seems my son would like to speak to me in private. Would you mind?" he asked the stranger.

"I will give you time to speak." He moved off down the path with his horse.

When the stranger was out of hearing range, Robert spoke as quietly as possible. "Father, do not buy this land. There is something strange about it."

"Strange?"

"Is it not strange that such desirable property is a few miles from home and yet you did not hear of it? Who is this man?" Robert asked. He looked down at the patch of strawberries with their bright red color. "This patch of strawberries should not be here. Strawberries do not appear ripe in the wild until early summer. Nothing about this seems right."

His father considered Robert's observation with a sigh. "This land looks good, but the price is just beyond our reach. It would have to produce a great crop in order to maintain what we have now." He looked at Robert. "I appreciate your observation. You notice things that I do not."

"What have the gentlemen decided?" asked the stranger. He rode back up the path toward them.

"It is a tempting offer, however, I will decline. We just cannot afford another parcel of land right now. Thank you for your time," replied Lord Stowe.

The stranger looked at his father with a sharp eye. His demeanor became rigid and much less friendly. "That is a pity, because this is a great price. I shall have to offer it to someone else." He turned round on the path and rode off, leaving father and son alone.

The stranger sold the land to one of their neighbors who spent everything he had to acquire the money. He was in a panic the next day when he rode to Lord Stowe's manor and begged him to come with him.

Robert again accompanied the men along the same countryside they visited previously. He remembered the creek that flowed on the right side of the road. They stopped short, surprised by the difference they saw. Instead of a green meadow teeming with wildflowers, they saw nothing but barren land that looked as though it harvested only boulders. Their neighbor was devastated.

"I sold everything I had because the land looked so good. How is this possible? I have the deed right here in my hand!" he exclaimed. Lord Stowe looked at the paper. It described the exact location, but he could see this was not the land he surveyed before. He was as perplexed as the man with the paper.

The two older men deduced that the stranger was of the Craft, and he enchanted the area to sell it for the money. The stranger disappeared, and their neighbor had no chance to seek justice and regain his money and property. He was ruined.

A strawberry alerted Robert that something was not right. He felt in his heart the stranger was not what he made himself out to be. As a result, he grew up hating those of the Craft for their special power and knowledge. He never forgot how easily people were deceived by their cunning. His wariness and disdain grew into prejudice; which eventually grew to the hatred of all things associated with the Craft.

He buried his face in his hands and wept. He looked back in shame on his part in Jason's murder. He stood by and allowed Joel to avenge Leanna's death by killing an innocent man. Now Joel disappeared and no one had seen him for almost two years. If Robert would have been a true friend to Joel, he would have used some of Lydia's well placed words to comfort and encourage Joel to mourn, grieve, and move on with his life. Instead, he allowed the hatred and evil in his own heart to fuel a vendetta against the couple who worked tirelessly to save the man's dying wife. Jason and Thena were strangers in Wildemere, but well respected. Robert wept for the world's loss of them more than for his pathetic existence.

Nafaria descended the staircase to the castle's dungeon. Andrew told her how to get there. He said it had been more than fifty years since the monarchs needed a reason to hold someone there. The law enforcement of Wildemere was able to handle most prisoners. It made Nafaria wonder why Nathaniel ordered Lord Stowe imprisoned there. She knew her husband left nothing to chance. He delegated very few tasks and those he did were usually mundane in nature. He only trusted her with secrets of importance. Lately she wondered if she were entrusted with even those.

The stone stairs spiraled as she made her way to the bottom. She carried a torch, but saw it was not necessary. The sconces held lit torches. The air felt damp down here.

She found a guard at the entrance door. The room was eerily quiet for a man condemned to die. The guard recognized her instantly. He bowed his head slightly, knowing it embarrassed her to be recognized more formally. "My lady, this is no place for you."

Nafaria stood before him, holding a small basket in her hand. "So, I am told. What is your name?"

"It is Hawthorn, my lady."

"Like the berries that grow rampant here in Wildemere."

"My mother told me so once," replied Hawthorn.

"I wish to see the prisoner, Hawthorn. A few moments are all I need."

"What is in the basket?" Suspicion tinged Hawthorn's voice. She smiled and threw back the cloth covering. A few pieces of bread sat next to a jar filled with clear liquid.

"You bring food for the man who killed your father?"

"Joel killed my father. Lord Stowe was merely present. Though he is guilty of allowing treachery to come to my family; I forgive him. I just want to visit with him before he dies. He is chained to the wall, and you will be right here standing guard. I am in no danger."

"Please do not tell your husband I allowed this. He would be very angry if he knew you were here." Nafaria heard fear in Hawthorn's voice.

"Is that what he said?" Hawthorn's words surprised Nafaria.

"It is what I fear, my lady. They say you knew Nathaniel Stone when he was a boy. Tell me, is the man you married the same as he was then?"

Nafaria heard apprehension in the guard's voice. She wondered why he would ask her such a personal question. What did others fear about Nathaniel that she could not see? He was impulsive and strong willed; always confident in any circumstance. Though he refused to listen to her father's last words, she felt that he had not changed in those aspects. "Yes, he is the same. He has always been willing to do what is just."

Hawthorn did not seem convinced, but he nodded his head and opened the door for her. Nafaria walked into the cell.

Robert looked up and saw the torch first. The bright ball of yellow flame was the only color he had seen for hours. A puzzled look crossed his face when he recognized the bearer of the light. "Why have you come?"

Nafaria sat down a few feet from him. She put the basket next to her and uncovered the bread. She took a piece and handed it to him. He took the bread and inhaled the thyme and rosemary scent. He looked at her again. Opening the jar of water, she set it within his reach.

"I wanted to see you before the execution. You are my best friend's father. I am sorry I could not persuade my husband to show you mercy. I regret the only thing I will be able to do is write Ephratha and tell her I witnessed your death. I do not know how I will find the words," said Nafaria quietly.

Robert looked at Nafaria as he drank water from the jar. He sighed and said, "I am sorry for the pain I visited upon you and your household. Your father was a man of honor."

"Why did you do it?" Her question came out in a whisper.

"I have distrusted anyone of the Craft since I was a youth. People who have special power and knowledge take advantage of those around them at will. It has happened before. My father almost lost all he owned to someone who tried to deceive him. I was with him one day and persuaded him not to buy a field made to look like good land, but in reality was not. When my father followed my advice and passed on the offer, the swindler went on and cheated another honest man out of all he owned. Some trickery of the Craft was used to hide the true nature of the land. When the deception was discovered, the man already disappeared. I have been wary of the Craft ever since. When Count Deveraux's daughter, Ana, was killed by being poisoned, I hated those of the Craft even more."

"I was ten years old when Ana was killed by Lya. That death cost the life of my mother's friend Analia. She and my mother were like sisters," said Nafaria quietly.

"Joel was suffering from grief at losing Leanna. He sought vengeance against your parents for failing to heal her. He was raving when he came to me. Leanna was such a special woman. It did not seem right that she died. So, I was one of the men who were there to mete out his vengeance on your household. It was a fool's decision that cost me my family; just as it cost you yours. I am so sorry I did not reason with Joel. I could not see past my own hatred," said Robert sadly.

"I forgive you," whispered Nafaria. "I must go." She stood up.

"Tell Ephratha I love her when you write her next," said Robert.

Nafaria nodded, tears brimming in her eyes. "Goodbye, Lord Stowe." She grabbed the basket and walked out of the cell.

Climbing the steps away from the dungeon, Nafaria pondered the depth of Hawthorn's question. Many of the castle guards feared Nathaniel. Was there truly something to fear? What was his goal? Nathaniel refused to follow her father's last request. He said he must not show favoritism. Why would he consider it favoritism to honor her father's dying wish?

She felt a draft in the stone hallway as she continued upward. Then, once again, she heard her mother's whisper as she had at Arioth, "*Train up your child*[31]."

Which child did she train? In her heart of hearts, Nafaria knew the answer. The only question she had was how? What else could she teach her daughter that would stand against Nathaniel in the days to come?

As Nafaria continued through the castle, she remembered a very important book she was given. She hurried up the stairs to her study. Of all the things she possessed, there was one book that would be most useful. She opened a drawer and pulled out a leather-bound book with a lavender flower embossed on the cover. She then took out another leather book that was blank inside. She sat down and opened both books. Picking up a quill, Nafaria began to copy Lady Cassandra's diary.

---

[31]   Proverbs 22:6

CHAPTER 21

The sun was warm and bright as it climbed above the hills and peeked through trees. Though the morning was chilly, the air refreshed Ephratha while she stood on the terrace off her bedroom. The world held great promise on a day like this. However, she could seize none of those promises for herself, or the baby sleeping quietly in his bed. A shiver ran through her body. She walked back inside.

The desk sitting next to the window held a single sheet of paper under a paperweight. She picked up the paper and looked at it once again. It was full of news from a life she wanted to be part of. She did not focus on the words. She looked intently at the neat, swoop of the letter *p*, and the crisp point in the tail of the *f*. The *m* held a certain beauty in it that enchanted her. Tears fell from her eyes as she walked out of the room, clutching the letter in her hand.

Jared came up the hallway, returning from hunting with Coleman and Raphael. They had an adventurous morning, and acquired two wild turkeys for dinner. When he saw Ephratha coming toward them, he stepped in front of her and wrapped his arms around her. She smiled as she hugged him.

"Is something wrong?" His voice was gentle and caring.

She sighed and looked at the letter in her hand. "I miss Nafaria. Though we lived a half day's journey from each other, we were at least in the same country. I wanted us to be able to share each other's lives. I wanted to watch our children grow up together. Her friendship is so special to me."

Jared held her close and kissed her forehead. "I know. Each time I get a letter from Andrew, it is filled with a desire to learn from me. 'Teach me how to be like you', he writes. I finally have the relationship I always wanted with my cousin; but because of how my uncle feels, I cannot tell him that face to face." He looked in her eyes. "We at least have each other. I hope that is enough for now."

Ephratha reached up her hand and placed it on his cheek. "Jared, I will never be sorry for the choices I made that brought me here. You have been my protector, my shelter. However, before you, Nafaria was my protector too. She never let me think of myself in any way but the most beautiful person in the world. Her special gift to me was her unending optimism. If not for her, I would not be the woman you see today. You are my shelter, but she is my rock. I miss her so." Her last sentence came out in a barely audible whisper. Jared held her as she sobbed.

"I have always marveled at the fact that you, a daughter of a noble who despised the Craft, have such love and devotion to one of its ranks. You have spent a long time with Nafaria as a friend. I know it is not fair now, but perhaps the wheels are in motion to bring a new time for our kingdoms. We may yet see our children grow old together after all. Write to Nafaria. Tell her everything that our little prince has been up to. I am sure she will be grateful for the news."

"Little Jerrik does nothing much but sleep and eat these days."

"Tell her about his eyes. I think she would like to know he has his mother's eyes: sapphire blue and bright as the stars." Jared kissed her lips then rubbed his nose playfully against hers.

"What will you do?"

Jared's expression darkened. "I have been up most of the night preparing something for Andrew. I must finish it and send it quickly. Something he said in his last letter troubles me."

"What could that be?"

"He thinks Nathaniel has changed, but is not certain. There is sharpness to him that Andrew has never seen before. It concerns him— and worries me."

"What could it mean?"

"I do not know. However, I will not leave Andrew without an answer. I will send him whatever wisdom my pen will afford." Jared squeezed her hand and walked back to their bedroom. Ephratha watched him go. She thought of Nina's distrust of Nathaniel again. "Oh Nina, what if you were right all along?" she whispered.

❈

Ephratha stood over her son's cradle, staring down at the tuft of light brown hair peeking over the soft blue blanket covering him. She reached down and touched her fingers to his cheek. She sank to her knees and knelt next to her son.

"I always thought you would grow up surrounded by playmates. I hope you will make friends around you. Maybe one day you will be friends with the little ones across the Anenderes. You need to learn to be wise like their parents," said Ephratha quietly.

"He will learn," said a voice behind her. Ephratha smiled and glanced up at Jared as he knelt down next to her. In his hand was a thick parchment roll.

"Have you written your letter?"

Ephratha nodded and smiled, handing him the parchment in her own hand. "It is not as large as yours, but I did tell her about his eyes."

"I will send it with Solomon tomorrow. I am anxious for Andrew to receive this."

"What on earth could take so much to say?"

"Andrew's last letter worries me. There was something I copied for him from our Annals of North Agea. I only hope he sees what I mean for him to see."

"Whatever it is, will it be wise for him to know?"

"I have no idea. So I send the letter anyway and leave it to YAHWEH."

"That is all that we can do." Ephratha placed a kiss on his nose. They rose and crept out of the nursery, leaving Jerrik to his slumbers.

The next day, Lydia rode into Arioth and stopped in front of the apothecary shop. She opened each of the two baskets strapped to her horse and took out the bundles inside. She proceeded into the shop with the bundles in hand and a cheerful smile on her face.

"Good morning Lydia," said Malcom when he saw her. He stood in one corner of the shop with a small bottle in his hand.

"Good morning, Malcom. I have a harvest of spearmint and lemon balm with me."

"Then it is a fortunate morning for me. I am in need of spearmint."

"What about the lemon balm?"

"I will take it, though I am not quite out yet. Your herbs are of great quality, second only to Lord Cade, so I will gladly take them whenever possible."

"Thank you. I never thought I would see the day I would make a business of harvesting wild herbs."

"Have you ever grown anything before?"

"Only roses; they were my joy when I lived in Wildemere."

"That explains the quality of your herbs. You are accustomed to putting care and attention into your plants."

Lydia was surprised at his remark. "This is not common?"

"No, it is not. All too often, care and attention are replaced with the urgency to harvest a great quantity to make greater profit. You cannot rush quality." Malcom handed her a cloth bag the size of her palm. It felt heavy in her hand, so she opened it and counted the gold pieces. Her eyes widened.

"Malcom, I cannot take this much for these herbs."

"I pay dearly for quality. I have had good luck in the last month with the herbs you provide for me. I am merely passing on the profits of your labor."

"Thank you." Lydia smiled.

"So, where are you off to now?"

"A visit to Arioth is not complete without seeing my daughter and grandson," Lydia said with a laugh.

"Enjoy your time with your family," he said as she headed out of the shop. He watched through the window as she climbed back on her horse. When she was out of sight, he returned to his work; a slight smile playing on his lips.

Lydia found Ephratha, Jared and little Jerrik in the throne room with the king and queen. On seeing her, the child instantly reached out for her.

"It seems you are wanted, Mother," said Ephratha as she gave her a hug, then handed Jerrik to her.

"I decided to stop in after my business at the apothecary shop. Malcom paid me handsomely for my herbs once again."

"I think he counts it an added bonus that you have become one of his many suppliers," said Jared.

"Do you think so?" asked Lydia.

"I do. I am glad you found something here in North Agea that makes you happy," said Jared.

"I am happy to be able to sustain myself selling herbs," replied Lydia.

Ephratha laughed. "Once again, mother, you have proved yourself able to handle anything."

"Your highness, you have a message from the prince of Nereheim," said the door guard. Jared saw the guard standing with two of Nereheim's royal guards who kneeled before him. He recognized Colin Greene.

"Please rise. What is the message?" asked Jared.

"I am afraid this news is as shocking as it is sudden. Prince Andrew himself sent us to tell you that Lord Robert Stowe is to be executed at noon tomorrow," said Colin.

Ephratha and Lydia looked at Colin. Ephratha's eyes grew wide. "Father?" she whispered.

"The prince knows you will not be in time to make an appeal or even visit him before the execution. However, he thought you should know." Colin walked closer to Jared and said, "Prince Andrew also wanted you to know this decision was put forth by King Rohn's Court Adviser. He implores caution in the future."

"Thank you for bringing this news. From the look of you and your companion, you must have ridden all night. Please stay until morning and get some sleep," said Jared.

"Thank you, your highness. I am sorry for the news," said Colin.

Jared looked at the door guard. "Find these gentlemen food and a room for tonight." The guard bowed his head and motioned for the visitors to follow him.

———— ···+++··· ————

Ephratha felt her breathing become shallow. Her head buzzed as she leaned against Jared for support. "Father," she whispered again. Slowly her thoughts of despair were replaced with another one. Perhaps there was one thing she could do after all. She dried her eyes and looked at Jared. "Please take care of Jerrik today. There is something I must do," she said quietly as she slipped from his arms.

"Of course, what are you going to do?" asked Jared.

"I recently read in the sacred writings about a man—a king, who pleaded before YAHWEH for his dying son.[32] I will plead before YAHWEH for my condemned father. Perhaps he will hear me, perhaps not. I must try." She went to her son and kissed him on his cheek. Walking out of the room, she resolved to lay her request before her creator.

Ephratha sat at the window of her room and looked out at her home. Arioth was busy about its day, unaware of her sorrow. She lit a single candle and put it in the window and closed her eyes. She did not know if her routine was correct, she only thought about the creator of the universe who watched her. Such was written in those sacred writings Jared and her mother had so much respect for. Perhaps it was only those of the Craft he acknowledged; but she would plead to him for her father's life. It was her only option.

A few moments later, she felt a touch on her shoulder. Turning, she saw her mother standing next to her with a soft look in her eyes. In her hand was a lit candle, which she put down next to the one before Ephratha. Lydia kneeled next to her daughter and bowed her head as well.

———— ···+++··· ————

---

[32]   2 Samuel 12:15-20

The day went about its business, the sun shining down on Arioth as its residents bought, sold, and continued their lives. It was a normal day in the royal city of North Agea except for a single story that spread throughout the market, residences, and even the great cathedral Jared and Ephratha were married in. Each resident who heard the story stopped at the candle maker to buy a single candle.

Ephratha sat next to her mother with her eyes closed. She recalled the past, one memory at a time. She stopped at one that was far off, but still as easily recognizable to her as the business of yesterday. She was maybe five or six years old when she awoke from a bad dream and could not get back to sleep. Her father heard her whimpers and cries and came to see what was wrong. She only sat and cried, saying she was afraid of the dark. He sat down on the bed and held her as she cried. After a few minutes, he looked down at her and said, "It is natural to fear the darkness. You do not live in it, so you do not understand there is nothing to fear from it, only what moves within it. I will show you what darkness can hold."

He lifted her from the bed and carried her outside, into the garden. She clung to his neck while he walked among the roses her mother so carefully tended. He sat down on the stone bench with her in his lap. He gently lifted her chin so she stared up at the sky. "This is what the night can hold," he whispered as she looked at the stars. They were beautiful; extraordinary lights so pure and bright to behold.

From that night on, Ephratha met with her father for thirty minutes every clear evening to study the night sky. She learned names of stars, and star clusters. Her father told her stories and legends surrounding those stars. He showed her how to gauge direction from the various patterns in the sky. "Be mindful of the heavens and you will never lose your way on earth," he would say.

Even now, in another country, Ephratha took time most nights to go into Queen Clara's rose garden and gaze at the sky. She would reflect on the day and whatever puzzles needed to be solved. She learned from her father that darkness itself was nothing to fear.

In her deepest heart, she knew her father was a good man. He was broken somehow by something that happened, perhaps long ago, that made him distrustful of the Craft. In all their long conversations, and time spent together, he never mentioned the strange people of YAHWEH who claimed to help others and use their gifts for the good of all. She would give anything to know how things became twisted in his mind so that he condoned killing Jason and Thena for revenge. Tears dropped in her lap as she silently pleaded for her father's life.

Long shadows on the wall gave the first clue of sunset. Ephratha felt a gentle touch on her shoulder again. She saw Jared standing next to her with Jerrik in his arms. His eyes were misty as if he were holding back tears. "Bring your candles and follow me. There is something you both need to see." He turned and walked out of the room.

Ephratha rose from her place and helped her mother up. They picked up their candles and followed Jared outside, through the courtyard to the edge of the palace property. Ephratha blinked in amazement. Standing before her were dozens of people from Arioth, each holding a single candle.

"They started gathering about an hour ago. Somehow, news of your vigil carried through the city, and everyone came here. They wish to support you in this dark time," said Jared.

Tears streamed down Ephratha's face as one by one, those who were present stepped forward to take her hand, or give a word of comfort. Behind her, the palace servants and royal guard gathered also. King Lian and Queen Clara came up to her and held her. Colin and his companion stood nearby; each with a candle in their hand.

As one: royalty, military, merchant, peasant and noble came before YAHWEH to plead for the life of Robert Stowe.

CHAPTER 22

Andrew spent the morning wandering through the market of Wildemere. He received his letter from Jared when Colin and Emil returned from North Agea. Nafaria received a letter from Ephratha as well. He began reading the letter in the castle, but after a few lines his brow knitted together and he looked around his room suspiciously. Jared had something important to say, and Andrew no longer trusted his surroundings. He told Nina he was going for a walk to clear his head. The object of his walk lay in front of him. Andrew headed for the doors of the Grand Cathedral and walked inside.

Once he crossed its threshold, he breathed a little easier. He felt at peace in this place. His home where he lived his whole life ceased to be as tranquil as this room. Perhaps it was because this was where he talked to Nina for the first time. Or maybe he truly felt a benevolent presence in this place held sacred to the residents of Wildemere. He sat on one of the benches and opened his letter.

Andrew,

Your last letter fills me with concern. When Nathaniel returned from his sabbatical, he seemed different to me then. I attributed it to his solitary time away. I did not think to give you a warning because I did not feel one necessary. For that I ask your forgiveness, for you not only have a powerful man of the Craft in your midst, but he is your Court Advisor as well. If your father and he truly do see eye to eye on matters and vengeance is what they seek, I fear we will be plunged into war.

There is something I wish to share with you from the annals of North Agea. There are two excerpts here. One is about a diary that a man named Marcellus kept. That diary is over 100 years old. The next is an account of a murderer named Michalis. Both accounts support a theory rolling around my brain for a while. I did not share it with you before because you would think some madness controlled me. There is one man who could tell you if what I suspect is possible. Nafaria's brother, Michael, is well versed in the Craft and highly regarded by many for his extensive knowledge of things both great and small. He would know if such a thing is possible. If you require further proof, show him this letter and ask his opinion. It may not be what happened, but the jigsaw fits together only too well. The following are the copied excerpts from the annals of North Agea...

Andrew continued reading. The first excerpt was about a book called the Grimoire Macabre. The creepy tale made Andrew shudder. He stopped and stared at the mention of blood. He recalled Nafaria's nightmare—the one that turned a lock of her hair white.

The next was a detailed account of a man named Michalis; a famous murderer in North Agea. From what Andrew remembered of the legend he heard from his history tutors, Michalis became more deranged every time he killed. He thought himself omnipotent, but in the end was executed. Though a lunatic, he was regarded as brilliant. Michalis was a prime example of how a person may respond when he feels above the laws governing a country—or even human beings themselves. Feeling themselves above written human law was a problem some nobles went through. The rich and powerful did what they wanted with no thought given to the rest. This was what drove his father to execute Count Vedan for the deaths of Lord and Lady Saintclaire. Andrew understood Nathaniel's vehemence. He became Court Advisor to mete out justice, and proved skilled at the task. However, Andrew felt Nathaniel's wisdom was tainted somehow. His judgments were harsh and not fairly placed. Was Nathaniel using his authority for his own design?

Andrew next read Jared's theory. It was too preposterous to think, but what if it was true? He must find out. He thought of Nina's great uncle, Lord Sallen. He could get word to Michael through him. It was the only way to keep from arousing Nathaniel's suspicion. He carefully rolled the letter back up. He put his head in his hands and thought through what it meant if Jared was right.

After a few breaths, he composed himself and rose from the bench. He walked out of the cathedral to the castle. He stopped in the center of the market square. The apple blossom trees were alive, but there was a large space left where some trees were removed from the grove. Andrew stood there for a few moments. How did Nafaria feel being back in this country—this very city, where her parents were murdered? He never really thought about it until now. He knew the pain he felt only too well for his own mother who was gone. Where did she find hope when she lost so much? He decided it was time to imitate the grace of the women around him as well as the wisdom of the men.

Andrew walked up the colonnade and saw Nina coming toward him. Her face brightened when she saw him. "You finally remembered your home!" she said as she hugged him. He held her in his arms and kissed her. She smelled like fresh roses.

"How could I forget?" he asked. He walked toward the castle with his arm around her. "Did you finish your letter to your great uncle yet?"

"I was about to send it out."

Andrew shook his head. "Do not send it yet. I need to write him as well."

"Is something wrong?"

"I am not sure," replied Andrew with concern in his voice.

Reinard sat in his study, lost in thought. A thick heavy book lay open in front of him, but the words blurred together into a mass of lines and circles. Lately, he spent many afternoons in this manner. He looked through his books and notes for anything that might protect his family. Nathaniel proved himself capable of anything in his quest for power and vengeance. What did he want most? If it was power, why silence Michael? He was Court Adviser. Only the king held greater authority. There must be something more. If Nathaniel was commanded by his dark master to destroy Denholm Glen just to silence Michael, why go to such length? What would a force so powerful be concerned about? "Michael knows something," Reinard said aloud.

Another thought begged for his attention. What was gained by destroying Illith? Why did Jason tell Michael both Illith and Denholm Glen were in danger? Count Deveraux was given jurisdiction over Illith after Count Vedan's execution, but why did that matter? Everyone knew of Deveraux's distrust of those of the Craft. Reinard pondered this. Count Deveraux was responsible for the deaths of Raymond and Analia Bernard. Nathaniel was thirteen years old when his father and Jason's family fled at his insistence. Did Nathaniel destroy Illith to settle that old business?

While he thought through these things, there was a knock on the door. "Come in." As the door opened, he was surprised to see Colin.

"Colin, this is a surprise."

Colin sat down across from his uncle. "I seem to make rounds here quite often these days." Colin handed Reinard a wrapped bundle.

"Andrew gave me another letter from Nina for you. He told me to wait for an answer."

"That is odd," said Reinard, opening the package. "Let us see why Andrew needs a response."

He found his letter from Nina right away. It took very little space in the bundle. The rest of the package bore Michael's name. "I have discovered why Andrew needs an answer. We must go to Mauldon Manor and give this to Michael. Is there any reason for Andrew to disguise a letter to Michael inside a letter from Nina?"

"The prince exercises extreme caution these days. There is quite a bit on his mind. This letter to Michael may explain why he does not want anyone but us to know he sent it," replied Colin.

"We need to get over to Michael and see if we can help ease the prince's mind." Both men rose from their seats and exited the study.

<hr />

Reinard and Colin found Michael in his library at his desk. Before him was a thick book at least twenty years old. He looked up when he saw them, but his surprise centered on Colin who stood next to his father-in-law. Reinard handed Michael the package with his name on it.

"The prince sends his regards," said Colin as he and Reinard found chairs to settle into.

"To what do I owe this?" asked Michael as he opened the package.

"Prince Andrew is sifting through things in his mind, and finds he cannot trust the Court Adviser. He asked me to use extreme care as I go about errands he needs me to run," said Colin.

"How is the king?" asked Michael. His brow furrowed as he scanned the first of many pages in his hand.

"The king is still recognizable as himself. I cannot say how long that will last," replied Colin. "I am to wait for an answer from you."

"He says that he apologizes for not being able to come in person. He believes it will raise suspicion if he leaves Wildemere at this time," said Michael.

"There are quite a few pages for just a small note," said Reinard.

"It is mostly a letter Jared sent him that has excerpts copied from the annals of North Agea. Jared has a theory as to what happened to Queen Susanna." Michael's eyes widened as he read the letter.

"What is it?" asked Reinard.

"Jared thinks someone may have summoned the spirit of a murderer from almost sixty years ago. From what I am reading about the details of Susanna's body, the life of a murderer named Michalis, and an account of a man who witnessed the passing of the Grimoire Macabre from one successor to another, he may be correct. He believes Nathaniel summoned this dead murderer to kill Queen Susanna," said Michael.

"Does Nathaniel have that kind of power?" Colin's face was grim as he spoke.

"He may. I believe Nathaniel possesses the sacred bell of Herron. This relic alone has strong power from the dark lord who created it. Though the bell is said to have been fashioned by spirits and work only for the pure in heart, I believe it was fashioned and set in place by the god of blood to wreak havoc on the world. Why else would the city of Herron be an abandoned wasteland?" said Michael. He put the letter down and sat back in his seat and looked at Colin. "Did Andrew say whether he believed Nathaniel was capable of this?"

"He wanted to wait until he heard from you whether this was possible before he came to any conclusion. He has been very quiet and pensive over the past few days," said Colin.

"It seems our young prince is learning prudence," said Reinard.

"Andrew has a reputation of being self-centered. What did he notice about Nathaniel that put him on his guard?" asked Michael.

"The prince is completely different since they returned from North Agea following the queen's death," said Colin.

"That is certainly a good reason to mature. However, most people as self-consumed as Andrew was said to be tend to focus on their own pain. This letter I am reading shows someone completely different from the prince I saw at his wedding," replied Michael.

"What are you suggesting?" asked Reinard.

"It is more than the queen's death that has Andrew asking questions. Has anything else happened lately?" asked Michael.

Colin thought a moment, and then nodded his head. "Come to think of it, there was something else. He and Nina took a day trip together recently."

"Why would you remember that?" asked Michael.

"Andrew came to me before they left and asked me to watch the king closely. He was concerned the king may not be himself. It was the day before Lord Stowe was sentenced to be executed for his part in your father's murder." Michael started.

"You did not hear of this?" asked Colin.

"No," replied Michael. "Who ordered the execution?"

"It was agreed between the king and the Court Adviser that Lord Stowe was to be executed for your parents' murders. This was to satisfy those in Wildemere who still had questions about what was being done about their murders, but also to send a strong message to corrupt nobles that those of the Craft were no longer to be brought up on false charges and exploited for their land. Nathaniel was adamant Lord Stowe be held responsible to the point of death for his part in their murders. Nafaria came to the throne room and pleaded with the king and Nathaniel to let the matter drop. She said her father told her no one was to seek vengeance for his death. Nathaniel refused to listen to her," said Colin.

"So now, the prince suspects something that is potentially dangerous for him. He would have been better off unaware of everything around him," said Reinard.

"However true that may be, Andrew is changing for the better. He takes the time to ask questions he never would have before," said Colin.

"What do we do now?" asked Reinard.

"The same thing we have been doing—continue to look for something to help us against Nathaniel," replied Michael.

CHAPTER 23

Rohn lay in the darkness and willed his eyes to close. He calmed his breathing and his heart beat wound down to a slow thump in his chest. He almost felt at peace as he lay in bed drifting between the conscious world and that of dreams.

Perhaps it was the tea that Nina insisted he have with her before he retired to his chamber for the evening. Maybe it was the heart filled talks he had with Andrew lately. He was growing closer to his family every day. Andrew insisted they spend time together, just the two of them, and it lifted Rohn's spirits so greatly not even Nathaniel stood between them. Sleep was the natural by-product of a healthy heart. One that was free from worries related to his wife's death.

"Rohn." His eyes opened wide as he recognized the confident female voice he missed so much.

"Susanna?" he whispered. Slowly sitting up, he felt a draft from the open window. He got out of bed and stumbled toward it. He reached out to pull it closed, when a shadow caught his eye. A faint light came from the garden. He closed the window, pulled on his boots and robe, and headed downstairs.

The night air was chillier than he expected for late summer. In the moonlight he passed the roses marking the entrance to his wife's cherished garden.

A few feet ahead, were the wrought iron table and chairs that stood in the middle. He stopped suddenly and rubbed his eyes. Susanna stood on the other side of the table; bent over a cluster of maiden's blush roses, taking in their fresh scent. Her eyes were closed, her lips pulled into a soft smile showing her enjoyment of the activity she was engaged in.

Rohn stood mesmerized. "Susanna?" His whisper broke the spell she was under. She opened her eyes and looked at him.

"Rohn." Her whisper was more in his mind, than from her lips.

"Is this real?" he asked softly, taking a few steps closer. Her smile was soft—her eyes sad.

"Avenge my death. Lian knows the murderer." She reached out her hand to him. He tried to grasp it, but she disappeared before he could touch her.

"Susanna!" Rohn shouted as he sank to his knees before the roses and cried in the night.

⁘⁘⁘

Sitting on his throne, a dark expression resided on Rohn's face. He was deep in thought, but those thoughts clouded his eyes and darkened his heart. Suspicion furrowed his brows. In his hand was a crystal orb that fit neatly in his palm.

Nathaniel walked into the throne room and saw him staring at the piece of crystal. "Your majesty," he said as he bowed to the king.

"Tell me, Nathaniel, do you think Lian knows who killed my wife?" Rohn lifted up the crystal orb and stared at it in the light.

"When Queen Susanna died, the king was in counsel a long time with the man who examined her body. They looked carefully for clues to her killer, but never reached a conclusion that was shared with anyone," said Nathaniel carefully.

"No conclusion?" Rohn's brow furrowed.

"I always felt King Lian was frightened by something he knew, and was unwilling share. He may not know who the killer is, but he knows something he has not disclosed to us," replied Nathaniel.

"Lian knows something," whispered Rohn. "I wish to know what that something is."

"What do you command?" asked Nathaniel.

Rohn set his jaw firmly. "I will ride to Arioth and speak to Lian personally. Stay here in my absence."

"Yes, your majesty," replied Nathaniel.

The king rose from his seat and left the throne room.

Nafaria busied herself with the girls. Each was in an amiable mood, but Fiona seemed more restless than her sister. She wrapped her tiny hand around Nafaria's finger and tried to pull herself up, while Leona lay still and gurgled happily.

She picked up Fiona and snuggled her. The little heartbeat on her chest was constant and Fiona settled down. Nafaria kissed her. "How would it be if you and I had some play time together?" she whispered.

Just then, Nathaniel walked through the door, and the moment was gone all too quickly as Fiona perked up her head, smiled brightly and reached her arms out to him. Nafaria sighed, passing her to him.

"Is something wrong?" Nathaniel kissed her cheek as he took Fiona in his arms.

"No. I was just enjoying holding Fiona for a moment. It seems the opportunities to do so are few." Nafaria walked over to the cradle where Leona lay. She was lying quietly and concentrating on her fingers. Nafaria looked down at her and put out a hand which Leona latched hold of and pulled toward her.

"Nathaniel, how would it be if I took Fiona with me today?"

"What do you mean?"

"I want to have alone time with Fiona like I have with Leona. I never spend quiet alone time with her unless it is to nurse or to put her to sleep."

"There is no need for you to trouble yourself. I spend my time with her."

"She is my daughter too. I simply would like some time with her the way I spend with Leona. You have never spent time alone with Leona. It would be good for both of us."

"What will you do?" Nathaniel's question was sharp in tone.

"I am going into the forest to look for herbs. There are not too many warm days left." Nafaria's tone was calm, but she felt hurt that Nathaniel seemed unwilling.

"There are too many things in the forest that are unsafe. I would prefer Fiona stay on the castle grounds."

Nafaria was surprised by his answer. "Do you not worry when I take Leona with me?"

"Fiona stays here." Nathaniel ignored her question.

"Why are you keeping me from my daughter?" Nafaria's tone was stern.

"Fiona is mine!" Nathaniel shouted. "Do not test me in this, Nafaria. Fiona stays with me."

Nathaniel turned and briskly walked out of the nursery with Fiona in his arms. Tears welled in Nafaria's eyes as she watched him go. She did not understand why he would act in such a way. "He has never raised his voice to me," she whispered. She wiped her eyes and went to the cradle.

"Well little one, it will be just us today." Nafaria sighed as she pulled a cloak over Leona's shoulders and then pulled one over her own as well.

She nearly ran into Andrew when she came downstairs. "I am sorry, Andrew, I was not watching where I was going."

"No trouble. I seem to wander around quite a bit these days." His eyes showed concern when he looked at her. "Is everything alright?"

"Yes." She forced a pleasant smile. "I am going into the woods this morning."

"Be careful. I understand you are of the Craft, but you can still be attacked by wild animals."

"I will be fine. Be sure to look after Nina today," she said as she walked outside.

⸱⊹⊱⊰⊹⸱

Nafaria walked through the forest with Leona wrapped in a soft blanket inside a long handled basket. Over her shoulder was a canvas bag to put herbs she found of interest. The castle grounds afforded excellent places to replant wild herbs, and the gardeners were as gracious as they were enthusiastic with her every whim.

The warm air was comforting. The changing colors of the leaves on the trees hinted that autumn was near. However lovely the morning was, Nafaria's thoughts were darkened by the argument between her and Nathaniel. She purposely waited until she was amid the trees and various bushes before she gave in to her tears.

After their argument, Nathaniel left with Fiona before they came to an agreement—something that never happened before. She sighed as she continued through the woods.

The concern Andrew showed her when she nearly ran into him surprised her. The look in his eyes told Nafaria he realized something was wrong, but wished not to pry. She never thought Andrew Catalane would notice the cares of another. He certainly had changed.

The forest thinned, and Nafaria stepped into an open area bordered by elm trees. Putting down her basket, she reached inside and picked up Leona. She then pulled out a wool blanket, and sank to her knees. She spread it out as neatly as she could with one hand, and then gently laid Leona down. Leona looked up at her, giggling and reaching her arms out for her. Nafaria felt the tears drop on her hand as she plucked a stem of lady's mantle from a nearby plant. The bright green leaves on the stem sprouted just below a lively yellow-green color flower. Leona took the stem with the flower in her hands and focused her attention on it.

Nafaria watched her daughter's fascination with the tiny plant. Leona drew her entire attention to this one thing, and was quite still. She seemed focused on the smallest details. This was so unlike her twin. Fiona would surely be crawling into the wood by now, exploring every crevice. She would seek out the dangers as well as the wonders of the forest. Both were traits she and Nathaniel exhibited at times: the need to be adventurous, and the need to contemplate. However, it seemed these traits were neatly split between the girls. Leona was the contemplative one, while Fiona made her surroundings fit her desires. Nafaria wondered if any greater strength was in one or the other.

Her tears continued as she sat on the blanket with Leona. More than once she wondered why Fiona was so special to Nathaniel. Why did he guard her so jealously? Why would he not let her have time with Fiona? She had no answer, so she sighed and wiped away her tears. She had to be strong for Leona.

Nathaniel had changed in more than one way, it seemed. Robert Stowe's execution showed Nafaria he was not above trampling the wishes of others to fulfill his goals. What was accomplished in that execution? Try as she might, Nafaria could not understand what was gained in usurping her father's last wish.

She felt a soft touch on her arm. Leona rolled over on her stomach and touched her with the flower, a broad smile on her face. She picked her up and placed a soft kiss on her forehead. "Well, little one; we have each other. I will teach you the way my mother taught me." With that she reached for the basket and gently put Leona inside. Then she gathered up the blanket, folded it, and put it in her sack. She picked up the basket, and went further into the forest.

Nafaria lost track of the time, and Leona fell asleep while she walked. As she went on, she began to feel she was not lost. She did not know how far she walked, but it had to be quite a distance. Her ears picked up the sound of running water. Following the sound until the trees thinned, she came out of the forest by a brook.

The brook lay ahead about twenty yards. Though it was threaded with wild plants and flowers, she could see a low bridge: one that was used to cross the brook from the property on the other side. She came out of the woods at the edge of her old home. Her breath caught. The figure of a woman with soft golden blond hair stood in the center of the bridge. Nafaria stepped cautiously forward. "Mother?" she whispered. The woman looked at her and smiled, and Nafaria knew it was indeed her mother.

"Mother!" she cried, hurrying toward the bridge. She stepped across and stood no more than a foot away from her.

"Hello, little one."

"Mother, is it really you?"

Thena smiled. *"Yes, but not for long."*

"How are you here?"

"The times you face are troublesome. I came to give you a warning, and a word of guidance. You must not worry about what you cannot control. Though Nathaniel is adamant about one child, you hold another in your hands. Train her up in all the ways you know. The time will come when she will face more evil than Nereheim has ever witnessed. She must be ready."

"I can only show her so much. I am not skilled the way Nathaniel is."

"You are skilled enough, Nafaria. You may not have great power, but you have wisdom. Your knowledge of plants and herbs is vast. Pass on the knowledge not only to heal, but also to cripple. The weapons you fight with are subtle as well as obvious. It is an awesome task to learn such things, but there will come a time when it becomes necessary to protect yourself and those you love."

Thena turned and looked at the manor behind them. *"Do you remember our home here? It is broken and forgotten. Rebuild the manor, not only to help heal the wounds of past sins, but as a haven for those who have no place left to turn. Michael can help you train Leona to be strong in the Craft and become a mighty foe to contend with. Raise her in YAHWEH's strength. Teach her to stay in the light throughout her life. Then when she uses the power she has been given, she will respect it, and it will not destroy her. Teach her that true strength lies in humility."* Thena turned back to her and blew her a kiss; then disappeared from the bridge.

"Mother!" cried Nafaria. She was alone once again.

Slowly, she walked across the bridge that still felt sturdy after so many years. Her brothers and father built it well. She walked through the gate and down the path to the manor. Everything around her was still and quiet. She heard the chatter of birds, but after a moment they died away. The great house stood ruined from the fire. The windows were gone, but most of the walls still stood, even with such obvious neglect. "A haven for those who have no place left to turn," whispered Nafaria.

She looked around the side and found the remains of the herb garden she planted and tended while she lived here. The various herbs and plants grew into a wild tangle of flowers and leaves alike. The land still produced, while its masters were nowhere to be found. She followed the path to the main road and headed back to the castle, the foundation of a plan taking shape in her mind.

CHAPTER 24

Lord Cade enjoyed the late afternoon. The sky would soon turn pink, as sunset approached. The hawthorn bushes bordering the front near the house needed to be trimmed. He would let the groundskeeper know in the morning.

A low rumble caused him to look out. Horses made their way toward Arioth. He scanned the group and caught sight of the banner before the entourage. It was the crest of Nereheim. Lord Cade was puzzled. Was Rohn visiting Lian for some reason? He knew Rohn vowed never to return to North Agea until Susanna's killer was found. Did that mean they found the murderer? Why would Coleman not have told him? These questions were in his head as he watched the horses turn and make their way up the gravel road that led to his home.

They stopped before the noble. King Rohn slowly dismounted and stood before him. "Lord Cade, I would like to visit the rose garden once again."

Rowen saw the king's firm jaw and noted the dark look on his face. His eyes were distant as well. Something put Rowen on his guard, but he bowed to the king. "My home is always at your disposal, your majesty."

"Thank you." The king turned to one of his subordinates. "Ride to Arioth and let King Lian know I am here, and wish to speak with him."

"You wish to speak with him here?" asked the guard.

"Yes, I will meet with him in Lord Cade's rose garden."

"Yes, your majesty." The guard mounted his horse and set off on his task.

"Now is the time for answers," whispered the king as he walked past Rowen to the garden.

Lian quickly left the throne room, with Rohn's messenger. Why would Rohn meet him in Lord Cade's rose garden? His mind was sorting through that latest question as Jared and Coleman approached.

"Your majesty, you seem in a great hurry to be off somewhere," said Coleman.

"Where are you going?" asked Jared.

"Rohn asked to meet me at your father's estate, Coleman. He is waiting in the rose garden," replied Lian.

Coleman furrowed his brow. "Do you think it wise to meet him there?"

"Why do you ask?"

"It seems a rather strange place to meet the king of a country," Coleman replied.

"Rohn lost his wife, the absolute love of his life, just a few months ago. He vowed never to return here unless I could tell him who murdered her. Now he is here, and though I have no idea why, I will meet him wherever he wishes. He is my brother-in-law— I am worried for him. I will go to him and try to ease his mind however I can."

The tone of the king's voice told Coleman he overstepped his place. "Your majesty, I mean no disrespect. However, I am your captain. It is my duty to make sure you are in no danger as you travel. For this reason, I insist on accompanying you."

"I wish to go as well, father," replied Jared.

Lian looked from his son to his captain. "Come."

They met Rowen at the front of his manor. Jared noticed the guards from Nereheim waiting as well. The landowner looked beside himself as he watched them approach. He bowed to the king. "He is in the rose garden. If I had to guess, he would be in the heart of the garden, near the maiden's blush roses. I remember they were Susanna's favorite."

Lian looked at them. "I will speak to him alone. I do not wish to upset him further if he expected to meet me alone."

"We will wait for you around the side of the manor, out of sight," said Coleman.

The king turned and walked around to the rear of the manor and entered the rose garden. He remembered the times when he and Clara sat among the roses when they courted. The garden was Clara's comfort. She was most at ease sitting among the flowers, idly arranging them as they took tea. The memory brought a faint smile to his lips. Things were much simpler then. Rohn looked intently at the maiden's blush roses. He turned to Lian when he heard footsteps approach.

"I vowed I would not return to this land until you told me who murdered my wife. However, your silence has caused me to break that vow. Tell me, brother, have you found her murderer?" asked Rohn bitterly.

Lian looked into the narrowed eyes of his brother-in-law and pursed his lips. He exhibited the look of the man Lian feared the most; one who would accept no truth except what he wished to hear.

"I have no clear idea who Susanna's killer is. We found many clues pointing to something inexplicable. I cannot even formulate a theory as to how it happened. This is why—" Lian began but Rohn interrupted him.

"You know something!" Rohn's eyes blazed with anger. "You know, yet you do not tell?" he shouted.

"I would only be telling you a fairy tale, not answering your question!" shouted Lian in return.

"You know something!" Rohn shouted as he drew his dagger from his side. He rushed at Lian and put the blade to his throat. "Tell me what you know!"

"I do not know for sure," replied Lian, his tone barely above a whisper. He looked at his brother-in-law with imploring eyes.

"Then you will join her!" shouted Rohn as he drew the blade across Lian's throat in one stroke.

Lian's eyes emptied as the life drained from them. Rohn stared at him, and then at the blade in his hand. He was so shocked, he threw it away. "What have I done?" he whispered.

Rowen and Coleman ran into the garden. Jared came up behind them. "Father!" he shouted when he saw Lian on the ground.

"I am sorry," Rohn whispered as he drew his sword and fell on it.

Coleman was too late to stop him. He lay on the ground, a few feet from where Jared sat, cradling his father's head in his hands.

⸱⸱✦✦✦✦⸱⸱

It was like an awful dream he could not be wakened from. Jared sat on his knees with his father's head in his lap. Blood flowed from the wound at his neck and spilled on the ground, on his hands, on his clothes—so much blood. He willed his father's eyes to open, but it was not strong enough to overcome the obstacle of death. His father was gone, and nothing could bring him back.

The others recognized the need for him to be left alone for the few minutes he was allotted. However, the time was still too short, when Jared felt a strong, but gentle grip on his shoulder. He heard Coleman's low commanding voice. "Your highness, we must go."

Coleman signaled two men who stepped forward and helped separate father and son. Slowly they walked out of the rose garden and back to the horses. Rowen waited there with two servants. Jared saw a bucket of water in each of the servant's hands. A white shirt was draped over his shoulder.

"Jared, you need to take off your shirt," said Coleman.

"You must clean yourself a little before returning home. Your family will be alarmed enough at today's proceedings. The sight of so much blood on you may be shocking," said Rowen gently.

Jared said nothing as he took off his shirt and grabbed a piece of cloth from one of the buckets to wash. He then took the shirt that was held out for him.

Rowen wrapped his arms around his son. "You have your duty, but be safe as you do it," he said quietly.

"I will, father," replied Coleman.

Rowen provided a cart and driver to take Lian's body back to the castle at Arioth. He also provided a cart for the Nereheim royal guard to transport Rohn's body back to Wildemere. The captain hitched the cart to two of their horses, and assigned a driver. He watched both groups of soldiers slowly proceed to their destinations.

Jared's mind flitted between mourning and trying to understand what happened. What could have been in his uncle's mind when he drew the dagger on his father? He knew there were times when the two kings did not see things the same way. He even knew there were times when they were at odds with each other over differing opinions. Whatever the situation, each had enough respect for the other to sit quietly and come to an understanding that would benefit all.

Jared remembered Andrew's warning the day Colin arrived with the news of Robert Stowe's execution. However, he doubted Andrew had foreseen anything like this.

As bad as he felt for himself, his heart broke for Andrew. In one moment, both lost their fathers. They would each be called upon to become their countries' new monarchs. Would they be up to the task? He spent his life preparing for this, yet he had doubts about himself. He was surrounded by people who knew him, loved him, and had the power and authority to make wise and just decisions. Andrew had only just begun to rise to the occasion of governing a kingdom, and there was a very strong authority in his midst neither of them trusted. What would become of Andrew if Nathaniel felt he was expendable?

"Your position is more precarious than any other, Andrew," he whispered.

Ahead, the castle gate was in view. He always looked forward to that sight when he returned home, for it meant he was among those he loved. Today, that gate would bring only blackness to those within. As he thought of his loved ones and this terrible news, he sighed.

Jared remembered his last homecoming. He was greeted by his and his wife's greatest friends. So much had changed since then. Was it really less than a year ago that Aunt Susanna, Uncle Rohn, and his father were alive and the future was so bright? The future no longer held promise, but its dark cousin; foreboding. What would become of him and Andrew as men, and North Agea and Nereheim as nations?

"Go see your mother and your wife." He was snapped out of his thoughts by Coleman's voice. He climbed down from his horse and headed for the castle.

⁘

Ephratha walked to the throne room with Jerrik in her arms. He was his lively and cheerful self. She thought Clara would like to hold him. At breakfast, she seemed tense and distant. It was as if she were burdened with knowledge that weighed her down like a millstone. The queen's energy diminished by degrees—taken by worries she was powerless to control. She remembered the scene in the throne room the day Susanna died. Clara knew something terrible happened to Susanna, but not what. Intuition told her something was wrong, and she fainted when the news was confirmed. Now Ephratha wondered if something worse happened.

Jared came into view before she turned down the hall of kings. His face was haggard, his shoulders slumped. Her smile faded as she took in his demeanor. For the first time since they met, Jared looked completely defeated. Tears fell from his eyes as he stood before her.

"Jared, what is wrong?" She made her voice as soft as possible. Anything stronger and she feared it would blow him away as a cyclone destroys all in its path.

"Father," he whispered, and slumped to his knees before her.

⊹⊹⊱•⊰⊹⊹

Lian is dead. The words echoed in Clara's mind like a resounding gong. The mere thought made her temples throb and ache. Her whole body was numb. There would be no growing old together—her life was gone. Her husband, the only man she ever truly knew and loved, was gone. He was her shelter, her mentor, her spirit. He was gone. What would happen next? Her sister was gone; her brother-in-law was gone. When would she wake from this nightmare?

Her fingers wandered aimlessly over the table next to her bed. With a loud yell, she swiped everything from the table, and finally her tears came. The sound of shattered glass brought Clara's attention to the crystal vase that held an arrangement of roses from the garden. It now lay in pieces among flowers and water on the floor. The crystal glistened in the fading sunlight. She slumped down next to the spilled water, roses and broken crystal. Tears rolled down her cheeks as she focused on the largest crystal piece. The edges were jagged to the touch. She picked it up, fascinated with the sharp point on one end. She peered at the rough jagged edge, and then placed the glass on her wrist, pressing it into her skin until blood came forth.

Her husband was no more. Her sister was no more. Her brother-in-law was no more. Slowly, Clara dragged the piece of crystal up her arm, exposing her vein. Then she did so with the other side. Clara Saint Marc was no more.

CHAPTER 25

Andrew stood with the sentry at the castle wall. He looked at the countryside that stretched in the direction of Burnea. He stood stock still. On the outside, he was poised and completely in command of his entire body. On the inside, however, he was agitated, stressed and worried. It was not like his father to take off, leaving the responsibilities of monarchy in another's control. He never trusted anyone else with that much power. Andrew feared his father truly was going mad. So, he stood and waited for his return. The day wore into twilight; still Andrew waited. The sky would be dark soon. The chill in the air increased.

Andrew considered going after him, but he would not leave Nina alone in the castle with Nathaniel. He was no longer sure Nathaniel could be trusted. Even Nafaria kept her distance lately. It was very subtle, but she spent much time in private with Leona. Nathaniel seemed too eager to have Fiona with him at any given time. Both still loved each other, but it seemed to Andrew that each had a very singular focus that drove them in opposite directions.

"Andrew." He was brought out of his thoughts by the sound of his name. He turned and saw Nina behind him. In one hand was a cup with steam wafting from the top. In the other, she held his cloak. "The cook suggested a cup of hot chicken broth. Apparently, Colin and Emil prefer it when they are on watch."

He took the cup and sipped the steaming liquid. The blend of salt and spice renewed his senses. He leaned over and kissed her cheek. "Thank you. This is exactly what I needed."

"I did not know how long you intended to stay here, so I brought your cloak." Nina spread the cloak over his shoulders while he sipped the broth. The twilight grew darker still. She followed his gaze.

"What do you suppose is happening there?"

"I have not the slightest clue. Father forbade us from going to North Agea until mother's murderer was found. Now he runs off in that direction, blinded by whatever fool notion has popped into his head."

"Perhaps we will never know what he was thinking."

At the sound of footsteps, they turned as Colin approached. "Your highness, I suggest you retire for the evening. You have been here since this morning. You need to rest."

"I am fine."

"Not even the royal guards have shifts more than four hours at a time. You must be well rested in order to stay focused. Go to sleep. I will keep watch for the next four hours," replied Colin.

Nina gently put her hand on his arm. "Colin is right. We should sleep tonight, and come back in the morning."

"Perhaps you are right." Andrew allowed himself to be led away by Nina. Colin watched them go, and then turned his attention to the direction of Burnea.

⸭⸭⸭⸭⸭

"Rohn!" Michael screamed as he sat up in his bed. He was covered in sweat, breathing heavily. Not since the death of his father, did he feel this pain of loss. It cut his heart as tears streamed down his face.

"Michael, what is it?" Lillia's light touch was cool against his perspiring skin.

"The king—I saw his death!" Michael sat shaking.

"Are you sure you saw it happen, or is it something that might be prevented?" asked Lillia.

"No, this feeling is the same as when father died. The king is dead, I am sure of it," replied Michael in a whisper.

"What will we do?"

"The country will be vulnerable. I will ride to Wildemere. I want to be there for Andrew. You must stay here with William. I do not want you anywhere near that castle."

"You must not go alone," replied Lillia.

"Peter will accompany me." Michael pulled her close. They held each other as they mourned the loss of their king.

Lillia moved about the kitchen as Maia prepared the morning meal. She could not sleep with Michael preparing for his journey before daybreak. As she packed a basket of food, she thought of what this loss would mean for Nereheim, but also for her husband. The Catalane family had endeared itself to the Mauldon family in unexpected ways. What started years ago as a friendship between Rohn and Jason became much more as Michael and Nafaria grew older. This loss would affect Michael as greatly as that of his father. She fixated on packing the basket so as not to cry once again.

Michael roused Peter and Stephen from sleep and asked them to come to the stable. When they both arrived he spoke. "Gentlemen, I have grave news. I wish I were wrong. I do not have details, but I know that King Rohn is dead." He looked at the ground before he spoke again. "Peter, you and I will be riding for Wildemere within the hour. I wish to be present for Andrew's coronation and Rohn's funeral.

Stephen, you will ride to Illith. You are only to speak to the Countess or Sebastian. Tell Alana the king is dead, and to be careful in the future."

The stable door opened and Lillia entered carrying the basket she prepared and a cloth bag. She handed them to Michael who strapped them to his horse. "Come see William before you go," she said as she kissed him.

"I will, right now," said Michael.

The men left the stable to prepare for their separate journeys.

Andrew climbed the steps of the castle wall. Colin's advice was indeed wise as he felt refreshed and more alert. He walked to the part of the wall that faced Burnea. Colin was standing there.

"Good morning, your highness," said Colin without turning to face him. "I trust you slept well."

"Yes, very well, Colin. Your advice was excellent. I feel better. Were you here all night?" said Andrew.

"I relieved the fourth watch sentry at dawn," replied Colin.

"Is there any reason you are spending so much time on sentry duty? You are second in command of the royal guard if I am not mistaken," said Andrew.

Colin turned and looked at him. "That is correct. I must confess I did not realize you knew as much."

"I am full of surprises these days," said Andrew quietly.

Colin turned back to the countryside. "My cousin Emil is one of the youngest members of the royal guard. When the king left, the stable boy informed me he was with the captain, and also accompanied the king to North Agea. Emil is capable, but I still worry."

Andrew sighed. "My father is king of a country, and I worry. I know how you feel."

Together, they watched as the countryside roused itself from slumber. After a few minutes, Colin furrowed his brow and took out his glass. He trained it far into the distance.

He handed Andrew the glass. "Something approaches."

Andrew looked where Colin indicated, and saw men on horseback moving with a horse drawn cart. After a minute, the banner was clearer. Andrew's breath caught. It was his father's crest, an eagle—the symbol of Nereheim. He watched the party draw closer to the castle. The cart was now noticeable, it carried a rectangular box long enough to be only one thing. He quickly scanned each of the riders, but did not see his father. He swallowed hard. Someone else rode his father's horse. Tears started as he watched the party draw nearer. Colin's expression was grim, for he understood what Andrew did. He saw his captain, but did not see his king.

At that moment, a guard approached them. "Sir, I am here to take sentry duty." He saw the expression on Colin's face.

"Your highness, you must meet them," said Colin quietly.

"You need to see the captain," said Andrew. They both headed down the steps.

Andrew, Nina, Colin, and Nathaniel were waiting in the stable when the party arrived. The captain dismounted and approached Andrew. "Your highness, it is with a heavy heart that I report to you that your father, the king, is dead. Your uncle, King Lian, is dead also."

"What? How can that be?" asked Andrew.

"Your father drew a dagger on the king in a fit of rage. He met King Lian in the rose garden on Lord Cade's estate. Your father wanted to speak with King Lian alone. We were told to stay behind. We heard angry shouts, but before we could separate them, your father killed your uncle and fell on his sword. The captain of North Agea's royal guard saw what happened, but was not in time to save your father from killing himself," said the captain.

Andrew closed his eyes and wept. Nina wrapped her arms around him as they grieved for their broken family.

Stephen reached Illith by midday. The village square was still in disarray, but under construction. The magistrate's office was one of the few completed buildings. He felt the Countess would be there.

He tied his horse to a pole and walked into the building. The room was small, but clean and neat. Orderliness was a Deveraux family trait. Each member was neat and graceful in everything they did.

She sat at a large desk in front of the back wall, reading a paper in her hand. Her auburn hair was pulled off her shoulders. Alana was as lovely as he remembered.

"Alana, it seems we have a visitor." Stephen felt a strong hand grip his shoulder. He looked to his right. Sebastian Cavanaugh stood next to him. He seemed taller, if that was possible. She looked up when she heard her name.

"I am a servant of Lord Michael Mauldon. He has a message for you," he stammered.

Sebastian smiled. "Relax. The Countess is quite beautiful, but she does not bite."

"What is the message?" asked Alana.

"King Rohn is dead. Michael left this morning for Wildemere to be present for the king's funeral and the coronation of Prince Andrew," said Stephen.

Both Alana and Sebastian were stunned at this news. She looked down at her paper for a moment and took a deep breath. "Did Michael give any details?"

"No, Countess. He only said you must be careful in the future," replied Stephen.

Alana sat back in her chair and looked at Sebastian, and nodded her head. "If Michael went to Wildemere, I shall go too. I also wish to support Andrew." She looked at Stephen. "Do you have a place to stay for the night?"

"No Countess. There was no mention of staying overnight."

"You should stay this evening and rest. You will stay at my home as my guest," said Alana.

"That is very kind of you, Countess. If you will excuse me, I would like to check on my horse."

"Of course," replied Alana. Stephen left the room.

"Is it wise to be at the coronation for Andrew? Nathaniel is sure to wonder how you made it to Wildemere so quickly from so far away," said Sebastian.

"I care not what Nathaniel suspects. Though he may be powerful enough to kill me, I am not afraid of him. I will do what is right and show support for our new king," replied Alana.

"So be it. We ride for Wildemere tomorrow before first light," replied Sebastian.

"Tomorrow," echoed Alana quietly.

Two days later, Michael and Peter arrived in Wildemere. As they rode through the market, Michael looked from place to place to see what changed. It was strange to him that he spent six years of his life in the royal city, yet did not consider it home. Elias Wheaton's antiquarian library was the only thing about Wildemere he missed. He did not even hold any memories of the apothecary shop that was his family's business.

"Something on your mind?" asked Peter.

"I was just thinking that I spent my adolescence here, yet it holds no sentiment for me. Perhaps my true home was always Denholm Glen," replied Michael. They continued toward the castle.

When they arrived, they left their horses in the stable and followed the colonnade to the entrance.

Andrew walked toward them. "Colin alerted me to your arrival. Lillia did not come?"

"William is still unable to travel here. I told her to stay behind," said Michael.

"Did you know about father?" Andrew's voice was barely above a whisper.

"Yes."

"How?"

"I saw him in a dream. He fell on his sword. It felt as if my heart was ripped from me. I felt the same when my father died. No words can convey how sorry I am for your loss."

Andrew gave him a nod. "I received the same sentiments from others over the past couple days." He took a breath and sighed. "However, you are the only person who can truly know how I feel. Alana and Sebastian arrived earlier today. They wished to be here for my coronation. She presented me with a large basket of lavender. It seems the doom that struck Illith did not affect its crops. The caretaker of Saintclaire manor sent them to remind me though these times are dark, we must never give up. There is always hope."

"We are here for you, Andrew. You are not alone."

Andrew's face held determination. "I will not let this evil tear the sister kingdoms apart. Our relationship is symbiotic—we need each other. I need Jared's wisdom. He needs my support. Together, we will be strong."

Jared stood on the terrace off his room looking at the castle grounds—his home. He spent his entire life here, and now it felt foreign to him. His parents were gone in a twinkling of an eye, and it seemed as if they took the life that was truly life with them.

Soon he would become the new monarch of his country. What would the future hold for his family? He sighed and said aloud, "I have prepared all my life for this moment, yet I feel as though I am far from ready."

A voice answered him. "Only the truly great kings ever felt that way." Coleman stood in the doorway. Both were surprised when they heard a voice behind them speak.

"My son is right." Rowen walked toward them. "Your father felt the same way on his coronation day."

Jared gave a weak smile. "In many ways, I feel just as nervous as when I married Ephratha. How will I ever manage without father?"

"You will manage with the aid of those you trust. That is also how your father did it." Rowen smiled as he reached out and embraced Jared. "I am very proud to call you my king."

Rowen turned to Coleman. "I wanted to let you know I am leaving for Nereheim after the coronation, so do not be alarmed if you do not find me. I will take Paul with me; he is my most capable servant when it comes to riding and dealing with horses.

"You are going to retrieve your cart?" asked Coleman.

Rowen nodded. "I also wish to give my condolences to Andrew personally."

"Will you give Andrew a letter for me?" Jared walked into his room to his writing desk. He picked up a rolled paper sealed with his royal signet. He handed it to Rowen. "I planned on sending a courier after the ceremony, but will you see that he gets this?"

"I will," replied Rowen. "Now, both of you be on your guard today. As far as I remember, Queen Susanna's murderer is still about. If ever there was a time to strike at the throne of North Agea, it is now."

"I was thinking the same thing," replied Coleman. "The royal guard will be prepared."

"Good, I will see you both in a few days." Rowen turned and left the room.

"You need to leave as well," said Coleman.

"I know," replied Jared. He took a deep breath as they both walked out of the room.

Rowen and his servant rode into Wildemere the next day. His heart was heavy as he thought of the letter he carried. Everything that happened in the past days also weighed on him. His country had been upended by evil, there was no question. Within the last two years, Jared and Andrew both wed, and all seemed well for the sister kingdoms. Now one of his greatest friends was gone, another victim in a wake of strange happenings in North Agea. What was next? Rowen feared for his son, the captain of the royal guard. Would the sister kingdoms be plunged into a bloody war? The only hope to insure that did not happen lay in the note he was to give Andrew.

They rode through the castle gate to the stable and left their horses. As they made their way down the colonnade, they were met by his quarry.

Andrew was with another young man who looked familiar to him. They stopped before the young men and bowed before Andrew.

"Your highness, I am Lord Rowen Cade. I give you my condolences for the loss of your father. I liked King Rohn very much. He was related to Lian, who was my closest friend. I believed in him, and knew that he and Lian were always willing to work together for the good of our two nations. When Jared heard I was coming here, he asked me to give you this letter." Rowen pulled out a sealed roll of paper.

Andrew broke the seal and opened the letter.

Andrew,

No words can express the sorrow I feel for you at this moment. In one instant, we both lost our fathers, and our countries lost our kings. Mother is also dead. In her grief, she took her own life. I place no blame on your father for any of these things. The blame I place is on Aunt Susanna's killer and those who orchestrated her murder. I propose we meet in Burnea, in seven days' time. You and I must agree on which direction we will take to make the sister kingdoms whole again. Be well, cousin, but more important, be safe. I look forward to our meeting.

Jared

Andrew's eyes misted as he rolled the letter back up. He turned to his companion. "I ask that you accompany me to Burnea. This will be an emotional time for us all, and I wish to have someone there who can be objective in all things."

"I am happy to accompany you, however, Nathaniel is your Court Adviser," replied the young man.

"He is Court Adviser, and will be there. However, I wish to have a friend with me," replied Andrew.

"I am happy to do so. I consider myself friend to both you and Jared," he replied.

Rowen looked at the young man carefully. "I do not know if we have met before."

"Lord Cade, this is Lord Michael Mauldon," said Andrew.

"You are the vineyard owner's son?" asked Rowen.

"Yes," replied Michael.

"Malcom Stone has told me much of you," replied Rowen. Michael smiled and bowed his head slightly.

"I have heard of you as well, Lord Cade. Your skill in the husbandry of chamomile and lavender has become quite well known even in the part of Nereheim I reside," said Michael.

"I take that as quite a compliment coming from one so learned as you," said Rowen.

"I am sure my sister would love the opportunity to speak with you if you have time before you return to North Agea," said Michael.

"I plan to meet Jared and my son in Burnea and head back with them. If she has time, I would be delighted to meet her," replied Rowen.

"She is very likely with my wife. They often take tea at this time in the rose garden," replied Andrew. He beckoned Rowen and his companion to follow as they went in that direction.

••••••

Andrew looked at the crowd before him. They were here to witness the beginning of a new era for Nereheim. They were here to see him crowned king.

He recognized people who gathered here from great distances such as Countess Deveraux and her ever faithful guardian, Sebastian Cavanaugh. When all the pomp and circumstance came to its close, he hoped to have time to ask Sebastian about the details that brought them together. They were friends, perhaps great friends, but Andrew caught a glimpse of them when they thought the other was not watching. Both had deep admiration and perhaps love for the other. He wanted to know what forged their relationship. The day they arrived in Wildemere offering their sympathies for what happened, they also offered sage advice: be strong and continue to strengthen relationships of those he trusted.

Michael and his servant Peter stood next to Nafaria. He too came from the West to offer his message: you are not alone. Though Michael had a reclusive tendency, he made his position clear. He would do all in his power to aid and protect his family and friends from his home in Denholm Glen. He would use his brilliant mind to thwart the evil that had sewn itself into the royal court. Andrew was far from alone.

There were others he barely recognized, still many more that were strangers to him. They all came forth to show Andrew their acceptance of him as their king. He felt overwhelmed and unworthy.

He passed each row of people gathered in the outer courtyard, toward the front of this great gathering. His uncle's last words to him came to mind: never be afraid to ask for help. He remembered Jared's challenge: what are you doing with your time? He remembered his mother's playfulness, but also her last encouragement: recognize your failings as soon as possible. You have time to learn and grow into a man of noble character.

Andrew walked up the steps and bowed before Nathaniel. As Court Adviser, he held the honor of crowning him king. As Nathaniel placed the crown on his head, Andrew thought of Lord Jason Mauldon. He remembered the apothecary's humility before his father. Andrew hoped he would be a humble king.

As one, every man, woman, and child went down on one knee before their king. Andrew shed a tear as he saw each of his subjects paying him this honor. "I only hope I am as wise as my father before me," he whispered. The crowd rose and cheers erupted throughout the courtyard. A new era for Nereheim dawned.

CHAPTER 26

The next day, the sun was bright and the sky clear. It was cold, though it was almost noon, as Michael and Nafaria walked the busy alleys and main roads of Wildemere. Michael soon realized they were heading toward their old manor.

"Are we going back home?" he asked.

"Yes," said Nafaria brightly. Leona looked up at them and smiled.

"I have an idea that I want to share with you."

The lane turned to cobblestone. Leona giggled with delight when she saw the fountain. Nafaria sat down on the edge and sat Leona in her lap. She looked toward the burned structure—their old home.

"A short while ago, I was in the woods with Leona. I planned to take both girls out, but Nathaniel forbade me from taking Fiona from the castle, so I only took Leona. I was gathering herbs and flowers, when mother came to me. She stood on the bridge that you, father, and Philip built over the brook."

"Did she say anything to you?"

"She told me to rebuild the manor to help heal past sins and be a haven for those who have no place left to turn. This is what I propose. We rebuild the manor according to its original design. Then we use the land and reopen the apothecary shop so the estate will pay for itself as it had before."

"Who will tend the manor?"

"It will be used for those of the Craft who have no place to go. Perhaps Elias Wheaton will help us oversee it."

"If he cannot, I am sure he will help us find one who can. There is a good chance he has an original layout of the manor we can use as a guide for rebuilding." Michael's mind was thinking through details of Nafaria's plan.

"Mother said that a time will come when we will need a safe haven. That is what I want to build here." Nafaria sighed. "Nathaniel has changed. He thinks I do not realize it, but there is something dark growing inside him. I feel it when I am with him. I love him, but I am afraid that one day he will destroy us all."

Michael sat down next to Nafaria. Leona climbed into his lap and studied him carefully. Her soft blue eyes made her look especially innocent. "It is much worse than you know, Nafaria. The reason William cannot be in the castle is because he is sensitive the same way Lord Saintclaire was. He feels the evil Nathaniel brought back with him from North Agea. He gave his loyalty to the god of blood and betrayed us all."

"You would never say such a thing unless you knew it to be true." Nafaria looked down at the ground. "Mother also said I must focus on training Leona to be strong not only in healing, but also the crippling effects of plants and herbs. She said you could help me train Leona in other ways that will make her able to stand against this evil.

Nathaniel will never allow Fiona to leave Wildemere, but I propose that for three weeks every summer I bring Leona to Denholm Glen at the time of her birthday. You will teach her all the mysterious things I cannot. I will teach her about herbs and their uses, even the deadly plants that I know. Perhaps it will make her strong enough."

"Strong enough for what?" asked Michael.

"To defeat the evil that has come to Nereheim." Nafaria looked at Leona and ran her hand through her soft hair. "I am afraid for all of us right now."

"I know. We will come through this dark time. There are others who are willing to stand up as well," said Michael.

"Look for me to visit when you arrive home. I have something I need to bring you. It is time for me to visit the vineyard again."

"Your old room is waiting. Come whenever you like." Michael put his arm around her.

⋅⋅◆◆◆⋅⋅

Andrew and his entourage rode into Burnea seven days after his coronation. The wind whipped the Anenderes into sharp waves that rode swiftly past the port city. Jared was waiting for them.

They stood facing each other for the first time since Rohn left North Agea with Susanna's lifeless body. Andrew winced as he thought of his father and uncle parting with such angry words.

Michael and Nathaniel stood next to him on one side and Nina stood on the other. She was now showing signs of the tiny life growing inside her— his child. Ephratha was with Jared as well, holding a baby boy in her arms, stretching and squirming about. He smiled as he watched his nephew, little Jerrik. Jared's faithful captain of the royal guard and longtime friend stood next to him as well. Lord Cade and his companion joined the captain.

Jared and Ephratha walked toward him. He and Nina advanced toward them. They stopped less than a foot from the other.

"I am sorry about Aunt Clara," Andrew said quietly.

"Thank you," replied Jared.

"We will get through this," said Andrew. "I need you, cousin. You have trained your entire life to be king. I can learn from you. As long as we support each other, we will get through this tragedy."

"That is well said, cousin." Jared embraced him.

"I never thought I would see the day I would admit you are better than me," said Andrew.

Jared shook his head. "I am not better. We both have our failings. Perhaps we will learn from each other how to be better kings as well as men."

"Today we shall have a new beginning. I want to leave this pain in the past and stand together against all odds," said Andrew.

"Together against all odds," replied Jared.

As the men declared peace, the tension drifted away as if taken by the river itself. Ephratha brought Jerrik to Nina and exclaimed, "Nina, you look radiant!"

"Thank you. I have been feeling well, but sometimes I have moments when I am exhausted," said Nina.

"Just wait until your child wants to play. Then you will know what exhaustion truly is!" said Ephratha with a laugh. The young women embraced each other, as others came to join in.

At the edge of Nereheim, peace was again declared in the sister kingdoms.

The bell of the antiquarian library tinkled as Michael walked through the door. He stopped in the middle of the vestibule and smiled as he took in the majestic sight before him.

"It never ceases to amaze me how this place affects you." Michael heard the familiar voice of Elias Wheaton.

"Elias, it is good to see you." Michael walked over and embraced the old man.

"How are you, my young friend?"

"Though troubles surround me, I still find peace in this place."

"Tell me your troubles, for I suspect they are what bring you here."

"It is true, but I should have come to see you sooner."

"Your father sent you away for your protection. I do not wish ill of you for staying away. I am happy you have lived this long if only to see you walk through my door once again. So, what brings you to see me?"

"I have two issues I wish to bring up. I have talked with Nafaria and we wish to rebuild our manor here in Wildemere to be a productive place. We plan to cultivate the herbs and healing plants my family began our apothecary business with. Since your son once owned the estate, I hoped you would oversee the rebuilding process."

"I would be delighted and honored."

"I wish to have the property tended and the manor cared for by those of the Craft who have talents in those areas. The manor will become a haven for those who need a safe place to stay in Wildemere. Cultivating the plants and herbs will make it profitable."

"We shall start with rebuilding the manor," said Elias. "Now, what else do you have for me?"

Michael pulled a piece of paper from his cloak. He unfolded it and handed it to Elias, who adjusted his spectacles to better view the page.

"This is an incantation I found in Joseph's diary. I can tell from the runes it is very old," said Michael.

Elias looked at Michael over his spectacles. "You know this language?"

"Before Reinard Sallen became my father-in-law, I grew up spending time in his private library. It was at my father's suggestion after I exhausted our books and that of my schoolmasters. His collection contained many books of runic language. He once told me it was the writing alchemists used to hide their most important information. Joseph chose to write his last confession in runes on the manor wall before he took his life. However, this page is different from any others he used runes for."

"Michael, not only is this writing very difficult to decipher, it is almost extinct. Very few people today even recognize it. How is it you are able to?" asked Elias.

Michael smiled. "My father often said perhaps my special gift YAHWEH blessed me with was constant study, because I always seem to be caught in it."

"The time period this incantation comes from is when Nereheim was barely a nation. Those of the Craft who first came here were said to have extraordinary power. Some could move things with their minds, and some were even said to fly. You cannot use this incantation simply because you are of the Craft the way you can with others. It is not enough to have the blood of the Craft in your veins. The person who speaks this incantation must also be given supernatural power from YAHWEH to equal its result. It is very dangerous, for the person who uses it can be corrupted and turned to evil if they are not disciplined in mind and spirit," said Elias.

"So, only one trained specifically can wield this incantation?" asked Michael.

"Yes and only such a person who has been given power enough to match its result. It is not for just anyone of the Craft. No one from my family line could have ever been able to use it," said Elias.

"Do you think Joseph called upon the god of blood because he thought he could have the power YAHWEH gave the ancients that first came here?"

"It is possible. The Coe massacre stayed on his mind since he was a young boy. I remember he sharpened his studies after that black business," said Elias.

Michael caught his breath. It was not often that people recalled the massacre that left his mother without her biological family. It was tarnish on the nation's past that many refused to believe actually happened. However, he knew it happened because his father took the time to write the entire account of the massacre and how his mother survived it in his family annals.

"Can you decipher it for me?"

"It will take time, but I think so. However, if you would like, I can give you a few books that will aid you in deciphering it for yourself," replied Elias.

"I would be most grateful if you would," replied Michael.

Elias walked over to one of the stacks of books near the back of the library. Michael followed, and watched as the old man pulled two volumes off a shelf.

"Michael, why are you seeking such power?"

"For your protection, I can only tell you that Nereheim is in the grip of the god of blood. I am looking for every resource available to fight for my country."

"Do what you must, but be careful along the way. Nereheim can ill afford to lose you." Elias handed Michael the books, then embraced him again.

Michael stood before the doorway to his old home. The damage from the fire did not seem to consume the greatest part of the framework of the house. However, time and the elements did their fair share to make the structure unstable. He walked inside. Though parts of the house were burned and destroyed, other parts were barely touched. When Joel's accomplices lit the manor, they must have only thrown torches about, not really aiming to bring the house to the ground. Otherwise the destruction would have been worse. He put his foot on the stairs and shifted his weight to test the wood. It seemed solid enough, so he carefully crept upstairs.

He came across the body of one of the servants who was killed, lying on the floor in one of the rooms. It was still in decomposition. His first thought was that Elias would have to arrange for proper burial for each body.

He continued down the hall and into the library. He recalled the day he first stepped in that room. Joel saved his life by pulling him out of the way of a falling bookcase. Six year later, Joel murdered his father. How quickly things can take a different turn with just one event.

He looked at the half empty shelves. These were books Nafaria and his parents used. He reached out and took a dusty book from its place. It was a book of plants Nafaria grew up with. She never returned to the manor to claim it. He held the book in his hands and sighed. He then spoke aloud—to the one person he wished he could receive counsel from at that moment.

"Father, September fifth fast approaches. Nereheim has a new king. Your old friend was deceived. If not for the courage and love Andrew and Jared possess for each other, the sister kingdoms would be locked in a bloody war orchestrated by another. Nathaniel's dark lord has been thwarted for now, but what of the future?" Michael looked out the window next to the shelf. "How am I to fight my best friend and brother?" he whispered.

"My son." Michael heard a voice behind him. He slowly turned with wide eyes in recognition of that firm but gentle tone. Jason stood in the doorway. *"You cannot live your life in grief because you know what happened. YAHWEH has blessed you with great knowledge, but the outcome will be decided by another generation."*

"Another generation?" asked Michael.

Jason smiled. *"Go your own way, Michael. Continue to study and prepare the next generation for battle. You will know when you see, the hope of the hopeless."*

Michael glanced at the book in his hands. When he looked up again, he was alone. "Father!" he shouted as he rushed to the door. He looked down the hallway. His father was gone.

The warm sun continued toward sunset as two horses trotted through Denholm Glen. The air was crisp for September, the leaves changing colors quicker than Nafaria remembered in Nereheim. Winter was sure to be hard. Colin was amazed at the coming and going of the people. Their monarch was dead, his son now occupied the throne, but everyone carried on their daily lives as if nothing was amiss. His angry demeanor was not lost on Nafaria. She rode carefully, holding Leona close to her. The child enjoyed the ride immensely. If she was uncomfortable in any way, Nafaria had no clue.

"Is something wrong Colin?" asked Nafaria.

"Nereheim has lost its king, and a nameless monster lurks in the shadows of the royal court. How can these people buy and sell as if nothing has happened? Do they not care at all?"

"You and I are privy to knowledge these people do not have. Even if they knew everything that went on this past year, there are as many ways to grieve as there are snowflakes that fall. You cannot judge how people feel merely by their actions. Village life is harder than in the city. People still need to feed their families," she answered.

When the village was behind them, they rode for another mile. They turned onto to a path leading to the vineyard she once called home. The sound of horse's hooves on cobblestone was heard and the manor windows came in view. A young woman with blond hair rushed from the doors of the house, a small child toddling behind her with a smile on his face.

"Hello Lillia," said Nafaria. Leona peeked out her head from Nafaria's cloak.

"Good afternoon Nafaria! You brought your child with you. Which one is she?" asked Lillia.

"This is Leona." Nafaria waited for Colin to dismount then handed him the child. She climbed down from the horse. Loosening the straps holding a saddlebag in place, she pulled out a velvet bag. "Is my brother around?"

"He is in the library," replied Lillia.

"Let me take Leona, so you may have a proper visit with Lillia." Nafaria held out her arms to Colin who handed back the child.

"Do you need any help?" asked Colin.

"If you will take the horses, I need to see Michael."

"The stable is this way," replied Lillia. She and Colin left with William.

Nafaria walked through the kitchen on her way to the study. She sighed as she walked toward the library. Standing in the entrance, she watched her brother. He sat in a chair looking at the fire, deep in thought. He reminded her of their father at that moment.

"Michael," she said quietly. His attention was snatched from the fire.

"Nafaria," Michael saw the child in her arms.

"Are you alone?"

"Only Colin is with me."

Michael rose and walked toward them. He reached out and gently took Leona's hand in his. It was pure and delicate, much like William's. He gave her a soft smile as she looked at his face. At that moment her blue eyes flashed.

There was a blinding light, and then he saw a beautiful young woman with midnight dark hair and bright sapphire eyes. She held out a necklace to a young man about her own age who took it. He then saw another young woman with her throat cut. A silver bell dropped from her hands as she sank to the ground. He then saw himself standing before a man on his knees, his head bowed before him.

A strange sensation emanated from the tiny hand. His eyes widened as he realized what Leona would become. "The hope of the hopeless," he whispered. His smile widened.

"Welcome Leona, to Mauldon Manor." Michael reached his other hand for her. She climbed into his arms and he hugged her tight. "I am so happy you are here."

ACKNOWLEDGMENTS...

As I think about my journey creating SCORPIO, I am reminded of the beginning line of "Duck for President." Only I would change it to read: Writing a book is very hard work.

Lack of confidence in my craft, and second-guessing myself has sent me back to the drawing board many times, often with tears. However, I have found that with every "back to square one," SCORPIO has become every bit the story I was hoping for. I have many people to thank for this.

Editors like Bill Greenleaf, Zach Cooley, and Hope Haugstad who helped with honest feedback and critique.

Professional writers like Michael Fitzgerald for your advice and encouragement, and Laura Kasischke who inspired me so long ago with your own writing and encouragement.

Friends like R.V. Alejaga who saw potential in the Books of the Craft from the beginning.

People like Cindy Martin, Elaine Sinclair, Amy Bacigalupo, and Tammy Collins who wrote reviews on Amazon, Goodreads and other places about how they felt about ARIES.

People like Sandy Gwyn at Pages Books and Coffee, Sharon Ritchie at Chapters Bookshop, Jane Derian at Barnes and Noble, and Travis Hiatt at Chef T, for giving me the opportunity to make appearances at your establishments.

People like the Spoken Word Society, friends, and my regular customers at Pizza Hut who are too many to name here, who bought ARIES out of curiosity or encouragement. If not for you, I never would have made it to the end of SCORPIO.

For everyone I have met through book signings in Galax VA, Winston-Salem NC, Cana VA, and in Mount Airy NC. Meeting you was a privilege and it was an honor to sign my book for you.

And for you, dear reader, who found this book and took the time to read it to this conclusion.

I hope the time you have spent reading it has been a pleasure!